SPECULATIVE FICTION FOR DREAMERS

Speculative Fiction for Dreamers

A Latinx Anthology

EDITED BY ALEX HERNANDEZ,
MATTHEW DAVID GOODWIN,
AND SARAH RAFAEL GARCÍA

With a preface by Frederick Luis Aldama

MAD CREEK BOOKS, AN IMPRINT OF
THE OHIO STATE UNIVERSITY PRESS
COLUMBUS

Library of Congress Cataloging-in-Publication Data

Names: Hernandez, Alex (Science fiction author), editor. | Goodwin, Matthew David, editor. | García, Sarah Rafael, 1974– editor. | Aldama, Frederick Luis, 1969– writer of preface.

Title: Speculative fiction for dreamers : a Latinx anthology / edited by Alex Hernandez, Matthew David Goodwin, and Sarah Rafael García ; with a preface by Frederick Luis Aldama.

Description: Columbus : Mad Creek Books, an imprint of The Ohio State University Press, [2021] | Summary: "A collection of speculative works, including short stories, poems, plays, and graphic short stories that address the breadth of Latinx experiences and identities, including those of DREAMers"—Provided by publisher.

Identifiers: LCCN 2021016476 | ISBN 9780814257982 (paperback) | ISBN 0814257984 (paperback) | ISBN 9780814281352 (ebook) | ISBN 0814281354 (ebook)

Subjects: LCSH: American literature—Hispanic American authors. | Speculative fiction, American. | Fantasy literature, American. | Hispanic American literature (Spanish)—Translations into English.

Classification: LCC PS508.H57 S64 2021 | DDC 810.8/0868073—dc23

LC record available at https://lccn.loc.gov/2021016476

Cover design by Nathan Putens
Text design by Juliet Williams
Type set in Adobe Palatino

CONTENTS

PART II ◆ Dreams Interrupted

PART III ◆ My Life in Dreams

PART IV ◈ When Dreams Awaken

PART V ◈ Dreams Never Imagined

Dreaming Latinx Realities

There's something thrilling about stepping into a world that we at once recognize, *and* that is fantastically and superlatively new. Mary Shelley served this up to readers of *Frankenstein* (1823) and so too did Jules Verne with *Journey to the Center of the Earth* (1864). Some of my favorite authors of the twentieth century dished up wildly imaginative new storyworlds and ontologies: Ursula Le Guin, Edwin Abbott, Philip K. Dick, William Gibson, Jorge Luis Borges, Julio Cortázar, Octavia Butler, Stanisław Lem, Samuel R. Delany, and Jaime and Beto Hernandez. *Speculative Fiction for Dreamers* brings to the fore contemporary new gen speculative narratives, creations that forcefully clear a space for us to reimagine Latinxs yesterday, today, and tomorrow. These vital narratives wake us to new ways of existing in mind/body, socioeconomics, politics, and ecogeographics.

In the past decades, there's been a pileup of speculative fiction in the mainstream. But it's a brand whereby the creative counterfactual thinking used to distill and reconstruct from the building blocks of reality contemporary falls short of *making new* our potential as human beings to exist in truly different ways. It's usually a rather creatively lazy extrapolation of a rotted-to-the-core reality governed by global capitalism. Newly barbaric forms of death, disease, and tellurian destruction are the order of the day. Anglo-led militaristic brute forces step in to bring temporary to calm. It leaves us lip-stuck with bitter tastes.

The alternative realities constructed by the many Latinx creators that make up *Speculative Fiction for Dreamers* step to the challenge of the speculative. They build storyworlds that imagine anew the future, and past, for Latinx subjects otherwise erased, ignored, or swept to shadowed corners. They create Latinx characters with entirely new affective and cognitive systems—and who shed conventional straitjackets of identity. They are creators of the speculative hailing from those otherwise identified *extraterrestrial* spaces. They are our dreamers of tomorrow.

These new gen Latinx creators build a whole range of storyworlds: from those filled with robots and high-tech, to those that reflect on new ways to relate to one another, to our communities, and to our planet, all while waking us to current toxic racist, masculinist, sexist, neoliberal practices. They choose to build storyworlds to revise yesterday, present an alternate present, or reimagine the future. For some Latinx creators, there needs to be a total reset for us to see critically our current destructive patterns: intersectional oppression and trauma. In others, it is the reimagining of our indigenous pasts and mythologies that clears affirmative intersectional spaces where we are allowed to blossom anew. For other Latinx dreamers, old tech can be refashioned into new tech respectful of culture, tradition, and people—a space to celebrate new ways of existing outside of nonbinary race, gender, and sexuality conventions.

As we face a reality that seems increasingly unbearable—climate change, border patrolling, children caged, families ripped apart—the space of the speculative seems more and more a place of reprieve for us Latinxs. It's also more and more a space for us to *see* a way out of these quagmirical, gelatinous masses. *Speculative Fiction for Dreamers* is testament to how the creative, mindful use of our counterfactual capacity today can imagine better ways for us to think, act, and feel tomorrow—where human and planetary organic life forms can productively and creatively cocreate in stunning and remarkable new ways a future for Latinxs—for all.

—Frederick Luis Aldama

INTRODUCTION

¡Seguimos en la Lucha!

Speculative Fiction for Dreamers is a compilation of US Latinx science fiction and fantasy stories. As the title suggests, this book is dedicated to the Dreamers, the young Latinxs who are navigating their identity in the ever-shifting, sometimes perilous but always promising, cultural landscape of the US. This book is likewise for dreamers everywhere, those whose imaginations take hold of them and never let go.

The book comes out of our experience with the previous anthology, *Latinx Rising: An Anthology of Latinx Science Fiction and Fantasy*, which demonstrated the hunger of readers for themes and characters that mirror the Latinx community. *Latinx Rising* is a tight-knit and powerful collection that sent out a signal of the strength of Latinx science fiction and fantasy. *Speculative Fiction for Dreamers* is something else, more like a large extended family of writers, so diverse, so bursting with energy, that we know you will be stimulated and inspired. In these pages you will certainly find something new: it might be a new take on a classic fantasy or science fiction story, a new futuristic or fantastical view of how Latinx culture can be expressed, a Latinx character in a place you had never imagined them, or a character just like you, but expressed through art for the first time. This is what makes us so excited about this book. We know that these Latinx speculative fiction writers and artists are remaking the cultures de las Américas.

Being Latinx, in its immense, beautiful, fractured entirety, is a kind of speculative fiction in itself. We don't mean that in the soft, subtle way of magic realism; rather, our reality bleeds freely and profusely from science fiction, to fantasy, and all too often, to horror. We live speculative fiction lives. We wear fluid speculative bodies to function in different, potentially hostile environments. We are the product of exploration, conquest, and colonization. We are a tale of technologically superior invaders and the valiant fight to repel them, a battle that still rages across our genomes, psyches, and social structures.

We, the hybrid survivors of that great and terrible clash, are now embarking on our own bold voyages to seek out new lives, heroic journeys to escape realities that make some of the most popular dystopian fantasies seem like viable alternatives. Our voyages don't just shunt us through space. We are thrown through time. Becoming unwitting time travelers, living, breathing time capsules sealed tight at our point of departure. When we, or our children, ever return home, our words are slightly dated, our connections to the old world, its music, fashion, TV shows, movies, streets, buildings, air . . . skewed just a bit by the cruel effects of time dilation. Our alienness is compounded.

As Latinxs in this nation, and in this ominous world, we find our multiple identities are often invisible. Not just in books but also in public history, international policy y en la cultura. Still in this twenty-first century, women cannot traverse the streets freely at any time of day or night, and it is not easy to chant for rights to govern our own bodies at the doorstep of patriarchy and borders, and it is not easy to preserve our culture. Yet, there is a united call to action; we have synced our ethnicity and genders to protest the way we have been oppressed and overlooked in our society—triggered by a man who holds office at the White House even after he has been accused of sexual harassment and repeatedly vocalizes insults toward women and immigrants. We are witnessing an apocalyptic nightmare, where each day in our future becomes more dystopian than the past our ancestors left in our native lands. Over the past centuries, muxeres and Latinx, through personal and political movements, have gained some victories; some even changed national policies. Pero, a veces a los demás se les olvida nuestras historias. It is as if we only exist in a parallel universe, where we have to abandon our happiness to obtain galactic triumph; we have to choose to live among zombies, live in solitude, or fight to our death against our own gente. It is why we're drawn to read and write Latinx sci-fi; it has become our call to revolt, our way of interpreting a futuristic conquest.

We are beings shaped by some of the most thrilling speculative fiction tropes, and yet, Latinx characters and stories are rarely represented in the genre, certainly not in movies and TV to any meaningful degree. That is starting to change, at least in the wild realm of print. Latinx writers are embracing the weirdness and wonder of their lives, mining their extraordinary experiences and producing stories that are rich, complex, and entertaining. Stories in this anthology, such as "Jean" by Stephanie Nina Pitsirilos, brazenly revel in the sci-fi nature of Latinx existence in which ghosts, wormholes, and superheroes exist side by side with a girl trying to make sense of her mother's death. In Karlo Yeager Rodriguez's story, "How Juan Bobo Got to los Nueba Yores," a West African deity struggles to hold on to his fluctuating identity after immigrating from Puerto Rico to New York, where even divinity can be eroded by the daily grind of survival.

There is much longing in these stories as well, for the health and wholeness of family and culture. In Lisa M. Bradley's "Tía Abuela's Face, Ten Ways" the longing erupts for a special beloved family member who is brought back through some new and challenging technologies. Longing for absent siblings appears often through the anthology, as in two postapocalyptic stories, Louangie Bou-Montes's "Like Flowers Through Concrete" and Sara Daniele Rivera's "The Music Box." In Grisel Acosta's "BlindVision," we encounter an increasingly common experience, the longing for reality in a life filled with virtual worlds. At the same time, many of these stories depict a more chaotic acceptance of what is present, as in Ernest Hogan's thrilling joyride "Those Rumors of Cannibalism and Human Sacrifice Have Been Greatly Exaggerated."

Gender and sexuality form much of the foundation of the collection. In Sabrina Vourvoulias's short story, "Saint Simon of 9th and Oblivion" the favorite daughter chooses to tinker with time, masterful embroidery, and gender roles to deter an extravagant alien sorcerer. Reyes Ramirez unapologetically depicts a supersheroe at the peak of fighting an insurgence of zombies and the resurrection of white supremacy, while also recovering Latinx history, in "An Adventure of Xuxa, La Ultima." Equally inspiring, in "Soledad," Ezzy G. Languzzi uses magical realism and shapeshifting to preserve her protagonist's traditional legacy as a muxer living in a patriarchal time capsule. These stories bend the borders of the speculative world and capture the intergenerational struggle of Latinxs. They all chant proudly: ¡Seguimos en la lucha!

—Alex Hernandez, Matthew David Goodwin,
Sarah Rafael García

PART I

Dreaming of New Homes

How Juan Bobo Got to los Nueba Yores

KARLO YEAGER RODRÍGUEZ

Back home, he was sure he had been better, less confused.

Even now, standing at the head of the class, he frowned at the big map and tried to remember where he'd come from. The blue parts must be water. Everywhere else was a green so deep he fell into it and came out on his mountainside, the one back home, where he ran and climbed and wandered; where he could spend a morning eating mangoes until his face was sticky and spend an afternoon following a single ant as it meandered through the tall grass—

"Juan," his teacher repeated. "Can you show us?"

A giggle rippled through the classroom. Juan liked hearing people laugh, even if sometimes they called him Bobo, like in all those fables. He liked listening to those stories. He liked listening to all the things he was supposed to have done, like he had lived so many lives. Juan blinked, seeing the map again. He dropped his hand and shrugged.

"Juan, where are you from?"

"Puerto Rico," he said.

"Yes." His teacher pointed at the map. "Porto Rico. Can you show us on the map?" The laughter was louder this time.

Juan stood taller and shrugged again.

His teacher's pale skin turned the color of hormiga brava. She glared at him, snatched her yardstick and snapped it against the map. "Do you even habla inglés?"

Juan felt a worm of fear wriggle into his gut. Pinned under her gaze, he nodded and sang what English he had learned from la missy back home:

Pollito, chicken
Gallina, hen
Lápiz, pencil
Y pluma, pen—

Mami came to get him after he spent the day in the corner. She took him home as fast as his legs could carry him. If he dragged his feet to stare at the airships floating as slow and serene as whales overhead, she tugged him forward until they reached their building.

She pushed him into the apartment and locked the door behind her. Before she left, Mami hissed they would settle things, don't think she'd forget. The apartment grew dark as he waited for Mami to return. He lay back onto his cot and let his mind wander.

He told himself the story of How Juan Bobo Got to Be a Shut-In to remember, but wasn't sure how much time had passed. Had it been yesterday? The day before? The old stories started with once upon a time, but Juan knew it didn't mean things happened for certain. Things could have happened already, are yet to happen, or never happened at all. Maybe his story followed the same rules.

One of the trains on the Brooklyn Manhattan Transfer punched past outside, all vibration and the sound of a thousand scissors singing snickety-snack. It shredded his story to tatters, leaving behind silence and the musty smell of old plaster dust drifting down.

Juan jumped when Mami slammed the door behind her.

Her promise to settle things—forgotten until the moment she returned—crashed over Juan, and he froze, wary. She shrugged a load of clothes onto the back of her sewing chair before she disappeared into the room she shared with the other girls. She returned, having shed her street clothes and wearing her house slippers.

Juan closed his eyes, pretending he was asleep. He watched Mami as she stood over him, her face in shadows. Was she going to pull him out of bed and punish him like she'd promised? After a time, she turned away. She picked through the clothes she had brought from work. She shook out a skirt, and sank into her chair. She turned the fabric over in her hands before taking needle and thread to the tattered hem.

She hummed a meandering tune while she sewed. Juan's eyelids grew heavy, every blink stretching out into what seemed forever, the fluid loop of once upon a time. Adrift, adrift in the gray place between sleeping and waking, between now, then, and what's-to-be, Mami sewing in her chair an island of light in the distance.

Juan dreamed, or thought he dreamed, of being back home.

He laughed, running alongside Abuela's three-legged pot bouncing along the road. Mami had sent him to fetch it. When he got to his grandmother's house, she urged him to carry it lest it get dented. Juan had good reason not to follow her wishes: the pot was as black and heavy as unconfessed sins.

"Here." Abuela had pressed her gnarled hand into Juan's and slipped him a paper cone full of gofio to sweeten the deal. The powdery combination of toasted cornmeal and brown sugar set Juan's mouth a-water. "I know it's your favorite," she had said, and her dark face crinkled into a sly smile. She knew the way to keep Juan's attention was through his sweet tooth.

He had been dutiful, oh, how dutiful he had been!

Now, he trudged along, blowing droplets of sweat out of his eyes, the sweetness on his lips long forgotten. The pot felt heavier than before, no matter how many times he shifted it from one aching shoulder to the other.

Then he noticed its three legs.

"You might've fooled Abuela, but not me," he grunted as he set the pot down. "Get going, lazybones! You can use your legs to walk the rest of the way."

The pot did not budge.

"Go!" Juan shouted at it, but it wasn't until he kicked it and sent it rolling along that it moved. All it had needed was the right motivation.

Now, he clapped his hands in rhythm with its hollow clangs, the black iron of the pot dull with the dust of the road. The clangor reminded him of the rolling beats of Papi's drums: trucu tác u-tác! Juan sang, weaving the beat between the ringing of the pot and the slap of his feet on the road.

Lola se murió,
Lola, lo lamento;
Mento, mentosán;
San, San Germán . . .

He ran, the grass-green of the cane fields on his right, the blood-red clay of the road stretching away before him, and the deeper green of the mountains stretching away toward the sky on his left. The air was full of the buzzing of mosquitos and the sweet, rancid smell of sugar cane left too long in the sun.

Then, the mountains spoke.

They rose, green and huge as the swelling waves in the deep, deep sea, frozen as they scratched the underbellies of rain clouds. The voices of the mountains rolled out of the forests, full of the rumble of faraway thunder and the whispers of leaves moving with the wind.

Does your Mami know where you're going, Juan?

Juan started to answer but spluttered as the first fat drops of rain stung his cheeks. Quick as a slap, he came out of his reverie. The pot had rolled to a stop in the road ahead, the rain pattering around it. The dust of the road, soon to be mud, would leave stains dark as blood on his clothes.

Imagining the look Mami would give him if he returned to the house covered in mud, he peeled off his clothes. He folded them into a bundle under his arm. Ahead, the downpour hissed toward him, driving the voice of the mountains before it.

Does your Mami know you're wearing your Sunday best?

No, he wanted to say, that's not true—but who could argue with the mountains? When he proffered his bundle of homespun clothes as proof, they had disappeared from under his arm. He looked under each arm, to be sure, muttering donde estás. He was wearing a motley, the crackling red of end-of-harvest cane fire on his right, the black of charred fields on his left.

The rain stopped.

A coqui made a single tentative peep, swallowed by the night. The smell of rain, clean and sharp as a knife, mingled with the flat musk of wet earth.

A low thrum in the air made Juan shiver, and he felt something slither loose, deep in his belly. He choked back loops and loops of crowing laughter, knowing once he started he could not stop. No one could, not Abuela, not Mami. No, it was time to go, to get back home, to let Mami make things better again.

When he turned to kick the pot again, an old jibaro stood in its place, his skin dark and dusty as black iron.

"Enough." The old man raised his hands in surrender. Old cast iron shears, machete blades, and crooked skewers fell to land in the red mud at his feet, as if he had them all hidden in his sleeves. "No more kicking. You found my hideout, Echu. I give up."

Juan felt a flutter of—what?

Recognition? How? He had no memory of the old man.

Was he feeling confused again? Had this happened on the island, on its mountains and red clay paths, or before then, when it was once upon a time? The paths had become all tangled, blended together so they all looked alike. Juan shook his head, but if he squinted, the old man looked like Abuela. Was he her brother?

"You hear me, Echu?"

"I'm Juan."

"Sí, Pepe," the old man said, and nodded with pursed lips. "C'mon, this is Tío Oggy you're talking to." His face crinkled into a wry grin and he raised one foot toward Juan. "Go ahead, pull the other one."

"I'm not Pepe, either." Juan patted his chest and repeated himself, louder and slower, "I told you already—I'm Juan."

Oggy scoffed but leaned in and squinted into Juan's eyes—first one, then the other, as if he expected to see something there. When he was done, he grimaced and spat on the side of the road.

"That's the best trick you ever pulled." The jíbaro chuckled, but the dull red of hot iron glowed through his skin. When he spoke again, wisps of acrid smoke curled out of his mouth. "How'd you hide from yourself?"

So many questions! His chest burned with their heat, thronging in his throat, but not one of them scrabbling past the others to be uttered. It would be like the thin spray of a leak before the flood, and like the laughing spell he had tamped down, he wasn't sure he could stop himself.

Instead, Juan shook his head and shrugged.

"She really did it." Oggy murmured, and Juan wondered if the old man was talking to him. "Snipped and tucked you away, tight as a pocket."

Juan wanted to know who had done the sewing, but he fell silent when the townspeople stepped out onto the road. They slipped out of the cane fields like phantoms, and each knelt to take one of the sharp irons from the mud. More people stepped out of the trees and long grass on his left. Juan recognized his teacher and the sugar mill's majordomo Don Peyo, their faces slack. They hissed accusations at each other from their ragged lines, a small town's old hurts and petty squabbles ripped open, bleeding poisoned words until one by one they fell silent, staring at Juan.

"He's red," the people to his right murmured.

"No, he's black," the people on his left growled.

They leapt at each other, shrieking, rusted iron stabbing—

Juan lurched awake to the snickety-snack of the el-train rumbling past. In its wake, the latest Johnny Rodríguez song wafted through the vents from the neighbor's apartment. It was the closest Mami and the other girls got to owning a radio.

Mami sat in her chair, humming, her hands moving needle and thread. The rest of the apartment was dark, still, the girls long since gone to their shifts at the shirt factory. The collection of blouses and skirts Mami had brought draped the arms of her chair in a tidy stack.

She stopped humming when she felt Juan slip out of bed.

"Johnny," she said, voice low. She frowned at the stitch she worked on, pulled it tight. "What are you doing awake?"

"No pude—" Juan flinched at Mami's hiss. He switched to his halting English. "I could not—sleeping? No. I could not sleep?"

Mami's eyes flashed in the low light, but she softened after a moment, waved him closer. When Juan tried to clamber into her lap, she set her sewing aside and murmured, wasn't he too grandesito for his Mami's lap? She relented, and he put his ear to her chest. He could feel Mami's hum through one ear and hear the music with his other.

"Ay, Johnny." Her sigh trailed off into nothing. Juan waited for her to settle things like she'd promised, or to tell him again how important speaking English was to fit in with things here. Instead, she stroked his head before she took up her sewing again.

"A bad dream." Juan shuddered. "What made me awake."

Mami made a small noise.

She folded the fabric of the skirt once, then once again as she pushed the needle through, pulled the thread taut as she finished the hem. Light flashed off the needle as she closed the stitch, but Juan gasped when Mami drew out her shears to snip the thread.

"What's the matter?" Mami tucked the needle into her sleeve, thread trailing. She shushed him as she brushed the skirt and folded it.

"Why do you do it, Mami?"

"The extra work?"

"No." He pinched his fingers as if holding a needle and rolled his wrist, mimicking Mami's movements. "What's the word for coser?"

"Sewing."

Juan nodded. "Why do you like sewing?"

"It's extra money." Mami shrugged. "I like it."

"Why do you like it so much?"

"Aren't you full of questions tonight?" She patted the finished skirt, set it aside, and peeled a shirt off her chair arm. "It's a good one, though."

Mami found the mark of tailor's chalk on a torn underarm seam. She pulled swatches out of her pockets, comparing colors against the fabric until she found a close enough match.

"Making old clothes new again is an old magic. It lets people tell the world new stories about themselves. You can almost be someone new if you're wearing new clothes."

"Did you," Juan said after a long moment, "ever make me clothes, all red on one side, black on the other?"

Her hands froze mid-stitch.

"Mami?"

"Time for bed, Johnny."

Juan shrank away from the tone of her voice. It was Mami's Nueba Yores voice, where the chill of the air, the hardness of the concrete had seeped into her words. She had used it when she found him playing on the corner with the other children. Come out of the sun, mijo—you want to look like some burnt-up thing?

Juan didn't understand why staying out of the sun was important to Mami when she was as brown as he was, but he stayed inside to be her good boy. Now, he looked yellow. If Abuela saw him this way, she would give him spoonful after spoonful of cod liver oil, convinced he was sick.

Silence stretched to fill the air until Juan slipped off Mami's lap. He climbed back into his bed, turned to face the wall. Mami stood, stretched, and turned out the light.

"Johnny?" Her voice was low, tentative. "Where did you see those clothes?"

"I must have dreamed it," Juan said after a moment before turning in the dark to face the wall. He lay awake a long time after Mami had gone to sleep.

◆

The story of How Juan Bobo Almost Fed His Sweet Tooth started the next day. He woke to Mami bustling out the door to work, past the other girls who lived in the apartment. Maggie and Alex chattered and joked with Juan while he searched the kitchen for something sweet. The empty sugar jar reminded him that Mami and the girls couldn't always fill it. Another difference between this place and back home.

He wished he could go out and get some sugar at the corner store, but Mami didn't want him outside and the girls knew it. They leaned against the end of the kitchen counter, sharing a cigarette as they played briscas. They gossiped in low voices while they took turns tossing cards into the pot until one of them scored the trick. Juan flounced back to bed and lay there until Alex and Maggie stubbed out their last cigarette and, yawning, disappeared into the next room.

Alex always called him Juancho, Maggie played rhyming games, and—best of all—both of them spoke Spanish with him. They had been the ones who had told him his Papi was off in the war fighting the animales.

For days, Juan's head had danced with visions of lion warriors, elephant generals, monkey spies, and his father standing tall against every one of them. Papi's black skin gleamed with sweat as he held his pistol in one hand, his machete in the other, and held off the vicious enemy.

When Juan asked Mami how the army Papá fought against held their weapons—didn't the animales have paws?

She corrected him.

"Not animales, Johnny." Her smile trembled and didn't light up her eyes. "Alemanes. Germans. Soldiers from far away."

His vision, which had transformed into Papi surrounded by enemy soldiers, lost its luster. In its place, he felt hollow and afraid he might never see his father again.

Now, in the apartment, Juan froze, his hand in the breadbox. Had he heard one of the girls stir in the next room? After a moment of silence, he moved his hand and felt the edge of a silver dollar Mami had hidden in there. He pocketed the money, took the spare key, and slipped out the door.

He took the stairs down and stepped out of the building into the barrio. The calls of hawkers filled the cool morning air with Spanish and English, drowned out by the sound of a streetcar zipping past, ringing its bell, trailing sparks.

Juan followed a crowd of people. He started to cross the street with them, but stopped short staring at a zeppelin crossing overhead, silent and enormous as a thundercloud.

"¿Tú 'tas loco?" Rough hands fell upon him, yanked him to the curb in one long frog-march step. Juan blinked at the old man's skin, black as an old three-legged pot. "Muchacho, didn't your Mami teach you sense? You can't just stand on the street eslembao like that."

"Oggy," Juan said. He was glad to recognize someone in this place. "How'd you get here? Things get bad back home for you, too?"

"Oggy?" The old man looked confused a moment, but then winked and gave him a sly smile. "Si, Pepe. Go ahead and pull the other one."

"Not Pepe, remember?" Juan knew this game. "Juan—or Johnny if you don't want to get in trouble with my Mami, too."

"Speaking of—" Oggy snapped his fingers. "Where's your Mami, kid? She know you're out of school?"

"Yeah," Juan said. "She's the one who talked to my teacher about not going back."

Oggy pursed his lips and started to step away when Juan dug into his pocket and pulled out the silver dollar.

"She gave me this." Juan brandished the coin. Oggy stopped mid-step, his gaze so fixed on the coin, Juan put it back in his pocket. "She said to buy her something sweet."

"Why didn't you say so?" Oggy tilted his head so Juan would follow him. "I know just the place."

Oggy urged him to go inside when they got to the store. The old man had made Juan's mouth water with his descriptions of the sweets inside. It was the best place in the barrio, Oggy told him, but when Juan set foot inside the owner shooed him out. In between scolding him, he repeated, "school, school" until Juan backed out of the store.

"What do ants care if I get some candy?"

"Ants?" Oggy looked confused.

"Sí. He said the true ants didn't want me in there."

"Doesn't seem fair." Oggy shook his head along with Juan. He stopped, and a smile spread across Oggy's face. "I know! If I act like your Papá, he'll let me inside and I'll get what you want. Just tell me what sweets you want."

Oggy held out his open hand.

Juan felt a sudden prickling of doubt. He should close his fist around the silver dollar and slip it back into his pocket, go back home and put it back where he found it.

"C'mon, muchacho." Oggy flapped his hand. "Think about how happy your Mami will be that you thought of her! I'm sure she'll share with you."

Juan imagined Mami smiling at him like she used to do so often back home, and the glow of pleasure made him forget he had made up the story about Mami wanting sweets in the first place. He planted the coin in Oggy's palm.

"Wait for me here."

He did. His mouth watered as he kept imagining how the sweetness would weigh on his tongue. Soon he would get gofio or a pilón lollipop encrusted with sesame seeds.

Where was Oggy?

The shadows had lengthened by the time Juan worked up his nerve enough to go inside again. The shop owner glanced at him before he returned to reading his newspaper. Juan peered down the handful of aisles, and once again because he sometimes missed things the first time.

Oggy wasn't in the store.

Juan felt a pang of fear. He had lost Mami's money, and he didn't even have any sweets to offer her as a trade. He raced back, trying to beat Mami home.

It didn't work.

When he cracked the door open, Mami raised her gaze from Alex and Maggie. Her glare drew him into the apartment. He saw the girls' wide-eyed faces for an instant before they scurried past him and out into the hallway.

"Close the door." Mami's voice was cold, calm.

Juan froze.

"Johnny!" Mami barked, making him jump. "What did I tell you?" Mami's voice was low again, trembling with anger. Juan leaned against the door to shut it, afraid to look away. Mami had never hit him, but he was afraid she might now.

"Why?"

Juan felt his face burn with the shame of not being the good boy his Mami wanted. He tried to think about the why of things, but it retreated into the same place once upon time lived in his thoughts, left no reasons in its wake.

He stared at his hands, his feet, and shrugged.

"Fine." Mami bit off the end of the word and put her hand out, palm up. "The girls told me you took their money, but I made sure they knew my Juan is no thief."

The heat drained away, left Juan cold. He blinked at Mami's empty hand. He wanted to say something, anything.

"Johnny." She waggled her fingers under his nose. "Give it back."

Juan stared at her hand. It filled his entire world.

"I don't have it."

Mami set her jaw.

"H-he promised, Mami—!" Juan started to tell her about how Oggy had agreed to buy him candy, but as soon as he mentioned Tío Oggy his mother cut him off.

"Not another one of your stories—!" Mami pressed her lips together as if to hold back the rush of words. She sighed, said, "I'll have to pay them back for what you did. Money I'd just made last night—" She stopped, raised a hand to her mouth.

She pinched her lips closed, like closing a coin purse, and shook her head. She reached into her pocket and pressed a silver dollar into Juan's hand. He stared at the coin, still warm from Mami's hand.

"You," Mami said, "will be who gives this back to them. Let's see how you feel when you see their disappointment in you. But be sure to say you're sorry."

Later, after the girls left, Mami asked him what had happened. He told her about meeting Tío Oggy, how he had promised Juan he would buy the sweets for his Mami, but had disappeared instead.

Mami bowed her head and sighed. She was in her chair, the light of the lamp at her back. When she spoke, her face was in shadow.

"I want what's best for you, mi amor," she murmured, her voice hollow. "Your father too—he wanted more than just cutting caña until you're old and bent, with nothing to show for it but scars on your hands."

She stared at the doorway to the bedroom. Juan's eyes sought hers, wanting her back from wherever memory had taken her.

"Why did you want something sweet?"

"I miss Abuela's gofio." He had almost told her about the dream, the sweetness so heavy on his tongue he woke up craving it.

A ghost of a smile flickered across Mami's face. She stood, gestured for Juan to sit at the tiny kitchen table. When he did, she had already taken out a pan, and the bottle of milk from the icebox. She poured milk into the pan and set it on a low flame on the stove. Once the milk simmered, she stooped to grab a fistful of rice, tossed it into the pan. She stirred it until she turned down the heat and poured out the rice soup into a bowl.

"Here," she said and slid it across the table, the steam caressing Juan's face. "Like Abuela liked to say, barriga llena—"

"—corazón contento," Juan finished the phrase, nodding at the wisdom. Often, he *was* happier after he ate. He took the spoon Mami handed him. He slurped at the steaming rice, remembering how Abuela liked to make this when she could get the rice she needed for it.

Between Mami standing behind him, stroking his hair, singing a meandering tune, and the warmth of the rice soup pooled in his belly, Juan felt today soothed away, smoothed away until he felt his eyelids grow heavy.

❖

How Juan Took His Piglet to Church began when he had taken his beloved Chencha wrapped in swaddling clothes to the chapel up in the mountains back home.

The folks from town called it Monte Arriba because of the long climb to get there, but the jibaros in the mountains called the tiny church the Chapel of Tides because it came and went—sometimes there, but gone others. Everyone agreed it lay at the center of a once upon a time place.

Yellow-green palm leaves woven into a cross hung from the rusted zinc roof, and Juan crossed himself like he'd been taught was proper. The green slopes of the surrounding mountains rose through the low-hanging clouds.

Mami had told Juan the family was going hungry. She told him to bring Chencha out of her pen. Juan knew what would happen next, and how he had cried!

After a full day, and half of the next, of Juan howling and drumming his heels against the floorboards, Mami snapped. The day she would go hungry, she said, was the day Chencha would be baptized.

Juan knew what he had to do.

Now, Juan bowed his head as he stepped under the eaves, cradling his piglet. Chencha was heavy as a stone in his arms, and she snored, but he loved her. She pranced and wagged her scraggly root of a tail when he came near, so Juan knew she loved him back.

He looked for the washbasin the priest used as a font. A quick splash was all Juan needed to save his piglet from becoming tomorrow's feast, then back before sundown. A small sound made Juan peek farther into the chapel.

A woman in white sat on the lone pew, her back to him. Her shoulders shook with quiet sobs, her hands folded together and pleading to the cross painted on the far wall, behind the altar.

Shelves flanked the cross, filled with clusters of flickering candles and the chipped statues of saints. The sorrowful, pained eyes of the icons gleamed in the candlelight.

A gust of wind slammed the door closed behind Juan, buffeted the chapel. The wooden slats creaked, and the small building shuddered and rolled like a ship at sea. Chencha squealed awake and squirmed out of Juan's arms. She trotted down the aisle, toward the altar, dragging her swaddling behind her.

He cried out after Chencha, but the chapel pitched forward after another gust. Out the tiny window, the green slopes of the mountains moved like gigantic swells trailing salt spray behind them. In the distance, the mountains grew more narrow, lights twinkling along their sides like rows of windows, and the low oblong shape of an airship hung low in the sky. Was this the steamer he had taken with Mami to los Nueba Yores, or was it another ship, from further back, from before they got to their island all those years ago?

A memory bubbled up, of being carried through the green peaks and valleys of the deep, deep sea. Squeezed down to fit, surrounded by shit and fear and death. The muted ting-ting of black iron chains, wailing in the dark belly of a ship. Carried, carried across the face of the compass rose.

Back in the chapel, the woman in white keened over the sound of the wind. She moaned and rocked, cradling a bundle in her arms. She repeated, "Se lo han llevao, why did you take him?" When he drew closer, Juan noticed it had been Mami all the while. He had not noticed it before. Maybe it was the magic thrumming through every board of the place, or maybe he had never seen his mother this sad.

"Don't be sad, Mami."

She could not hear him. Juan wasn't sure if it was over the full throat of the wind, over the creaking sounds of the chapel moving like a galleon over the swells, or because he was now a phantom, a dream-self.

Mami whispered, "They took him," and looked up at the wall of saints. "One of your own," she said, her gaze darting from one porcelain face to another. Their collected eyes looked away, upward. Juan peered over her shoulder.

He had thought she had Chencha, once again wrapped tight in her swaddling, but instead it looked like a stone. When he blinked, he realized it was fire-hardened clay, black and rounded as a river stone on one side, the bright red of fresh blood on the other. It had cowrie shells for eyes, a mouth.

Was he feeling confused again?

Juan knew he was both the clay baby in Mami's arms and himself floating over her shoulder. He knew it the same way old stories and dreams feel like slipping on familiar clothes after visiting and revisiting them.

Mami stroked the curved surface of the clay baby.

Something vast moved behind the wall of saints.

He felt it like an indrawn breath, or a sudden gust of wind laden with the taste of rain upon it. Its gaze moved over him, the cloud of a thunderstorm sliding over rolling hills. It peered out at them through the eyes of the saints on the wall, each of them a mask through which it watched the world.

"I'll hide him, sewn up. Safe as God's own pocket." Mami leaned forward, a quavering smile on her lips. "Please."

The chapel groaned, tilted, a ship climbing the face of a wave. Outside, skyscrapers squeezed between the mountains, lights glimmering like sprays of seaward stars. Mami cocked her head, as if listening to a whisper. Her face beamed her thanks and she rocked back to sag against the pew. She murmured her thanks over and over while her hands moved. Juan watched in horror as she drew out her shears and cut a Juan-shaped hole in the air around the stone. What was left in its wake was a simple doll-shape. She drew the shimmering cloth over the seashell eyes. She set aside the shears, blades stained red, smoothed out wrinkles. With a long needle, she started stitching.

He saw the needle flash, felt stitches tighten at the nape of his neck, and—

He thrashed awake. The snickety-snack of the train, a soothing lullaby. Mami stood at the washbasin in the kitchen, the gray light of dawn all around her. He panted, shuddering as the last shreds of the dream faded. The green hills of home a knife of yearning piercing his heart.

Mami sang in a low voice, washing dishes. Her song lulled him, his eyelids heavy. It had been a dream, nothing more, nothing less.

She slipped her shears a-drip with blood into her apron pocket. Sleep fled. Juan clamped both hands over his mouth to keep a scream from clawing its way out.

Mami stopped.

She turned her ear, and Juan saw her face in profile. He willed his limbs to ease back into bed and closed his eyes as if asleep. Juan didn't dare open his eyes because Mami might be standing over his bed, watching him.

He jolted awake when the door snicked closed.

Had it all been a dream? Had it happened? Juan shook his head. Why had she done—what? Cut him down to size? Was he some kind of cloth Mami was ready to sew?

In none of the Juan Bobo stories he had told himself had Mami ever wanted to hurt him. In every one of the stories, she loved him just the way he was. Was he feeling confused again?

Back home, whenever he had felt like this, he would have run off into el monte. He would have tramped up and down back trails, surrounded by the green hum of living things, to help him think. Here, his thoughts were the dull gray of concrete and steel.

He had to go, even if it meant defying Mami again, somewhere green with trees and grass and maybe the chuckle of water, trickling somewhere unseen.

After he left the building, Juan wandered the streets of el barrio asking for directions to someplace with trees. By mid-day, he caught a glimpse of treetops overhanging stone walls, but even though his feet ached and his stomach felt like it flapped against his ribs, he felt renewed by the faint smells of loam and water and green leaves.

A sign hung next to the entrance to the park:

NO
PORTO RICAN
GODS
ALLOWED

Juan blinked, clenched his brow while he mouthed the English words over and over. His head hurt trying to understand, but he shrugged his doubt off and entered the park. In the distance, people walked on the arch of a bridge crossing a stream, wearing fancy clothes and tossing crumbs to the swans. The low burble of the stream called to Juan, the sigh of a breeze ruffling his hair.

A whistle pierced his calm and he turned.

"Mano, pa' dónde va?" Oggy stared at him. "Where you think you're going? Didn't you see the sign?"

Oggy tried to grab him by the arm, but Juan danced back.

"Leave me alone." He glared at Oggy, Mami's scolding still a fresh hurt. He wanted to scold Oggy for taking his money, but Mami didn't like him lying, either. "You took the money I gave you."

"Sure." Oggy looked like he'd bit into something bitter and ducked his head in a half-nod. "If that's what it takes to keep you out of the park."

Juan felt an odd vertigo as he said, "No."

He turned away, walked farther into the park, breathing the smell of dirt and green living things. Ardillas bounded off the cobbled path, and one chattered at him from its perch in a tree, its bristling tail twitching. Juan remembered ardillas back home were fierce and brown furred and snake eaters.

Mami told him the right word for those was mongoose.

He felt the old confusion cloud his mind, and sat until it passed. He sank onto one of the many benches lining the path until the feeling passed. Who was shouting?

"Vamo muchacho!" Oggy dashed forward, his furtive movements like the squirrels'. "Let's go before there's trouble."

People from el barrio crowded at the entrance of the park. Some pointed and cast dark looks their way, and Juan waved at them, gestured them closer. Why didn't they want to sit on the benches and enjoy the shade like him?

"Come on," Oggy said. "If you follow me, I promise to get you some sweets."

Juan clicked his tongue, shook his head. No, he had wanted some quiet time under the branches of a tree like back home. No longer—first Oggy, now this crowd, and those distant cries—who was shouting?

Two police officers trotted across the grass, clubs in hand. They made sweeping gestures as they approached, the way Juan shooed away his little Chencha when she was in his way. On the bridge, more people in fine clothes gathered, watching. The way they moved reminded him of when officers came looking for Papi back home, after what happened at the sugar mill. Papi had turned, told him to run even as he stood blocking the door.

"No!"

Oggy stepped between them and Juan, hands together in supplication. The officers shouted in an English broken in ways Juan didn't recognize. He stared at their skin—more pale than his—and orange hair, and wondered if it affected how they spoke English. How they swung their clubs at Oggy made it clear what their words to Oggy meant.

Oggy blocked their way to Juan, holding his arms out even as one of the officers swung his club. Juan cried out, sprang up to pull Oggy away. They fell back, a jumble of limbs. When he saw blood running down half of Oggy's face, he shouted for help. One of the policemen pried him off, wailing, and swung his club at him. Juan scrambled back, ran toward the crowd.

The gathered people from el barrio had spilled into the park. Some of them shouted to the others, do something, lo están matando! Others said nothing, or muttered there will be trouble for everyone. He recognized one voice.

"Let me through!"

How could Mami be here? She should be at work, right? No, he heard her shout his name. "Johnny, mijo, come here." She reached through the crowd.

He glanced back at Oggy, held up between the two policemen with blood streaming from his scalp. Juan clutched at Mami's hand, and she pulled him through the crowd. Once out, she turned, eyes blazing.

"May this be the last time," she spat through gritted teeth. Her hand flashed out and slapped him on the face before she crushed him to her and sobbed.

◆

Back at the apartment, Alex and Maggie had felt the long, tense silence loom over them and left earlier than usual. Each smiled at Juan when Mami was looking the other way.

She had yanked his arm all the way back from the park, snapping him forward step by step. Juan had stopped when he saw the warning sign again, its block letters shouting:

NO
PORTO RICANS
DOGS
ALLOWED

Juan blinked at the words, mouthed them again, but Mami tugged him along in her wake. He craned his neck to keep looking at the sign as he stumbled behind his mother.

Back in the apartment, he touched his cheek. The sting of Mami's hand—light and dry against his skin—lingered. She took a long breath, smoothed back her hair.

"Juan," she said. He blinked, surprised. She had insisted on calling him Johnny ever since they got here. "Things can't go on like this. Do you know how much you scared me?"

Juan stared at his hands.

"I just—" Mami murmured. "Why can't you mind what you're told?"

"Mami, I—"

"I don't want to hear about it—!" She slammed her hand on the kitchen table, but bit back whatever else she had meant to say. "I'm sorry. I'm so sorry, mijo. Forgive me, but I'm so—angry."

Juan dropped his gaze, cheeks ablaze, lips quivering.

"No!" Mami rushed forward, kneeling to take his hands. "Not at you, mi amor." A ghost of a smile softened her face. "We—your father and I—had hoped this place would be a better place for you, just like in the stories."

Juan knew all about the stories he loved best. They began, once upon a time, but they could happen whenever—yesterday, a hundred years ago, or not yet. Mami's once upon a time had been this place, los Nueba Yores. Did Papá think the same?

"Was this before Papi had to go prove he was brave?"

"Yes," she whispered. "Brave. The police came for him."

"¿Y qué pasó?" Mami shot him a look, and Juan ducked his head. "I mean, what happened next?"

"They made him choose." Mami scoffed, a grim smile pressing her lips together. "He had the freedom to choose between Sing Sing, or going into the army."

Juan squeezed Mami's hand.

"I couldn't let that happen to you, too." She raised a hand to cup his cheek in her palm. "I want you to be safe, stay safe, fit in."

Juan felt the dizzying dream-sense of being in his body while also watching himself far away through a velvet tunnel. His ragged edges fluttered in the wind between who he had been and who he was, now.

"Safe?"

"Your Abuela has a favorite saying: vestir un santo con el saco del otro. I didn't know I could do it, Johnny, but I had to try."

Dressing one saint with the other's clothes?

"I saw you, Mami." Juan shuddered with the effort of dragging the memory to light. "In the chapel back home. After, too. Is that why Oggy was in the park?"

"Stop it, Johnny." Mami's face hardened. "Dreams are just that—dreams."

"He called me Echu," Juan said. Was he talking too fast? "He laughed at me, hiding behind new clothes—"

"The old man in the park? Look what all his nonsense got him. Is that what you want?"

Juan opened his mouth, closed it without saying anything.

"Is it?" Mami's voice lashed him, her eyes gleamed like wounds. "Tell me. Is that what you want to happen?"

Juan shook his head, murmured *no*.

"Then help me, mi amor." Mami put her arms around him, pressed him to her. He stiffened before he let her enfold him into her embrace. "Help me keep you as safe as being in God's own pocket."

Juan made a small sound of assent. He trusted her to keep him safe, but the cost of living in a place like once upon a time was not being tied to any time at all. There was no before, only a now and the happily-ever-after, which is to come.

Juan wasn't the only one who wanted to fit in. Like a child's game, every person dared others to snip away threads to who they were before. Folded, then once again, until it was hidden from view, even their own. He felt the old, familiar confusion lift as the song of a thousand scissors singing snickety-snack filled his ears.

◆

Juan walked to school, let the sounds of el barrio wash over him. English, Spanish tangled in the air, became something new, something different. The streetcar zipped past, trailing sparks, filling his nose with the acrid smell of ozone. Once it was gone, the slow simmer of old food rotting in the gutters enveloped him.

Airships floated overhead, under steel-colored clouds.

The gray peaks of skyscrapers rose like mountains, not yet crowned by mist or thunder. If he looked out of the corner of his eye, he thought he saw mountains, hazy with distance. Every time he repeated his story to himself, they grew sharper, greener, until one day the skyscrapers would become the mountains back home. He started the story again, from the beginning.

Once upon a time, Juan Bobo got to los Nueba Yores, and was sure he had been better back home. He was convinced he had been better, less confused. Juan knew—other people called him Bobo, just like in the stories. This confused him even more, because he dreamed of a time when he had yet another name, but not today.

He repeated it until the story flowed seamless, without a hitch.

Those Rumors of Cannibalism and Human Sacrifice Have Been Greatly Exaggerated

ERNEST HOGAN

The frankentruck left Pie Town and headed toward the Very Large Array when Lola yelled, "Cowboy alert!"

"And it don't look like he's from around here," said Chuncho, who was driving.

Down the road a white kid in a cowboy hat, ostrich-skin cowboy boots, jeans, and a Virgin of Guadalupe T-shirt stood, backpack on his shoulder, sticking out his thumb, smiling.

"Yeah, pard, muy suspicioso. Better give him a ride. Check him out."

"You never know these days."

"Besides, we're ahead of schedule, and it might be fun." Lola leered.

Chuncho slid the truck off the pavement, raising a cloud of dust as it came to a halt a little too close to the white boy for comfort.

He didn't run, but his eyes were closed, and his thumb was still up as if it would offer some kind of protection.

"The kid's got faith," said Lola, whose hair was tucked up into a baseball cap decorated with a cowboy riding a giant scorpion.

"Or maybe a death wish," said Chuncho, whose long black hair spilled out of a classic red bandana.

"What kind of truck is this?" the white boy asked once he got his eyes open and climbed in.

"Just a Joe Typical truck like you find out here these days, made outta parts scrounged here and there from various sources where you can't tell the junkyard from the parking lot." Chuncho smiled, tweaking the moustache that spilled down under his chin. He turned down the energetic, accordion-driven music.

"The engine. It's really quiet. And makes a strange sound—like a spaceship."

"You can find all kinds of raw materials, especially since they started making cars down in Mexico." Lola crowded him with her ample, tattooed bosom.

"I've never seen anything quite like it." The kid was wide-eyed with wonder. His blond hair and beard made him look like a baby Viking.

Chuncho shook his head. "I knew it! You ain't from around here!"

The white boy blushed. "I thought this outfit would make me blend in."

Lola leaned back, got ready to lecture. "First, cowboys don't hitchhike. Unless there's something obviously wrong, like a burning, upside-down vehicle, and they're covered in blood."

"Also," Chuncho added, "around here, most of the cowboys are Indians."

"And shiny new boots and the T-shirt of La Virgen are the stuff you'd wear to go partying at night, not wandering around in midday."

The white boy pulled out a device, and started typing with a nimble thumb.

"That's all very interesting. Let me take some notes."

"What?" Chuncho asked. "You a spy or something?"

"No. I'm an anthropologist."

Lola suppressed a laugh. "A what?"

"An anthropologist. I'm here to study your culture."

Lola chortled. "Since when do we have culture around here?"

"Aztlán has been developing some interesting cultures lately."

"You really ain't from around here," said Chuncho.

"I'm from the American States."

Chuncho shot Lola a grin. "The Americano States."

She twitched one eyebrow. "Or what's left of them."

The kid tapped his device. "I'm here on a Kerouac grant from the Center for Cultural Futurism."

"What?" Chuncho grimaced.

"It's a think tank that's keeping track of neocultural developments in order to better understand the direction of civilization."

"Didn't they used to be called the CIA?" said Chuncho.

"How interesting!" Lola put an arm around the boy.

He blushed again.

"How long have you been in these here newfangled United States of Aztlán?"

"Just a few days. I entered through Utah. The Center figured it would be easier for a person of my coloration."

She sighed. "Damn Mormons. Always letting more white people in."

Chuncho shook his head. "They aren't happy with being part of Aztlán. They keep proposing secession, but their growing brown population keeps out-voting them."

"The same thing keeps happening in Texas. Democracy. Gotta love it!"

The kid nodded. "Yes. Just like Afrolatinization keeps the Neo-Confederates from leaving the American States—say! You seem to know a lot about local culture, and you're willing to talk—" The white boy held up his device, a shiny piece of virgin corporate technology. "Mind if I record our conversation? It'll be a great help in my work!"

"Work?" Chuncho groaned. "You actually get *paid* for this farting around?"

"It's so hard to do anthropological research these days. You find an interesting phenomenon, then when someone goes back to verify, it's vanished without a trace. So any form of informal documentation helps. Like with the UFO a while ago—I tried to take some video, but it came out all blurry."

"It was probably a drone."

Lola nodded. "We get a lot of those around here."

The white boy's finger was poised over his device, ready to hit the glowing "record" spot.

"I don't know," said Chuncho.

Lola jabbed him with an elbow to the ribs.

"We'll be happy to talk to you, kid. You look like good company. And besides, it'll be *fun!*" She winked.

Chuncho suddenly smiled. "Oh yeah, sure, why not? It could liven up a dull drive."

The radio telescopes got smaller in the distance. A few bison grazed on the flat expanse. A *Zia Logistics* truck passed in the other direction.

The kid made some adjustments on his device.

"This is Oswald Parker. I just got a ride on a truck that's near the Very Large Array in New Mexico, and the drivers agreed to talk. Can I have your names, please?"

"Lola."

"Chuncho."

"Could we have your surnames, too? Just for the record."

Chuncho snorted. "Sorry, but we need our privacy."

"That and the people we work for may not want us to be fully identified."

"Well, Lola, I can understand that. Who do you work for?"

Chuncho laughed.

"I'm afraid we can't tell you that either, Oswald," said Lola. "They're real privacy freaks."

"A lot of people, particularly in business, are. But that's okay. I mostly want to find out about life here in Aztlán, but I would like to know what you're hauling."

Both Lola and Chuncho laughed.

"Afraid that telling that would be a *big* no-no!"

"So, I should assume that my taking pictures is out of the question?"

The truckers howled.

"Besides," said Chuncho, "it's a technical thing, and kinda hard to explain."

Lola pinched Oswald. "Are you sure you're not a spy?"

"I'm just an anthropologist with a healthy curiosity. This truck is such a radical custom job, un-logoed, and non-self-driving. I thought it might be something interesting."

"Oh, it's interesting all right."

"So interesting that they gave us guns to protect it." Lola lifted her shirt, revealing her fire-apple-red bra and holstered gun.

Taking a hand off the wheel, Chuncho flashed his own sidearm.

"Wow! It must be pretty important."

"I guess so. Like I said, it's technical. I don't really understand it myself. I think it might be a new power source."

Lola jabbed Chuncho in the ribs again.

"Oops! I guess I should be more careful."

"Don't worry," said Oswald. "I'm going to consider you to be confidential sources. By the way—am I in any kind of danger?"

"Nah, those rumors of cannibalism and human sacrifices have been greatly exaggerated."

"We hardly ever do that kind of stuff anymore."

Oswald gave a nervous laugh, and fingered something under his shirt.

"What's that? A St. Christopher medal?" Asked Chuncho.

Oswald pulled it out to show. "It's a John Wayne medal. The Indian woman who sold it to me in Kanab said he was the patron saint of white people, and would watch over me."

Chuncho laughed.

Lola reached between her breasts and pulled out a medal just like Oswald's. "San Juan de la Hollywood is the protector of the people."

"John Wayne is a real saint?"

"Sure," said Chuncho, "like Pancho Villa, Emiliano Zapata, Jesus Malverde, Santa Muerte . . ."

"Oh, those new, unsanctioned saints."

"People make saints, not some medieval bureaucracy from across the ocean."

"This is Aztlán," said Lola, "the Land of We Don't Need No Stinking Badges!"

"But John Wayne is American. Isn't that cultural appropriation?"

"Las Américas ain't nothing but cultural appropriation," said Chuncho.

"Besides," added Lola, "Hollywood is in Aztlán."

"That's right," said Oswald, "it is now."

"Always was."

"Always will be."

"Amen."

"So John Wayne should protect us from being attacked or robbed?"

Lola waved her hands across the windshield, and the radio telescopes that were giving way to cannabis fields. "Here? You never can tell, maybe someday, somebody will steal them while they're listening for aliens."

"Have they ever picked up any aliens?" asked Oswald.

Chuncho laughed. "Think they'd tell us?"

"Actually," said Lola, "a lot of shamans come here. If you asked me, they're probably translating messages."

Oswald sighed. "If only I could talk to them!"

"The multinationals who finance all this since the secession like to keep that stuff to themselves."

A car with blacked-out windows cruised by in the other direction, its Yang and Yin flag flapping in the breeze.

"There goes a pack of shamans right now," said Chuncho.

"Why shamans? Why not linguists? Or scientists?"

Lola shrugged. "Quien sabe, compadre? We only know what people tell us."

"Who? Where?"

A truck logoed *Lone Star Logistics* passed like it was in a hurry.

"Y'know, people, in bars, pizzerias, pie shops."

"Speaking of people. Are you Indians? Latinos? Hispanos?"

"What kind of racist shit is that?"

"Sorry, it's just that I'm an anthropologist. It's my field of study."

"Chill, Chuncho. He's just doing his job. I'm Comancheroid."

"And I'm a Karankawa."

Oswald raised an eyebrow.

"Karankawa? I hope you were just kidding about the cannibalism."

"Hell, no. I'm proud of my cannibal heritage. Why should the Mexicans have all the fun?" Chuncho grinned, showing his very sharp teeth.

"Aren't the Karankawas extinct?"

"You shouldn't believe everything you learn in school."

"That's why I'm on the road doing research. I know about the Comanches and the Comancheros—I saw the John Wayne movie about them in preparation for this trip—"

"San Juan made movies?" Lola's smile made it hard to tell if she was kidding.

"—but I've never heard of Comancheroids."

"They're something new."

"One of the new, improved lost tribes of Norteamerica."

"Like the old-time Comancheros, we're renegades, forming new alliances."

"Are you involved in any quasi-legal activities?"

"What?" Chuncho shot Oswald a dirty look.

"Don't worry. I'm a scholar. As an anthropologist, I'm a non-judgmental observer with no affiliation to any law enforcement organizations."

"You think we look like gangsters or dope dealers or something?" Chuncho gave a half-smile.

"There hasn't been much of that since the cannabis business out of Colorado became a major force in Aztlán's economy." Lola smiled, but hers went all the way out.

"That along with Hollywood and Las Vegas."

"Not to mention the tech industries that multinationals are sponsoring all over Cali, Arizona, and Tejas."

"And the secret labs here in New Mexico."

"And don't forget the spirituality business."

"Yeah, one dude's Mickey Mouse is another dude's Buddha!"

Oswald smirked. "Uh-oh! You two are starting to sound like the Aztlán chamber of commerce!"

Lola gave him an elbow to the ribs.

Chuncho gritted his very sharp teeth. "We don't have nothing to do with those cabrones!"

"Chuncho, are your teeth filed?" said Oswald.

"Damn right they are."

"Why?"

"Makes me pretty." Chuncho laughed. So did Lola.

Oswald joined in. "Is tooth filing popular in Aztlan?"

"In some circles."

"What about other kinds of body modification?"

Lola shrugged her shoulders, squeezing her breasts and causing tattoos of the Virgin of Guadalupe and Wile E. Coyote to almost touch across her cleavage. Then a nipple with a ring popped into view.

"A Mayan guide in the Yucatan once told me that it's all coming back . . . facial tattoos, scarification, skull shaping . . ." She stuck out her split tongue, rubbing the halves together.

"Wow!" Oswald raised his device. "Could I get some video of that?"

"Knock yourself out." Lola did some oral acrobatics for the lens.

"They're trying to outlaw that sort of things in the States," Oswald said as he reviewed what he had just shot.

"Pendejos." Chuncho looked bored. He opened a compartment on the door and pulled out a colorful, resealable bag. He grabbed an oblong green object that he popped into his mouth and chewed.

"Anybody want any Cee-Cees?" He held out the bag.

"Come to mama!" Lola reached over, grabbed a handful, gobbled them like candy. "You want any, Oz?"

"Uh, I don't know . . . What are they?"

"Shit!" said Chuncho. "You've never seen Cee-Cees!"

"That's right." Lola's smile grew more intense. "They're doing their best to make everything illegal in the States." Then she leaned on Oswald. "My dear boy, Cee-Cees—"

"Not to be confused with chi-chis," Chuncho interrupted.

"I don't think he's *that* confused." Lola continued, "Cee-Cees—"

"Like saying 'Yes-yes' en español!"

"Would you cut that out? Where was I? Oh yeah—Cee-Cees—" Lola shot one to Chuncho's ribs, again, "—are a great new product out of Colorado, and research facilities in Cali."

Chuncho interrupted again. "It's a chocolate-flavored delivery system for a scientifically blended combination of caffeine and cannabis!"

"Keeps you awake and energetic. And feeling good! It's the working person's best friend! And it doesn't make you pee all the time!"

"It's rapidly replacing coffee throughout Aztlán!" Lola grabbed one out of the bag and waved it in front of Oswald's nose. "You should try one!"

Oswald focused on the Cee-Cee, crossing his eyes.

"It'll help you understand our culture," said Chuncho.

"And us," added Lola.

Oswald stared at the Cee-Cee.

A car with Ohio plates and a bumper sticker in Arabic passed them.

"I don't know," said Oswald.

"There's a helluvalot you don't know," said Chuncho.

Lola's eyes opened wide. "I know! I know! How about we make a deal? We'll let you have a peek at what we've got in the back if you eat a Cee-Cee."

"And it will prove that you've got some huevos."

"I'd really like to see what you've got back there."

Lola waved the Cee-Cee in front of his lips.

"Could I take a picture of it?"

"No," said Lola. "Besides, it wouldn't do any good."

"The nature of the beast," said Chuncho.

Oswald fingered his John Wayne medal, then took the Cee-Cee and popped it in his mouth.

"Good boy!" said Lola.

Oswald chewed, swallowed, closed his eyes, then opened them.

"Nothing's happening."

"It has to go through your digestive system."

Chuncho hit a button on the complicated dashboard, and a panel behind the seat whirred open. A soft yellow light leaked out.

Oswald twisted himself around to see, or at least try to see, a glowing shape, pulsing. Focusing on it left afterimages on his retinas. "We're getting kinda *Kiss Me Deadly—Repo Man—Pulp Fiction* here."

"What is that?" asked Lola. "Some kind of NeoAmericano prayer?"

"I minored in cinema." Oswald turned away, blinking. "And you don't know what it is."

"They pay us not to think about it."

"Whoever they are."

The panel whirred shut.

Lola and Chuncho smiled.

"Maybe it's a new kind of energy source." Oswald blinked, and rubbed his eyes.

"Yeah. Esoteric physics or something like that."

Then Oswald looked scared. "Could it be radioactive?"

"They said no."

"And there's no kind of shielding."

"I'm not feeling any ill effects . . . so far."

Another *Lone Star Logistics* truck passed.

"I feel . . ." said Oswald.

"What?" asked Lola.

"I feel . . . Great! It just hit me."

"It's the Cee-Cee," said Chuncho.

"I should take notes." Oswald pulled out his device and started typing, and mumbling. "Feeling energetic, mild elation, and . . ."

"Confident," said Chuncho.

"Yeah. Like I could take on the world. Say, this could be dangerous."

"It helps folks all over Aztlán get their work done. Coffee sales are tanking. If we could just start exporting them . . ."

Lola grabbed Oswald's shoulder. "Say! You should take some back with you!"

"Nonono! All cannabis-based products—even hemp—are illegal back in the American States. The Center wouldn't approve."

"Your loss," said Chuncho. "These new products are taking over."

"Bet they'll come up with things that'll replace opioids, coca-oids, and meth eventually," said Lola.

"The gangsters wouldn't like that," said Oswald.

"Too bad." Chuncho shrugged while extending a middle finger.

Oswald looked out the window and did a double take. "Wow! What are those?"

Lola leaned over him to look at windmills, solar panels, and strange towers.

"It's an energy farm!"

"They're popping up all over."

"Yes! I've heard of them." Oswald aimed his device and took some pictures. "Is it true that they're harvesting carbon from the atmosphere to make fullerene materials?"

"Beats me," said Chuncho.

"Fuller said that pollution is an unharvested resource." Oswald scribbled more notes.

"Who's Fuller?" asked Lola.

"Sort of an Americano saint." Oswald smiled at his own quip.

Then a red light on the dashboard blinked and beeped.

"What?" Oswald jumped, almost losing his hat.

"We're being followed," said Lola.

"Sure took the app long enough to notice," said Chuncho. "I've been tracking it in the rearview for ten minutes."

Oswald squinted.

"I don't see anything."

"You're looking too low."

Oswald looked up into the sky full of top-heavy, puffy, flat-bottomed New Mexico clouds.

"A UFO! Just like the one I saw earlier!"

"It's probably a drone."

"We get a lot of those around here."

Oswald frowned. "It's getting awfully close."

Chuncho sped up. So did the UFO.

"Seems to want to be near us," said Lola.

"Maybe we should take it out."

Oswald gulped. "Uh—take it out?"

"Yeah, they didn't give us these guns for nothing."

Chuncho slowed down. The UFO got closer.

Lola undid her seatbelt, took off her hat and handed it to Oswald.

"Hang on tight to this for me, dear. And yours too, if you don't want to lose it."

Oswald white-knuckled the hats in each hand as Lola got out her gun.

Chuncho lifted an arm, exposing his own gun. "Better take mine too."

"Good idea." She grabbed it with her free hand.

Chuncho hit another button. A panel overhead whirred open. Lola's hair flew wild as she stood up, raising the guns.

The two truckers gave out yells like attacking Indians in an antediluvian John Wayne movie.

Lola aimed and fired.

Oswald closed his eyes, gritted his teeth, and held his breath.

The sound of an explosion cut through the wind blast.

Oswald opened his eyes. In the rearview, he saw the UFO raining down in flaming pieces.

Lola and Chuncho screamed and yipped. She reholstered her gun and handed Chuncho his. Chuncho gave her a high five. Then Lola grabbed Oswald and gave him a hard kiss.

As the panel whirred shut, Oswald sat paralyzed, his hair sticking up and his lip twitching as he stared into space while Lola got back into her seatbelt, grabbed her cap, stuffed her hair back into it, and screwed it on tight. After a while she pried his hat out of his hand and put it back on his head.

"So how do you like Aztlán so far?" Lola asked.

Oswald stared at the oncoming road.

"It's . . . overwhelming."

Chuncho and Lola laughed.

Talking into his device, he said, "Honest, that really happened."

Then he turned it off and just stared out at the road ahead for a while.

Lola and Chuncho glanced at each other and smiled.

Farther down the road, the landscape got rocky, and deserty. On a hill by the roads a woman was being crucified. She wore a Mexican lucha libre mask and dress that billowed in the breeze. She was attended by a group of masked people wearing robes with pointy hoods.

The car with Ohio plates and the Arabic bumper sticker had parked. A family of black people—a woman and three girls wore hajibs that glittered in the sun—were taking pictures and selfies with the crucifixion in the background.

"What the fuck!" Oswald snapped out of his daze.

"Penitentes," said Chuncho. "A religious group."

"They've come out into the open since the secession."

"They help the poor and stuff."

"It's good to see more women being crucified these days," said Lola.

"What about the masks?"

"The law requires facial covering during these rituals."

"And it looks cool."

Oswald turned around as they passed them. "Could you stop and let me off here?"

"Sure." Chuncho slowed down, pulled over.

"Why?" asked Lola.

"I need to interview them. It's just the thing that I need for my research."

"Maybe they just look safer than us."

"I'm not sure I know what safe is anymore," said Oswald. "Goodbye! Thank you very much!"

He was out of his seatbelt before the frankentruck stopped. He opened the door, leaped out, and ran toward the crucifixion.

The truckers laughed as they got out and switched seats.

"My turn to drive!" Lola turned up the accordion music.

"Do you think he really was an anthropologist?" asked Chuncho.

"I don't know. What's an anthropologist?" said Lola.

"We sure did scare him."

"It's about time for us to head out. Let's give him something really interesting to report."

"Yeah." Lola did some mysterious dashboard work. The frankentruck pulled back onto the road, then took off, straight up, for outer space.

After the g-forces melted away into weightlessness, they couldn't stop laughing.

Back in Aztlán, Oswald sent a text on a hyperencrypted link:

It's weirder than we dared imagine.

Saint Simon of 9th and Oblivion

SABRINA VOURVOULIAS

As it was in the beginning, is now, and ever shall be

Saint Simon wasn't a plaster saint, and his Oblivion Oratory was not a church. But people filed in and out of the three-bay rowhouse on 9th Street as if from a basilica, singing his praises. Miracles were said to have been delivered from the dark innards of this ordinary sacred place, and the neighborhood's devotion to the flesh-and-blood resident within was fierce and proprietary.

I had just turned ten when I met him, and was, by most accounts, a tractable and pleasant girl. My mother had always told me I was pretty, so I believed it, but I cared less about that than she did. Mine was a different obsession: I alone had seen an airship of impossible proportion and great speed transiting high in the sky when I was three, and I never stopped searching the skies for another like it. My love for that shiny mystery (and others like it) wouldn't change even after I started living far from my mother, in Little Italy.

But I didn't think about any of that when I disembarked at the city's port dressed in my best lawn dress and my first real hat. No, that day, I stood beside my steamer trunk, worrying about whether I'd recognize a sister I couldn't properly remember, fifteen years older than me and so long a resident of this city she had forgotten how to write to us in Spanish.

I shivered while I waited for her, and not only because my dress was more suited to the warm and humid climate I'd come from than the day I arrived to. The city was filled with unfamiliar noise, and the noisome fumes of steam and coal and camphorated winter woolens. But my greatest shock came when Alta finally strode onto the pier to meet me. The sister who came to stand in front of me at the pier was dry and hard, like a plantain left unattended after its dark and sweet prime. She looked older than our mother.

I soon came to understand that many of the immigrant women in the city looked just as worn and tired. Long hours of punishing work was the price they paid to live in a city where balloons transited the high sky, steam whistled out of iron at the rail palace midtown, and emporiums of every sort of wonder dotted the streets.

Alta was actually the most daringly made of the girls at Mrs. Pasarelli's boardinghouse, and my arrival didn't change her habit of slipping out to see her beau in secret. I spent my first night in a new house (a new city, a new country) by myself, trying to identify the unfamiliar sounds that traveled from street to house, as I sewed up the snags and rents the long walk from pier to boardinghouse had produced in the delicate fabric of my dress.

Without intention but by grace or unknown quality, I became Mrs. Pasarelli's favorite boarder. Which was a good thing, because Alta worked long hours at the garment workshop and if Mrs. Pasarelli hadn't been looking out for me I wouldn't have learned Italian, let alone English. I wouldn't have eaten much, either. All the girls got an evening meal for their boarding fee, but nothing was prepared during the long hours while they were at the factory. Mrs. Pasarelli dragged me with her on her rounds to her vendors, all of them Old World in custom. The bakers, butchers, and purveyors along 9th Street thought I was Mrs. Pasarelli's granddaughter and she never disabused them of the idea as they gifted me with tidbits of buccellato, cured meats, and marzipan.

She taught me the ways of the city: how to ride the horse-drawn streetcars, how to dodge horse pats in the street without so much as a glance, and how to layer all my light clothing together for some semblance of warmth.

It was in Mrs. Pasarelli's company that I first met Saint Simon.

We were outside of St. Mary Magdalen de Pazzi when she sank to her knees and pulled me down to the ground with her. She kept her eyes downcast as the saint and his entourage passed in front of the church. I didn't know to avert my eyes, so I stared.

He didn't stand either tall or small but solidly in the middle, though the hat he wore pushed back on his head gave the illusion of a couple of extra inches. His hair was dark and curly over a high forehead. He was dressed impeccably in a bright white shirtfront, a five-button waistcoat, well-tailored coat and trousers, and shiny leather boots. He wasn't so much handsome as well-formed and polished to the smoothness of fine-grained wood.

His people noticed me looking. One of them started to admonish me, but Saint Simon held his hand up for silence. After a few moments he removed the small cigar in its bone holder from its home at the edge of his lips. "And who are you?" He asked it in English first, then in Italian, and after a pause, in Spanish as well.

I heard Mrs. Pasarelli's intake of breath. My accent had become so native none but she and Alta knew that the honeyed words of Spanish were ever poised on the tip of my tongue.

"My name is Carmen," I answered. In Italian.

"A boy's name," he said.

"Sometimes," I said. "And at other times, as you can plainly see for yourself, it belongs to a girl."

He laughed. "Pretty girl Carmen. Do you know who I am?"

I shook my head.

"You will," he smiled as he extended his right hand toward me.

I wasn't sure what to do after touching my fingertips to his but, whatever it was, I didn't do it. A hiss erupted from his followers. Saint Simon looked amused. "They all kiss it, you know," he said to me conspiratorially. I noticed his gold pinky ring then. Like a signet, only smooth and unmarked.

"Sorry," I said, and ducked my head to comply.

But he reached with his other hand and pulled my face up by the chin.

"Do nothing solely to fit expectation," he said, meeting my eyes. Then he let go of my hand and touched his fingers to the upturned brim of his hat. I watched his devotees engulf him as he walked away, forgetting I was still on my knees until Mrs. Pasarelli yanked on my arm.

"Pray you never need his intercession," she whispered fiercely in my ear as we walked home. "Pray you can live to a good old age without asking for his boon."

"Who? What?" I wanted to please this woman who had been kind to me, but her words confused me.

"Saint Simon of 9th and Oblivion," she answered. "The patron saint of impossibilities."

"Saint Jude Thaddeus is the patron of the impossible."

"I didn't say the impossible but impossibilities."

"Oh," I said, though I didn't see the difference.

After a moment I added, "I thought you couldn't become a saint until you were dead and your body stayed uncorrupted and smelled of flowers, and you performed three miracles."

"And what makes you think he hasn't?" she said.

That night I watched Alta prepare for her rendezvous. She dusted under her arms with talcum powder, dabbed some toilet water on her wrists and on her bosom. I got out of bed silently and went to stand behind her at the dresser. It was the first time I hadn't protected her privacy by pretending to sleep through her preparations.

Her eyes met mine in the mirror. I took the hairbrush from her hands and started brushing the hair glowing mahogany in the buttery light of the kerosene lamp.

"I won't apologize for my dalliance," she said, jutting her chin out just a bit. "I can no more wait for a properly disposed courtship than I can wait to pay our board to Mrs. Pasarelli."

I brushed in silence as Alta finished her ablutions.

"I want to ask you a question," I said after a while. "Do you know Saint Simon?"

She started, then measured her words. "I know of him, certainly."

"He's well-formed and worldly, but why would anyone think he is a saint?"

She studied my reflection in the mirror. "Someone asks him for something and he procures it."

"Like a merchant?"

"If a merchant could sell you what hasn't been invented yet."

"A tinkerer, then?" I felt a shiver pass through me. Whimsies and gadgets that fit in your palm were second only to airships in my affections.

"It's more than things, Carmen," Alta said. "They say he can make riches land in your pockets, or make your fondest desire meet you as you round a corner."

"Then why isn't everybody in Little Italy camped out on his doorstep?" I asked.

"Have you seen the queues?"

I shook my head. "Mrs. Pasarelli says that particular threshold isn't one we want to cross."

Alta took the hairbrush from my hands and laid it on the dresser, then deftly pulled her hair into a twist. I waited while she pinned it.

"Mrs. Pasarelli is a good woman, but perhaps not as canny a businessperson as she should be," she said finally. "Everything has a price, Carmen. Sometimes you have to think of it as an investment."

She turned on her bench to face me. "While we're talking about investments, I have a question. I remember Mother starting to teach you to sew when you were tiny, before I left. Have you grown to show the same ability with the needle as she has?"

"More. She used to give me all the silks to embroider. Why?"

"It's well past time for you to start earning your keep. Either do contract piecework or begin working at the workshop. There are no other choices."

I felt myself bristle at her words. I didn't know exactly what I wanted to do in this city of wonders, but I knew it had nothing to do with stitchery—whether by hand or by machine.

"Willy wants me to marry him," Alta said. "At my age I won't get a better offer. I cannot go into marriage dragging a sister along with me."

"I guess I could take in piecework," I said after a time. "Even though I'd prefer to perform contract work for myself, not a shop."

"If I show Mrs. Pasarelli your handiwork, she'll spread the word," Alta said. "She knows everyone in Little Italy, and maybe some in the Irish, Polish, and German neighborhoods too. Enough people, maybe, so you can make a living for yourself. Especially if you are willing to range far, and offer your services to those folks the Italian clothing workshops will not serve." After a moment she added, "But all of this depends on whether you really have the talent."

I walked over to my trunk and rooted around until I found a silk case covered with my best embroidery, and several of the fine linen and cotton handkerchiefs I had trimmed with cutwork. I handed them over to my sister.

"Yes," she ran her fingers over the stitching, "extraordinary. Mother's magic is in your fingers too. I'll show these to Mrs. Pasarelli tomorrow." She placed the pieces on the dresser top, but kept her hand on them, stroking them as if she were considering something. She was so long thinking it was me who broke the silence.

"I don't want to be beholden," I said. "Even to someone as well-intentioned as Mrs. Pasarelli."

"We are all beholden," she answered. "Sometimes the only choice we get is to whom."

She stood up, gathered her purse, and made ready to leave.

"Is he a good person?" I asked at the same moment she turned the glass doorknob.

"He is both good and bad. Or neither, Carmen. Like all of us."

I knew she thought I was asking about Willy, but her answer rang true for the real subject of my question as well.

Do nothing solely to fit expectation

Years later I'd remember the times that followed by which sort of stitchwork was most in demand, and what indulgence I was able to afford by it. The first year nearly every piece called for herringbone and cross stitches—and I treated myself to an afternoon at one of the city's museums, lingering among glass cases filled with fantastically jeweled beetles, and huge chunks of amber with bits of life caught in their frozen, honeyed centers.

The next year called for chain stitch designs that wandered in and out, and above and beneath each other to form intricate knot-work borders. I took a short trip in an air balloon, the flames roaring in my ears as we climbed above the patchwork city.

The sixth year—my sixteenth—it was cutwork fine enough to resemble lace. I saved up for a tiny brass kaleidoscope I hung around my neck; its tumbling glass gems melded into new shapes before my eyes—at my leisure, and at my pleasure.

I was making enough money to afford to live in a walk-up by myself, but I stayed at the boardinghouse. While I still received regular letters from home, it was Mrs. Pasarelli's face that popped into mind whenever I heard the word *mother*.

Alta and Willy, and their baby, Edgar, came to visit on Sundays. I didn't much like Willy—he seemed too much the eager salesman to me—but Alta didn't wear the hectic look she had during her years at the garment workshop, and Edgar was a grand baby, impossible not to love wholeheartedly.

"It's hard to remember I once lived at the boardinghouse," Alta said to me as we walked to get the streetcar after a Sunday dinner together. "It seems a lifetime ago and as if it happened to a different woman."

She turned her face to look fully at me, and smiled. "You should have a tintype made to send to mother. So she can see that you've grown into a well-formed woman."

I laughed. "She is quite worried that I haven't yet entertained a single marriage proposal. She's even more concerned that I am untroubled by it. It puts in jeopardy her plan that I should move back there with my new family in tow."

"Funny how she doesn't seem to need me to return," Alta said. "And I've already given her a grandchild."

The truth hung, unspoken, between us.

Despite her Peninsular features, Alta was the darkest Zelaya born in three generations. I was lighter. Here both of us were assumed to be Southern Italians or maybe outdoor-working Greeks, but at home it was understood we had significant indigenous and African blood coursing through our veins.

Our wholly European-appearing mother had sent me away to find an unknowing, and suitably pale, American husband ("Para mejorar la raza, nena"). Alta had simply been sent away. And no matter how much bleach, arsenic, and powder my sister used before sitting for the tintypes she sent home over the years, our mother had never once asked her to come back.

At the stop we stood and waited, the two of us with Edgar, and Willy standing well apart watching the passersby with the intensity only salesmen seem to muster. "You've noticed he has an eye for the ladies?" Alta asked, returning her eyes to mine after glancing at her husband.

There was no correct response to a question like that, so I didn't venture one.

"Saint Simon told me that would be the cost," she said. "Insecurity amid security."

"What do you mean? You petitioned him for something?"

"Yes, that night so long ago when you brushed my hair and made me feel cared for . . . like no one before had ever bothered to make me feel," she said. She touched my arm, a forlorn little tap of gratitude.

"But why, Alta? How could you be so desperate you'd go to Saint Simon for anything? Willy had already asked you to marry him, you knew you'd have a life away from the workshop, and those were the two things you always wanted."

She dropped my arm, moved a step away from me. "Don't be a child, Carmen. Did I ever say such to you? No, others said it to you about me—Mrs. Pasarelli perhaps, or more likely, Mother. But when does what people think we need or want correspond to what we really wish? When do their words and imaginings match what is inside our hearts?"

She was right, of course. My own heart filled with shiny things not yet invented, which neither real nor loan mother would ever understand.

Alta laughed then, but not from amusement. "I wasn't engaged that night, Carmen, I was pregnant. Willy had no thought to marry me. I wasn't meeting with him."

"But you dressed up, got ready the way you always did . . ."

"Saint Simon is a man, too."

Something ugly twisted inside my chest when she said it. "What happened to the baby?" I asked after a moment.

"I lost it a week after I saw Saint Simon," she said, and though there was no emotion in her voice, I saw her twist her favorite ring round and round her finger after speaking the words.

The streetcar trundled to the 12th Street stop. Willy sauntered back to join us moments before it came to a standstill, grabbing Edgar's pram to haul it inside.

"Good things will come to you," I said to my sister before she got on the streetcar. "And they will come without having to pay a price to any saint, real or false. You'll see."

Alta gave me an oddly wistful look. "Embroider a pillowcase for me, Carmen. Put your thoughts for good things into every stitch. And next time we meet, give me that sample of your art so I can rest my head on that certainty every night."

"Of course," I said. And even though I didn't understand her request, I went home and did exactly as she said.

Others found hardship in the next year: factories lost workers in fires, lung weaknesses abounded from the motes that swirled thick in our sky, and many children begged on street corners, or offered themselves for money.

I thrived.

I was doing piecework for churches across the city, and they paid hard coin. Mr. Spagnolo, the butcher, talked to Mrs. Pasarelli about his son, Joseph, still laboring in the Abruzzo. He was convinced I'd be a good match, and wanted to pave the way for a future union. Mrs. Pasarelli never said yes or no, thinking the butcher would continue to bribe her with choice cuts of pork while she equivocated. I took care never to ruin her ploy, even when a tintype of Joseph indicated a man rather older and more dour than his father's description.

Seeing Joseph's face and shoulders reproduced on the metal square reminded me that I had never sat for a tintype to send to my mother, even now that I had the earnings to easily cover the cost.

There was one photographer who catered to the Italian and Greek clienteles, and he set up his camera in a corner of the cordwainer storefront near Little Italy once a month. Three days after my seventeenth birthday I walked over to consult the schedule posted on the shoemaker's door.

"Will you be sitting for a portrait?"

Saint Simon stood behind me. His devotees were some twenty or so feet behind that. He hadn't changed.

"Yes," I said. His followers waited for me to kneel. I didn't. Their displeasure with me was expressed in exactly the same way it had been years before; his motion to silence them was also the same.

"Ah. Pretty-girl-Carmen. I wondered when I'd meet up with you again. But no longer a pretty girl."

"Do you mean no longer a girl, or no longer pretty?" It was insolent, I knew that, but something inside me longed to shatter the bell jar of solicitude around him.

"No longer either of those. A woman now. And rather more beautiful than pretty."

"You have a love of trinkets?" he asked after a long moment, his eyes drawn to the kaleidoscope hanging around my neck.

"A love for what allows me to experience the ordinary in extraordinary ways," I said, a little defensive.

"Are you yourself a tinkerer?" he asked.

"Only with the poor materials allowed to women: needle and thread and cloth."

His eyes darted from the kaleidoscope to the blouse beneath it. It was heavily embroidered with my best stitchery—a sampler of sorts—and wearing it was a sales technique worthy of Willy. But I caught myself wondering whether the saint's eyes lingered to notice my unusual skill or the swell of my body beneath it.

"Magic is magic, no matter its method," he said thoughtfully. "That is an extraordinary collection of the mythological and the scientific you have embroidered there—I believe I discern both the Trojan Hector and a rendering of the Hector's dolphin found so recently in New Zealand."

I secretly thrilled that he had recognized both figures within the extravagance of embroidery, but made my tone one of censure. "Whatever skills I have, I've bought them by earthly toil, not magic."

"Really?" he said. He smiled a little at that and studied my face for rather longer than was the custom.

"I, too, have come to sign on for a portrait," he said finally. "Shall we initial the hours for our sittings?"

"Why don't you sign up first?" I suggested, suddenly nervous that he'd sign up for the time slot next to whichever one I initialed. Or perhaps I was fearful that he would not.

"That would be a breach of courtesy beyond measure," he half bowed to me as he took a couple of steps back to give me room.

I initialed a slot that already had initials for the sessions before and after it, then indicated to him that I was done. I had taken several steps away when I heard him exclaim.

"Why, look at this," he said. "How fortuitous. It appears one of my friends has already signed me up without my knowing. Here are my initials, right above yours."

"Impossible," I said, stepping back to look at the list. I distinctly remembered "JT" as the initials before mine on the photographer's schedule. But there they were, two sinuous esses, snakes on parallel paths.

"It seems I will have the pleasure of seeing you again next week," he said.

I nodded mutely. Before I knew what he was doing, he reached for my hand and brought it up to his lips. I had never been kissed before so I didn't know whether all kisses stood the hair on your arms on end.

He gave another quick bow then disappeared as he had years ago, hidden by his people. I waited until I saw the whole group turn down 9th Street, then looked at my hand. By some trick of light his lips had left a luminescent mark there. The two esses-snakes again. My stomach fluttered uneasily at the sight.

The first present to arrive at the boardinghouse was beautiful and not entirely out of custom for courting gifts. It was a Mantón de Manila shawl, heavily embroidered with fine turquoise silk thread and finished with an extravagant foot-long fringe. I knew it had come from Spain, was frightfully expensive and something I could not keep. Mrs. Pasarelli, though scandalized that the saint would woo me, was equally scandalized by my decision to send the gift back without comment.

The next day the gift was more suited to what the saint knew about me, but again, not entirely out of the norm. The embroidery set included a gold thimble, bodkin, and case full of good German needles, and the finest scissors I had ever held—tiny and elaborately wrought, with blades honed enough to draw blood when I tested them. I sent it back with a shade more regret than the first offering.

The day after that a thing both suited and marvelous arrived by the usual courier. The slender golden tube was no ordinary kaleidoscope. When held to the eye it yielded the refracted images of a city from some other world, a place that had never existed, its streets dissolving from one to another with a mere flick of the fingers. By some trick of the lens, the city appeared peopled and full of life. The courier waited a long time until my wonder was satisfied enough to send that back.

My favorite—the one it tore my heart to unhand—was a silver automaton of spherical shape that hummed in my palm until it opened and released a strange and sleek airship—like and unlike the one I had glimpsed as a child. It shimmied on the end of a slender, silver tether as if waiting for me to do something.

As I watched, a door in the ship's side opened and a metal walkway slid down, like a tongue, until it touched my palm. I walked two fingers up it while I imagined myself boarding the ship, but stopped short when I remembered both Mrs. Pasarelli and the courier were watching.

One gift arrived each day at the boardinghouse and each was returned the same day to the oratory on 9th Street.

The day before I was scheduled to sit for the photographer, the delivery was of a small, and very heavy, velvet pouch. It felt as if there were a measure of lead shot in there. When I pulled the drawstring, a single gold ring rolled out onto my palm. It shouldn't have been so heavy, but it was, until I placed it on my finger. Then, it fit itself to size and instead of weighing down my hand made it feel so buoyant it might have floated away if not attached to my wrist.

Mrs. Pasarelli gasped when she saw the ring, and not only because of the symbolism of it on my finger. It was the saint's pinky ring, which hundreds of petitioners had kissed in tribute. I took it off and turned it over in my hand. What I had once thought a blank bereft of signet was actually inscribed with his initials—this time the snakes or letters came just shy of forming an eight.

"You cannot send that back," Mrs. Pasarelli said. She looked awestruck, and a little fearful.

I thought about it.

"Tell Saint Simon I will return this to him in person. Tomorrow. At the photography studio," I said to the courier.

I put the ring back into its pouch and tied that to the chatelaine at my waist. Throughout the day I felt its heavy tap at my hip, like a metronome marking time.

I arrived at the cobbler's shop exactly on time for my sitting but, as I was ushered back toward the makeshift photography studio, I saw Saint Simon still holding the pose he had been asked to take during his session.

He had dressed exactly as he had the day I first met him, down to the small cigar tucked in the corner of his mouth. One of his hands rested on a damask-covered occasional table placed there by the photographer. His other hand rested on his hip.

His head turned to me as he felt me enter the space, and I knew by the smile that ghosted his features that he cared not that he had ruined the tintype with the motion. The photographer squawked but Saint Simon just tossed the cigar in his direction and came to stand in front of me.

"You didn't return the ring."

"Not yet."

"Should I take that as encouragement?"

"I have it with me."

"But perhaps not to return?"

I dropped my eyes. I didn't rightly know what I wanted. His attentions had already filled and overflowed the corner of my heart I had set aside for a suitor. But that corner was small, and my heart crowded with other, more compelling desires.

I heard him laugh again, and as he did when I was a mere girl, he picked my chin up and tipped my face to look into his. But this time he kissed me. It didn't last long, but I could tell from the burn that remained on my lips that he had marked me with the same luminescence I had seen on my hand. It made me angry to think he had staked his claim this way, and at the same time I felt strangely anxious to return to his lips.

He stepped back and held me at arm's length as he met my eyes.

"I am no saint, Carmen." He spoke in Spanish but I was so used to my adopted languages that it took me a moment to realize the throwback to my childhood.

"Are you a demon, then?"

"No, not that either. I did not believe you were a creature of vision limited to the angelic and the demonic."

"And yet you are no ordinary man," I said. "You don't age. You give people what they ask for. And you know both too much, and too little, about women."

"I could tell you my story, and trust your imagination to take in its meaning, but will you hear my offer instead?"

He waited for my nod, which I offered grudgingly—I would have preferred the story.

"I do not offer you the mundane," he said. "No promise that we will grow old together, or bring up a tribe of children and their children. I will provide you with no servants to attend to you, no social engagements to plan, no society by which to improve the lot of your loved ones. But none other can give you the materials I will give you to tinker with. None will more willingly provide the means to fashion the marvels you can now only create in your mind. And none will rejoice as I will when you succeed in bringing them into the world."

It was not what I had expected, but what I wanted. As if I had gone to his house on 9th Street to whisper my most personal petition in his ear.

And I wasn't easy with it.

"Why me, Saint Simon?" I asked. "Is it just that the way I look pleases you?"

"It pleases me, of course. You are lovely to behold." He sighed, let go of my arms, and took a step away from me. "But that is not the reason. I am used to tribute traded for fulfillment of desire. You make no petition; you create what you want, with me or without me. You don't need me."

"And if I were to keep the signet ring, wouldn't that indicate need? Wouldn't that be both petition and tribute?" I felt sad asking it.

He took off his hat and ran his hand through his hair so his curls tumbled in disarray. It made him look younger, vulnerable. "You cannot imagine what you are turning down."

Without him touching me I felt my lips and the hand he had once kissed flare again with his luminous seal, and thoughts of the novel courting gifts he had sent to Mrs. Pasarelli's boardinghouse crowded my head.

"Of course I can," I said, untying the little pouch from the chatelaine. I reached for his hand and placed the pouch with its heavy ring in his palm, wrapping his fingers around it.

I moved away from him then and went to stand in front of the photographer. When I looked up from my pose, he was gone.

That night I read the latest letter from home and thanked whatever fate had brought me to this gray city teeming with workers and immigrants and the buzz of eternal striving. There was no appeal in returning home to the life my mother outlined in her letter. Certainly none in the men she listed as potential suitors, stolid types who swore to repair my odd ways by dint of routine and eternal bond.

As I set aside the paper crisscrossed with my mother's neatly inked entreaties, I thought on how, even without accepting his ring, Saint Simon had ruined me for all other suitors. Mrs. Pasarelli stroked my hair and murmured consolations in Italian while I cried. She didn't understand my tears. And why should she? Neither did I.

Are you yourself a tinkerer?

I made enough money in the next four years that Mrs. Pasarelli didn't have to take in any other boarders. Alta moved from Little Italy to a fine home at the northern edge of the city and I rarely saw her, though she sent me weekly letters that spelled out, in her extraordinarily graceful Spencerian hand, the happier details of her life.

The butcher had stopped hoping to marry me to his son, but he remained fond of us and often gave us his most select cuts of meat for less than what he charged others. My embroidery adorned the vestments of priests, including the archbishop, and the altars of so many churches across the city I lost count. Mrs. Pasarelli grew fat from the rich, exotic treats I bought for her in the other sections of the city when I made delivery of my embroidered goods.

Saint Simon was still around, of course, because need and desire never go away, but I didn't run into him again. Sometimes, in middle of the night, my skin would burn and I knew then that he still thought about me.

We received word that my mother had passed away and I asked Father DiStefano at St. Mary Magdalen de Pazzi to celebrate a memorial Mass for her. When Alta walked through the door neither Mrs. Pasarelli nor I recognized her. My sister had turned into the picture of immoderation while I wasn't watching. Her hat required not one but three citrine-tipped hatpins to hold down its extravagance of trimmings.

Later, as we walked to the streetcar, I linked my arm through Alta's as I had in the old days. We walked slowly. Edgar ran ahead with his father.

"Do you know whether Saint Simon still grants petitions?" my sister asked.

I ignored the twinge that followed the name. "Whatever do you lack that you'd think to ask?"

"When I went to him years ago, I petitioned for security. Later, your own gift to me brought us financial luck. But now that I am thinking of moving my family even farther from this octopus of a city, I would ask for the smallest share of what you have."

At my blank stare, she said, "Mother's magic. Every stitch she took, every one you've taken, has brought the certainty of good fortune with it. She made you her unwitting apprentice until you learned so well you surpassed her abilities. That's why she implored you to go back before she got too feeble to baste, much less embroider. And you stayed away. How I've thought on that. She chose the wrong daughter."

"My skill with the needle isn't magic," I said after a long silence. "My success comes from how wildly I imagine and how meticulously I execute. Not magic, not fortune, just me."

"You've always had an exceedingly high opinion of yourself," she said, then shrugged. "Perhaps that, too, is part of the gift Mother chose for you."

After she left I thought more on her words. I loved my sister, and I knew that in her sin-pelos-en-la-lengua way she loved me just as well. The idea that I had been given an unearned magical gift distressed me, even as I disbelieved it.

And maybe it was that disbelief that made me put down the needle for a while. I had plenty of trunked merchandise so I didn't stop peddling, or fulfilling standing orders, but I didn't make anything new.

I filled the hours of my day wandering the city, discovering its most remote and hidden charms, though several weeks into the new routine I started noticing that many of those charms were built on the labor of people who were barred from enjoying them. And everywhere I went, I scoured the skies, too, hoping to glimpse the metallic shape remembered from my childhood and Saint Simon's miniaturized automaton.

The remainder of my time was spent helping Mrs. Pasarelli do whatever needed doing. Her heart had gotten weaker after a bout with pleurisy, and sometimes I found her out of breath and clinging to furniture to keep herself upright.

Slowly, the churches stopped clamoring for my handiwork. The private requests from clients citywide—for christening gowns, fancy shirtwaists, and embellished tablecloths—dried up. The clothier who had placed an order for as many of the exquisitely hand-embroidered wedding gowns as I could produce saw his storefront go up in flames, and the whitework with which I had filled curtains and handkerchiefs seemed to go out of fashion all at once.

When I finally picked up my embroidery hoop again my mind went blank and my fingers, driven only by memory, turned out workmanlike but uninspired stitches. No good fortune accompanied them.

Once I understood that sewing would never again offer me a livelihood and my independence, I considered other options. I was neat-handed and strong, resolute and a quick learner—so I became an apprentice at Mr. Spagnolo's butcher shop and started brandishing knives and saws instead of needles.

A lady butcher was something of a scandal, but Mr. Spagnolo paid me to be there and to learn his trade for his own reasons: he had started to think of me as a match for himself. I didn't encourage it. I had always been unfit for marriage and even after my turn of fortune there was no space left in my heart for a kind man with calf eyes and a blood-stained apron.

His gentle but unwanted affections made me toy with the idea of apprenticing for another trade. I went sometimes to the local clockmaker's shop and asked him to open up the cases of mantel and pocket clocks to examine the tiny springs and ratchets powering the timepieces. I talked long with him about caliber and escapements, and found that I liked even the words of his craft.

But then the clockmaker, too, started making eyes at me.

Like the clockmaker and Mr. Spagnolo, there were other men who followed my comings and goings with interest. I was a woman of robust good health, with lively eyes and usually upturned lips, whose interests were as varied as the city. I was well past marriageable years but delighted by my solitary state—a woman unneeding, as Saint Simon had once noted. I found the extraneous masculine attention a bother and a bore, but I paid it little heed as I bided my time at Mr. Spagnolo's butcher shop.

The boardinghouse was dark one night when I came home from a full day of sausage-making in preparation for the city's Italian festival. I walked up the staircase of our house without lighting a lamp because I did not want to wake Mrs. Pasarelli, who slept more fitfully these days. When I opened the door to my room, it slammed back and sent me sprawling.

It wasn't the clockmaker lurking in my room.

It wasn't Mr. Spagnolo.

It wasn't my brother-in-law, nor my beloved saint, or any man I could name or recollect meeting.

But just because I didn't know him didn't mean he didn't understand what I valued about my life.

He brought a splitting maul down on my right hand while I scrambled to get back on my feet. The next blow, to my other hand, was badly aimed and caught the tips of my fingers as a press catches overripe fruit.

For the second time in my life I had Mrs. Pasarelli to thank for my survival.

I don't know how she withstood the heart-stopping screams that roused her, or how she ran up the stairs, but the sound of her approach sent my attacker out the window onto the porch roof and then down to the street.

Lucky, the surgeon called me.

Lucky that the assailant used the blunt side of the maul instead of the ax side. Lucky that Mrs. Pasarelli had some bone-setting skill so that an amputation wouldn't be necessary. Lucky to be alive.

As if he, or any man, could understand what my life (and Mrs. Pasarelli's) would by needs now become.

In the days that followed, Alta sent money for my convalescing, but it was not enough to keep us living forever as we had, and there would be little more forthcoming.

Mrs. Pasarelli managed to rustle up enough paying boarders to fill the house again, but not without sacrifice. Her knuckles and knees were swollen and bruised once more with the harsh work of cleaning and maintaining; her rounds to buy from purveyors took her out early and late in the cold, even when the pain in her joints overwhelmed her and her step faltered. Every night she would fall abed with the wheezing of those whose bodies were not meant to be laboring so hard into their twilight years.

I stayed in the room I now shared with her so that mine could be rented out, hands lying still in my lap, my mind yearning for the impossibilities that my life would no longer yield.

A woman unneeding

Mrs. Pasarelli had never been outside so late at night and her steps weren't as sure as they had been, but she knew most of 9th Street by heart and she didn't fall . . . her greatest fear of late.

There was a moment of vertigo as she climbed the steps to the double door she had never before allowed herself to knock upon. Not when her husband was spitting up blood. Not when her cupboard had held a single box of biscuits. Not when her last remaining biological kin moved to the other end of the continent, as far from her as they could get before hitting ocean.

She lifted the heavy snake-twined knocker and let it fall twice. She would have liked to say it was a woman who opened the door, but the metallic cast of the skin pointed to something other: a tinkerer's construct. "I came to petition," she said anyway.

The mechanical being chugged and huffed. Mrs. Pasarelli followed it down a dim hall to a doorway leaking light unlike any she had seen before. The room was filled with things, almost all of them moving: waves of small metal spheres ebbing and flowing across the polished hardwood floor; dark, wingless shapes hovering in perfect formation in the air above her head; orbs emanating the strange and pure white light that filled the room.

A piece of piano music played, somber and plaintive. When Mrs. Pasarelli finally located its source, it turned out to be a strangely shaped glowing rectangle on the desk in a shadowed corner of the room. The same corner where Saint Simon stood—something glinting metallic in his hand—watching her as she examined the surroundings.

When she saw him, she averted her eyes and started slowly to her knees. "Saint Simon, I beg your intercession."

"You don't need to get on your knees. I don't care for it and there's no one else here to appreciate the theater of it." He moved out of the shadows when he said it and motioned to a chair close to her. "Sit instead."

The music stopped as he came to perch on a chair directly in front of hers.

She allowed herself to study him. "You are not really a saint."

"No," he said, a smile passing fleetingly over his features. "People name what they don't understand according to their natures, and in this neighborhood, at this moment, you are all a very Catholic lot. It won't always be that way . . ."

He waited a moment, then went on. "I doesn't matter what I am, I have the ability to grant most of what your people can think to ask. Tell me why you call on me."

"I want to see your true face."

"Is that all?" The smile stayed on his lips this time. He tossed the small metal object from one hand to another. "A flattering but very silly petition."

"No, that is not my petition," she said. "I just want to know who I'm dealing with."

"I see." He kept tossing the object between hands, each time quicker than the last so it became impossible to discern its shape in the blur. He took a long time considering her request, then he flipped the metal object he had been playing with straight at her.

She surprised herself by catching it. It was a smooth sphere, but there was something in it because it shimmied in her palm. As she held on, it fractured in curved lines, collapsing away from its center, and reshaped itself into a miniature airship like one she had seen years before when looking over Carmen's shoulder at the boardinghouse.

The airship levitated over her palm—the air visibly shivering around its fusiform shape—buzzed up to her face, then sank and grounded itself again on her hand.

She leaned forward with some difficulty and set the ship on the carpet by her feet. "Why do you create such strange things?"

"Because I can. Because sometimes you have to see things writ small to remember how to create them writ large. Or maybe because this is an oratory and creating them is as close as I get to prayer." He shook his head and sighed. "But you did not come here to talk about my gadgets. You came to ask that I insinuate a particular thought in someone's head to prompt the outcome you desire. Or you crave an achievement, a windfall, wild success you believe is beyond your ken. Or perhaps you wish something dark and cruel to befall someone you detest, but you are ashamed to ask it of your familiar saints, and scared to ask it of the neighborhood's familiar sinners."

"No. None of those interest me in the least," she said. When his eyes met hers she saw the spark of curiosity.

"It is my daughter I came to ask for," Mrs. Pasarelli said. "You have met her. In fact, after your interaction with her you likely understand her better than any but me."

The spark guttered out and turned into something different. "How extraordinary. You believe I understand any of the thousands of you who have bent your knee to me? What have any of you given me to know you by, except your dull and small-minded petitions?"

Mrs. Pasarelli pulled a heavily embroidered handkerchief from her sleeve and dabbed at her perfectly dry eyes as if they were over-flowing. Then she held the cloth over her mouth as one artful sob followed another. When she was done, she offered him the crumpled linen, as old people sometimes will when they are distracted.

He hesitated, then took it, and when he realized it was dry, smoothed it to square on the leg of his trouser. His fingers traced the raised satin stitches.

"I remember the hands that crafted this magic," he said after a moment. Then he got up and walked away from her.

"Neither magic nor hands serve her now. And whatever she once envisioned, whatever wild imaginings she once entertained, what-ever kept her going from one happiness to the next—she has left off doing it. As if all that mattered about her was the skill of her hands. I do not rightly know what to ask you to do for her, Saint Simon, except that it help her find a way back to herself."

When he said nothing, Mrs. Pasarelli continued. "I know there will be a price in petitioning for this, but I am willing to pay it—even if it means she will loathe me when she finds out I've come begging you in her name."

He turned back to her. His eyes grew larger as he studied her, and duskier, until they rivaled two enormous pools of India ink spilled out onto the lucent, hard surface of his face. "It is not you she will hate."

After a moment he added, "She still thinks of me with something like love sometimes. I can feel those thoughts on my skin. It might surprise you to know—as it surprises me—that I am not yet ready to give that up."

Mrs. Pasarelli stood up slowly. "Then you are not as different from the folk whose petitions you disdain as you'd like to believe."

He grabbed her hands, held them tight in his. Long minutes passed, their gazes locked in unspoken challenge. "What have these hands created?" he asked her, finally, in Latin.

Mrs. Pasarelli knew nothing of alien beings who pretended to be of her time and of her people, for their own complicated reasons—but she held seven decades of Roman rite in her memory, and she recognized the hard questions that preceded a ritual of acceptance.

"These hands have cooked, these hands have cleaned, these hands have counted money," she said after long thought. "They have swaddled the young, they have tended the old, they have fought back death. But these hands have created nothing."

Saint Simon dropped her hands and turned away. The strange contraption in the corner started playing again, and the orbs overhead dimmed to half their light.

"Then they must learn," he said. "Come back in a fortnight."

World without end

The imagination is life viewed through the distortion of an isinglass curtain.

I may have imagined Saint Simon.

I certainly imagined a gadget like one of his, but properly mine, a metal sphere whirring, clicking, and cracking open to reveal—tiny, perfect, whole—my city. Urbi et orbi.

I held the sphere-city up to my eye (as if my hand had no problem holding the fractured orb), and found Alta's rambling house. Inside it, my sister sat at a quilting frame, teaching herself to sew magic with stitches. I may have imagined the world fairer than it actually is, and so her stitches were tiny, perfect, and perfectly fortunate.

In the cracked-open city's south, I let my eyes retrace my first journeys—from pier to boardinghouse, from boardinghouse to 9th Street, from St. Mary Magdalen de Pazzi to Oratory.

I may have imagined Oblivion Oratory as well.

I certainly imagined crossing its miniaturized threshold (as I never had in life) and found, in its labyrinthine rafters, a room of bright, moving wonders. Inside it, Mrs. Pasarelli toiled at a tinkerer's workbench. I may have imagined the world more advanced than it actually is, and so the array of tools and materials at her hand were marvelous in their mystery, and impossible to name.

I let my eyes travel the rest of the sphere city—east, west, and north—remembering streets in neighborhoods I hadn't seen since I was younger, back in the days when I made delivery of my embroidered goods to all corners (if a sphere can have corners), and then again when I went searching out its mysteries. I may have imagined the world more fluid than it actually is, and so my past was also my present and my future on those streets.

I may have imagined all of it.

Except this: Somewhere hidden in city or world is a silvery airship waiting for me.

I remember the speed with which it transited an empty tropical sky. I remember its miniature iteration opening to me. I remember how that unspoken wish made material unfurled its long ramp as invitation. I remember that it was held by only the slenderest of restraints.

I remember and know beyond simple imagining. If I ever find my airship, I will climb up, step inside its alien space, and cut it loose.

Because there must always be an impossibility to believe in. Am I right?

So be it

"Wake up," Mrs. Pasarelli repeated until I opened my eyes.

Morning light streamed through the window's wavy leaded glass. My fingers were motionless on the linen sheet I had long ago embroidered with feather, seed, and spoke stitches: Buon Giorno it read on one side, Buona Notte on the reverse.

After Mrs. Pasarelli had helped me dress and I was seated at my usual spot at the window, the old woman knelt before me and took my hands in hers.

"I have had such odd dreams," I told her. "Bitter and sweet at once."

"Like life then," the old woman said.

"I imagine so." I sighed then, and looked down at my hands. Mrs. Pasarelli's gnarled, swollen fingers wrapped around mine so tightly I could see the blood pooling in my fingertips. But I felt nothing.

"What have these hands created?" Mrs. Pasarelli asked unexpectedly.

It seemed such a cruel question, and yet I felt no malice in it.

"Good fortune. Rancor. In the end, they created nothing," I answered.

"Not nothing," Mrs. Pasarelli said. "These hands created our lives."

She released my hands and plunged one of hers into the deep pocket of her apron. I looked away from the movement, out the window, to the city coming alive beyond the glassy barrier. Maybe I'd go outside today, just to hear the noise and see how the street had changed since the last time I had walked it, months ago. Maybe I'd borrow one of Mrs. Pasarelli's aprons so I could tuck my hands, out of sight and out of mind, in the pockets, so none would look on me with pity. I could find some joy in this plan.

When I looked back to ask her about the apron, Mrs. Pasarelli had placed something in my right hand and wrapped her fingers around mine so I could cradle its smooth metal curve.

I couldn't feel the sphere vibrating, but I could hear it humming. Or maybe it was me humming.

Either way, something was breaking open, and I caught my breath to see what would emerge.

Ancestral Lines and Other Tall Tales

SAMY FIGAREDO

Notes from the Playwright: *Ancestral Lines and Other Tall Tales* was originally written in 2017 for Teatro de la Séptima Generación / Seventh Generation Theatre.

Casting: This play can be performed with as few as four and as many as six actors. The characters Imani and Aleja are both envisioned as queer people of color, and the pronouns used in the text are deliberately "they/them." The Ancestors are led by one "femme figure," Zemi, who must be played by a performer of Indigenous or Latinx origin. There must be at least two Ancestors (including Zemi), but there can be as many as four. If performed, the director can divide the Ancestors' lines up in whatever way they like.

Text: A lot of the dialogue between Imani and Aleja, and some of the dialogue between Aleja and Zemi, is meant to be rapid-fire. The two friends talk over each other in ways that only friends can do. A forward slash in the text (/) indicates that one line overlaps with the next: one character might keep talking for a little bit, but they eventually trail off as another speaks over them. An em dash (—) similarly represents a character being interrupted, but in this case the interruption is abrupt: one thought is suddenly cut off by the next.

Lights up on a sloppily furnished bedroom: a haphazardly made bed topped with mismatched pillows and throws, a cluttered desk, a drawer with clothes spilling out of every one. There may be a hideous knockoff Oriental rug on the floor. In the corner, an end table has been converted into a makeshift altar replete with candles, incense, and statuary.

ALEJA can be heard arguing with their roommate IMANI. The argument is fairly low-stakes at first—it's more like the casual sparring of wits that goes on between old friends. The conversation starts offstage.

ALEJA enters first, carrying plastic grocery bags full of beverage cans, sunscreen, Tupperware containers full of leftovers—looking like they just came from a cookout. They are pursued by IMANI, whose carefully groomed outfit suggests they did not go to said cookout.

IMANI: So, this white lady—whom you've never met before—just walks right up to you and says you have a /

ALEJA: "female ancestor watching over my right shoulder" **IMANI:** "female ancestor watching over your right shoulder"

IMANI: And you *believed* that shit?

ALEJA: I didn't say I believed her. I'm just saying, I thought it was kind of cool that she came up to me / and said

IMANI: What was her "spirit animal?"

Standoff—both understand the implications, and ALEJA doesn't want to give IMANI the satisfaction of being right.

ALEJA: A maned wolf.

IMANI: Yup.

ALEJA: Okay, but come on. You have to admit, it's at least kind of cool that she came up to me of all people and—

IMANI finally throws their hands up, exasperated.

IMANI: Dude, you know why! You *know* why she came up to you.

ALEJA: No, I don't!

IMANI: You went to a Samhain / ritual

ALEJA: It's pronounced "Sow-in," / not

IMANI: Do you even *celebrate* that shit?

ALEJA: No but the pagan group hosting it said people of any faith could come / not just Wiccan

IMANI: Okay, so how many other people of color were there?

Another standoff, as before.

IMANI: She went up to you because she wanted her brownie points. She saw *one* POC and wanted your stamp of approval on her fucking church of cultural appropriation just so she can keep—I don't know, worshipping Buddha and Odin and being a fucking Voodoo priest-ess / at the same time

ALEJA: Okay. *Okay.* I get it. Okay? I get it. I just . . . thought it was kind of cool.

An awkward silence settles in. IMANI realizes they've hit a nerve.

IMANI: . . . and anyway, didn't you get your Ancestry results like, last week? You don't / need

ALEJA: I mean, yeah, but it's—it's not the same thing. It's weird, you know. The way they break down your results. And it's all, like, pop science bullshit. And the labels, the labels are totally arbitrary. It *says* I'm part "Native American," and "Andean," and "Amazonian," and "South American," but like . . . which parts? Most of my rela-tives don't have any documents. Especially on my dad's side. I just wish I could trace that path back, you know? Figure out exactly who came from where. Maybe then I'd feel like . . . I don't know, like I had a real community or something.

IMANI: Okay, first, that's not where community comes from; and second, we can't all trace ourselves back to Charlemagne or Henry VIII or Shakespeare—

ALEJA: Shakespeare doesn't have / any living relatives

IMANI: Will you just / listen to

ALEJA: But I get it / I get it

IMANI: At least you're not "descended from Thomas Jefferson."
I'm trying to tell you. *We don't get to trace ourselves back.* It doesn't matter if you came without documents, or someone brought you here without documents, or you brought your own documents but someone made you change your—look, *fuck* a document. You and I don't just get to go online and trace ourselves back like that, and look up our long-lost cousin with some huge English countryside estate, and call ourselves the descendants of Vikings and classical composers—

ALEJA: I know already, okay? I know. It was just . . . in the moment . . . it was nice in the moment, okay? It didn't mean anything.

IMANI: . . . did you have fun?

ALEJA: I mean . . . the food was pretty good.

IMANI: Whaaat? You didn't tell me there would / be food!

ALEJA: Yeah, it was like first you had this ritual and then there was a potluck—

Their conversation is interrupted by the sound of a ringtone. IMANI checks their phone.

IMANI: That's my ride.

ALEJA: Oh. Cool.

> *Deflated, ALEJA starts busying themselves with their altar—lighting a candle, incense, etc.*

IMANI: You're okay, right?

ALEJA: Yeah, of course.

IMANI: . . . you really okay?

ALEJA: *Yes!* It was just a ritual, no big deal. Now go. Tell Ell Jay I said hey.

IMANI: You want to come?

ALEJA: I'm good. Kind of tired, so . . .

IMANI: . . . okay. Well, I'll see you tonight then?

ALEJA: See you tonight. Have fun.

> *IMANI leaves the room. Seconds later, we hear another door closing. ALEJA is now alone in the apartment, sitting at their altar.*

ALEJA: "Fuck a document." . . . Maybe there was one, once, that could've proven you existed. It would have been written when you lived . . . and burnt, too, so that no one would know your name after you died. Now, the only link I have to you is some meaningless pop science percentage and the words of a pussy-hatted pagan, telling me you're there on my shoulder, telling me—

| **ALEJA:** "you're on the right path." | **ZEMI:** "you're on the right path." |

> *Softly, slowly, ALEJA's ancestors emerge from the darkness. The ANCESTORS' lines can be divided up however you choose, depending on how many actors there are.*

ANCESTORS:
So, child, you are finally ready

to know us
to speak us back into existence
back into the world—
to pull us from the soil our bodies have nourished
for centuries.
Come, feel the earth from which you grew
like grass without roots
each blade now indistinguishable from the next
forming a lush blanket over this rich earth
Its beauty taken for granted
because no one can ever understand it—
Nobody ever takes the time
It is your earth, child,
the land of high mountains
where fertile land stretched beyond the horizon
All we ever wanted grew in abundance
All we had, we gave freely
and all we did not would be stolen
along with our names—our histories
Come trace the tapestry of where we've been
It may be frayed
but so long as you live, it survives
You are, after all, on the right path.

ALEJA stands, hesitant to approach. They tentatively reach out to pass their hand through the ANCESTORS, as if they are ghosts. It doesn't pass through. One of the ANCESTORS looks at it, then takes and lowers it. ALEJA sighs, loud and passive-aggressively.

ALEJA: *Dale que te dio,* if I had known all it took was going to some bullshit pagan potluck, I wouldn't have thrown down two hundred dollars on a DNA kit.

They stare at the apparition of their ancestors. The ANCESTORS don't respond.

ALEJA: You're supposed to be my ancestors?

ANCESTORS:
We don't suppose anything—we are.
We are your ancestors

or, at least, some of them.
A font of them,
We give a face to the unseen, all for you—
for you to look upon us, as you've always dreamed,
and for us to regard you,
our blood,
our legacy.

ALEJA: Then which ones? If you're only *some* of my ancestors, which ones? Where are you *from*?

The ANCESTORS laugh.

ANCESTORS:
From?
What is this "from"?
Your mapmakers and lawmakers,
they draw their lines differently than we did
or would have done.
We were first on the land
The land chose to host us
accept us
nurture us
first
And we gave back
We loved our island
before anyone else did—
and they did
and they did
and they did.

ALEJA: Then . . .

A femme figure, ZEMI, steps forward.

ZEMI: We are the Taíno people.

ALEJA: Taíno? Then—my family—we were Taíno?

ANCESTORS: Are. *Are.* You are.

ZEMI: You *are.*

ALEJA: Then . . . the test. The "Native American" / thing

ZEMI: Is not . . . all wrong. Your tests paint the Native peoples of the world in broad strokes.

ANCESTORS:
>We are not a monolith
>Every land has its Native people
>Some have many people
>of many nations
>But do not speak of us in the past tense
>The four of us
>right now
>may be an illusion
>But the indigenous people of the world
>are as real as you are
>They walk the earth with you
>and you share their legacy

ALEJA sits, processing the information.

ALEJA: I really thought the Taíno people didn't exist anymore. I didn't even learn about them—

ANCESTORS: Us.

ALEJA: *(Hesitates.)* You . . .

ANCESTORS: *Us.*

ALEJA: *(A breath. A two-letter word has never been more difficult to say.)* . . . us. I didn't learn about . . . *us* . . . until college. And even then, everything I read told me that we had been killed off hundreds of years ago.

The ANCESTORS trade looks. ZEMI kneels before ALEJA, taking their
hands in hers.

ZEMI: My blood . . . do you think we wrote your books? Is mine the face you saw in your lectures? When did I—

ANCESTORS: When did we tell you these lies—

ZEMI: And wasn't there anyone in your life to correct them?

ALEJA pulls away, retrieving an unopened beer can from one of the plastic bags. They stare at it for a moment, then crack it open and take a sip. They're still drinking, even as they turn around and see the ANCESTORS staring at them. ALEJA offers them the beer. The ANCESTORS look at it, unimpressed. ALEJA awkwardly sets the open beer aside.

ALEJA: My grandfather came from Spain. I know that because he used to say so, all the time. He was so proud of it. He'd say they had baptismal records tracing his family back to Andalucía for four hundred years. You can look them up, if you want. I did, and he's right. Baptismal records. And that's not even all. You can see his family coming in through Ellis Island before they finally settled in Puerto Rico.

ZEMI: And your grandmother?

ALEJA: That's where the well dries up. I found a couple of things on her dad, but her mom . . . and their parents, and their parents . . . it's like they never existed.

ANCESTORS:
They existed.
We existed.
Someone told you a lie one day—
one you had no choice but to believe—
when they said "no papers, no person."
No one can blame you
It doesn't take much to enforce a lie
All it takes is
fire
and blood
fear

and greed
the might of the righteous
and their ships
and their guns
and the rest of us have no choice
but to believe.
What proof have we to the contrary?
What voice have we to protest?

ZEMI: Someone once spoke our names—and we had names—but they took our names with us when they died. Either someone chose not to tell you, or they were not able to tell you; but it is no accident that you were not told.

> *ALEJA turns back to their altar.*

ALEJA: You know, one time, my mother told me . . . when she was pregnant with my first sister, her aunt told her—

ALEJA: "make sure you eat plenty of oatmeal. You wouldn't want your children to turn out dark like you."	**ANCESTORS:** "make sure you eat plenty of oatmeal. You wouldn't want your children to turn out dark like you."

ALEJA: My grandmother was always serving me oatmeal when I was a kid. I hated it. I thought it was stupid then, but now . . .

> *ALEJA sits again, and again, ZEMI goes to their side. They rest their head on ZEMI's shoulder. The ANCESTORS encircle them.*

ALEJA: It feels like she just wanted me to be white. Maybe because . . . maybe because she couldn't be. She couldn't "pass," and she was obsessed with this . . . old wives' tale, or whatever, because she wanted me to. *(Beat.)* Why didn't she tell me that I'm part Taíno? Was she ashamed?

ANCESTORS:
    Part Taíno? Which part?
    Do you have a single fingernail that is indigenous,
    while the rest are not?

ZEMI: You may choose to show certain sides to people to survive, but the features you conceal are still with you. The moon does not dissolve to form a crescent: it only chooses to show us less of itself. You are like the crescent moon, only allowing a sliver of yourself to shine through the dark night. But you are the sum of everything and everyone that came before you. You are always every part of you at once—and you are always Taíno. You will always be Taíno.

ANCESTORS:
> Your other ancestors come from other countries
> and you are their legacy
> You are the next chapter in their narrative
> You carry their histories,
> their ancestral lines and tall tales
> their faces and hair and teeth and their gods,
> yes, their gods,
> and their laws both written and un.
> They are all you.
> We are all you.
> And now, you decide what that means
> for those who will come after you.

ALEJA: After me? I'm not having *kids*! I'm pretty sure my parents have given up on me ever getting married. I mean, look at me!

> *ALEJA gestures at themselves. The ANCESTORS don't understand*
> *what they're trying to say.*

ALEJA: . . . I'm queer?

> *The ANCESTORS are unfazed.*

ANCESTORS: What of it?
> The name is new, but your identity is not.

ALEJA: Okay, great, you're all cooler than my parents, but you're also *not* my parents. You're not the people I grew up with, and the people I grew up with? Not so cool. I'm the one nobody talks about—or to. I've been cut out. The only people I call "family" these days aren't related to me by blood, and the people who *are* my blood want nothing to do with me. I have cousins and nieces and nephews that *I* know exist, whose pictures I've seen, but . . . we've never met. They have no idea who I am.

. . . they have *no idea* who I am.

I'm going to be the one whose story is forgotten—deliberately forgotten. When they have kids, and their kids have kids, and their kids have kids—no one will remember me at all.

The ANCESTORS exchange looks again.

ZEMI: You can change all of that, child. You have a weapon more powerful than any paper: you have your life. You may never know the full history of your ancestors. You hardly even know *ours*. But you can preserve yours for future generations.

ANCESTORS:
If you want to honor us—
truly honor us—
use your voice to preserve our memory
and yours.

ALEJA: But you can't know that'll work, right? It's like you said. If anyone, even my own parents, wanted to pretend that I just don't exist . . . it's all in the lies they tell.

ANCESTORS: *(Laughing.)* You don't understand.

ZEMI: No one can erase you while you live and breathe. Your existence is the antidote. Once your family knows you, they can never unlearn you. That is your path. And you are, after all /

ANCESTORS: "on the right path."

Lights shift as the ANCESTORS (including ZEMI) disappear. A door opens offstage. The sounds of someone rifling through their belongings. ALEJA stands.

ALEJA: . . . hello?

IMANI: *(Offstage.)* Hey, it's me. Have you seen my wallet?

ALEJA: . . . no?

IMANI: (Offstage.) Shit. I'm already late.

> ALEJA looks back at their altar, pensive.

IMANI: (Offstage.) God, I'm stupid. It was in my other jeans.

> IMANI enters, pocketing their wallet.

IMANI: Okay, take two. You sure you don't want to come?

ALEJA: . . . yeah, um . . . actually . . . (Taking their phone out of their pocket.) I actually have plans for tonight? Thanks, though.

IMANI: Plans, or "plans"?

ALEJA: What are you, twelve?

IMANI: But are they, though?

ALEJA: (Gently pushing IMANI out of their bedroom.) Oh my god, go! Have fun!

IMANI: Remember to Fleet before you meet!

ALEJA: Bye!!

> IMANI exits. ALEJA waits by their door, listening for the opening and shutting of their apartment door. Once they know they're alone, they turn back to their altar. They stare at it for a few more seconds, then look down at their phone to make a call.

> A long silence passes.

ALEJA: . . . hey, Mom.

> Blackout.

Quetzal Feathers

TAMMY MELODY GOMEZ

The quetzal feathers magically appear
in my outstretched fingers,
and as my hand closes upon them,
a force greater than me sweeps me off my feet
and suddenly the feathers have swollen up
within my fist to become an entire
shimmering wing carrying me higher
and higher to the land of my beginning.

I close my eyes to keep this dream alive
and let myself release all fear,
as the winds seem to carefully part,
making our flight now smooth and sweet,
and I notice that one wing has
doubled to two and soon a tail and head emerge
to form a complete magic bird.

As I climb up the muscled back of the quetzal,
we aspire to higher elevations,
and I do not question this uprise.
I glimpse down below us,
recognizing this terrain,
a mountain place of winged fish and fluorescent frogs,
where I have forced my dreams to take me, again and again.

We then cascade down, one feather at a time,
a shower of plummet, and I feel my arms
open wide as if I too were a bird.

We race swiftly downward: the bird, my body,
to the place of my dreams.
I will be landing soon,
as the campesinos raise their eyes in welcome.
They have been dreaming of me for centuries.
One upon another, our visions will finally blend,
and when I touch Mayan ground,
my arms will remain open as I run towards
the deepest embrace I have ever dreamt, ever known.

Tía Abuela's Face, Ten Ways

LISA M. BRADLEY

On satellite video, via the tablet propped on the tray table beside her hospital bed

In the background, bag-eyed, Papá drones a monologue of medicalese I hardly hear as I study her closed eyes, closed face. It's like she's already dead. Even after Tía Abuela lost her speech, she never missed my calls. She'd peer into the camera, fascinated by the new skies and weird landscapes behind me, bouncing up and down a bit whenever I introduced her to an "alien." That's what our fellow galactics were called in the pulp novels we once read together.

Now, in chairs drawn around her, abuelas aunces cousins weep. It's so unfair. Why do they get to sit so close while I'm half a galaxy away? They never sat with her at the kitchen table, reading dreams of the future while marranitos baked in the oven. I shift impatiently in my bunk, furious that physical and emotional proximity aren't proportional. Even by blood we are distant. Technically, Nevaeh's not my grand-aunt, but a great-aunt. Just an extra generation to drive the sting deeper.

Papá continues explaining her swift decline in scrupulous detail. I don't complain. This is how he copes. As if the future can't come so long as he's describing the present. Why not believe? Maybe he'll prolong the vigil until I make it home to say goodbye. Like in those books Tía Abuela and I read, maybe he can stretch time.

Upside down, crowded around her coffin with the cousins

When I realize I'm silently willing her to open her eyes, to share those epically dark galaxies once more, I force myself to examine the rest of her. The mortuary beautician plumped out the wrinkle at the corner of her mouth, the one forged by her perpetual smirk, perhaps thinking it was a scar we'd like erased.

I mention it as we return to our pews—the further the relation, the farther back the pew—and Tía Yasmin overhears, turns to snap at me. "It's easy to criticize but you weren't here, were you?"

She is wearing mourning mascara, the kind that runs if you cry, to show how distraught you are. Tía Abuela Nevaeh never wore makeup. And I cried all my tears while waiting to get through quarantine.

"No, you were gallivanting around space," she says, "sticking your nose where it doesn't belong."

Seeing I'm speechless, Cousin Er tries to intervene. "Mom, it's her job," ze hisses. "She's an anthropologist."

Tía Yasmin stands, the better to chide me. "No, if Lo truly cared for Tía Nevaeh, if she cared for this family, she would've been here, not studying bugs."

Uncle Jaden, now craned in his seat, raises an eyebrow at me. Not ironically, to show dismay at the xenomisiac slur—he could care less about the Crooshayn, the galactics with whom I'm working. No, he's challenging me to deny Yasmin's criticism. After all, how many times has he lectured me about not taking sufficient interest in my own people, la raza?

Gossipy whispers rake through the room until even Papá, standing at the entry, notices the commotion. He finishes greeting an elderly mourner before turning in our direction and frowning hard enough to give himself a unibrow. Yasmin sucks her teeth and flounces away, but I worry Papá's frown was meant for me.

After the mourning period, in the hallway of her house

Tía Yasmin wants to donate all of Tía Abuela's paper books to a museum. Cousin Er slants a glance in my direction, and Papá clears his throat. He suggests I might like to select a few that are special to me before they're donated. Yasmin speaks as if I'm not even in the room. "Don't be ridiculous. She can't possibly spare room in her vessel. Besides, what adult needs books about dragons and killer robots?"

It's like, while crying in quarantine, I wept away my spine, too. Or maybe I'm just exhausted from the breakneck journey, because I don't bother arguing. I leave the sorting of possessions to them— later I'll steal some well-thumbed novel anyway, one with pages dog-eared to mark her favorite lines. I offer to clean instead.

I dial the windows from black to clear. Feathers and fur appear in the corners of every room. Tía Abuela's pets are gone—while she was in the hospital, mis abuelas adopted "The Owl and the Pussycat"— but they left plenty behind. Wondering what else will materialize, I go from room to room to uncover the fabric-shrouded mirrors.

Once we covered mirrors to keep the deceased's spirit from getting caught; now it keeps us from primping when we should be grieving. As I reach for the black fabric, I consider how the Crooshayn might interpret our mourning ritual. They have no concept of vanity (at least, not the ones we've met).

At the end of the hall hangs a small, rectangular mirror Tía Abuela used for meditation. I remember it's old and very plain: no buttons for a diagnostic overlay, no slideshow when it's idle. I pull the fabric and am turning away when, out of the corner of my eye, I see Nevaeh in the mirror.

Skin prickling, I whip my head around. She's not there. Of course she isn't. It was merely my reflection, a delusion born of bone-deep desperation to see her again, alive and vibrant. I jeer at my reflection (*If you'd gotten here in time . . .*) and notice a wrinkle at the corner of my mouth.

Maybe I did see her. A piece anyway.

In digital albums, as I search out images and video of her

I'm staying at Papá's but he turned my old bedroom into a studio. I sit at his desk, under a framed collage resembling my vessel. It's crafted from painted snippets of anthro textbooks, star charts, horoscopes. Apparently our agreement not to discuss astrology has no bearing on his art, even if it's about me.

I'm not here to look at that anyway. The family's been sharing digital albums, and Papá made copies for me. I search for pics and vids of Nevaeh when she was my age. An idea I don't dare verbalize percolates in my head.

Laughter bursts from the living room. Cumbias are in vogue again, and half my cousins are trying to teach the moves to Tío Benny and his husbands. Being jazz not pop fans, the three men are apparently hopeless, providing much-needed merriment to Papá, mis abuelas, and the grown kids. Listening to the happy chaos, I can almost smile.

Cousin Er, followed by Tunas, zir purple chow chow, comes to ask if I want dance lessons, too. I'm glad to see zem, though ze had to sneak out of zir parents' house to get here. (Yasmin and Jaden don't approve of Tío Benny's "lifestyle.") And true, my cumbia skills *are* rusty, but I tell Er I have to finish some work first. Tunas, perturbed by the crashing in the living room, stays to sleep on my feet.

My set of reference images grows, and my idea turns into a plan.

Superimposed over my likeness in the surgeon's office

The consultation suite smells like rosemary, rather than the antiseptic I expect. Were it a Crooshayn actualization chamber, it'd smell of hot metal and charred carapace.

My armchair is angled toward the doctor's in a way that makes me nervous, as if I'm about to be interviewed for a media stream. Dr. Vasquez massages the console disguised as a side table, and my face, a meter tall, replaces the wind-ruffled prairie grasses projected on the opposite wall. He drums his fingers on the table and Tía Abuela's face, just as large, ghosts over mine. I've been doing photo manipulations for days, but seeing the overlapping here, beside a surgeon . . . I rock in my chair, thrilled.

He notes a more than passing resemblance and asks if she's a relative. Delighted he sees the similarities, I tell him our exact relationship. Then I assure him there are no copyright issues. Even before I left home, people were trying to emulate neo-Bollywood stars and resurrected Vocaloids, but Nevaeh (a school nurse) was never famous.

Dr. Vasquez purses his lips and twists them to the left. At first I take his silence for dispassionate professionalism. When the silence grows awkward, I stop rocking. Sweat erupts on my upper lip. Is he going to say it's not possible?

"There must have been some kind of miscommunication," he finally says. "I don't do honmods."

"I don't know what that means." (I ignored the term on the forms I completed, overwhelmed after the first twenty acronyms and various medical jargon I'd had to look up.) "I've been off-world," I say.

He taps his console and the overlapping images disappear. Loneliness creeps over me.

He doesn't notice my feelings, perhaps too busy trying to mask his own. "There's a growing trend," he explains crisply, "of people seeking to honor their relatives, recent and ancestral, via reconstructive surgery. Such surgeries are called 'honorary modifications.' Honmods, for short."

Despite his barely concealed disgust, I'm elated. I'm not the only one! There are others like me. Enough, even, to necessitate a portmanteau. "So it's possible?" I say, and my voice shrills with glee.

Dr. Vasquez gives me a look worthy of Tía Yasmin. Then he gives me a referral.

Blurrily, in a nurse's mirror

Everything is swimmy. Which I guess is appropriate, since the serum in my irises is modeled after the chromatophores in octopus skin. Eventually I should be able to change the color of my eyes as easily as dialing a window black, clear, or anywhere in between. I blink impatiently and ask for a mirror.

The nurse, a round blur of dark skin and lilac uniform, tells me to settle down. "You just got out of surgery. There's nothing to see but bandages, if you can even see that."

She introduces herself as Ruti. I realize she has a prosthetic hand when one of her fingers becomes a small flashlight she shines in my eyes. She asks me to look this way and that, and I comply. Then she reviews my vitals, quite leisurely, and reports them to me. I take stock of my surroundings, trying not to scream in frustration. The private room is dimly lit. Tulips brighten a bedside table, and the word *tulips* reminds me of Tunas, my cousin's dog. Remembering the fluffy weight on my feet soothes me in a way the nurse's deliberate pace can't.

Ruti holds up her tablet. "I will let you have a peek, but I'm warning you, you won't be able to see well until you've watched the calibration video. That's normal. And remember, even after the bandages come off, your face may not look that different. The first phase of alterations has to be minimal. Regulations."

"Do that many people change their minds?"

Ruti shrugs, setting her tablet to mirror mode. "Maybe 15 percent. Some people find they aren't good patients. Once they experience the first mods, they choose to make do with cosmetics, hair, mannerisms."

I nod. I myself now sport the undercut Tía Abuela preferred in her thirties.

Ruti finally gives me the device, which I seize with trembling hands. She was right. Half my face is covered with gauze and anesthetic patches. But I can see my eyes are darker than before. It's like Tía Abuela's looking up at me from a rippling pond. Once I've calibrated and practiced, I'll be able to embellish my irises with even darker flecks, to more closely match Nevaeh's eyes.

I can't cry yet. The surgeons did something to my tear ducts to avoid a histamine response. As I hand back the tablet, Ruti squeezes my shoulder. I look up to smile gratefully. Now I can see her eyes. They're golden.

As a mosaic, between surgeries three and four

I can cry again, and I do. I thought healing from surgery two was the worst physical pain of my life—until surgery three. The only way I can endure the thought of surgery four is by telling myself that it's probably the last. And, no matter how awful, it can't compare to the emotional blow almost a year ago, when I docked my vessel and reopened the com link to learn I was too late, Tía Abuela was dead.

Between crying jags, I send pics and video of myself to my colleagues. Human and Crooshayn alike will need to adjust to my new appearance. My transformation is also a fabulous opportunity: my colleagues use the images to discuss with the Crooshayn delegation the complexities of grief, mourning, familial connection, bodily autonomy, medical tech, and social sanction in human cultures.

The images are, objectively speaking, hideous. My eyes work perfectly now, and in the pics I see Tía Abuela's face like an ill-wrought mosaic, familiar features pushed apart by surgical "grout": red cuts, puffiness, healing scars, sometimes even the glint of gossamer stitches. I send photos to Papá too, who's sworn to secrecy, but those are never as graphic as the ones I send into space.

The vids are worse, because they show the mangled mosaic is moving. I *never* send those to Papá. One of my roommates in Recovery watches her bots operate as avidly as other people watch sex-crime shows. She says it hurts less when she can see what's happening, which is the bots working beneath her flesh to reconnect nerves, create new ones, and restore capillaries. Our bots will make it possible for us to blush, sweat, and wrinkle.

I think the last one is funny; most people want to *avoid* wrinkles. Not me. At age eighty, I want to look like eighty-year-old Nevaeh. Ruti says when I hit 110, I may reconsider.

I hurt most at night, even if Ruti doses me up before bed. Among some Crooshayn, the worst pain is called (as best we can translate it) "burrow blight." Individuals in burrow blight make an extremely loud, rhythmic, scratching sound—not so different from the ululations one might hear at a human funeral. They say the sound relieves suffering. I'd try it, but I don't have the proper mandibles.

Instead, I stare into a mirror by moonlight. I'm not looking at my face, just the narrow strip around my eyes, like Tía Abuela looked into her hallway mirror to meditate. I stare into my/her deep dark eyes and find comfort.

I'm catching up.

In the expressions on my family's faces

Tía Yasmin disowns me. I have stolen Nevaeh's face, I'm told. It's a sacrilege, no one will ever replace her, especially not some pocha who's more interested in bug genealogy than her own culture. Tío Jaden threatens a lawsuit.

Papá isn't thrilled, either, but at least my photos prepared him. He doesn't disown Yasmin in return, partly because Abuela Tiffany is already crying, but he kicks her and Jaden out of his house. They try to drag their kids after them, but Er—who took one look at me and began to weep—and Er's youngest sibling fight to stay. Tunas also stays, but that's loyalty to Er, nothing to do with me.

Zir parents banished, Er hugs me harder than I've ever been hugged in my life. "It's beautiful," ze whispers in my ear. "What you've done, Lo. What you've sacrificed."

I scoff through my tears, aware of the wrinkle at the corner of my mouth deepening. "What sacrifice? I just couldn't bear to be without her."

Abuela Tiffany looks anguished. She grips my hand and says, "Tía Nevaeh never would've asked you to do this. She loved your face, querida."

"And I love hers," I say, smiling helplessly.

Abuela Chris, who's never cried over spilt milk, says, "It's weird, and I don't get it. But more importantly, won't this be a bureaucratic nightmare? What about all your IDs?"

Papá snorts. "She willingly broke the bones in her face. You think she gives a flip about her pilot's license?"

I laugh and Papá manages a weak smile. Tío Benny asks to take a photo with me, which he sends to his husbands with an invite that reads, "Yasmin, Has-been. And she won't be back. Bring the kids."

There are plenty more people to tell—or show—and from the abuelas' bewildered expressions, I know I've got a lot of explaining to do. But just now, my relief is so vast, I literally can't stand it. I sit on the floor.

Tunas approaches me and tilts her head. I offer my hand. She sniffs it and, seemingly satisfied, she plops down on my feet. Within minutes, she's snoring.

In the corner of my new identification card

When I've finally slashed through all the red tape—a turn of phrase my colleagues needed a history book to explain to the Crooshayn delegation—I show Abuela Chris my new ID card.

"Will you look at that," she muses. "How does the system distinguish you from Nevaeh? Other than her being dead, I mean."

Cringeworthy as I find the addendum, I remind her that, though my irises have changed color, my retinas are the same and could never be mistaken for Nevaeh's, nor could my fingerprints. Even my blood type is different.

Abuela rolls her eyes at herself and says, "Of course, of course. It's still you under there."

"Exactly."

"Well, I guess it's all really real now," she says, hugging me with one arm.

I lean into her love. "Really real," I say. My cheeks feel warm, and I realize the bots did their job: I'm blushing with pride.

Now, every time I look in a mirror

Back at work, I smile at myself in every reflective surface I see. It's a good thing the Crooshayn have no concept of vanity; I wouldn't want to give them the wrong idea. Sometimes I force a smirk in front of the mirror, otherwise the wrinkle at the corner of my mouth won't take hold like Tía Abuela's did. Wearing her face requires some upkeep, but it's worth it to see those eyes, dark and shining like galaxies, and the wonder lifting her cheeks.

Nevaeh is always with me. I'll never be too late again.

PART II

Dreams Interrupted

Jean

STEPHANIE NINA PITSIRILOS

OBSERVATION: Wormholes are triggers that drag you
back in time to relive the painful scars of family history.

—Rigellian Recorder 211

My mom's story is legend. It all played out during what the industry
said was the Bronze Age of Marvel, though I gotta disagree, to me
it was Golden, classic. She fulfilled every expectation society had of
a Nuyorican young female in the seventies: sexual to sinvergüenza-
level, prone to drugs, poverty-stricken, and with a dab of the mys-
tical. She has the kind of story that gets immortalized by a plastic
sleeve and white backing board of a comic book protector. It's a burden to try to live up to the stereotype, but my mom was up for the
task. At least you can say that. I don't have any living memories
of her except for one; the rest are family tales extracted from my
grandmother and aunt with a little coaxing, plenty of Budweisers,
and wormholes. Those little rips through the fabric of time are how
she peers in from yesterday, denying Grandma a fresh dawn of the
promised, holy tomorrow—me, a grounded sense of the present. No
surprise; my mother had a supernatural ability to fuck things up
good—not just for herself but the universe around her.

Wormholes. I'm notoriously good at documenting a trip down
their tunnel, and it drives Grandma crazy—she not understanding
my obligations as The Rigellian Recorder 211. *¡Embuste!*, Grandma
likes to protest, not buying that wormholes exist when I bring up
the past, nor that I'm a robot made by the Rigellians to aid in their
colonization of space. *I gotta write this stuff down, Grandma. I'm a witness to Earth's events, removed from its consequences.* But she hasn't ever

read *Thor* Issue #132 to understand my origins as companion to Thor in his Viking battles in The Black Galaxy, and later, sidekick to The Watcher. She doesn't understand how anything is possible in deep space.

Even if Grandma doesn't believe the space robot-witness-writing bit, she shouldn't refute the existence of wormholes; they're *everywhere* in our neighborhood, and a particularly nasty one resides in our apartment. Science, in our situation, backs that they are traversable: our colonized, non-White bodies provide the "exotic matter," and the fucked-up abundance of negative energy density that surrounds us account for wormhole stabilization. Plus, they get *everyone*—this ain't no invisible boogeyman that one tripping homey in our projects shouts is eating him up. Yet still I get the ¡*Embuste!* from Grandma. Perhaps (though too convenient an explanation) she's routinely shot by an obliterating memory beam upon exiting a wormhole's winding narrative, like Kirk on Amerind. But Ghosts? Yeah, *those* Grandma believes in.

Sometimes I'm not traveling these wormholes and my feet are firmly touched down in Earth's present. Like now: I can report how, with Aunt Ceci's help, Grandma's getting ready to do a séance for Rita's daughter Esmeralda, another junkie who OD'ed. Because of these circumstances surrounding Esmi's death, Grandma's about to be sucked into the Sankofa Wormhole's gravitational force and I'm getting ready to go down with her.

Sankofa Wormhole

The photograph was a wormhole like no other—*the Sankofa Wormhole*—the one just before the hallway curtain of glass beads separating the tucked-away bedrooms from the rest of our apartment. No fronting whom it rep'ed. The tattered edges of its Kodak Bromesko paper camouflaged a gnarled spheroidal mouth that spewed out radiation as it licked its chops in eternal hungriness. The photograph was always something Grandma walked past, eyes avoiding its entrapment. It had been in the living room on top of the television set for years, until Aunt Ceci finally decided that it did more harm than good there staring at us, locking the room in a somber silence and forcing us down continuous trips of her universe. Aunt Ceci moved it into the hallway one day; like Talky Tina and Willie the dummy, we knew we could never get rid of it.

"It must be so hard, seeing that picture," Rita's cousin now says, gesturing to the photograph. "It's gonna be that way, especially for Rita."

Circumstances of death were one thing. But Rita's cousin, in her immense stupidity, helped activate the Sankofa Wormhole with acknowledgment of existence. Of course, Grandma fights it.

"I wasn't looking there," Grandma answers curtly, drawing her eyes away from the photograph of my mother. "I was looking at the closet." Spirits always like to hide there until Grandma calls for them.

And, of course, she doesn't win against the laws of wormhole physics, the hungry mouth. The pull is too strong. Down we go.

◆

My mother had chestnut hair (when she didn't dye it that ridiculous red color), autumn brown eyes, and a motherfucking mouth *like no other.* She was Grandma's eldest, but showed none of the responsible traits that you burden a first-born with. Aunt Ceci says "buck-wild" is how Grandpa Juan described her when he complained about Grandma's "inability to raise respectable girls." The way Aunt Ceci describes him saying that, you get the sense that he was pointing out Grandma's failure at her sole purpose in life. A concession that his daughters had become the slur that islanders used to describe the diaspora contaminated with New York's urbanity: *Nuyorican.* You could hear the shame in his voice. Then he'd shuffle out of the living room to get another beer.

Grandma had tolerated his shit-faced behavior as something that came along with the unfortunate luck of being born with a Y chromosome. But soon, less and less money came into a house barely making ends meet. As far as Grandma knew, Budweiser hadn't gone up in price. He'd come home later and later and was irritable. And—more notably—*down.* Finally, it all came out one day, the day he popped the question to Grandma. She had been putting away some socks in the dresser when he called her from the bed.

"Come here. I got something for you."

"I don't need any more of what you got."

"Shit, I don't need that from you *too*. But come here."

Grandma says that she turned around not really expecting any-thing special. His hands were empty. Then she saw that his sleeve was rolled up and there was an elastic band around the top of his arm. The needle was lying on the comforter of the bed.

"Come on," he said. "It's good. Do it with me."

She had stared at him for five long seconds without any response. Not a refusal to join him man and wife into his spiral down the big bad world of heroin, not an acceptance of his invitation to say so long to life, fuck my mom and Aunt Ceci—they could fend for them-selves. In what I would call a space-time anomaly—because really it was just five seconds so how could she have seen and felt all of this in that small time frame?—Grandma says that she saw her fin-gers maneuvering a thin needle into buttonhole after buttonhole of an unholy number of shirts, hours and hours day after day in the midtown factory that was her job. She felt the start of a tremor in her hands from working outside the labor laws, and without the later benefits of Social Security because you think those greedy fuck-ers of owners made them official on the books? There was no "car-pel tunnel syndrome" for a female Puerto Rican or worker's comp or anything remotely like that. You worked until you were worth-less. Red buttons, blue buttons, red buttons with white polka dots, striped buttons, black buttons, black buttons with white polka dots. She sewed—what—five million of those fucking blouses, pants, and sweaters, only to return home to wait on a charity line of Church of the Holy Name of Jesus to get her girls some clothes? Meanwhile, her eldest daughter was becoming wilder and wilder because she wasn't there to watch her. The Thanksgivings with a malnourished chicken, not a pernil. The Christmases without Santa. *So. This. Is. Where. The. God. Damn. Money. Went.*

Grandma says he picked up the needle from the bed and waved it to her. That it was then when she saw my mother staring at them from the bedroom door. It was the one time in Grandma's memory that my mom had chosen to be silent instead of having something smart to say. So, Grandma made up for my mom's sudden meta-morphosis into Saint Benedict by pulling out the drawers of the dresser and hurling them at Grandpa Juan with an explosion of curses that my mother mentally added to her already notorious vocabulary. After he'd been released from the hospital he moved out.

Here is how the ride through the Sankofa Wormhole ended, an infuriating *question* after such a journey: Was it "What did you do to my poor daddy?" that drove my mother away? Or, "What was Daddy doing that felt so good that it drew him away from us?" Did the answer matter? Because it was what my mother spent her last days in 821 Columbus finding out.

And here is Rita now, sitting at the edge of our sofa, describing her own daughter-calamity, Grandma preparing to resurrect her.

Legs tucked in, head resting on the knees, arms splayed open . . .

"That's how they found her, Doña, mi Esmi." Rita sits with her hands folded in her lap, giving Grandma the details of Esmeralda's death. Rita's eyes are puffy and red.

Nobody seems bothered that I'm writing in my notebook at the dining table documenting events (the good Recorder that I am), like suddenly they aren't going to resurrect the dead and have a conversation with them.

In a derelict brownstone on Manhattan Avenue . . .

Grandma turns her eyes to the hallway, walks toward the closet. She knows where Esmi is. She always knows where they are.

"With the needle still in her arm, in a corner of the stairwell, she was wearing—"

I try to imagine what my grandmother's thinking. It can't be easy going from wormhole to underworld, but that's Grandma's life. I'm thankful that, at least, I never have to go *there*. I'll take being whipped through wormhole after wormhole and traveling the past over being an unwilling medium for the dead, jerking her head, shuffling her feet, and clapping her hands Michael-Jackson-style with some *Thriller* zombies. *Ten times over.*

Dark blue jeans, pink jellies. Yeah, that's what she was wearing the last time we saw her.

"Why'd she get into that life?" Rita finally sobs. "A mother has the right to know."

Grandma lifts her hand and turns the knob of the closet door. The door opens. She has a look on her face that's gotta mean: *There's Esmi, sitting there.*

I imagine what Esmi might look like. What she does in the afterlife. Maybe she lifts her head and touches Grandma's hand. I know she doesn't have eyes. Grandma says they never do.

❖

To know *her*, you had to know *him*, and that's why that photograph was troublesome, maybe acting more like a black hole than a wormhole, because it's hard to say if you ever really emerged fully back on the other side when it was done with you. It inevitably left you at the doorstep of another wormhole, functioning as some cosmic highway that spilled out in a plethora of exits to shady side streets.

When Grandpa Juan left with his heroin, Aunt Ceci says the house settled into an uncommon quiet. Ceci doesn't seem to mind telling me these stories as much as Grandma—though push her too far and she gets lost in anger. Aunt Ceci remembers Grandma returning home at seven from the factories, holding her hands together to help calm the tremors she'd get after hours of sewing. My mom and Aunt Ceci would be eating dinner and Grandma would join them, only to get up a few minutes later to cook tomorrow's dinner. The times when she looked into the refrigerator and would see it was bare, she'd tell them to stop by Holy Name the next day and ask for food. It didn't take too long for Grandma to catch on. Aunt Ceci would recall one epic scene:

Genesis Wormhole

"I don't want you staying out late no more." Grandma said this close to two in the morning or—*how the heck would I know, Nova, why you gotta know all these details?*—some ungodly hour that my mother had snuck in.

"Yeah, Ma," Ceci says she answered. "Sure. But only because I'm pregnant."

Just like that. She was one cold bitch.

Aunt Ceci says she watched Grandma's face turn white, then simmer into a blazing sazón con culantro y achiote red.

"Puta," she recalls Grandma erupted. "That's what I raised!" To concede Grandpa Juan was right was no small defeat. Here's where I broke the non-interference doctrine of Recorder protocol, asking mid-story: *So, good things can come out of bad, Grandma?* Grandma was rocking in her rocking chair, well into her fifth Budweiser, her record player blasting a nostalgic La Lupe or melancholy Daniel Santos bolero. *The announcement of my coming-soon-to-the-world.* Grandma seemed none too pleased that Ceci allowed me to dredge this memory up. The anger probably provided her with the sobriety to answer carefully: *Si, pero . . . That's no the point.*

Here's where I lucked out: The heroin didn't start 'til after I came.

Grandma says she thought perhaps, just perhaps, they had a chance of turning around their lives with this. Becoming a mother could sometimes do wondrous things to the most wretched women. It *did* work for a while. They said she was a doting mother for the first few years (wasted, because I was too young to remember), though they did question whether she was of right mind when she told them she was naming me Nova Odyssey. *Nova: expelling light to become something greater,* she schooled them like a PBS special. As for the Odyssey part, she had never told them. She stuck around the house, avoided old friends. She didn't have a job, but Grandma didn't want to push it. But by the time I was five, my mom was back to her old ways, hanging out late—*Why the fuck you can't watch her? She's asleep anyway.* The belligerent fights in the house about what she was doing and with whom. It went like that, until she just stopped coming home.

"Ma. I think she's doing heroin."

Lit up like a Christmas tree, Grandma cried how when Aunt Ceci said this, she could not help but think of that *piece of shit* Grandpa Juan waving his heroin needle from the bed, my mother watching coyly at the door. *To know her, you had to know him.* And any trip down Manhattan Avenue led you to where their stories merged.

Manhattan Avenue Wormhole

When my mother hadn't come home for a week, when my sulking began to weigh heavily on them, they set out to comb the Avenue to find her. For Aunt Ceci, it was a familiar trip. She had to do it for Grandpa Juan, when curiosity, perhaps even love—this truth I can never unlock for her—made her reach out one last time to him. Grandpa Juan could read the grooves of a record like the rings of a tree. He could tell you where Juana Peña cried in a Hector Lavoe / Willie Colón vinyl, which groove held Celia Cruz's pine for the land with color, that two and a half inches from the perimeter of a black world you'd meet with wailing NYC sirens—*ready or not*—the badass Pedro Navaja (that last song *if* he had lived that long). But he never did read the instructions on the dust sleeves of his Columbia records.

> "Take care of your needle . . . no needle is permanent. A worn needle irreparably damages the delicate grooves of your records . . . check your needle for wear at your dealer's . . ."

Grandma told me this once while rocking so violently in her rocking chair one day that I thought she really was going to go back in time, a decibel-piercing Julio Iglesias song her rocket fuel. There were cans of Budweiser beer everywhere, and by now it should be obvious: Budweisers are good triggers for opening up spontaneous wormholes to unknown destinations, Grandma having a propensity for traveling through the particularly shitty ones. There wasn't much good for her to look back on in life, so statistically speaking, most of them were going to be shitty, anyway.

When Aunt Ceci discovered that Grandpa Juan was holed up in one of the brownstone apartments on the Avenue with other users, she told Grandma. Grandma refused to see him. So, Aunt Ceci spent the long, hot summer months visiting him as his ravaged body slowly succumbed to some new apocalyptic virus disease people were starting to call AIDS.

For *her* we walked down the Avenue toward a chocolate-colored brownstone with the Sankofa bird welded into its door-gate, Grandma with a clenched fist. Its old, wooden door was scratched and smeared with the occasional markings of graffiti. Even the gold lock on it looked dull and worn. Grandma had spotted one of my mom's old friends hanging outside the stoop. Pushing a five in her hand, it was easy to get her to spill where my mother was holed up.

"Stay out here with la niña," Grandma had ordered Aunt Ceci.

I thought I didn't remember this.

She didn't want me to see how she knew she'd find her. In a corner of a scarcely furnished apartment, head slouched down, arms to the side, palms up like she was carrying something, her pink jellies reminding you of her youth, that she was only twenty-two when she OD'ed on heroin.

◆

Finding Esmeralda is easier, even after all the wormhole trips. Dead Esmeralda starts to say, in a jarring exchange of bodily possession of my grandmother in the living room, what we already knew. Been through. What the wormholes remind us of every time we travel them:

I liked it.

It felt good.

What do you care, what life I'm gonna have anyway?

She was pumped up with needles, her veins a river of heroin.

Grandma is fully with the spirit when the cops knock on our door, asking questions about Esmi's death not because they heard a misa is taking place or because they believed Espiritismo would give them clues on the latest death in 821, but because Grandma's house was where neighbors said her family had retreated to.

After confirming their uniforms from the peephole, Aunt Ceci undoes the locks (leaving the chain in place) and opens the door to the wormhole with a pistol.

Franklin Simon & Co. Wormhole

The uniforms had changed somewhat since the ten years we had opened the door to them before, a different pair of cops who had come to follow up on what had happened to my mother. The house was dark then too, venetian blinds down all day in mourning, me too young to understand the sorrow that had consumed my grandmother and aunt. When Grandma had let them in the house that day, they entered the living room uncomfortably, refusing her offer to take a seat.

"She simply OD'ed," the officer had told her.

"OD'ed?" Grandma spat back. Her selective understanding of English had kicked in.

"She doesn't believe it, Officer. Why would there be so many needles in her, then?"

"Look," the officer continued, shifting his weight and adjusting his belt. His physical movements etched the scene indelibly in our memory as the gesture moved his hand closer to the handle of his gun. His partner had his eyes fixed on different parts of the room, anywhere but on us.

"That's the evidence. Maybe it was *intentional*, catch my drift? Quick way out."

That was something Grandma wasn't *ever* gonna hear. To live in hell in this world was one thing. Suicide, Grandma's Catholicism damned, meant an eternity of my mother suffering.

"She was a junkie. What did you expect?"

"Not only a junkie, señor. My *daughter*."

And just like that, they left.

Aunt Ceci had waited a few minutes, then grabbed her keys and a pair of sunglasses and left too. I stayed with Grandma, wondering if Aunt Ceci was going to disappear into the same unspeakable place that held my mother captive. They needed something to bury my mother in. They didn't want my mom sitting in no morgue anymore. Ceci made her way down to Franklin Simon & Co., entered the women's sleepwear department and quickly spotted a white lace nightgown displayed high on the wall. "Excuse me," she had called to the saleslady arranging some blouses on a rack.

This. *This* is the wormhole's signature.

The White woman had been wearing a white blouse and spectacles and had a neat bob of chestnut hair.

Aunt Ceci pushed her sunglasses farther into her face, hiding the swollen eyes behind the lenses. "I'd like to see that nightgown there," she'd said, pointing up. The gown, she remembered, looked angelic.

"Oh, that's too expensive for you," the woman snorted, immediately turning her back to Ceci and walking away.

How could the woman have known how her prejudice would be such a trigger? 'Cause Aunt Ceci went *ballistic*.

"*You fucking bitch,*" Aunt Ceci screamed, skipping all polite doubts that perhaps she heard wrong, because she knew what went down. "How dare you," Aunt Ceci screeched. "I told you I wanted to see it, I didn't ask you *the price*, and you don't know what I can or can't buy!" Enraged, she stormed toward the woman, daring her to continue walking away. Terrified, the saleswoman slipped into the back, where staff had begun to converge from all corners of the floor. Suddenly, a Black saleswoman emerged from the crowd and approached my aunt.

"*Oh-No-You-Don't,*" Aunt Ceci says she screamed. She tells me this story with a bit of pride, and I don't tell her how pathetic I think it is that rage is all we have left as a sign of dignity. "They sending you to me because you Black? To *appease* me? I want the White bitch that refused to show me the dress. Send *her* back here and have her get it for me. I didn't ask her the damn price!" Aunt Ceci ripped off her sunglasses and tore at her black clothes. It's here where I imagine my aunt's skin having turned green. "My sister was killed, you piece of shit!" she yelled out to the back of the store where somewhere, the saleswoman was cowering. "That nightgown is the only one you have that will cover all the bruises on her fucking arms so that we don't have to look at them when we bury her!"

By now crowds of customers, managers, clerks, and tailors had amassed to watch the spectacle. Showers of apologies from the store managers followed.

"*Inappropriate.*"

"*So sorry.*"

"*Condolences.*"

They never allowed the saleswoman back out with Ceci there, probably in fear of her life. A few days later, with my mother buried, Aunt Ceci had received a letter from the store with more apologies, and regrets that she had canceled her account with them. Seeing her sister in the coffin, her arms covered in white cotton lace—without the potty mouth going off, without the visible needle marks because the nightgown covered them—Aunt Ceci believed my mom truly looked like an angel. It's what Aunt Ceci had wanted. A myth, for whom I don't know. What she couldn't erase though were the words and vision of the saleswoman dismissing her. Countless times she replays the Franklin Simon & Co. scene to me as if it were yesterday, whenever she experiences the smallest racially tinged slight. It's like some Vietnam flashback that won't go away; how my mother was buried in a storm of rage that had nothing to do with her death, but the fact that society always reminded us of our place in it.

It's a cruel fact of life. How many healthcare dollars are wasted every year, spent on skinny out-of-state nutritionists paid to scold *people like me* in school-based outreach programs on how unhealthy our rice and beans are, when really, the core to understanding heart disease is the stress of constantly being a US Defense Department casualty Bruce Banner, taught to keep all that rage in by harboring a dissociative personality, lest you be shot down as a race-rioting Incredible Hulk.

At the burial, what had been the sedative keeping Grandma together was the sight of seeing me staring into the pit of dirt where the sexton laid down the coffin holding Mom. The flowing night-gown gave my mother a softness I was unfamiliar with. The black ribbons in my mother's hair—wasn't she supposed to be admiring bright ribbons carefully secured by her own hand, in my own curls? I shudder at the thought; I would have seen the track marks along her spent veins as she tied a ribbon into my hair like a lie.

Later in memory the whole thing would remind me of a different ritual entirely: she was *bagged* in the brownstone apartment by the coroner, *boarded* in the morgue for viewing, and *boxed* in a coffin, sealing her from light. The same steps used to preserve comics. The only difference being comics are stored upright in their boxes, ready to be pulled out again. My mother was laid flat.

❖

The wormhole closes up, and after collecting Esmeralda's history of drug use from Rita and her cousin, the present-day set of cops leave. Rita and kin leave next, the mournful faces that they walked in with now also showing signs of wormhole travel vertigo, confirmed in the premature whispers as the door closes behind them: *What the fuck is up with that house?*

❖

Grandma may hold Jesus Christ as our savior, especially in sorting out shit like this, but for me it's the Marvel Universe and comics. The Uncanny X-Men are more than mutant wonders marginalized by society with dire expectations to me. My world is awash in the fire of Jean's song. *Jean.* Flaming red hair, emerald green eyes, arms splayed out in the open air in self-immolation over Central Park. She was responsible for the genocide of billions; Jean was addicted to eating stars. I reckon here is where forgiveness is supposed to fit in, looking at the good of Jean before the darkness eclipsed her. The part of Jean that selflessly took her own life so others could be spared all the hurt she was capable of inflicting. Or was it selfishly? Those closest to her are left with a black hole—not a light-emitting nova—in place of Jean's star. So, it's my own universe that she fucked up that concerns me. To echo Nightcrawler: *How then can I forgive Jean?* This Jean can't be my mother, but then again, society doesn't give us accurate mirrors, so why can't I dream?

Claremont's Universe

After all that's happened today, I walk myself up the stone stairs of Butler Library. Columbia University's Rare Book and Manuscript Library houses the donated archives of legendary X-Men writer Chris Claremont, and noted of Claremont's work, among other accolades, are the complexities and strengths of female characters. It's like visiting a church; here I'm provided a narrative that I accept, accounting for my existence as an emotionless recording robot, the existence of wormholes, her. Here, I like to glimpse some of the genesis of his creations, how he constructed strength in characters faced with adversity. The Dark Phoenix Saga, of Jean, to be specific. Taking it back: the story of the Sankofa bird that looks to the past in order to move forward, where Grandma and I can finally agree. And there it is, the original encased in a glass tomb. I do what can only be a religious rite: pull out my copy of *The X-Men* #137 from my satchel and visit her in legend. It's the hardest wormhole for me to visit because it's here where her story ends for me. Inside, it's never the past but always the present, a state of existence I crave. This wormhole offers you a choice as to whether to enter.

I open its pages and get sucked in.

X-Men #137

I stare into a crater that disappears into the blue area of the moon. The Kree weaponry is set up neatly in a cavern, the cannon aimed with the precision of a needle to the dark alleyway where Jean will soon kill herself, again, to save the world, to save the universe.

It felt good, Jean says. Why she chose to be a world-destroyer. How she'd do it all again, just to get that high.

I watch Jean step in front of the Kree technology.

Choose life, Jean, I whisper to her, afraid someone will hear me. Afraid that others will discover wormholes exist, will discover that here is where Jean resides.

It's better this way, Jean says. *Quick. Clean. Final.* She says this to the vacuum of paper space, not to me. Me, she never sees.

I witness the blinding flash of light that ends Jean's immortal life.

Jean, I plead into the silence. *You never came back. They said you would rise again.*

Why? The Watcher's Recorder asks on the page.

I look at my robotic self, drawn by the pencil of John Byrne, defined by Terry Austin's ink. Glynis Oliver has given my metal skin a copper color, my chest a sparkling emerald cavity holding a recording grid of circuits where my heart should be.

Why did Jean have to die? Even a history-recording robot wants to know. It's an answer I don't want to hear. It isn't enough.

Because she was human, the observant Watcher answers back.

I wanted her—I want myself—to be something more.

◆

When I return home, all traces of the séance for Esmi have been erased. My grandmother is sitting on her chair in the kitchen—unaware that I've walked in—warming up next to the riser pipe by the window and looking out into the Avenue. A record crackles. Grandma gets up and with trembling hands flips the album, *Good Morning Starshine,* to the other side. She smiles at the song: "Jean." It had been one of Jean's favorites—the Jean, that is, I can't seal away in a comic book sleeve. The Jean who loved this song really was my mother, a Jean that was young and alive. Grandma plays the song when she thinks she is alone. I start to think, perhaps this is my grandmother's escape to her own fictional Jean, a trip down a musical wormhole she doesn't admit to. Because with all the other puzzle pieces where they should be, this is the one that forever remains out of place for Grandma. Why she never sees Jean, in a dream, in her séances for the dead, in her visits to that uncanny middle world where extraordinary things happen. If Grandma believed in wormholes, if she read comic books, would she feel better?

The spell breaks because Grandma finally notices me staring at her from the door. She gets up and turns off the record player. She switches on the television. The house can never be quiet. She smiles at me before disappearing quietly behind the hallway beads, giving the photograph of my mother a look before entering the bedroom. Peter Jennings is blabbing away, alone on the screen. I want to hurry to the television set to switch his anchor-god-sorry-ass off before getting indoctrinated from the smooth voice promising an angel among demons—The Person of the Week—but that would upset my grandmother further. She looks tired—from today, from yesterday. Shake up the world of the dead and there's no way of knowing how far back into the past you've reached to understand a story. Where a wormhole's taken you.

I feel kinda bad that I watched her so I follow her inside (*STATE-MENT: Time to be a Care Bear!*). The hallway beads stroke my skin like fingers grabbing something fleeting. Their trick almost works on me—the cool, amber fragments that sparkle, the smooth coax of a soothing hand—the sinister mask of an event horizon. But I'm done traveling for the day. I've made enough trips to last a lifetime. I don't look up at the unwelcome tombstone, the wormhole, the picture of my mother, Jean.

Like Flowers Through Concrete

LOUANGIE BOU-MONTES

Wyatt enjoyed his job. It took little focus and consisted almost entirely of walking around the woods, collecting soil or water samples for the local scientists to examine and deem safe or unsafe. He liked the quiet of it—getting up early in the morning to kayak along the canals crisscrossing town, spending the rest of his day walking around a few forest blocks and keeping an eye out for the well-being of the plant and animal life. He preferred it to spending time in his home in the dead center of town, surrounded by the near-constant screaming and laughing of his little cousins.

He had no real issue with kids screaming and enjoying themselves. Wyatt just preferred the outskirts of town: the trees bursting up through the roofs of the long-forgotten rectangular buildings, the mounds of moss and grass growing over hunks of rusted metal, the forest smashing its way past the concrete and asphalt that had once tried to contain it. Mamá Aurora, his great-grandmother, used to bring him and his older brother Seymour to the outskirts to show them how nature healed all her wounds, given time.

However, Mamá Aurora rarely left the house in the years since Seymour's death.

Wyatt paddled closer to the bank of the canal until he could climb out, boots holding their grip on the slimy rocks underfoot. He pulled the kayak up by the bow until it sat safely at the bank and set off into the forest with his backpack slung over his shoulder.

Many of the trees in this block bore green markers to signal the mostly clean and viable air, earth, and water found here. Wyatt's job was to monitor its condition and keep an eye out for fluctuations or missed dead spots. The farms provided the vast majority of the food, but without clean air, earth, and water, the forest wouldn't thrive enough to keep the game animals around.

He pulled his various energy and atmosphere readers out of his backpack and turned them on in turn before hooking them into his belt loops. They beeped their quiet, rhythmic patterns at his side as he walked deeper into the forest, ducking under low-hanging branches and peering into forgotten, moss-covered doorways.

Mamá Aurora told him that long before she was born, these ruins served as a college for women. Some of the buildings withstood the ravages of time to an extent, hollowed-out skeletons made of concrete and some even made of brick and mortar. The library still stood whole and recognizable, even buried under vines and moss, windows like gaping eye sockets. The townspeople salvaged the books long ago and moved them to a safer facility, but sometimes Wyatt couldn't resist a quick peek inside just to admire the plants and roots bursting past the tiles.

"Not today," he sighed, pausing to pat the moss-covered side of the building as if petting a horse or a dog. "Next time I'll remember a sketchpad."

Past the library, Wyatt ran by a swath of young trees and stopped at the top of a hill overlooking a sludgy pond surrounding a tiny, brush-covered island.

Or, at least, it had been brush-covered just the other day. Wyatt frowned, squinting against the amber glint of the sun against the murky pond water, but the image didn't change. Someone, in the week since he last swept through this block, had removed the brush and brambles from the tiny plot of land at the center of the pond, leaving only dark soil and vestigial sprays of grass at the edges of the island.

Wyatt ran down the steep curve of the hill to the edge of the pond and shoved the cuffs of his jeans deeper into his rubber boots. The pond scum squelched underfoot as he trekked across the short stretch of shallow water, particularly loud as he stepped up onto the island. Someone—whoever took it upon themselves to clear the land—had also prepared the soil for growth. The rich, earthy smell of manure permeated the air here, and the soil looked soft and dark, tilled into neat rows. Wyatt swung his backpack onto the ground and squatted down, rifling inside it for a sample cup. He dug his fingers into the soft, cool earth and scooped a few pinches into the cup.

A dog barked, the sound cutting through the air—loud, sharp, and close.

Wyatt scrambled up to his feet and whirled around in time to see a brindle dog the size of a small pony leap into the pond, heading for him. The dog's ears and jowls flapped as it splashed through the murky water, barking all the while.

"Whoa, whoa—" Wyatt held his backpack in front of himself, backing up hastily and trying not to slip over the loose soil with his wet boots. "Nice dog! Good doggy! It's okay, buddy!"

His voice sounded unnaturally high, even to his own ears. He slipped as the dog bounded onto the island, landing hard on his butt and barely catching himself with his elbows.

He heard a voice in the near distance.

"Get him, Maruka."

"No, no," Wyatt said quickly, scrambling back on his butt. "Sit, Maruka!"

Maruka ran through the dirt, drool flying off his jowls in ribbons, stopping only when he came close enough to Wyatt to stick his cold wet nose into his face. Wyatt yelped, but Maruka only licked him from chin to forehead, painting him in spit and drooling all over the collar of Wyatt's shirt.

Wyatt laughed shakily in relief, reaching up with both hands to pet Maruka's massive head.

"Thank god," he said, shrinking away from Maruka's wet, spongy tongue. "You're a good dog, huh?"

Maruka's owner came into view, towering over the both of them. He looked down with a bored expression, his dark brows set low over his light-colored eyes.

"What are you doing here?"

Even when Wyatt pushed himself up to standing, the guy still stood over half a foot taller, wearing an unwavering frown. In spite of his height, however, he didn't look much older than Wyatt, if at all. He looked him over, gangly and long-limbed, grass-stained knees, hair pulled into a sloppy bun at the nape of his neck.

This guy didn't strike him as any kind of threat.

"I'm, uh, doing my job?" Wyatt raised his eyebrows and shrugged. "What are *you* doing here? This area hasn't been sanctioned for farming."

"It's a garden," he corrected, resting his hands at his hips and looking at the disturbed soil. "And the trees all say this is a green zone, so I don't understand how this hasn't been sanctioned yet."

"We're keeping an eye on it." Wyatt turned to nudge the displaced dirt back into place as best he could. "The council hasn't come to a decision yet, so I have to check up on it every week until there's a ruling."

The guy heaved a sigh and rolled his eyes. "So, what, then? You want me to abandon this land?"

Wyatt looked around at the small plot of land, lovingly tilled and conditioned. He winced and shrugged his shoulders helplessly.

"I mean . . . I'd get a serious talking-to from my boss if I didn't ask you to cease and desist, man. I'm sorry."

Maruka barked and circled around their legs impatiently while his owner looked around the island, black brows furrowed and green eyes thoughtful.

"Are you the only scout who comes here?" he turned his eyes onto Wyatt's face, still frowning. "I haven't seen any others yet."

"Um." Wyatt saw where this was going. "I . . . yeah, it's just me . . ."

"Then you don't *have* to report this."

Wyatt stared at him for a moment, then laughed.

"What? I mean—I thought you were gonna *ask* me not to tell, but . . ."

"There is literally no need for you to tell anyone. It's a green area and no scouts come here but you."

He stared at the guy again in disbelief. Surely, he had to know that just because other scouts didn't come here didn't mean *no one* who could divulge this came here. Mamá Aurora brought him here even before the block received a green clearance, Seymour used to sneak off to plenty of restricted areas, and now this guy himself was tilling land out here. Obviously people came here apart from scouts—there was ample opportunity for word to get out.

Wyatt could feel his argument falling apart even as he made it. It just proved the guy's point that it didn't matter what he did out here since plenty of people went out here anyway.

"Look," he said finally, closing his eyes for a second to recollect his words. "I know you're not the only one messing around in the woods. I just can't risk my job, you know?"

The guy looked down thoughtfully, then turned his green eyes back up to Wyatt's face after a moment.

"I'll grow you something. Do you have any seeds you want grown?"

Wyatt felt his eyebrows crawling up toward his hairline. The guy was serious about setting up his garden—he couldn't question that. It almost made him laugh again.

But . . . Wyatt's black thumb was legend among his family. And he couldn't deny there *was* something he needed grown.

"So, first of all," Wyatt held up his finger, drawing his shoulders up straighter. "I just want to say that I don't believe in bribes. But I don't actually want to take away your garden . . . and I do have something I need grown."

The guy responded quickly, as if afraid Wyatt would change his mind if he reacted too slowly.

"Bring it tomorrow at this time. I'll grow it for you, whatever it is."

Wyatt laughed. "Whatever it is? Anything at all?"

The guy nodded, face completely earnest.

"What's your name?" asked Wyatt, shaking his head in mild disbelief.

"Simón," he said. "From the Norwottuck area."

"Simón what?"

Simón looked at him quizzically, but stuck his hand out, unsure of the level of formality Wyatt wanted. "Simón Bellot-Alvarado."

Wyatt took his hand and grinned.

"Wyatt Miramonte-Vincent." He shook his hand a few times, squeezing his fingers around Simón's broad knuckles. "You have a deal, Simón. But if anyone catches you out here, you can't tell them I let this slide."

Simón nodded again, seriously. "I understand."

❖

Seymour's side of the attic room still looked the same as it did when he was alive two years ago. At one point, Wyatt folded up Seymour's stray laundry and made the bed, but everything else looked identical: the patchwork quilt Mamá Aurora made for him one birthday lay folded at the foot of his bed, the stack of heavily dog-eared books on the floor—borrowed from the library years before his death and never returned, the chalk drawings scrawled over the dark brown wall.

Seymour's chalk caricatures still brought a hollow ache to Wyatt's chest. He had always loved them. Mamá Aurora's caricature stood out in particular with her big round ears and her thin face, and the twins with their exaggerated gap-toothed grins and surrounded by smelly clouds of flies. Some of Seymour's drawings had grotesque features, like demons pulled from nightmares. He used to point at the ugliest ones and tell Wyatt, "That one's you."

Wyatt's side of the room was almost empty. The bed stood alone, drawings scrubbed off his side of the wall, dust gathering in the corners where his belongings used to lie. He slept in the twins' room now, much as it pained him to sleep with a pair of thirteen-year-olds who both snored and talked in their sleep. Unfortunately, having left the attic room meant it stood out to everyone whenever Wyatt went up there. Nobody forbade him from going, of course, but any mention of Seymour made his parents swan dive into depressive episodes where they would forget meals, sleep for eighteen hours in a row—cease to function, essentially. It upset his grandparents, and his Mamá Aurora, and the twins acted out even more than usual—it threw their household into chaos.

Luckily, he knew where Seymour kept the seeds. He wouldn't have to be there long. If that kid—Simón—could really make them grow, it was worth the risk of getting caught.

He climbed up into the room, stepping on the floorboards he knew to be the quietest. Keeping one ear open for his family downstairs, he sank down into a crouch and reached under Seymour's bedside table. The envelope taped to the bottom had thinned with age, the tape waxy and delicate at the corners. Wyatt pulled it free and flipped it open to look at the dark seed pods inside. The front of the envelope read *For spring!* in Seymour's messy scrawl.

Wyatt tucked it into his flannel pocket.

"What are you doing here?"

Wyatt nearly tripped over his own knees, all the hairs on his arms standing on end. He whipped his head around to find Quinn, one of the twins, poking his head up into the room from the stairs leading up to the attic. Quinn ducked his head as Wyatt feigned a swipe at him and poked back up again, raising his thick black brows.

"None of your business," Wyatt hissed, crawling toward the stairs. "Shut up and get down before Mami and Papá see you."

Quinn backed down the stairs. "Rory's keeping watch."

Wyatt sighed, waiting for Quinn to climb down far enough for him to climb down too. Back on the ground, he pushed the stairs back up, standing on his toes to make sure they clicked back into place.

"I was just getting something."

"What?"

"Something me and Seymour kept in the room," Wyatt snapped, flashing Quinn an impatient look. Quinn looked back up at him, narrowing his black eyes suspiciously.

Rory's head poked into the hall, eyes wide and braids slipping out of place like always, no matter how tight Mamá Aurora made them.

"Um, Quinn—?"

As soon as Quinn opened his mouth to respond, Mamá Aurora came into view, pulling Rory into the hall along with her. She let go of him and fisted her hands at her hips, looking at the three of them through narrowed eyes.

"Why are the three of you sneaking around?"

Wyatt shot Quinn a scathing look. The twins knew how to be nosy, but nothing about how to be sneaky.

"Sorry, Mamá Aurora," he said. "I just . . . didn't want to upset anyone if I went upstairs real quick."

Better not to mention anything about grabbing something from the room, and better still not to mention it had to do with someone he'd only just met today. Mamá Aurora didn't know about the seeds, but knowing any of Seymour's belongings might end up in the hands of someone outside of the family would bring up feelings in her, no matter how much Wyatt insisted Simón gave him an honest vibe.

Mamá Aurora looked past him at the string to pull down the attic stairs, expression softening. She tugged fondly at the end of one of Rory's braids and reached out to play swat at Quinn's head.

"You two. Worse than Wyatt used to be with Seymour." She smiled, eyes still heavy with sadness. "He used to follow him around everywhere, never wanted to give him privacy."

The twins pursed their lips, making near-identical expressions of silent protest.

Wyatt remembered making the same face when Mamá accused him of idolizing Seymour.

Mamá Aurora came closer to him, reaching up and patting the side of his face. She stood tall for her age, straight back and square shoulders, only a few inches shorter than Wyatt. Her sadness didn't shrink her—if anything, she looked bigger when she talked about Seymour.

"You should spend more time with your little brothers, Wyatt," she said, reaching out to trace her thin, gentle fingers over the tight strands of his braids. "Share Seymour's memory with them. It'll do all of you good."

Wyatt looked down at his feet and nodded. In the last few years, his memories of Seymour all tangled together, tainted by the fact of his death. Mamá Aurora still managed to tell beautiful stories about him, somehow, but Wyatt didn't know how to talk about him anymore without clenching his jaw so hard he feared his teeth would crack. The twins were better off asking anyone else in the family for stories, except for their parents.

"You're right, Mamá," he said.

She patted his cheek again, then turned and placed her hand on Quinn's shoulder.

"Come on. Let your brother have some space."

Quinn looked back at him as Mamá Aurora led him away, eyes still narrowed in suspicion. Wyatt almost laughed; he looked like Seymour when he made that face.

That night, Quinn needled him about what he took from Seymour's room for so long he fell asleep in Wyatt's bed instead of the bunk he shared with Rory. Rory fell asleep long before both of them, either uninterested or too shy to help his brother needle, but Wyatt struggled to sleep at all even after Quinn drifted off. Quinn slept restlessly, tossing and turning in every direction and calling out in his sleep.

Wyatt placed a hand over Quinn's head late in the night, the touch pacifying him swiftly like a sheet draping over a caged bird.

"Shut up," he whispered to Quinn in the dark.

Quinn mumbled sleepily under his breath, brows furrowed. Wyatt heaved a sigh and settled closer, draping a heavy arm around his little brother. He still twitched and mumbled every so often, but the contact soothed Quinn's nerves. Wyatt had been the same at Quinn's age—plagued with nightmares that left him more exhausted after sleeping than before. Seymour always told him it was a gift, that it meant spirits noticed him and wanted to speak to him.

But spirits didn't reach out to him anymore. Now, dreamless sleep or dull gray dreams plagued his nights. He felt stupid missing the nightmares, but losing such a regular part of his life felt like losing a tooth or a toenail; nothing vital, but still glaring and painful.

"You know something," he whispered, watching Quinn's sleeping expression. "Seymour used to wake me up when my dreams got too bad. I wish he'd been here when you started getting your dreams. He always knew what to say when it got overwhelming. I never felt scared or alone when he talked to me about it all—the spirits and our ancestors and all that. He was a really good brother. Way better than me."

He stopped, throat painful and tight like his heart wanted to climb up out of his body. He swallowed and squeezed his eyes shut, angry at himself. He couldn't even talk about Seymour when his little brothers were asleep.

"Sorry," he said, covering the crown of Quinn's head with his palm. "I don't know why I'm still like this."

Quinn said nothing at all, breathing deep and even, face smooth with peaceful sleep. Wyatt settled close beside him and let sleep take him at last.

◆

Wyatt almost made it into the canal early the next morning, only to be stopped just as he pushed the kayak into the water by his mother's voice.

"Where are you going, *mijo?*" she asked, standing a few yards away on the grass with her arms crossed over her cotton nightgown. "You don't have work, it's Saturday. Don't think you can get out of helping the twins clean that pigsty you call a room."

Wyatt winced at her but didn't pull the kayak back onto the shore yet. He straightened up, gauging the look in her narrowed eyes. She looked tired more than anything, her brown cheeks tinged pink and eyes puffy with sleep.

"Sorry, Mami," he said, still holding onto the kayak. "I just have to do something real quick. I'll be back in like an hour, I swear."

She sighed through her nostrils and placed her hands on her hips. "What do you have to do at this hour?"

"I'm just gonna see a friend, just for a second. Please Mami? I bet I'll be back before the twins even wake up."

"You better be," she said, holding a finger out toward him even as her expression softened a fraction. "What friend are you seeing? It's been a while."

Wyatt smiled at her, waving her concern away. Simón was the exact kind of guy she liked seeing him with—serious, dedicated, and a bit rebellious. "His name's Simón, he's from Norwottuck—you'd like him, don't worry. I'll be right back, okay?"

His mother stood her ground a moment longer, looking torn. She looked out at the canals, the trees in the distance, and sighed through her nose. She cast her eyes back on Wyatt, her thick black brows furrowed, but nodded and waved him over, opening her arms for a hug.

Wyatt heaved a sigh and left the kayak's side, coming over to her with his arms open and letting her tug him down and squeeze him until he wheezed. She kissed the side of his face and let him go.

"Please be careful. Don't wander out of the green zones. Understand?"

"Yeah, Mami. He's meeting me out by the old library ruins."

She smiled, losing some of the tightness in her eyes. The ruins were familiar ground. Just as quickly, her face became stern again and she pointed a finger at him.

"If you come back late, you're cleaning the bathrooms. The ones on your Tía Carmen's side, too. Got it?"

Wyatt grimaced, but nodded his agreement and slipped off into the kayak, waving goodbye. Tía Carmen and Tío Connor lived in the apartments attached to the house. They had a mess of children—seven altogether, the oldest eighteen, born around the same time as himself, and the youngest two years old. Their bathrooms typically looked straight out of a horror story and the younger children were so annoying even Quinn and Rory refused to spend time with them.

All the more reason to hurry. Luckily, he knew the path well. He whizzed through the canals and double-checked his pocket for the envelope full of seeds when he hopped out of the kayak at the bank of the forest. He ran through the forest, past all the mossy green ruins, and stopped at the top of the hill overlooking the murky pond.

He saw Simón down on the island, sitting at the edge of the water with his dog, his head bowed over a pile of slim branches beside him. The sun gleamed off his black hair, his shoulders hunched over as he worked. Wyatt whistled sharply from the top of the hill and waved at them when they both looked up, Maruka hopping up to his feet and barking. Simón waved him over with a wide upward sweep of his arm and Wyatt rushed down the steep side of the hill.

"Hey!" he called as he waded across the pond. Maruka leapt into the water to meet him, splashing him all over with pond muck. Wyatt laughed, holding his hands up to shield himself as much as possible.

"Sic 'em, boy," said Simón in his usual sullen drawl.

Maruka ignored Simón's command, bounding around Wyatt and splashing mud and water around with his great paws. Wyatt shrugged at Simón, climbing up onto the bank and sitting a few feet away from him.

"You know, I think your dog likes me a little."

Simón rolled his eyes and turned back to the slim branches in his hands. He was tying them together with coarse twine, bending them into a small arc.

"He likes everyone," said Simón.

Wyatt watched him a moment longer as he pulled out his pocketknife and sharpened the ends of the branches.

"What are you making?"

"Mini-greenhouses," he said, nodding at the clear plastic sheeting folded up beside him.

Wyatt raised his eyebrows. "For what?"

Simón rolled his eyes again. "Plants that need greenhouses."

He nodded, petting between Maruka's ears and sitting between them. Two things Wyatt could say for sure about Simón so far: loved plants, hated speaking. It caught him off guard how charming he found it. Something about his moody, silent disposition soothed his nerves.

"Oh!" He sat up straighter, fishing the envelope out of his pocket and holding it up. "I have the *stuff*."

Simón looked up and furrowed his brows, reading the envelope. "'For spring?'"

"Yeah, sorry, uh—they're my brother's. Were my brother's." He smiled, handing them over. "He was good at this kind of thing but . . . I'm really not."

Simón flipped open the envelope, peering at the seed pods inside, his thick brows knitted close. He turned a few out onto the palm of his hand and hummed thoughtfully, uncertain.

"Some kind of—tropical shrub, or?" He shook his head and corrected himself before Wyatt could. "No, maga tree." He looked up at Wyatt, expression flat and disbelieving. "You brought me tree seeds? Tropical tree seeds?"

"I know it can be done," Wyatt said, holding back a wince. "My brother had plans to do it, so I know it's possible."

Simón sighed through his nose and turned his disbelieving gaze up toward the sky, waiting for some celestial being to tell him it was a joke.

"How long have these seeds even been in here?"

"Two years and three months."

Simón huffed, almost laughing, rolling the seeds over in his hand.

"These seeds have to be dead by now. Give me something else to grow."

Wyatt's insides prickled, hot and sharp. "They're *not* dead," he snapped, harsher than he meant to.

Simón and Maruka both looked at him, Simón's eyebrows rising high and Maruka's head cocked in confusion. Wyatt cleared his throat and straightened the sleeves of his flannel shirt. He didn't know much about plants, but he knew tree seeds were hardy. He *knew* the seeds still held life.

"You said you'd grow me anything. This is what I want. Please."

Simón looked at the seeds in his hand a moment longer, then huffed again and poured the seeds back into the envelope. He tucked it into his jacket pocket and gave Wyatt a withering look.

"I can't promise you anything. But even a small tree like that takes a while to grow from a seed. If they're viable."

"I'll take it." Wyatt ducked his head gratefully and patted Maruka's head. "And if there's anything I can do to help, just tell me."

Simón grunted in response and nodded at the rest of the branches still piled up beside him.

"You can help me with these."

"Oh." Wyatt didn't have time for much now. Staying here meant coming home to filthy bathrooms in need of cleaning.

But, if he was honest, he wanted to stay. Leaving so soon after snapping at Simón felt wrong. Giving up Simón's cool, collected company to avoid a dirty bathroom felt like a bad deal.

He squinted up at the sun's position in the sky. He still had a bit of time before his parents began to get nervous. They knew where he was, at least.

"Where's the twine?"

❖

Wyatt regularly checked in on Simón's garden as the weeks passed, even though Simón told him he had to try to germinate the seeds and grow at least a sprout before even thinking about planting them in the ground. Though nothing in the garden had grown larger than sprouts yet, he loved listening to Simón explain to him how to build simple structures to guide the tomatoes up as they grew, or what the purpose of planting something on a raised bed was. He still didn't talk much about anything else, but he had plenty to say about gardening.

Wyatt tried his best to keep up. He didn't know much about raising plants, but he knew a lot about soil, air, and water.

"I brought you this," said Wyatt, still sweating from lugging a bucketful of water mixed with coffee grounds from the bank all the way to the pond. "My boss told me that soil sample I brought back was pretty alkaline. So I thought your tomatoes could use some help."

Simón came over and took the bucket from him, lifting it up to smell it. He raised his eyebrows and looked over the bucket at Wyatt.

"This is helpful." He looked down into the bucket for a long moment before looking back up at Wyatt's face. "Thanks, Wyatt."

"Yeah," said Wyatt, smiling and squatting down to rub Maruka's belly. "Anytime, man. You know, that soil might convince them to sanction this land for public use. That'd be good."

Simón offered no opinion on the matter. He carried the bucket over to the area where they'd planted the tomatoes and set it down, hunkering down on his knees and examining the young tomato leaves. He pressed his fingers gently against the soil around the tomatoes and then brushed the dirt off his hands, sitting back on his heels.

"Still too wet?" asked Wyatt.

Simón nodded. He looked up at Wyatt as he came over to examine the young tomato sprouts too.

"Did your boss teach you about coffee grounds?"

"My *bisabuela*, actually," he said, smiling fondly. "She isn't really much of a gardener, but she taught me and my brother Seymour what she knew. Seymour took to it like a duck to water but I took to it like a duck to cement."

Simón's eyes lit up in amusement, though he tried not to smile.

"You've been helping me a lot. Maybe you don't give yourself enough credit?"

"I give myself exactly the right amount of credit, trust me." Wyatt shook his head. It encouraged him to hear Simón found him helpful, but the scores of withered and shriveled plants in Wyatt's past begged to differ. "I think you're just good at what you do. It's easy to help you when you always know exactly what you need."

Simón shrugged off the compliment and looked back down at the young tomato plants thoughtfully. Wyatt crouched down beside him, reaching out to feel the dampness of the soil. It clung to his fingers, cool and soft from an early morning drizzle. He brushed his hands off and crossed his arms over his knees, resting his chin on them.

"Later today they'll be ready for a soak."

Simón nodded. He stayed quiet for a long moment, still gazing down at the plants thoughtfully. Wyatt waited for his thoughts to finish brewing, tapping his fingers over his upper arms and tilting his head to watch him think.

"I've been wanting to ask," he said at last. "How did your brother end up with those seeds? Those kinds of trees don't grow in this area."

Wyatt's head swam as soon as the question left Simón's mouth. He dropped his forehead against his forearms and squeezed his eyes shut against the sudden nausea.

"Sorry," he said, shaking his head to try and clear the feeling.

"It's okay," Simón said quickly. "You don't have to tell me. I've just been curious about it."

"No, no. I'll tell you. Just—hold on." Wyatt sat back on his butt, pressing the heels of his hands against his eyes and taking a centering breath. The spinning in his head slowed and he took a minute to gather the pieces he still remembered clearly about that time. "My Abuelo Weston brought them up when he moved up here with us."

Simón smiled, small but his whole face glowed. "Abuelo *Weston*?"

Wyatt smiled back in spite of himself and shrugged. "He's *raza*, I promise." He wrapped his arms around his knees and pressed his face against the rough denim again for a second, then sat back up, taking a deep breath before starting again. "He came up here a little before we—before Seymour died. He brought the seeds up because he had to leave his *flor de maga* tree behind back in Florida, but he knew Seymour could grow a new one. Mom used to brag about him all the time to all our relatives."

Simón listened to him with rapt attention, his light-colored eyes trained on Wyatt's face even though Wyatt's eyes stayed mostly glued to the tops of his knees. He waited for more, so Wyatt pressed on.

"Seymour only told me about it. He wanted to surprise the whole family. But then . . . everything just happened so fast. One day we just—I got in a fight with Seymour about something stupid. I can't even remember what it *was* anymore. He was sick of fighting with me, so he took off—he wanted to clear his head out in the woods." Tears prickled at his eyes and he rubbed at them angrily. "Then he didn't come back. Me and all the other scouts went looking for him . . . and then my friend Lila found him a few weeks later—washed up on the riverbank."

Simón placed his hand between Wyatt's shoulder blades, leaning into him. Wyatt couldn't bring himself to look at him yet, but he could feel Simón's eyes still watching his face.

"He drowned. I don't know how or why, but that's what they said after they finished looking at his body." Wyatt pressed the heel of his hand against the dull ache between his eyes. "Now it's like—I don't know. It's like my brain shuts down when I try to think about that time. I forgot about the seeds. Abuelo did too, I think."

Simón looked at him for a few seconds longer, then finally tore his eyes away and looked down at the tomato plants.

"I'm sorry about your brother," he said.

"Thanks." Wyatt rubbed at his eyes again and pressed his face against his forearm. "Are my seeds dead?"

"A lot of them are dead or empty," said Simón, voice gentle. "But I'm not sure about a couple of them."

Wyatt looked up, raising his eyebrows. "Really?"

Simón nodded. "I can't promise you anything, but I can tell you that much. I want you to know I'm taking this seriously—I can tell how much it means to you. And now I know why."

The back of Wyatt's neck turned hot and he rubbed it self-consciously. "Yeah. Look—if they do all turn out to be dead, I'll understand. I know it's a little dumb."

"It's not dumb at all." Simón looked down at his hands, picking fastidiously at the soil under his nails. "I understand."

Wyatt waited a beat in case Simón added anything more. When he didn't, he pressed his shoulder up against Simón's. His fidgeting and lowered eyelashes, the tight set of his shoulders, and the distant tone of his voice told him enough. He'd lost someone too.

"Sorry," he said, squeezing his shoulder. "I'm glad you don't think it's stupid."

Simón turned his eyes up to Wyatt's face. "You're stupid in other ways."

They looked at each other for a moment, holding the most serious expressions they could manage. A second later, they snorted and leaned into each other, laughing so loud they startled Maruka and prompted him to bark and leap toward them. Simón stood up, holding his hands out toward the dog and trying to stop laughing enough to command him to stay away from the tomatoes.

Wyatt sat back on his hands and watched them, grin spreading wide across his face.

◆

Summer's end came with a torrential downpour that lasted for a string of several days. The sun finally came out from behind the thick gray clouds not a moment too soon. Wyatt felt himself going slowly insane with his little brothers and cousins constantly buzzing around him, pressing their noses against the window and singing *Que llueva, que llueva* over and over again. Mami and Papá didn't allow them out in poor weather and Tía Carmen and Tío Connor subscribed to the same rules.

When Wyatt finally left the house and took off for Simón's pond, he found the garden almost completely swallowed up by the water. Simón, of course, was nowhere to be found.

None of the plants were salvageable. Wyatt waded through the murky water even though he could tell by looking that nothing could have survived—even the greenhouses they'd constructed together washed away in the rains. He sat down at the center of the muddy spot of land still above the surface of the water and dropped his head in his hands, resolving to wait a while for Simón. If he came and saw the destruction, he would need someone with him.

But an hour passed, then another, and still no Simón.

"He's fine," he assured himself, standing up and squinting toward north, as if he could see all the way to Norwottuck.

Possibly, Simón already knew what had come of his garden. Maybe his family didn't have the same rigidity about traveling during bad weather. Without his garden, however, what reason did Simón have to come down to Nonotuck? Wyatt never told him so much as what block in Nonotuck he lived in.

Why had he never asked *where* in Norwottuck Simón lived?

❖

The Nonotuck area end-of-summer gathering happened in the Meadows, in between the farmland and the floodplain. Wyatt's family regularly attended every seasonal Nonotuck gathering; they set up their bread stand, his mom and dad took turns singing with the musicians, and his Mamá Aurora regaled crowds with stories. In years past, he and Seymour took charge of the bread stand. The twins ran it now, bartering hard for the best trades and only getting away with it because they were still babyfaced enough to be considered cute.

"Brats," Wyatt said coming into the cool shade of the tent and looking around at their gains. A basketful of fat, sunny peaches, a small basketful of berries, what looked like a fairly new motherboard, a large sack of fertilizer, and a bolt of fabric. "It's still morning. You know hustling people won't work so well when you're grown, right?"

Quinn shrugged and flashed his most innocent grin. "No one's hustling. Some of these people put in extra orders! We're just making sure everyone walks away happy. Right, Rory?"

Rory nodded, in the process of eating a big piece of casabe, his braids already falling out of place. Wyatt rolled his eyes and gestured for him to move out of his chair, moving into it himself. He pointed down at the ground between his feet.

"You guys obviously shouldn't be left alone. Sit, Rory, you're a mess."

Rory sat down on the ground, untying the ends of his braids and shaking them loose. Just a quick toss of his head left his hair pin-straight down his shoulders, like the braids were never there in the first place.

"I can't help it, they always fall out," he sighed.

"I know, I know," said Wyatt, gathering his smooth, slippery hair in his hands and trying to braid it tight from the roots like Mamá

Aurora did. He waited for Quinn to boast about his ever-immaculate braids despite also being born with his hair almost as straight as Rory's, but he kept a thoughtful silence, measuring his words.

"So," he said slowly. "Do you mean you're gonna hang out here? With us?"

Wyatt looked up, letting up a little on Rory's hair when he whined for the third time. He hadn't meant that, but now that Quinn *thought* he did, he looked cautiously hopeful.

He turned his attention back to Rory's hair, already looking to escape from the new braid as it formed.

"Well, it's traditional for siblings to run this stand together, right?"

"Yeah," said Quinn, a grin spreading across his face. "Papi and Titi Carmen used to run it together."

"And me and Seymour."

Rory turned his head back to look up at him and Quinn nodded, chest and shoulders proud.

"I used to be just like you guys," Wyatt said, rolling his eyes and smiling fondly. "When it was me and Seymour here, I tried hustling people a little. He always checked me, though. Remember how much we used to fight?"

"Not as much as me and you fight," said Quinn, raising his eyebrows pointedly.

"Yeah, right. I guess you guys were pretty young when we fought a *lot,* but trust me, Seymour wasn't always my biggest fan." He sighed, chest tight, and nudged Rory's head straight again so he could finish. "I loved him, though. Still love him."

"He loved you too," said Quinn, quick and certain.

His brothers didn't press him for more, content to sit in each other's company. Quinn turned his interest to laughing at Rory's braids already unraveling and Wyatt took the opportunity to take some slow breaths. It still hurt deep in his lungs to talk about Seymour, but the twins longed to hear it. He owed it to them to keep working on it.

By the afternoon, Rory's hair sat loose about his shoulders even though he kept complaining about the heat. Try as they might, nothing managed to grab a good hold of Rory's hair in the late summer swelter. Bread sold well enough, but Wyatt and the twins gazed longingly at the river and the glittering canals as the day went on.

"Rory, look at that guy," said Quinn, nodding at the crowd milling about the stands. "His hair's even messier than yours."

"Be quiet," groaned Rory. "Look, I bet he heard you, he's coming this way."

"There's no way he heard me." Quinn scoffed at the idea, pushing himself up off the chair to man the stand. "He probably wants bread. Hey! What can I do for you?"

From his place on the floor, lying with his head under Quinn's vacant chair to evade the blinding glare of the sun on the river, Wyatt immediately recognized the voice that followed.

"Are you Wyatt's little brothers?" asked Simón, serious as ever.

Wyatt scrambled up to sitting, almost knocking over the chair in his haste. Simón stood there in front of their stand, looking awkward but otherwise fine. He met Wyatt's eyes and his expression immediately relaxed into comfort.

"Oh," said Simón, tone softer. "Here you are."

"I knew you were okay," said Wyatt before he could stop himself. "I looked for you like—"

"Me too. We must have kept missing each other."

"I saw the island, Simón. I'm so sorry—all that work you did . . ."

Simón shook his head. "*We* did. And it's okay. It was bound to happen."

Wyatt frowned at him, squinting at him scrutinizingly. How could he be fine after losing so much work? But he really did look fine—his brows sat low over his eyes like always, but he was almost smiling.

"Simón—"

"Hey!" Quinn raised his eyebrows and jabbed his thumb back in Simón's direction. "You know this huge guy?"

Wyatt rolled his eyes and sighed at his brother. "Quinn. Be nice." He gestured at both his brothers in turn. "Simón, Quinn and Rory. They're thirteen."

"Hi," said Simón, nodding at each of them. Wyatt noticed belatedly that Simón's arms hung down heavily by his sides. Leaning over the stand counter, he realized Simón held a flowery hanging plant in one hand and a bucket covered with a towel in the other.

"Bringing me flowers?"

Simón smiled, looking down at the plant and shrugging.

"I guess I am, yeah. Mostly I wanted to talk to you. Can I borrow you for a minute?"

Wyatt nodded, shoving his hands in his pockets and coming out from behind the stand. He glanced at the twins over his shoulder, raising his eyebrows at them seriously.

"Don't hustle folks while I'm gone."

Quinn and Rory looked back at him with matching puzzled faces. They shrugged agreeably, exchanging quick glances before waving him off.

Wyatt sighed and looked up at Simón as they walked toward the floodplain. He looked a little flustered, but Wyatt attributed that to his unruly hair and the stifling heat. He reached out for the covered bucket, wrapping his fingers around the wire handle before Simón could object.

"Let me help," he said.

Simón snorted, but handed the bucket over. "We don't have to go that far. I just wanted to show you something. And to give you this."

He held up the hanging plant, the long green vines pouring over the top of an elegant wide-mouthed clay pot. Wyatt reached out to touch one of the resplendent purple blossoms, thin and veined like butterfly wings but smooth as satin.

"You're really bringing me flowers?"

Simón looked down at the plant, thinking for a moment before answering.

"I started propagating this for you the day you brought me those seeds," he said finally, looking up from the plant. "I was worried they'd all be dead, and I didn't want to leave you empty-handed."

"Oh," Wyatt said, setting down the bucket to take the pot from Simón instead. "That's—you didn't need to do that for me."

Simón pressed on as if Wyatt hadn't spoken. "It's from a bougainvillea at my house. The original plant belonged to my mom."

Wyatt's chest clenched tight. He reached out, squeezing his hand around Simón's forearm, and swallowed hard against the sudden lump in his throat.

"It's beautiful, Simón." He grinned, lifting the pot up closer to his face. "I promise I'm gonna do everything I can to keep this alive. I mean, I've never gotten flowers before. You really know how to set the flower bar high."

Simón shook his head. "I know you can keep it alive. I've seen you take care of plants before."

Wyatt laughed, but he didn't argue. Even if he couldn't figure out his way around a garden trowel without Simón, he couldn't fail at taking care of a piece of Simón's mother's plant.

"I'll take care of it like it's Seymour's."

Simón smiled, pulling the towel off the top of his bucket. Inside, in the center of the packed, dark soil, sprouted a pair of bright green, spade-shaped leaves.

"And I'll take care of this like it's my mother's," he said, stepping aside so Wyatt could lean over the bucket and look. "Because I don't trust you with it just yet."

Wyatt set down the clay pot, carefully so as to not jostle the bougainvillea, and dropped onto his knees to look closer into the bucket at the tender young leaves. He opened and closed his mouth a few times—he knew exactly what it was, and yet he was afraid to ask for confirmation. He swallowed, throat even tighter than it had been a moment ago, and blinked fast against the uncomfortable prickling in his eyes.

"One made it?" He choked out, finally. "It's alive?"

"Yeah," said Simón, crouching down with him and sidling closer. "Maybe two, but this one sprouted first. I wanted to show you."

"I thought—I don't know. With the garden flooding, I thought—"

Simón smiled gently and ducked his head lower to catch Wyatt's eyes. "I took your seeds home with me, Wy. They needed a lot more care than I could give them at the garden. I wasn't going to give up on them just because I lost the island."

"Thank you," said Wyatt, voice thick with tears and eyes blurry. He threw his arms around Simón's shoulders without thinking and squeezed him as tight as he could. "I wish I knew how to show you how much this means to me."

"I know how much it means to you."

Wyatt tightened his arms around him again before letting go, sitting back on the ground. He placed a hand against the white plastic bucket, wishing he could see the thin, sprawling roots within the soil. He imagined them in his mind's eye, reaching down toward the ground, planting themselves right beside Wyatt. He leaned close against the bucket, resting his cheek against the plastic lip, and watched the shiny green leaves standing proudly. The leaves themselves reminded him of Seymour, straight-backed and proud— young and vulnerable. He wiped his eyes with the heel of his hand and pressed his forehead against the lip of the bucket instead.

He and Simón stayed that way a long while. Simón kept their silence warm and patient, his hand eventually crossing the space between them to cover Wyatt's. Wyatt turned his hand upward so their palms touched.

As the sky darkened from orange to pink to purple over the floodplains, the music and joyous voices behind them carried on. Wyatt, tears still in his eyes, chest aching, stood and pulled Simón up by the hand, locking their fingers together.

"I wanna celebrate. Do you dance?"

Simón winced but shrugged, pulling Wyatt a few steps away from the plants. He glanced around self-consciously.

"I'll try. I feel like celebrating too."

Wyatt laughed and wiped his eyes again with his free hand.

"Come on," he said.

On the floodplain, under the cover of the dim twilight, they danced around the maga and the bougainvillea with a lightheartedness Wyatt never thought he'd get to have again. As he laughed at Simón's lack of anything resembling coordination, watching him try and fail to catch the rhythm of the music behind them, he thanked god for serious boys with two left feet and green thumbs.

A Flock for the Sandhill Crane

ROMAN SANCHEZ

San Antonio, Texas, 1931 CE

Cruzita Valdez is ninety-seven years old. She is talking to her daughter's garden. She doesn't know, but I'm listening too.

An oak tree of comparable age stands tall inside the wooden fence, creating green shade for her and the tiny plywood shack her family lives in. The roses, tulips, lilies spread their petals open to the light of the sun piercing out at them from the distant horizon, like the sparkle in the eye of her many alcoholic children and grandchildren, ready to fill and be filled with weak red wine. Cruzita takes note of the dozen unique bird calls twinkling in the nooks and creases of trees and bushes surrounding her daughter Maricela's small yard: flycatchers, jays, chickadees, bluebirds, mockingbirds, sparrows, cardinals, and a titmouse.

"Ay, and Apá with his broken shovel, mis queridas, the one Amá gave him before she died giving birth to me. My Apá would sleep with that dusty shovel. It had a broken handle. The blade was made of steel from the shop in Piedras Negras, Jaime's shop. Jaime was old and cranky his entire life, could not walk as good as I do now, that's right babies. His granddaughter, Ximena, and I would gather up rocks from the dirt floor of his steel shop. I did not mind the heat— I was happy to rest from tending the goats and cows and chickens all week with Graciela and Apá," Cruzita hums softly, giggling. Her shoulders seem to shake with a constant chuckle. Her white hair is tied back in a strict bun.

She stands, huddled over from the weight of changing time, her ankle-length cotton dress a white cloud of flowers, like her mind. She holds a tin watering bucket, administers water slowly, drop after drop filled with the morning's stories: the Mexican-American War of 1846, when she was too young to understand, the Mexican army marching past her small rancho on the edge of the desert in Piedras Negras, purchasing two cows, five chickens, and a goat from her Apá, almost everything they owned.

"Where were they going chiquitas? Off to fight the americanos taking our land, I think. Daddy told me many stories of the white men, oh how they drank and fought all over our northern borders, took girls like me to do bad things when they weren't digging for gold. ¿Yo? No, I would never go with those bad men!" she laughs at the audacity of bluebonnets. "I was too busy feeding the goats and their babies, and milking the cows in the hot sun. Or I was inside all day making beans and tortillas, since Amá was gone, que Dios la bendiga."

"Yes, yes, they are very easy to make niñas: you soak a new batch of corn every night, you grind the kernels on the metate, crush them until they fill the holes, you dry the mush so you can mix in the water and salt."

"My favorite part was taking a break to go gather sticks or grass hay for the cooking fire, and you put the grass under the sticks, and with your fire rocks you can light them with a clap!" She brings her frail hands together with hidden force.

It is early March and the Texas mornings have not yet begun to fill the air with fire as they often do during summer months. She inches slowly through the garden path as it winds backward and forward among the crowd of flowers and trees, winding to the road, to the house.

She stops for a moment in the crisp grass, her feet bare and skeletal, her withered body hunched and hidden among the jungle-high plants around her. She puts down the watering can, and, fumbling in her other pouch, pulls out a small bag of leaves and grass, rolls the tobacco in its own leaf (slowly, given her shaking extremities), dangles it to her lips, lights it with a match. The smoke is slow-burning but not hot. She fills her lungs with the world, looks up and around.

She is tired of talking and watering the grass. She ambles back to the front porch of the house, climbs with pain-filled precision, unapologetic of the waddle in her gait, the pause after each step up the stairs. Her hands are a dark red-brown, like her whole body, hidden as it might be by a white dress; those hands reach now to sweep the dust from the woven porch chair, probably the carpentry work of her son-in-law, Ramiro, and his brothers. The crows are out in the neighborhood, a full battalion. She turns and sits, after a slow careful descent, into the wicker chair perched near the front steps.

Up over the curb squeals a battered Ford Model A, coming to a halt in a teeter-totter just before ramming the front chain-link fence. Cruzita is at attention now, after a long morning of self-absorbed gardening. She realizes her great-grandchildren José, Gregorio, Tomás, Arabella, and Maria—she may be perpetually lost in thought but she prides herself in recalling names—have been running in and out of the garden all morning, perhaps all their lives. She watches them as they sprint out of the yard to the newly arrived A Model, its driver stumbling now from his seat onto the sidewalk on which he has parked. Bottles of cheap red wine fall to the ground alongside him, but remain unbroken. The kids run to their father, Cruzita's grandson Lupe, who appears in all likelihood to be quite enjoying this so-called Great Depression at the moment. It is around 12:45 in the afternoon.

"Ya!" Lupe yells as they swarm him. "Hijos malcriados! Métense a trabajar todos," he slurs, struggling to find his balance, stumbling upright and into the garden yard on his hands and knees.

"Apá, Apá," Tomasíto calls in his high-pitched voice. "How 'bout you too, no?"

Laughter floats through the garden. Cruzita huffs smoke through her nose.

"Pinche niños—" Lupe says and lunges toward them all like the jaguar strangling his heart, though his unfortunate position on the ground gives them plenty of time to dart away like many giggling mice.

Lupe flips onto his back in a drunken haze, mumbling to himself in sympathy, occasionally wrenching between tears and hysteria. He does not notice La Grande, Cruzita Valdez, his beloved abuela, who has lived through the creation of Texas, through a civil war, a world war, who has lived to see the arrival of the railroad, electricity, the telegraph, the telephone, and the car, like the one even now splayed on the lawn, who has seen the white man massacre forests and drill for oil. This very same ninety-seven-year-old woman, who just before had been smoking through her drifting mind on the porch, has shuffled like a squirrel down the staircase and across the garden, cane now in hand, towering above Lupe, prone as he is.

"Lupe!" she rasps through the last of her smoke, the bark in her voice resounding. She is una madre del rancho. "Get up right now, desgracia! You are the one who should be working, old man. What kind of thirty-seven-year-old man drinks all day while his seven kids run around town ruining our neighborhood and tarnishing our name? What kind of man cannot get a job two years after he got fired from the foundry?" Cruzita is poking him forcefully with her cane, ignoring his grunts and "Ay Abuela no!"

He stumbles to his feet to escape her but is still too drunk.

"And are we talking about Lupe, the hero of the Revolution, who decided out of the blue one day to build gardens to feed refugees! Fifteen-year-old Lupe, getting the kids to help las familias running from Mexico, giving them squash and tomatoes and beans and eggs. Look at you now malcriado! Virgen Purísima, help me now because I'm about to—" Cruzita is interrupted by a fit of coughs, doubling her over.

Lupe has stopped crying, laughing, running—is on his knees with a dazed look, her words a needle piercing through the buzz.

"Guadalupe—" Cruzita is coughing and coughing, on her knees.

Lupe's wife, Celia, and his mother, Maricela, have come out onto the porch in the commotion, as have the mothers and grandmothers on either side of their house. The great-grandchildren, other children from up and down the block, begin to congregate in nervous giggles. Even the workers at W. C. Johnson Lumber across the street pause to watch the old Mexican woman pause from beating and berating her grandson, calling "Lupe" with anger ringing out violently from her lungs.

And when her ninety-seven-year-old heart stops beating mid-cough and she stumbles taut onto the grass, everyone—the garden flowers, the family, the gringos—feels it, in the muzzle of the soil, the gaze of the sun, the shake of the trees. Even I feel it.

Lupe, Lupe, Lupe . . .

A Valdez invokes my name.

So I get involved again.

◆

300 years later, 2231 CE

But not right away.

I take my time, test out my feet. I watch for signs.

My friend, Luun, disappeared yesterday. I think that is a clear enough sign.

Fifteen miles southwest, in the San Antonio region of the Plains Megacity, an abandoned town once named Natalia is being made into a launchpad. The town is completely devoid of human life, one-story houses left derelict along its twentieth-century roads, small government buildings from that time period tilting into the soil. The asphalt and sidewalk are graying, cracked throughout, roots of oak and cedar and mesquite pushing through and attempting to reclaim. Indeed, non-human life has hit a boom here, with front yards and gardens expanded like full spring. There are gardenias in living room sofas, zucchini in cable televisions. I see a shopping cart fallen on its side outside the H-E-B grocery store, itself now a gymnasium of rose vines, wood sorrel, and box elder. There is a paper bag filled with expired yogurt, Fritos, and apple cores.

The UN reconstruction effort somehow overlooked this abandoned town, a curious oversight in the middle of the Plains, an enormous city that extends from the southern tip of what used to be Mexico up into what used to be Canada. I'm no longer curious though. Soon every building will be overturned, recycled. Every empty space will be a launchpad for the rich.

I haven't taken form like this since Europeans arrived in the Americas, seven hundred years ago. I so rarely take form and, when I do, I make sure I'm needed, the Great Lady of Guadalupe, here to save the day.

I need to practice in this empty space. I walk with slow footing, wriggling into my leggings and silky white blouse. I've chosen to wear men's leather boots. I like my clomping gait. I am brown, my hair falls down my back in black waves, but is not overwhelming. I always like to test my limits, so here in this abandoned town I spin on one foot. I sprint as fast as I can, then jump to a halt, calm my breath quickly. I grab a pipe fallen along the road and begin to whack fences, mailboxes, windows of sleeping cars. I find a piano at the western edge of town, one leg missing, the whole thing kneeling before me. I kneel as well, attempt to play Debussy's "Clair de Lune" and "The Entertainer" by Scott Joplin, which always brings a smile. I practice smiling and move a strand of hair from my face.

Walking into the patch of cedar woods at the edge of this abandoned town, getting closer to the largest launchpad, I move quickly, skipping over logs and stacked granite. I pull my weight along, tree trunk to tree trunk. I climb a tree even, sure of myself, foot over foot. A sparrow and a titmouse see me coming, tweedle laughter at my hijinks. Sing! I say, Sing! We are all singing together now, whistling a morning tune. The sun rises on our backsides and the air feels crisp like a leaf's edge. A rocket sits on the launchpad in the distance, the travelers starting to climb aboard. The thought of Luun boarding among them looms over me but I need to focus my efforts for a few minutes longer.

I celebrate the absence of people in these woods. Momentary absence perhaps. It has been too long since my body was free of people. I bend down and plunge my hand with precision into the soil, wiggle my fingers around an earthworm. I pull her up to me, wriggle my torso with hers, then place her on a moss-covered log decomposing onto the carcass of a cardinal youngling. I try to nourish when I can.

Noise, noise above me, approaching. I stand in place, feel a drone on the wind, a vibration. I let it near, listen to my increasing heart rate. A hovercraft passing by, unusual in the industrial district where I've found this hidden launchpad. Is it on patrol? Have I triggered some surveillance camera, a laser trip-wire? I crouch down, hands and knees, elbows huddled in tight. The drone of the craft is a mountain waterfall, an erupting furnace. Then it is past, seems to speed up, off on its way to another launchpad I know of in the west. The wildlife and I emerge from hiding, gather to each other, huddle our foreheads together. Squirrel eyes, rabbit eyes, crow eyes, mountain lion eyes: black nights filled with laughter. We part ways and I continue on my trek.

I have to practice taking form away from people, away from busy energy. I'm afraid of artificial light as well, the eerie orange or blue glow it casts against your eyelids, the insecurity it brings. True fire is a different hue of light, different intensity. Are artificial lights merely fire shot through a tube? Fire contained? I think not. There's a gaping difference, I know it.

Buildings are like caves filled with fire, but the fire, the walls, are man-made and, thus, often tainted with violence. The woods, in their long lives, tall breaths, know this and they dream of an escape, always scheming. Scheme, I say, before they eradicate this patch of forest and abandoned town! Reach out your roots a little farther, turn over every table, every air-conditioner unit. Reclaim, reclaim what you have lost. I support you, I do.

Into a clearing, crunching my toes into humus and compost, boots in hand. I find an abandoned car, a '94 Honda Civic. All of its windows have been smashed, its rear driver's-side tire and rotor are missing. The gas tank is open and leaking unleaded fuel drip by drip into the carpet of oak leaves and wild mushrooms. I laugh with disgust, thinking of how long it will take the processed fuel to seep back through the bedrock from which it once came, how long until it recomposes itself, forms up again as a marker of contact with humans, of borders crossed, worlds made and destroyed. I think of how long it must have been since anyone walked through these woods and noticed this two-hundred-year-old car sitting here.

I am suddenly aware of a new purpose here in the blood rush of the day, though not the one I came here for. I walk around to the front of the car, where the front bumper has fallen into the forest floor. A young fawn is trapped underneath at her hind leg, which is twisted and bloody, bone showing. She sees me, actually looks into my heart, understands who I am, but is unable to stop whimpering. Pain is evident in the wet creases of her eyes and her mouth jitters open and closed. There are claw marks on her lower thighs, where she has attempted to escape by clawing off her own hoof, has tried over and over again for the last few hours. She seems aware of the mistake she made by reaching for the berries tucked under the car. She is pleading and miserable. I bend down and brush a hand against her soft cheek. I coo.

I'm worried about Luun, who has cut himself off from me. I cannot sense him. There is a silence where, for countless millennia, there was Luun. Luun, my oldest friend, the only other one like me. I have an idea of where he has gone or where he is trying to go. That is why I came to the launchpad—to intercept him before he leaves. To plead and beg him to stay or take me with him. My mind is clouded with envy.

I'm bonded with every being that lives inside me, deep in my brown skin, my plains and deserts and mountain terraces. But Luun is different, made of something more than just the Earth.

Luun is from the Moon.

First: the issue at hand. I clear away the leaves and branches around the deer, remove the decaying log poking at her neck. Clasping hold of the bumper, I lift with a grunt and the Civic shifts in the ground, then rises up entirely at its front end. I tighten my grip and swing as hard as I can, to my right. The car is airborne for a brief moment, almost immediately crashing into an old oak, which shakes in response to the impact. The deer's eyes are shut. She is quivering.

I hear a shout in the distance. Two shouts. Instantly, I know there are two others nearby. *Them.* I am not surprised to know they are here, at the precise moment I want to escape in pursuit of Luun, to flee my body before pollution and negligence burn it to a complete crisp. For seven hundred years, they and their family have been close by, have found me when I least expected it.

Stepping back to the newly freed deer, I reach down, place my hand on her abdomen: *Calm mi'ja.* She stills in anticipation or fear. I move my hand without a change in emotion and grasp tightly onto the broken leg, reach my hand deep into her wound. She reacts immediately, honking and roaring in pain, attempts to run for safety.

Then she stops bleating. Without understanding how, her efforts to escape are fruitful and she pulls herself up, forward, healed and fresh, no longer any sign of breakage.

How is it possible to be stuck with one family out of so many others? Out of so many millennia? Why do they continue to come up, to draw my attention? Why do they place such demands on me, even now?

The descendants of Juan Diego were marked forever when he met me. I do not know if it is a curse or a gift.

The deer and I are face to face, staring. She wishes so much to apologize, to give thanks for what I have done. I require no such affirmation.

"It is okay, child."

"Go."

She seems to nod softly, then turns and bounds away into the forest, hoping to catch up with the rest of the pack.

I turn back to the Civic and watch as cedar, ash, beech, chapote roots reach up out of the ground, their tendrils to the sky, and clamp down on the body of the crushed vehicle, begin pulling it down, deep down into the Earth that is my true body.

❖

When Gerald Z. DeLamonte introduced the first near-light-speed-capable rocket produced by his corporation ALTERO, he did not mention that the global upper class had known about the project for years or that it had been intended only for them. He spent months after his initial announcement touting the possibilities of his rocket technology to the UN—the world's dominant political body since the nuclear war of the twenty-first century—and to the capitalist class, what few remained after the UN implemented its Cooperative Economies Project. Corporations had been at odds with UN and its project during the two centuries after the war, but the project had won out, making corporations, corporate-run jobs, corporate-made products of any kind a political minority by the time DeLamonte made his announcement and embarked on his promotion efforts in 2231.

ALTERO, a new company, a merger of two tech companies led by wealthy families that survived the war, became the planet's savior overnight. They had spent a decade perfecting a design that was easy to scale into production and could be affordable for families, UN government officials, or Cooperative companies looking to expand. The UN could multiply its postwar reconstruction efforts with the new resources space could provide, maybe even begin a new era of prosperity and advancement. The rift between the UN and the capitalist class could finally be healed—a compromise reached. Every city street was abuzz with excitement and hope in the months after DeLamonte's announcement.

But few except the handful of families around the world—like the Valdez family of Valdez Corp.—knew that ALTERO had also spent that very same decade organizing the capitalist class, devising a plan to escape the common people and their socialist UN.

They had never intended to give the world the opportunity to begin life in the stars.

While DeLamonte kept the UN and its citizens distracted, the capitalist class began boarding his rockets and preparing to flee.

For the Moon, and then: *beyond*.

I saw it all happen, watched the trends, and felt the implications immediately. Every white person with the means will take the escape route. Why stay among the colored riff-raff, the socialists, the radicals blaming global warming and the nuclear war on corporations? Why continue to be hounded by the UN to conform to the new Cooperative Economy and its non-hierarchical structures? Why give up proprietary knowledge and resources? Why continue to lose money and customers when you could populate the stars for just one month's salary and never have to deal with the UN again?

The European-descendant citizens of the Earth had been signing up in secret for years. The few dozen capitalist corporations that remained knocked on those citizens' doors, funded those who could not afford it, wrote them checks, even recruited them to do the door-knocking themselves. *Soon, only non-whites will remain,* they told people in secret corners of the megacities of this earth. *Let them deal with the suffering planet. Live and let live.*

Whiteness is not dead in the twenty-third century. It is packed into rockets that sit right now on secret launchpads.

Ready to go.

◆

At the edge of the forest now, near the launchpad fence. Irene and María Valdez are just beyond me, unaware of my presence. Off in the distance, little white figures climb ladders onto rockets, carrying suitcases and backpacks, blankets, stuffed animals wrapped in bow ties. The lines to each rocket stretch for hundreds of feet to the motley assembly of hovers soon to be abandoned on the field surrounding the pad. Luun could be anywhere, masquerading as another of the wealthy travelers or a ladybug clasping to someone's back.

"Pretty crazy, huh?" I say in a clear voice.

"Shit!" María and Irene jump back from the small hole in the fence they had been cutting with bolt cutters. They turn to me, cutters in hand, anger and panic mixed in their brown eyes.

"Who are you? What do you want?" Irene spits at me.

I hold my hands up in the air to sign harmlessness. "It's all right, it's all right. Just came to see, like you." I take a step closer, out of the woods now. Contact made.

"What do you think you're doing, sneaking up on us like that?" Irene says.

"Well, how was I to know you were trying to break in? I just came to see, like I said." The wind blows through our shirts, the sun dances above us.

"We're not trying to break in," María says in a hushed tone. "We want to get a better look."

"No, we don't have to answer to her," Irene snaps at her younger sister. "What's it to you if we're breaking in?" she calls at me. "Are you some kind of spy for those assholes?" She points her cutter toward the launchpad.

"No, no, I don't work for nobody," I say. "Anyways, there's nothing good for people like you that way."

Irene's eyes are roses on the sun. "What did you say?"

"What do you mean people like us?" María asks.

I smile inadvertently, causing the anger on their faces to grow. "Girls, you were raised to be nice to strangers! This is unbecoming of you."

"You don't know anything about us!" Irene yells.

"Who the fuck are you?" María says, inching toward me.

"People call me Guadalupe," I say, standing tall with hands turned toward them, presenting my harmless face.

They look at me like I'm a rabid dog. They see I'm expecting recognition or acknowledgment.

"Are we supposed to know who that is?"

"What—the—fuck—do—you—want?" María is tired of this exchange. Violence brews in the girls' veins. For wealthy teenagers, they are actually starting to frighten me.

"I want you two to leave this place and go back home to your parents," I say without hesitation. I feel like I'm losing grip on this conversation.

"Our parents are dead, asshole!" Irene is done talking. "Get outta here and leave us to it."

I cannot control my laughter so it comes forth, a wonderful, pleasant feeling like swirling grasses or hawks dive-bombing prairies. I let it continue for some time, cognizant of the incredulousness on their faces. *Just you wait, chicas.*

"Your parents aren't dead, ladies," I say. "They're at home right now, putting groceries away after a trip to the store. I'm not a child, you know."

"They're dead!" María says, wavering.

Irene has begun to suspect something. She grips the cutters tighter.

"You can't hurt me, Irene," I say and she gasps at my invasion of her thoughts. "Nor do I think you want to. You either María."

Their eyes are slits, they glance around and behind themselves. The deer from before is nearby, reunited with her pack now and leading them to me. She is eager to show them her savior.

"I said they call me Guadalupe. I've gone by many other names too. But that one, I like the most, que no? It best summarizes the situation for the moment."

They are disarmed by my comment, not likely to understand the symbolism of my name, with its Nahua and European influences, how it connects to the rocket ships currently waiting to flee with the descendants of those same Europeans. I walk forward slowly, past them, toward the fence. I grab it, shake it. It gives a little, the hodgepodge of wiring and tie-downs only haphazardly secured last month.

"Think about it. Here they all are, falling over themselves to finally get away from people like you—"

"You look just like us! You are one of us—" Irene interjects, still angry. I ignore her.

"—so many centuries trying to put all of you into ghettos, in inner cities and forgotten rural towns. Crafting laws that allow them to discriminate and exploit. Laws to keep you away from them. I mean really, it's been crazy girls, just unreal. I mean, y'all wouldn't know but I was there, every day, every year." I'm upset now and they can tell when I glance at them. Even without glancing I know they can sense my anger and it has canceled out their own. They are quiet.

"They put so much effort into dominating this continent. Running from their King and Queen, running from their Church, but bringing their enemies with them. Looking to make a buck, make it big. Making new enemies. Building their capitalist empire over centuries. Using nuclear weapons to destroy anyone who disagreed, who disobeyed, and then refusing to participate in the reconstruction efforts, preferring instead to do everything in their power to maintain their position of dominance."

Irene and María have gone completely silent now, unsure of what to say or how to decipher the guilt they feel at my words. I'm breathing heavily. Talking tires me.

"And they've convinced people like you, whose ancestors they massacred and enslaved, whose land they stole—they've convinced you to be like them, think like them, to wear their clothes and spread their Good News."

I am still gripping the fence, watching the boarders. I cannot see Luun anywhere.

"I've been pretty disappointed in what you Valdez have become," I say, grinding my teeth.

◆

A few months past, Irene and her family flew down to Laredo to shop for the abuelos, who liked mementos and nice things from the mall-globes floating above that region of the Plains Megacity, who could afford such things. Such places were only built for corporate heirs and their families, what few remained, and the Abuelos Valdez did not mind flaunting their access.

"Chopping, chopping," María said. "Papi, why does Grandma say *shopping* with a *ch*?" The kids were strapped into the backseats of the hover. Everyone laughed.

"Why can you not roll your R's, like a true Mexican?" Rodrigo mocked. Elena, smirking, smacks his driving arm.

"Dad, that's not the same!" María said.

"Totally the same dude," Irene jumped in. "All of our friends think you were sent away to some gringo boarding school at some point." She giggled at the truth of her joke and turned up the volume of her Gameboy, because Dad was blasting rancheras and sing-yelling into the space between their seats.

The early winter sky in south Texas was gray like cigarette smoke and there was a lone sandhill crane perched on a tower balcony as they pass. The crane catches Irene's eye. How did sandhill cranes still exist? Did they always perch so high?

"Baby, I want a new purse for Christmas," Elena said as they neared the Laredo region. Other hovers passed by frequently and the area could not be distinguished from any other part of the mega-city, except for one or two unique architectural landmarks.

"'Pa que?" Rodrigo asked, mimicking his father brother mother sister second sister everyone he's ever known. "You don't got no money!"

"Grammar!" Elena yelled over the snickers in the backseat, still self-conscious that the stockholders might be listening into their con-versation, in those final weeks before the rockets left and everything changed. Rodrigo glanced back at the girls through the rearview, making "'*Ta loca*" eyes at his teenage audience. "What would the Board say if they heard Mr. Valdez talking like a *hoodrat*, like a com-mon person?"

"I'd get a lot more political support—"

"Dad!" Irene interrupted, eyes up from the game, roaming out on the urban maze around her.

"Que mi'ja?"

"Isn't this where our ancestors used to live and work, by Laredo?"

Rodrigo frowned, glancing out the driver's-side window, then across, out the passenger's side. With a furrowed brow, he shakes his head. "I'm not sure mi'ja," he said. "It's possible I guess."

"Do you think they liked it here, Dad?" Irene asked.

"What's there to like about being a poor farmworker?" Elena interjected. "Our family doesn't deserve to be—"

"Here she goes," Rodrigo said, quieting his wife down with a glance, she huffing at his tendency to speak over her. "Irene, love, I'm sure they loved this land and always did." His eyes were straight, the word *land* dancing off his tongue. "But I bet they hated the work, baby. The Valdez deserve better than a farmworker's life."

"We might still get a better life too," Elena mumbled.

Irene nodded at her dad's answer and continued to look out the window, her vintage Gameboy forgotten on the white leather of the hover seat.

I was the lone sandhill crane that day, flying alongside their hover for miles until I was slightly ahead and could stop and rest. Many flew the airways that day but no one else could see me. No one thought—*how peculiar, a sandhill crane without its flock.*

The sandhill crane is one of my favorite forms to take aside from the female human form. Its expansive wingspan lets me lift high into the sky with little effort, gives me a chance to look at the contours of myself, the crevasses and plateaus, the mountains and rivers and valleys. Sometimes even the sea, though I rarely push my limits out over the water.

I've taken the sandhill form often over millions of years, long before humans grew into their own. I think Irene watched me out of the corner of her eye during most of that trip. My wings were her wings. My spirit was her guide, calling her back from the halls of luxury.

◆

"Irene are you kidding me?" María shouts. I had drifted into a memory, spaced out, and in that moment, Irene had reached her breaking point, had cut a few more snips from the fence, crawled under, and started running toward the rockets. She had chosen black tights and a loose-fitting shirt for just this moment so she shot quickly across the field separating the fence from the launchpad.

"What do we do, what do we do?" María asks me, tears in her eyes and panic in her voice. The majority of the rockets have sealed their hatch doors in preparation for their ascent.

Irene wants to board. She doesn't care about my disapproval. I can't actually read minds but I know this to be true.

I know this because I gave her life. Gave her people life.

I watched the Spanish create her people, create a continent of mestizos through murder, exploitation, plague.

Created mestizos who always had to decide: join or run.

Run from Catholic missionaries and conquistadores and colonial administrators. Or join them.

Run from lynchings in the South Texas brush, killed by Texas Rangers while their brothers and sisters fought a revolution back home. Or join the lynch mob.

Run across the desert, moving quickly from cactus shade to cactus shade, dying from thirst in the Santa Catalina Mountains of Tucson, being buried under empty water bottles, tattered backpacks, tennis shoes. Or be the desert guide, bash in the skulls of your countrymen. Empty their pockets for meager coin.

Run through tunnels dug by drug cartels, themselves formed to make money off the US's need for narcotics and its continuous strong-arming of the Mexican government since the Treaty of Guadalupe Hidalgo in 1848.

Run from the nuclear blast descending upon your city, fired at you by the enemies of the capitalist class, you caught in the middle of a fight that has nothing to do with you. Run from the angry mob, looking for food during the years of nuclear winter, willing to kill and eat anything.

Or join the mob.

Join the UN and help rebuild the world. Or join the capitalists, help them exploit the situation. Make a fortune, barricade yourself against the mass of bodies that look like you.

Bodies shot and draped over fences like blankets drying in the wind.

Millions of Europeans trying to eradicate the indigenous bodies of this land, treating them as less than animals. Hundreds of years of destruction, each moment, the question: run or join?

Irene has clasped onto the steel ladder of the first rocket she could reach, but the doors to the rocket have been sealed, not to be opened until the ship arrives at the Moon.

Her timing is poor: the ships have begun lift-off proceedings, passengers secured, fuel primed. One by one, they ignite booster rockets, ride the wave of fire and pressure into the atmosphere. María and I are too far away to see Irene's face very clearly, but we can tell she is torn between fear and resolution. She just wants a chance to fly, to get away from all this.

Like Luun does. Luun who is in one of those rockets. Luun who I will never see again.

Do I run or join?

And, at the moment her rocket ignites, she is jolted free, tumbling down a short distance directly into the blaze of the rockets. Blood and bone and nervous system burn up in superheated fire. I am there too now, clasping Irene's hand as it falls away from her disintegrating body, pulling it toward me.

Then we are hundreds of feet away, though still inside the fence. I hold Irene's hand until it has regrown its radius, ulna, humerus, entire skeleton, its veins and nerves and muscles and tendons and organs, its sheet of skin, its brain with memories intact—all forming together in seconds under my grip.

The last of her hair returns just as María arrives at our side, her hysteria and disbelief gushing forth through tears and sobs. She reaches us, kneels, throws herself onto Irene.

The young woman who seconds before had ceased to exist gasps back to life, unharmed, held by María and I like a newborn child. She gulps in a panic, her eyes jolting open. She is aware of all that has just happened and I know I will have to soothe her, help her deal with the trauma of being disintegrated and then reborn. She understands who I am now, like few of her ancestors had before her. We meet eyes and she sees: multitudes, the vast pantheon of life that has lived and died in me, including her family and her own self. María sobs, Irene goes unconscious, and I kneel on my haunches, energized.

On the outside of the fence, a pack of deer look on, the youngling I saved watching me with calm understanding.

María's gaze shifts up, past me, to the rockets ascending into the vacuum of space above us. I slowly let go of Irene, leave her in María's arms, and turn to watch my children depart in a dozen cloud trails, heading somewhere far away, somewhere they might be given another chance to learn from their mistakes. Or maybe continue to make more.

And Luun will be there too.

Fancy

DIANA BURBANO

A woman, STRAY, sits on the floor of a jail cell. She is older, beautiful. She has been abused badly. The sound of another woman, FANCY, young, a person of color. She is hollering and making a huge fuss. She is thrown into the cell.

FANCY: I have all my permits! It's all together, recheck the microchip! Goddamn it! Why I gotta be in here? With this ugly old lady!?

Fancy reaches for her eyelash, removes a magnetic eyelash strip. It's an electronic device. She gently presses a button and puts it back. She laughs.

FANCY: Idiots. Think I'm too stupid to figure out what you were looking for. Looking in all my cavities— These fools need to get a beauty consultant. Hey Mama— *(addressing the woman on the floor)* hey—it's cold down there— Hey—Mama—

The woman on the floor looks up dully. Fancy crouches down to her. Looks into her eyes and shakes her head.

FANCY: Dang what they got you on, elephant tranq? Hold on Mama.

Fancy removes a small tablet from under her nail. Puts it in the older woman's mouth. The older woman shudders, then anguish passes in front of her eyes. She sighs a ragged sigh and lets Fancy sit her down on the bench.

FANCY: You in there?

STRAY: Are you here for me?

FANCY: Shh . . . don't say nothin' okay? Hold on—

Fancy does a quick assessment; the woman is in bad shape. Fancy uses another elaborate nail to check the woman's vitals.

FANCY: *(as if to say "Jesus Christ!")* Bader-Ginsburg! You in bad shape.

STRAY: They keep pumping me full of drugs. And they took my cyanide tablet.

Stray is crying.

FANCY: S'okay. Hey. Hey—

STRAY: I lost them. All of them. We were so close to the border. They let us get so close.

FANCY: Not all of 'em, baby. Three of 'em made it.

STRAY: Three girls. Out of twenty.

FANCY: Three girls in freedom.

STRAY: I made a rookie mistake. I miscalculated how much water we would need. The Biloxi waste stretched farther than I've ever seen it.

FANCY: The Megafracking destroyed the last of the wetland. There's no fresh water left in the Old South.

STRAY: I told them I would get them out.

FANCY: They're too many girls to save, love.

STRAY: Every girl deserves to be saved.

FANCY: Mama—

STRAY: Stop calling me that.

FANCY: Shit, you getting mean in your old age too.

STRAY: I've always been a mean bitch.

FANCY: Bitches get shit done.

STRAY: I'm tired.

FANCY: Mama. We blow up the tower the day after tomorrow. We so close to ending this thing.

STRAY: Close? We're farther than we've ever been.

FANCY: The church's decree that women need to report to the city center during their menses. That's tough, reduces our forces, but we have it planned for the green moon cycle.

STRAY: The noose is tighter than ever. My last mission. So many young women refused to come with me.

FANCY: Mama—

STRAY: Like sheep, like cows, without fighting.

FANCY: Fighting like you do gets people killed. Or thrown in jail— We got other ways to rebel.

STRAY: I want to save them.

FANCY: Most of us want to stay and fight. I got my real mama and my grandmama. I'd like to liberate them from slavery too. Can't do that by running over the border. Gotta stay here and fight. Liberate ourselves *in* our own homes.

STRAY: *(suspicious)* I don't know you.

FANCY: Shit, Mama. Of course you do. Look!

> *Fancy lifts her shirt and shows Stray a brand or tattoo. Stray runs her finger over it.*

STRAY: You came back and they caught you, enslaved you.

FANCY: Hell no, lady.

STRAY: False bravado.

FANCY: Nah—I came back to be a Fancy girl. Papers and all. All access to some of the leading bedrooms in the city.

STRAY: That's awful.

FANCY: Nah. No one suspects a Fancy girl of having brains.

STRAY: I didn't spend my life sacrificing so that you could come back to be a whore.

FANCY: Tsk. You older folks are so judgmental. My body, lady. I do what I want with it.

STRAY: We fought so you could have agency over your own body.

FANCY: And I do. Who else you see coming to rescue you?

STRAY: Shameful.

FANCY: *(annoyed)* Lady. I'm good at my job. I have a say in how and when the sex happens, *and* I get paid. *And* people spill all sorts of good shit around me, that I then use to help the cause. I ain't ashamed.

STRAY: We fought to liberate you.

FANCY: Consider me liberated. I'm on full birth control. No enforced laboring, no kids taken away. For that alone I'm grateful for what I do.

STRAY: Oh, my child.

FANCY: Don't get sentimental. Women have cried enough. Sex is *my* fiercest weapon.

STRAY: Keep telling yourself that.

FANCY: You're the one who got caught.

STRAY: I had two girls who were so pregnant they almost couldn't move. One was eleven.

FANCY: Shhh—

A sound from outside the jail cell.

STRAY: They're coming for me.

FANCY: Hurry, Mama. Where are you hiding the rest of the girls?

STRAY: I won't tell you.

FANCY: Dear Leader is furious. I think this is the end for you.

STRAY: Dear Leader can go fuck himself.

FANCY: *(smiles)* Hell, yes! That's the lady we know and love. He still mad you alive. The day you went rogue. Legend.

STRAY: For all the good it did me.

FANCY: You miss the good life?

STRAY: What part? Bound into ridiculous clothing that displayed me like a doll? Forced to smile and bow and sleep with a man I hated? I spent my youth imprisoned by my beauty.

FANCY: You married him to better yourself.

STRAY: I was just a kid.

FANCY: Aw, Mama—

STRAY: I walked down the aisle at his vulgar club, my back in pain from being weighted down with jewels on the ridiculous gown he made me wear. He gave me a coat made of the last wild leopard. He liked me covered in gold and he liked me quiet.

FANCY: But you listened. You heard. The resistance owes its life to you.

STRAY: To hell with all of it. You should go. Let me die. It won't take long.

FANCY: *(decisive)* Mama. I know your son.

STRAY: *(pain)* My son.

FANCY: I'm one of his coterie of Fancy girls.

STRAY: I have no son.

FANCY: Mama, he's *your* son. He's been helping us.

STRAY: Helping you? He's a playboy.

FANCY: He is. He is also a good man, and a fighter.

STRAY: There are no good men.

FANCY: He's the one keeping the supply tunnel open.

STRAY: My son?

FANCY: Yes ma'am. He's helped us smuggle many girls beyond the border. In full view of Dear Leader and his cronies. Girls we *never* could've smuggled out on our own. The ones the other leaders want, he takes for his own. No one fights him 'cause he's the heir. We get them to the Tower, and they join his coterie. If they disappear, no one bats an eye. They're just Fancy girls after all.

STRAY: How many?

FANCY: Hundreds. He's got quite the rep.

STRAY: I wish I could believe you. He's his father's son.

FANCY: Check it: he managed to convince Dear Leader that his taste for brown girls was a kinky quirk. Otherwise, we'd be dead. I'd be dead.

STRAY: I don't like it. Bartering bodies for freedom. It still means we are just meat.

FANCY: Meat that will live to fight another day. We fighting for our rights. To exist. To have agency over our bodies. Ain't that what you taught all of us?

STRAY: What I tried to teach everyone was just common sense. We frighten them because we bleed.

FANCY: To them our blood means one less baby to fight their wars. They don't like that.

STRAY: *You* have the right to decide when you wanted to have a child. *You* have the right to own the shell of your own body.

FANCY: We always own our souls. And in our souls we dream.

STRAY: Dreams don't keep you alive. Actions do.

FANCY: Mama. Where are you hiding the rest of the girls? I don't have much longer before the authorities discover that my papers are in order. Their racism is my camouflage. C'mon Mama. Where are the girls?

STRAY: My son will know. If—you see him. Tell him. Mama's favorite place.

FANCY: He'll know?

STRAY: Yes. He'll know. If he's who you say he is.

FANCY: Thank you. We'll get them into California Nueva and freedom.

Sound of the approaching guard.

STRAY: Tell him. I don't regret birthing him. He's not his father.

FANCY: We're still fighting Mama. I know it looks different to you. I know it looks like we have given up, but the young fight in a different way. You can't see it, but we do. We know we have to play by certain rules in order to win. We teach each other, we tell the stories, we educate, we advocate.

STRAY: When I was young women could drive, and have credit cards of their own. We were almost equals.

FANCY: Nah, Mama. We were never equal. We were better. These bloated sick leaders. They gotta die sometime.

STRAY: We said that years ago. When there were still birds in the sky.

FANCY: *(at the sound of a turning lock)* Here.

Strips off her magnetic eyelashes and hands them to Stray.

It's a beacon. When they transport you to the Death Site, we'll know. We'll get you out.

STRAY: No! Let him kill me. Just make sure someone films my execution. Make me a martyr. Use my body for good.

FANCY: *(kisses her)* The mothers are the peacemakers. We will remember you.

> *The door opens. Fancy walks out. Stray looks at the eyelashes in her hand. She puts them on, and flutters them. She starts to laugh.*

> *Blackout.*

Time Traveler Intro

ELIANA BUENROSTRO

What does grief and trauma even look like after you're expected to heal or even after you yourself think you can heal. I am convinced it changes shapes and forms. I carry it with me all the time, it's just different now.

I live so many multitudes and in so many realities. There's the me in Chicago. The me in el Distrito. The me in Guadalajara. The me in La Piedad. The me on Prozac.

I am grateful and in pain from my past time as a time traveler. I am everywhere and split into so many directions. Split into multitudes. I am here and not at all.

The Music Box

SARA DANIELE RIVERA

The stage is set, lights are up, and tonight's audience is speeding toward the Music Box!

It stands, the only sight for miles, in a desert blank as a page. Once, there were hummingbird yuccas and acacia trees, rose-bellied lizards and fragrant mesquite. Now the land is stamped and burnt. But look at how the Music Box shines, magnificent in its isolation! Bright as a moon on earth.

Look, people say when they see it. *Something good came out of this.*

Barely visible, a long line of darker sand stains the ground. The Music Box is built to bisect this line, a pathway with a strange shredded look to it like one long eyebrow. The remnants of a wall. The acid at the base of the wall contributed to the discoloration.

If the sand is an eyebrow, does that make the building the eye? Its mechanized roof does part like a lid when there's a show. But in this analogy, a whole body is missing.

❖

The lights of incoming cars, low-fly limo and valet, appear in the flat arena as if the Music Box were a bulb drawing all energy to itself. The cars are quiet. Cicadas would be louder.

The people who arrive at the doors of the Music Box are delicate mosquito-cicadas. Beautiful blood-suckers, humming with anticipation. Tonight they drip from their mouths. They fluff their feathers. They want to look their best because they're here for a special show, the second ever held at the Music Box. They will see *her*, the great soprano of their day. Her life will intersect with theirs; they'll own a piece, a moment. Something beautiful will happen.

After all, how could anything ugly have happened here? Here, where the violins are already playing like crickets to the moon?

◆

Their payment is programmed into their clothes. As they walk under a particle-sensitive portico, everything is registered: name, payment, corporate affiliations. They follow the hovering lights of usherbots (they didn't pay this much for long lines) that lead them through the lobby, the first ring, and the outer edge of the dome.

There's a dress code at the Music Box. Dresses, suits, high heels, low heels, ties, bow ties, what matters is the quality of the material. Fabrics are noted upon entry, and nobody wants cheap or repeat clothing reported. The Music Box requires clothes that can be traced to within-year designers.

The floor is carpeted red. Stereotypical, but these associations run deep. Ceilings fly high, bathed in rose-gold illumination. The seating that rings the dome features exorbitantly cushioned, throne-like seats, spaced out in pairings and groupings according to party size. In the left armrest of each seat is a discreet mini-fridge. The patrons need only run a finger over the menu for their beverage of choice to slide up into the cup holder.

The other armrest serves as the base for a small, fist-sized contraption, a gold, jewel-studded hand-crank, reminiscent of an organ grinder, that serves as the logo of the Music Box.

What's this remnant of another era doing here? Jack-in-the-box crank, pencil-sharpener crank? The cranks connect to opera glasses that patrons receive upon entering the Music Box. The glasses act as two screens that manipulate the singer's appearance and performance to suit the patron's tastes. Change the color of her dress? Turn the crank. Change the color of her hair? Turn again. Make her slimmer? Turn turn turn. Transpose the octave she's singing in, make her sing in a rain forest, make her hold out a note longer, auto-tune her? Turnturnturnturnturn!

(Want to remove her clothes? Pay more. Know the right person. Sit in a certain seat. Then turn.)

◆

Her name is Ignacia Dove. She's performing in the round tonight. Before the show, the stage is a closed black disc. Ignacia waits below on a platform that will elevate, part the doors, and become the stage floor. She's kept in total darkness. At this point in the programming, patrons require the illusion that she is not there. She must exist only as ephemera.

Shhhh. It's starting.

There's a pre-show programmed into the glasses. Thousands of cranks turn in tandem, their gold sheen glinting in auditorium shadow. Silence settles, but don't worry, these patrons didn't pay this much to be silenced. They want to have their say when they want. For this, there are mouth-mutes and person-to-person voice connections; patrons can talk to the people they want to talk to, talk to themselves if they must, and block out all non-performance sound. Those who want to commiserate can turn on the live forum at the bottom of their screens.

Shh. Mouth-mute. Her body rises like a beacon in the dark. Her dress is red unless you change it, deep silken red, almost liquid when crossed by shadow. Her hair is black unless you change it. Her skin is just-white-enough. She looks out at the audience and sees the pinpoints of light (the e-embroidery on their clothing). Like a bobbing night sky, illuminated by pockets of stars.

Ignacia opens her mouth. Already thousands of eyes have changed her. The note that pierces and trembles at once becomes a French syllable, then a French word, *sombre,* and finally the disembodied flutes begin, and her first aria.

If she could, she would sing in Spanish. If her mouth could still shape the words.

◆

Queridísima hermana,

Here at school I have a lace curtain. I have a windowsill full of flowers. You remember how I always tried to bring flowers back to life, the wildflow-

ers that came up through the sidewalk back where and when we lived. But I don't water these. I'm sitting by the window and writing to you and the thought of watering them turns my stomach into an anvil. They're flaccid. I'll get in trouble for this.

Do you recognize the way I talk? Would you recognize my singing? What does your voice sound like? I wish I knew.

I'm writing to you after not writing for so long not because anything has changed (you'll still never read this) but because I've remembered something and want to corroborate it with you. I won't say too much, like what side of the wall we lived on or what language we spoke.

Won't say. Can't. I get very scared, MariE. Because I actually think sometimes that I don't remember, not even the basics. Where we grew up. Where we were born. What language I learned first. The gaps in my mind fill with music and nonsense. I'm desperate for you, like a friendship necklace, to complete the other half of this.

When we were little we had a volleyball. It was disgusting, gray and scrunched and just a little too flat, but we loved it. We dreamt of school teams. There was a morning we went out to the rusted posts behind the house, and behind you, opposite me, I remember thousands of adobe rooftops. There was something in your eyes (maybe I imposed this): something hard and flat. You threw the ball up to serve and it smacked, popped, wheezed, then hung on the net and slapped into the dirt. I remember the dent of your hand, right in the center.

You had this way of inspecting things. We were both looking at it and you know me, I was already crying. You held the ball and showed me where the heel of your hand had made a perfect coin-sized hole.

You pronounced it dead and said we had to bury it. We processed, solemn as church, and you carried your red plastic hand shovel. It took us a while but we made a grave and then you said: "Dear God. This volleyball died because I hit it too hard. The End." I told you God wasn't going to let your ugly ball into heaven. You said that He might, if I sang a nice song as a eulogy. I didn't know what a eulogy was, but I knew what a lullaby was. I sang one of Mami's. She listened from the window; I saw her drying the vermillion plate. That night, she said my voice would be my salvation.

Maybe you wanted to hit something so hard it broke. Maybe you wanted to love something enough to bury it and give it a name. I only wish you could respond, and tell me for sure that this happened, that I'm remembering right.

❖

Take a step back. Retreat from the Music Box. The singer's voice tunnels away from you, you leave the comfort of your seat.

Imagine this same land, ten years ago. Easier to imagine it as something constructed, as if the whole thing were a theater set made of dragged-in foamcore, painted to look like the devastation that was actually there.

With a particular radius of the city gone, one could see more, see farther. Gone were the skeletal levels of highway, gone their scaffolds, their winding limbs. Gone the homes that climbed the hillside, gone the billboards and neon stars. A field of human remnant stretched out from wherever your feet contacted the ground. A line could be drawn between you and any point on the horizon, and each square foot along that line was a burial site.

Hammers pounded and clinked. Tractors, pulleys, drills. The whir and crank of the build had begun and sound came from everywhere, overlapping rhythms of a new song. Progress. Forward motion. Rebuild. Reclaim.

Whose reclamation? Whose song? What remained of a neon star was a hollow metal starfish, burnt and grayed out.

But never fear! The people of this country were promised: soon, this sad desert would no longer be sad. There was a project in the works. No, the cities wouldn't be rebuilt—just one building. One place, one special, protected place, where citizens of the new world could have the experience of a lifetime.

Promos punctuated every bus stop, interactive videos lined the exteriors of buildings all over the country. On the internet, every click had the potential to be a portal. Clues were dropped, and already people were buying into the treasure hunt: an image pop-up of an old organ grinder. You touched your finger to the screen to turn, and three lines of text cropped up:

WELCOME TO THE MUSIC BOX
OWN YOUR ENTERTAINMENT
COMING SOON

❖

Queridísima hermana,

Parents were like bats in those days. Shine a light on them and they departed. First a flashlight at the door, then lamps ignited in the street. Flares went up and parents went away.

We assumed they went somewhere. We knew they went back over the border, that some were held in detention. But I'll share what was whispered to me as a child, because I have no way of knowing what you do or do not know: those parents who disappeared ended up in arroyos or in fields. Sand-caked shoes in the middle of the desert, dirty bras knotted with tumble-weeds. Bones and wind and quiet.

It took me two months to fully understand I would never see you or Mami again. That was the first time I tried to get out, the first beating I received. They held out my arms, my legs, but avoided my throat, face, chest, and stomach. The places that could affect my voice.

I feel like I'm bleeding out. The memories are coming whether I invite them or not. I'm so tired. I can't feel the slightest pressure or I collapse around myself like every wall I've ever seen demolished. I picture myself as that house Tío Marco lived in, the one we called casa rompecabezas because its components littered the ground. That was post-wall, pre-bomb.

Or was it? The wall was when? The bomb was when?

Dios santo. I don't remember when I died, MariE.

◆

She exists for your entertainment.

She makes for glittering eye candy.

She makes you cry, laugh, scream, every sound that starts deep in your gut and heart.

Her place in the world is here, standing in presentation.

She's a dress-up doll, a slice of the make-believe.

You don't care who she thinks she is.

Once you leave the theater or shut off the screen, she ceases.

She dances backward, a twinkling melody in her steps, and climbs back into the treasure box where you keep her until she's needed again.

She looks cute, sometimes, trying to say something. She doesn't understand: the only words of hers that matter are scripted.

You remind her to obey.

When she exits, she must shut the door niceandsoft.

It's time for her to go back into the dark.

You'll consult her when you want something red and shiny again. You'll crank the organ grinder. Make her dance.

❖

Ignacia has one song left: grand finale. So far, the live-forums seem content. She stands waving, smiling, playing with the crowd like a seasoned performer. Silk roses land at her feet.

She hushes the crowd. They wait; the usherbots hover.

"Hello, patrons of the Music Box!" she calls out, her voice like a beauty pageant. The crowd cheers.

"It has been the greatest honor of my life to perform for you in this venue, which is such a historic part of the bright new world we built from the ruins!"

Confusion, then applause. They like hearing about the brightness but bristle against any mention of the ruins.

"A society that innovates while remembering the best of its glorious traditions."

This they love. But her voice cracks at the word *traditions.* Her pause, her swallow, is barely perceptible, and she gathers herself to say one last thing.

"And so I will see you tomorrow night, here! And the night after, right here! We have a fantastic program for you *every night* at the Music Box!"

She can't quiet them! They roar with joy. A tremor in the finger that rises to her lips, and gradually, languidly, the roar becomes a simmer, then silence, oh what an experience. They are ready for her now, their precious wildflower.

Once she knew wildflowers; she spoke to them to keep them alive.

Now the turning cranks, the intent eyes.

❖

And this is the moment the forums will critique for weeks.

The full sum of their disappointment, when all they paid for is not given to them: Ignacia Dove's mouth hanging open, making no sound.

The shape of her mouth warps and wanes as if trying to execute some sort of transformation. The orchestra loops through the intro again, but she can't sing. She isn't. Her mouth gapes, hovers, tries to form a word, and now it's a rigidity that trembles up through the pillar of her body, from the calves that shake beneath the cling of her dress to the chest that rises and falls in hyperventilating rhythm, to the eyes that start to glaze with tears and read as gray in fading light.

A *malfunction,* more than one user-patron will say. *Not what I paid for.* But she was born, not engineered.

❖

Wall, war, bomb.

That's how it went.

This isn't news.

Maybe this is too direct.

Maybe I should've used a smoke machine.

Step back further, twenty years: the day the bomb dropped. The sun shone *bravo,* glaring off rock and mud brick, and lizards were out basking, their throats flapping with breath, chambers soft and round as human thumbs. Two ghost towns, half-unknowing. The cicadas flew and hummed their warning.

Four thousand miles away, a little girl whose life began on the border sobbed on the floor of a dorm room in the new music school where the historical contexts of her operas were sanitized. She lay with her cheek to the ground, her arm winding halfway into a hole in the wall where she'd been hiding letters to send to her sister. Someone had taken them. Her fingers trembled between knots of dust and lint.

On the outer edge of the bomb radius, the other Paloma sister, María Elena, sat on the front steps of their casita. She was alone. Mami was gone, a bat hanging upside down somewhere. MariE kicked at the dusty ground, hoping to start a hurricane on the other side of the world. She would survive that day. Years later, the letters would find their way to her through the hands of a woman who swept dorms after hours, who collected one girl's loneliness and took the delivery upon herself.

MariE, always forceful, inspecting, dramatic. She would sit one day in the audience at the Music Box, watching Ignacia's mouth open and close with all the voicelessness they both had gained.

She tells this story now as best she can, in a voice that no longer sounds like hers but like something constructed.

◆

There's only one thing to do: end the night. The mechanism of the stage engages and the audience makes their dissent heard, first through the typical *boo* and then something more animalistic. Before she starts her descent, my sister's eyes go hard and flat as slate. She clamps her lips together, though she still shakes throughout, and there's something resolute in her, a faltering transformed.

Sister, queridísima, I would never paint over any part of you. Your eyes travel ghost-like over me. Maybe you've been robbed of sound because your body can feel it: the way we rise, the way we change. I won't leave without you. I won't allow distance and silence to hover over us again like a sustained note. I see it. I see you. I know what you're trying to say.

You want to tell the story of that day. The harshness of the sun, how very few eyes turned up to watch the sky. Instead, our people looked down at their hands. They looked at each other, they watched the calliope hummingbirds. Hunger made their mouths drip but they believed, they believed something beautiful could happen. Maybe, one day, something will.

But on that day the sky sliced open. Bright as a moon on earth.

PART III

My Life in Dreams

My First Word

WILLIAM ALEXANDER

Mama drove the lead garbage truck under storm clouds.

"Looks like it might rain," I said.

"No. It won't." She chewed on the stem of her pipe. It was a curved and elegant thing made out of wood, the sort that wizards and detectives loved. She didn't actually smoke it, not with me riding beside her. She just chewed the stem and talked around it. "No rain. Not here. But we are close to the coast, and the storm. Close enough to see its outer rim."

"*The* storm?"

She smiled. "Yes, Leita. *The* storm."

We passed mile markers and highway signs. I thought I recognized the name of the place we were headed, but found it unpronounceable.

Mama drummed a steady beat against the steering wheel with two fingers.

"The eye of the storm is stable," she said. "It gazes down on our home. The whole island is safe there. Survivors are thriving. But they're surrounded by walls of water on every side." Her voice was resonant and washboard rough.

I looked out the window to keep from saying *You can't possibly know any of that.*

Sunset lit up the storm clouds overhead.

She clicked her turn signal two miles before our exit so the whole caravan would know it was time.

"First they learned how to fish sideways on those walls of water. They learned how to delight in centrifugal force. Then they built larger sailing ships with masts perpendicular to the ground. Right now they're hard at work on a whole space program. One day soon they will navigate up and out of the spiraling storm, out of the world's gravity well. They will catch the solar winds in their sails. And then they'll look down from orbit. They will see us and come sailing to bring us home."

We left the highway. Mama steered us into a big, empty parking lot at the edge of town. Then she circled back until the caravan of garbage trucks bit its own tail. The RVs clustered inside that larger circle.

I practically fell out of the lead truck. Mama hopped right down, somehow spritely after a twelve-hour drive. She grabbed a crate full of wooden scrap and commenced to build a campfire in the very center of our caravan circle.

She did this every night. Maybe it was meant to be a bull's-eye. *We're here. If anyone is sailing overhead and looking for us, we are right here.*

Cousins spilled out of other trucks to laugh, complain, and set up camp. But then they all stopped talking, all of a sudden, which meant that the spokesman had found us already.

A local man picked his way in between the trucks. He didn't hold his nose. It looked like he wanted to, though. He wore a stiffly pressed uniform and walked stiffly inside it.

The spokesman approached Tío Gustavo and opened his mouth, but Gus backed away with his hands in the air and called for help. "We need some translation over here!"

Mama left her campfire burning on the pavement and went over to the spokesman.

He spoke to her in shredded paper. Reams of it emerged from his mouth, spilled over his uniform, and made a pile between his polished shoes.

Mama was the only one of us who understood the local lingo. She scrutinized the patterns that the paper made.

Papi and Gus both went about their business, ignoring and ignored, but the cousins clustered together to watch—Braulio, Felix, Hector, Kassia, and me.

"It's nice when they say recyclable things," Kass pointed out. "Remember the last one? Each word a Styrofoam packing peanut? And she would *not* stop talking."

"The one before that spoke plastic shopping bags," Hector remembered. "Torn ones. Couldn't even use them to scoop up dog shit afterwards."

"Remember the guy who spoke diapers?" Felix asked, grinning.

"Do not remind me," said Kass.

This local seemed to be wrapping up his list of instructions. He spit out one more authoritative mouthful, turned right around, and left the shredded pile of his discourse on the pavement.

Mama swept it up and put it in the proper bin. Then she came back to her fire. Papi and Tío Gus joined us there.

"What's the job?" Gus asked.

She wouldn't answer until after she had set up her little grill and soot-scorched espresso maker.

I could not possibly explain why Mama needed to brew her nightly shot of weapons-grade caffeine outdoors. We had perfectly good stoves inside the RVs. But the woman required her fire.

We waited until she was ready to translate.

"The kids get the park," Mama finally told us. "Easy work. They also get an apartment complex overlooking the park, which shouldn't be too bad. The residents have been using their own roof as a flying landfill."

"And what do we get?" Gus asked.

"The hospital," Mama said.

Her brother laughed, satisfied that the work would be exactly as awful as he had expected.

Papi looked worried. He usually did.

"Are you okay with this job?" he asked. Mama was the only one meant to hear him, but I watched his lips move in the firelight.

"Not really," she said. "Hospitals are hard. They need to be sterile, but the doctors say things that leave nasty stains."

"That's not what I meant."

"I know what you meant."

I didn't know what he meant. But I'm the youngest, so I'm used to everybody acting like they know things I don't.

The espresso picked that moment to boil over. Mama actually giggled as she poured herself a cup.

Everyone else drifted away to their own evening rituals. I stayed. Mama offered me a tiny cup, just like always. I refused, just like always, because one sip would keep me awake all night.

❖

Fog covered the whole city in the early morning. I couldn't see the sky, or the storm—unless we were inside the storm. Maybe that's what the fog really was.

Kass and I got started on the park. It was right downtown, and carefully manicured, but whole swaths of grass were dying underneath piles of old conversations. Cold dewdrops covered both the grass and the trash.

We set up four bins for compost, salvage, recyclables, and irredeemably hopeless waste. Then we got to work.

Mama always said that sorting salvageable from unsalvageable things is an art and a science. Papi said it's more a matter of mood and wishful thinking. I usually start my day believing Mama and end it agreeing with Papi.

We found several broken musical instruments—a green ukulele with no strings, plastic kazoos with no wax paper inside, and a harmonica so flattened that breath wouldn't ever pass through it again.

"I wonder what this conversation was about," I said.

"I don't," said Kass.

I wished that I didn't. Every time I tried to understand the local lingo I got a headache right in the center of my forehead. And I could sense that same headache of incomprehension coming on already. Maybe if I stopped trying then it would go away. But I couldn't stop. Those drifts of plastic straws and snack wrappers meant something. I wanted to know what. But that wanting made me feel like a cyclops poked hard in the eye.

Kass was watching me. Sort of. She kept her eyes on her work. But she was also aware of me with a sideways kind of focus, like we'd both regressed a decade and she was stuck babysitting me back at the caravan.

"What is it?" I asked her.

"Nothing," she said, too quickly, and then moved away.

Two local women crossed the park. Both of them were dressed for important, pinstriped business. Every word of their conversation was a single-use coffee pod, already used. They hocked those pods out like whole mouthfuls of snot. I waited until they were well out of sight before I retraced their steps, scooped up every pod, and tossed them into the hopeless bin.

Someone was still watching me.

"Stop it, Kass."

It wasn't Kass.

A boy stood behind the bins. Not one of my cousins. A local boy. Unmistakably local. He wasn't supposed to go near the bins. He looked right at me. He wasn't supposed to do that, either.

The boy spit out a plastic soda bottle. Then he waited for some sort of response from me. I didn't have a response. I didn't know what an empty bottle meant to him, or what it was supposed to mean to me.

He seemed disappointed, and then angry. I looked around for Kass, but by the time I looked back he was already running away.

The bottle that he said to me belonged in the recycling bin.

I tossed it in with the irredeemables instead.

◆

Mama seemed tired at the end of that first day. No, that was the wrong word. I was tired. She was something else. Weary. She pulled down pipe smoke like it was oxygen and chewed hard on the stem.

I sat next to her. "You okay? Need anything?"

"What I really need is to stop hearing that question," she said, so I didn't ask anything else while she busied herself with her campfire. The ritual relaxed her. It settled the evening into its proper shape, and spoke clearly about that shape without making a mess. She offered me fresh espresso, just like she always did. I said no. Then she told me about sky-whales.

"They migrate. Like butterflies. We don't see them because they stay deep inside the thickest clouds to hide from predators."

"What kind of predator eats sky-whale?" I asked.

"Giant squid," she told me. "*Trampoline* squid. The largest among them can stretch far enough to grab neighboring islands in an archipelago. Smaller ones leap from the water, bounce on their parent-trampoline, and rocket through clouds to snare whales for their dinner. One day we'll set up our own huge trampoline between the trucks and catch a few sky-whales."

"For our dinner?"

"No, no, no. We'll tame and ride them. They can swim right through storm clouds, you know. They'll be able to carry us all the way home."

The spokesman showed up then. He told us our wages. Mom unfolded the spitballs of wadded bills and clipped them to a clothesline to dry, but in the morning they still smelled like morning breath.

◆

The apartment building was a dingy kind of respectable. It had an old lobby and a brand-new elevator. The floors were clean. At first I thought that the residents kept to themselves in order to keep neighborly small talk to a minimum. But then we found the roof. Massive piles of spent words sat baking in the sun.

Kass and I surveyed the damage while Hector and Braulio set up drop tubes down to our dumpsters below.

"I wish they would just shut up sometimes," Kass said.

I kicked a cast-iron skillet. "Do you think this rusted out here, or was it rusty from the start?"

"Rusty from the start. They never say anything useful."

I tried to imagine casually uttering a word that scraped rust against the back of my teeth.

We got to work. Kass pretended that she wasn't watching me sideways like I might toddle right over the edge of the roof, or be stupid enough to use a drop tube as a playground slide.

It was a clear morning. No fog. We could see the long shape of storm clouds spiraling like the arms of a galaxy. Maybe galaxies are really storms. The quiet in the eye of the Milky Way is a massive black hole, though. It isn't home. It isn't some kind of safe haven. It isn't a place where survivors can thrive. And no light or sound or communication of any kind has ever escaped from beyond the event horizon of a black hole, or from inside the hurricane that has raged over our island for as long as I've been walking and talking.

We could also see the hospital where Mama, Papí, and Tío Gus spent their day sorting through medical waste.

"What happened to her there?" I didn't mean to ask that out loud.

"You did," said Kass.

"What?" I turned and looked at her feet, half-expecting to see those two words taking up space. They were heavy words. They should have been there. Instead they had already vanished to wherever our words go. I looked up at her face. She stared back, wide-eyed and stricken.

"What did you say?" I asked, even though I'd heard the first time.

"Forget it." Her voice squeaked like Styrofoam.

"What did you just *say*?"

"Please forget it! Don't get any ideas about what it means. Doesn't really mean anything."

I pointed at the hospital. "I was born there? I'm local?"

"Not really," Kass insisted. "I mean yes. You were. But no."

"I'm not from the island?"

"You are in every good and every awful way that matters."

I looked back at the storm. There has always been a storm. A hurricane has always raged between us and the place we were from. But now I wasn't from there anymore.

A horrible grinding noise came from the alleyway. Felix had screwed up the truck hydraulics. Again. Kass fled with the rest of her brothers and went down to fix whatever he had just broken.

I stayed on the roof. But I wasn't alone for very long.

The local boy found me. Maybe he lived in this building. Maybe he had seen us come in and followed us upstairs, through the roof-access door that was usually locked. Now he stood between me and the door.

"What do you want?" I demanded.

The boy took two steps closer.

I judged the distance between myself and the drop tube that led to a dumpster full of paper and cardboard, just in case I needed to sprint for an emergency exit. Maybe I really was stupid enough to use it as a playground slide.

The boy uttered a refrigerator. He didn't seem to have any trouble producing an entire fridge from inside his distended jaw. It was dark beige. It thunked against the rooftop, several times his size. He could have fit inside it. Instead it had fit inside him. He seemed very pleased with himself and his eloquence.

I felt my forehead start to throb. I didn't understand. I didn't know what he meant by the word *fridge*. And he could tell. His satisfaction turned sour. He spit three bottle caps at me and missed all three times. Then he opened the fridge, grabbed my arm, and shoved me inside.

It was warm in there. Smelled like mildew.

I counted slowly to sixty before I kicked the door back open.

The boy was gone. I threw his bottle caps down the appropriate slide and then shouted for backup from burly cousins. "We've got a fridge up here!"

Locals paused on the sidewalk below at the sound of my voice. Then they walked faster without looking up.

◆

My headache lasted all day. I brought it back to the caravan with me.

Mama's campfire was already blazing. Her rustic espresso had already brewed. The spokesman had already come and gone. He had left the soggy spitballs of our payment behind him. Mama sat, sipped her coffee, and chewed on the stem of her pipe. It was clearly broken. She had made it useless by chewing it.

I held back, unsure how to sit next to her now that I knew.

She took the pipe away from her teeth and examined it. Then she tossed it in the fire and spoke herself another one.

The new pipe looked pristine. The local lingo always came out useless, but Mama's word was unbroken.

I sat with her. She offered me espresso, and this time I said yes. It helped with my headache.

"The storm is a song," Mama told me. "One day we'll learn how to sing right along with it. We will harmonize with family singing on the island, inside the eye, and together we'll bring that endlessly spiraling wrath into harmony again. We will reach the tonic, the key-note that the storm has been singing toward for decades, and once the song is over those huge walls will all come tumbling down."

I didn't get any sleep that night. None whatsoever. Mama filled the RV with her mighty snoring, but the espresso made me forget what sleep even was.

◆

Once upon a time there was a storm. It split itself into ten thousand small shapes with spindly legs. Every one of those little mini-storms spoke devastation, negation, and waste. They spoke entropy and endings. Their words filled up landfills while we spun in circles, migrating around and around. We cleaned up the mess as best we could. But then we learned how to speak beginnings.

◆

On the third day we finished the job, even though I wasn't very much help. Kass and the other cousins watched me from a respectable distance and picked up my slack without teasing or complaint.

I didn't ride back to the caravan with all the trucks and dumpsters. I wanted to walk. That took me through the newly pristine park, alone, where the local boy found me again.

I ignored him. He followed me. His words littered the path behind us.

"We just cleaned this place," I muttered.

"Pay attention to me!" the boy shouted. His shout was a broken bike chain that whacked hard against the back of my leg.

I spun right around and said something to make him stop.

My word was a sword. It stuck in the ground between us. The blade looked new and sharp. I wondered how I had uttered it without cutting my own tongue.

The boy stopped, astonished by what I had just said. Then he lunged for it. But I was faster. Quicker on the uptake.

Understand me when I tell you that my word felt good and solid in my hand.

Do as I Do

PEDRO INIGUEZ

Maria dipped a single hand into the cool, silver stream and cupped it into the form of a saucer. "Now, do as I do," she said to the robot staring blankly at her. It put down the assault rifle, and dipped its hand into the running liquid. Its metal hand closed and imitated her as best as it could.

She lifted her hand, now holding a small amount of water. "Go on, try it."

The robot lifted its hand and water spilled through its fingers.

"No, no. Try it again. You have to learn. It's important."

The robot plunged its hand into the water again. Its digits shut together and formed a curved hand. It raised its hand and looked at Maria. She lowered her head and saw the small puddle of water. "Yes, that's good."

She raised her cupped hand close to her chest where she cradled a puppy no older than a few days. The pup's mouth opened, making sucking motions as it whimpered in high-pitched tones. She angled her hand so that its mouth suckled on the edge of her palm. She tipped her hand slightly and water trickled into the pup's mouth.

Maria nodded at the robot. The robot held a pup who stared at it with closed eyes and a protruding mouth. The robot tilted its hand and water spilled onto the puppy's face. The small creature squirmed and shook in the robot's grasp.

"No, you have to be gentle or you'll drown it. You understand me? It'll die. Your motions have to be slow and graceful."

The robot stared at her dumbly. "Graceful?" it said in a voice that sounded like metal scraping against metal.

"Yes. Delicate. Tip your hand slowly so that only a trickle escapes your palm. Try again."

The robot cupped a handful of water and lowered it to the puppy's mouth. Maria watched with a subdued breath. It had been difficult trusting a machine. She remembered when it happened so many years ago. She was just a girl then. The news reporters said some sort of corrupt programming had caused the world's military machines to turn on all living things. They said their infrared sensors had become faulty and began targeting anything with a heat signature. That meant most living creatures on Earth. But by the time the world had figured out what was wrong, the machines had begun constructing their own children, passing on their source code along with all their faulty programming. They were so resourceful. But Maria knew nothing of science or even of the technology that had made her television work. All she knew was the fear that drove her. It had been months since she had seen another survivor. That's what made this so important.

She looked up. The sun started to cross the hills to the west. In about two hours it would be dark. She turned her attention to the robot. It lowered its hand slower this time. A steady palm tilted downward and a trickle of clear water funneled into the puppy's mouth. The puppy gleefully drank it up.

"That's good. See? You can do it."

The robot regarded her for a moment, nodded, and then returned its focus on the pup. There was hope for the robot yet.

"All right, we have to move now. It's going to be dark and our heat signature will stand out like a sore thumb. Give me the puppy."

"I do not emit heat, Ms. Maria."

"I meant me and the puppies."

"I see. I am sorry."

The robot extended its hand and Maria took the puppy from its grasp. She put both of their naked bodies into her backpack and zipped it nearly shut, allowing just enough of a gap to let some air in. Their muffled whines broke her heart and she tried to ignore them until they could find a place to sleep. She slung the AK-47 toward her chest and brushed off trace amounts of dust from the barrel.

"Will we be returning to the cave again this evening?" the robot asked, retrieving its own Kalashnikov.

"No. We have to keep moving south. We need to find survivors."

"Statistically, there may be more survivors north, in the US."

"No, no. That was the source of all of this. There is less technology down south. I heard there is an elaborate cave system in Oaxaca with an underwater lake. We could live there and they wouldn't be able to detect our heat signatures from above. If we move fast enough we can reach it in about a week."

"Have you been there?" asked the robot.

"No, I've never seen too much of the countryside. I know that they lived in poverty and that technology was scarce in that part of Mexico. The government always seemed to disregard those people and their requests for modernization. Now it's the only thing that may have staved off total annihilation." She sighed. "Why am I even telling you all this? You're just a dumb robot."

The robot said nothing and looked away.

Maria filled her canteen and strapped on her backpack. The extra weight from the provisions and the puppies made her back pain flare up again. She suppressed a moan and walked forward. The terrain on the slope of the hill was rocky and uneven. As she walked, she felt the sharp pebbles stab through her soles and jab at her feet. In short time, she would need new shoes. *Just ignore it*, she told herself. She wanted to climb to a higher elevation to get a better grasp of her surroundings. She knew, though, that the robots had utilized smart-drones in the air. It was a calculated risk.

The robot slipped a few times but readjusted itself. Its hands probed and pulled on rocky fissures and footholds as it clambered behind her. It wasn't designed for any outdoor trekking; it was a city robot made for city jobs. It had been a prototype protocol model on display at the Mexico City Technological Exhibit when the world went to hell. The robot was marketed as a maid for the wealthy.

Maria had found it a week ago under the rubble of the convention building, pinned against a construction beam. For all she knew it had been pinned there for years. At first, she thought it was a person, and she pulled and heaved trying so desperately to save its life. When the beam came loose she reeled in horror.

It had hobbled toward her and thanked her. Its right leg had sustained damage. It said he was at her service. She didn't know what to do. Ultimately, she had thought the robot stupid and only good for menial tasks and small talk. She decided to take it with her even though she didn't quite trust it. It seemed harmless enough and it wasn't a military robot. And after Isidro, the robot was her first shot at companionship. She had laughed hysterically at the irony before the tears came.

After a few minutes of hiking up the hill, the puppies stopped whining. She knew her legs were going to be sore. They already felt heavy, like they were dipped in drying cement.

As she reached the top of the hill she took off the backpack and paused for a breath. She arched her back and felt the pain kick in again. The robot reached the top and stared blankly ahead. They had a panoramic view to the south. Plain green fields and small hills rolled as far as the horizon. The sky was clear and violet and a cool breeze swept in. Maria closed her eyes and thought about Isidro. She had only known him for a few days before she lost him, but he had filled that time with more life than all her nineteen years of living.

She turned north. Off in the far distance were the ruins of Mexico City. Skyscrapers sat broken and jagged and the urban sprawl lay deserted. She had spent years there, scurrying like a rat, avoiding the onslaught of robot scouts who picked off the last survivors of civilization. One by one everyone she knew had succumbed to starvation, disease, or mechanized murder. That's when she decided to leave.

The sun sank below the western horizon. The day's last light would be snuffed out before long.

"Come on. Let's go." She reached for the backpack, but the robot had already strapped it to its back. "Thank you, Robot," she said.

"You are welcome, Ms. Maria."

"Just call me Maria. I suppose I should give you a name, I'm getting tired of calling you Robot all the time. What would you like to be called?"

"I do not understand, Maria."

"Pick a name for yourself, something that describes you." She forced a smile in an attempt at warmth.

"I understand. I am Robot."

Maria sighed and shook her head. Below, the unknown awaited. She gripped the rifle tight against her chest. She descended the southern edge of the hill.

"Come on, let's go, Robot."

◆

"Now, do as I do," Maria said as she opened a small can of beans.

Robot pulled back the lid of his tin can. His other hand slightly crushed the sides of the can. He was trying to be as gentle as possible.

It had been two days since she taught Robot to cup water from a stream. Since then she had let him help with other small tasks like bathing the puppies and checking them for fleas and wounds. She'd found them amidst a dead litter on the outskirts of Mexico City. The mother was nowhere to be found and Maria had to assume that she had been eaten by some wild animal. She took pity on the surviving puppies and decided there was enough room for them in her backpack.

Maria retrieved a spoon and handed it to Robot. She made sure he was looking before taking her spoon and mashing the beans together into a smooth pulp. She picked up one of the puppies and cradled it on her lap as she sat on the floor against a tree.

"When they're young they don't have teeth, so they need to ingest something smooth. You understand?"

Robot nodded. "Yes, Maria. I understand."

"And we won't have beans forever. You can mash berries into pulp, too."

She brought the spoon to the puppy's mouth. Its mouth jutted out and a small tongue lapped up the bean paste. Maria looked at Robot.

Robot mashed up the beans inside his can and pulled out the spoon. Inside the can was a smooth brown paste. He held the puppy in one hand and fed it with the other just as she had showed him.

"That's good, Robot. You're learning."

"I am pleased to serve you."

"You serve them, Robot. We have to take care of them. All life is precious and we need to make sure no harm comes to them. We have to stick together."

"Like a family?" asked Robot.

"Yes, like a family."

A sharp pain twisted in her insides and she leaned across the tree. She regurgitated the water she had drunk that morning. Her guts felt like spilling out her throat as she spewed her lunch onto a patch of grass. The feeling had been getting more frequent. Her abdominal muscles were contracting violently now.

"Is everything all right, Maria?" Robot asked.

"Yes, I'm fine, Robot. Must've been a bad batch of water." She leaned against the tree and closed her eyes.

"Very well. Would you like to take the puppy back?"

"The puppy? Oh, yes." She had a thought. "Robot, would you like to name one of the puppies?"

Robot stared at her blankly.

"Go on. Just like you named yourself. Mine's a boy, I'll name him Roberto, like my father."

Robot stared at the puppy in silence.

"You have a girl puppy. Go ahead and name her."

"I will name her Robot Junior."

Maria grit her teeth. She fought the urge to scream, took a breath, and said, "You don't quite get how the name thing works do you? That's not exactly a girl's name."

"Why?" asked Robot.

She opened her mouth to explain the differences between male and female names and stopped herself. It would take too long. "Never mind. You win. She can be Robot Junior."

Robot held Robot Jr. in his hands and nodded. He gave her back to Maria.

She placed Roberto and Robot Jr. in her bag and finished the rest of the bean paste in silence.

Robot stood upright and stared off into the distance. She wondered if he could think like she could. What kind of thoughts ran through his head?

"What are you thinking about, Robot?"

"I do not think, Maria. I only react to my environment. Abstract thought, hindsight, foresight: I am incapable of such things."

Maria nodded. She was placing all her trust in him. It was crazy. Maybe she had gone mad.

"Robot, how long do you have to live?"

"I am afraid that question does not apply to me. I am not alive. My battery cell has another thirty years left of charge if that is what you refer to."

"I see. So, Robot, you've never felt alive?"

"I cannot answer that question. Is there anything else I may assist you with?"

Maria sighed and bit her lip. "No. Let's get a move on. Oaxaca is a couple of days away. We've been lucky avoiding the other robots so far. After this point we'll be walking through open fields, and we'll be more easily spotted. Once in Oaxaca, we'll be near the jungle."

"As you wish, Maria."

As she stood, her stomach ached. Her muscles felt like knots. She put a hand on her stomach and her belly felt warm.

She walked out from the cool shade of the tree. Her face felt flushed as the open sun beat down on her.

As she turned, Robot strapped the backpack on before she could get to it. He limped to her side and awaited her command. She patted his shoulder and said, "All right, let's move."

◆

The sky boomed with the sound of jet thrusters. Maria knew the familiar sound of the drones. She sprinted as fast as her aching legs would let her. Robot hobbled behind her, the whine of puppies at his back. If they even got a read on her heat signature it would be over. She knew the protocol: the drones would alert the others and they would deploy ground units to verify the liquidation of the target. If the drone missiles didn't get her first. It would be over only when the target was acquired and destroyed.

The trees were thick and tall and thin slivers of sunlight pierced the canopy like spears. She had no time to focus on the dense, sticky air of the humid jungle. Leaves and palms slapped her face as she jumped over vines and barbs.

Sweat trickled in her eyes. She stopped to rub them and catch her breath. The drones hovered above her position. She couldn't see anything above the veil of trees. Had they detected her? A small stream ran under her feet. Just a trickle, but the water forged a small path through the jungle floor. In the distance she heard a dull roar, like static on a radio.

Maria looked at Robot and pointed in the direction of the sound. They jogged forward. A few miles deep into the stream the air became cooler and the sound grew louder. The stream widened into a small river, its current grew rapid and violent.

Ahead, the river ran off a rocky ledge. Mists of water shot upward and Maria could see small rainbows materializing in the air. The line of trees ended here and the sky opened up above.

"That must be it," she whispered to Robot under the shade of a tree. "The waterfall leads to the underground caves. If we can get down there, we could hide and live off the land."

Robot nodded as he surveyed the sky. "We will be exposed," he said, pointing at the empty sky above. "The descent would allow the drones to target us easily."

Maria kneeled on the ground. Her insides churned. She groaned and leaned an arm against a tree.

"What is the matter?" asked Robot.

"We have to get to the caves. No matter what."

Robot slung his rifle behind his torso and placed an arm on her shoulder.

The air burst with fire and cracked with the sound of thunder. It sounded like the sky was tearing apart.

Behind them, a half a mile to their north, the trees caught fire and swayed viciously.

Another explosion lit the trees a few hundred feet from their position.

"They know I'm here," Maria shouted.

Robot swept Maria off the ground and cradled her in his arms. He hobbled along the river as fast as he could. Another explosion decimated the tree where they had just stood. Robot crossed the end of the tree line as he ran exposed under the clear sky. He heard the hum of a drone overhead but didn't stop to look. Robot ran to the edge of the cliff and jumped. Another eruption echoed at the edge of the cliff as he saw the cascade of white water fall into a wide lake below.

Together, the woman, the robot, and the puppies plunged into the cool pool of water.

Robot released Maria from his grip. She swam for the surface. He unshouldered the backpack and raised his arms upward as his feet pedaled swiftly. Two hands plunged in the water and took the bag.

He breached the surface of the water and saw Maria quickly opening the backpack on a small, rocky shore. Behind her was a small oval opening to a cave where the water seeped briskly through. Robot pulled himself onto a flat rock where Maria pulled out the still bodies of the puppies.

"What is their status?"

"They're not breathing."

Maria laid the small body of Roberto flat on the rock and pressed her lips to his. She blew into his mouth and pushed her hands against his chest. "Robot, do as I do."

Robot cradled Robot Jr. in his hands and placed her gently on the rock. "I am incapable of breathing life into her."

"Press against her chest. The pressure should cause her to spit out the water."

Robot pressed against Robot Jr.'s chest with his palm. Her small paws hung limp and lifeless at her sides. He looked back at Maria. Roberto coughed up water and began moving his head. His eyes opened for the first time and let out a small whine. Robot looked back at Robot Jr. He pressed at her chest with his finger. He pressed again. And again.

"Please breathe, Robot Junior."

He lightly caressed the puppy's face with his finger. Her mouth opened. Robot pressed her chest again, rhythmically now. Water spewed down the side of her small muzzle. She opened her eyes and whined.

Maria picked up Roberto and touched Robot's shoulder. "You did it, Robot. You just saved all our lives." Tears streamed down her cheeks.

"I am pleased to serve you all. Shall we go inside now, Maria?"

She wiped the tears from her face and nodded. "Yes, let's take a look inside."

Robot carried the pup. She squirmed in his hands as her eyes darted at the world around her.

They crouched through a four-foot entrance. Inside, a dark, open, humid world welcomed them. A few beams of sunlight pierced the dark ceiling from above, lighting the space around them. The stream of water ran through multiple passageways. At the nexus of the cave was a large, spacious area lined with moss and craggy walls.

Maria picked a path and walked forward. The path led through a tight, winding trail. Maria brought Roberto against her chest and squeezed through bumpy cave walls. Robot did the same with his pup as his back scraped against rock.

They walked into another spacious chamber where much of the stream water collected into a small lake. Maria handed her pup to

Robot and grimaced. She sat on a large, flat rock and held her belly. She moaned and her cries echoed through the cavernous chamber.

"What is the matter, Maria?"

"It's time, Robot. I'm having a baby. My water just broke."

"I am confused. You are pregnant?"

"Haven't you noticed? My belly? My aches? My vomiting?"

"I know little about human biology. How may I help?"

"Just stay with me," she said as she rested against a wall.

Robot sat beside her and placed the puppies down. They tried to walk but toppled over on their clumsy legs. After a while they fell asleep at his side.

Maria reached over the rock and cupped a hand of water and drank.

"Why did you not inform me of your condition?" Robot asked.

"You have to understand, Robot, I don't know how many survivors are out there. I didn't want anyone knowing I harbor life inside me. The risks were too high. And, well, you're a robot."

Robot said nothing as he stared at the slumbering pups.

Maria placed a hand on Robot's shoulder. "But now I know you're a friend."

A sharp pain pulsed inside Maria's gut. She held on to Robot's arm and squeezed. She lay on the ground and took off her pants. She closed her eyes.

"I'm in pain, Robot."

"Tell me about the male who impregnated you."

Maria stared at Robot, and then nodded.

"His name was Isidro. He was a little older than me. He was the only survivor I had seen in over a year. At least it feels like it was over a year. He was nice. He taught me how to use the rifles. I don't know any more about him," she moaned.

"Stay focused. Please tell me more."

She screamed at the cave ceiling. "He had darker skin than me and had beautiful brown eyes. Told me his family was killed by robots when he was fifteen years old. He had been hiding in the subway station, sleeping on the rails. He had to come out of hiding because food was running short. That's when I met him. I was scavenging an old pet store for food. It had been looted long ago, but there he was, frightened and joyous all at once. Like me."

Robot moved his hand to hers and curved it shut. She squeezed as her moans roared down the cavern.

"We were only together a few days before we were separated. A drone spotted us from above and fired on our position. He told me it would be best to split up. The drone chased him while I ran away. My mother would've liked him."

Maria broke into a heavy sweat and spread her legs. As she screamed, Robot watched as a small head appeared from under her.

"Catch the baby before it falls on the ground."

A body slid out and Robot extended his hands. The baby took the shape of a small, wet human. Robot held it in his hands and pulled it completely out.

"There is a hose attached to this child," Robot said as he delivered the baby to Maria. She cradled the baby in her arms as it cried with small outstretched hands.

"It's an umbilical cord. Find me a sharp-edged rock."

Robot looked on the cave floor and found nothing that suited. He slammed a fist against the wall and a few pieces of rock broke loose. He found the sharpest one and handed it to Maria. She severed the cord. She squeezed the baby to her chest. It was like nothing she could ever describe. All she knew was peace.

"It's a beautiful baby boy, Robot." Maria smiled.

Robot nodded and stared in what Maria assumed was curiosity.

She extended her arms and said, "Hold him."

Robot held out an open hand.

"No. Do as I do," she said. Maria cradled the baby with both arms against her chest and rocked him side to side.

Robot took the baby and did as Maria instructed. He cradled the child and rocked him side to side. The baby stared at the robot for a while and closed his eyes.

A sound in the distance. The echoes of hums and loud footsteps filled the cave.

"They are here," Maria said.

"We must go," Robot said, slinging his rifle around.

"No. They already know I'm here. They'll keep hunting until they've found me. Then they'll discover all of us."

Robot stood quiet and stared into the darkness.

"I think you understand, Robot. This is goodbye."

"I am confused. I do not know what to do."

Maria walked back toward the cave entrance and turned to Robot one more time. Her shoes were tattered and her clothes bloodied. "Just do as I did." She smiled, cocked her rifle, and brought it up to her bosom. With that she vanished into the dark and toward the raging rapids of the waterfall.

For a while there was silence. Robot looked at the baby and crouched by the lake. He dipped his hand in the blue waters and scrubbed some of the blood off the baby's face. Robot said, "I will name you Isidro," and tapped the baby's nose.

He turned to the puppies, sleeping on the rock, and sat beside them with Isidro in his arms.

A loud burst thundered through the caves, the unmistakable sound of machine-gun fire. Then silence once more.

He looked at the pups and the baby. Their sleeping bodies, still and peaceful.

Beyond the cave was a world of death. But in the cave he was sure of one thing: there was life.

"Do not worry. I will be here," he said, looking at the three small lives around him. "Perhaps we can look for more family."

As day fell and the sunlight faded from the ceiling above, Robot stared into the dark and waited for his children's hungry cries.

The Clarification
Oral History Project

PEDRO CABIYA

Welcome!

The Clarification Oral History Project is a nonprofit organization powered by people just like you. It was created on October 25, 2016, by majority resolution no. 42ACXM5–2016 of the Suzanne Comhaire-Sylvain Foundation for Clarification Research and tasked with collecting the experiences of victims and firsthand witnesses of the Clarification. This colossal endeavor is made possible by the collective effort of selfless volunteers who loan the project their varied talents and valuable time. And by those of you gracious enough to share your experiences of the Clarification, helping us understand better, and more about, this baffling event.

This brochure aims at providing you with the necessary information and motivation to have you pledge us your time, your stories, or both. Be sure to read the essay "The Clarification: An In-Depth Look," published here by courtesy of its author, Clarification correspondent Jomairy Heredia. There you will find a general description of the event, a condensed overview of current scientific research, an abridged timeline of the social and political fractures sustained as a consequence of the Clarification, a sneak peek at the intriguing story of the Exception, closing thoughts on the relevance of oral history and the ambitious goal of our project, and a basic Clarification bibliography.

There is a wealth of knowledge in the stories waiting to be told. Knowledge of the world as it was before the Clarification; of the turmoil following the mysterious disaster—during which the plate tectonics of our societies moved about and rumbled as they sought to regain stability—and finally, knowledge of the world as it is now.

Best regards,

Dr. Isadore X. Bellamy Pierre-Louis

Project Director

Santo Domingo

May 15, 2021

About Us

The Clarification Oral History Project is a nonprofit organization created by the unanimous vote of the board of directors of the Suzanne Comhaire-Sylvain Foundation for Clarification Research on October 25, 2016. It is governed by an independent committee and assigned minimum funds. The project's directive is to record and process the experiences of victims and firsthand witnesses of the Clarification.

The project's headquarters are located at Calle Las Damas no. 34, Zona Colonial, Santo Domingo, Dominican Republic. The COHP maintains thirty-one offices, staffed by volunteers and spread out over the island of La Hispaniola. All offices are equipped with a soundproof booth and recording equipment by kind donation of the government of Japan.

The project is led by anthropologist and botanist Dr. Isadore X. Bellamy Pierre-Louis. Interviewers—by far our largest team—are coordinated by ethnomusicologist Dr. Franklin Genao. Poet, linguistics expert, and literary scholar Dr. Sinny Navarro oversees the work of translators and transcribers. Curation is a joint effort of all team members, including volunteers, who read the stories stored in an online database and vote. Stories are never lost—votes only move them up or down in the priority level. Winners get to be transcribed, translated, and published first.

The COHP has been the grateful recipient of important grants, endowments, and financial pledges by many supportive institutions, chief among them The National Endowment for the Humanities, The Guggenheim Foundation, The Ford Foundation, The Martí Endowment for Culture and the Arts, and The David Ortiz Recon-

struction Fund. It also survives thanks to the kind support and generous donations of individual persons like you.

Our logo is the vévé representing Papá Legbá, an important loa in Haitian vodoun. Legbá speaks all human languages and is the guardian of the threshold to the spirit world, where the secrets of the Earth are kept. A vévé is a religious symbol that acts as a beacon, a signal for the loa to come. By it we are reminded of our values and goals, always bearing in mind that just as Papá Legbá, the great elocutioner, facilitates communication, speech, and understanding, so must we.

Our Mission

To record, organize, analyze, evaluate, and curate the many testimonies of the victims and firsthand witnesses of the Clarification, and make them available to the general public in written form.

Our Vision

We believe that we can arrive at a deep understanding of the social and cultural events leading to and following the Clarification through the experiences of those most affected by it, shared willingly.

Our Values

While *empathy* guides our interviews, we strive for *accuracy* in our transcriptions and translations, and for *relevance* in our curation, certain that *knowledge* accumulated through oral testimonies will lead to *improvement* of the affected groups.

Frequently Asked Questions

What is the Clarification Oral History Project?

The Clarification Oral History Project is an initiative of the Suzanne Comhaire-Sylvain Foundation for Clarification Research tasked with recording, curating, and archiving the myriad testimonies of victims and firsthand witnesses of the mysterious humanitarian disaster commonly referred to as "the Clarification."

What is the Clarification?

The Clarification is an unexplained event that took place in the early hours of January 12, 2016, during which Haitians and Dominicans of Haitian ancestry—up to the third generation—turned, without exception, into fair-skinned, blue-eyed, mostly blond Caucasians.

Were only those groups affected?

Only Haitians and Dominicans with Haitian ancestry *living at the time anywhere in the island of La Hispaniola* were affected.

Why is it called "the Clarification"?

Two weeks after the event, when everybody had already understood what had happened, self-appointed specialists and pundits during a morning talk show were asked their opinion on the "Haitian issue," a term regularly used as an euphemism for Haitian migration to the Dominican Republic, but one that had suddenly acquired a very different meaning. The most distinguished among the speakers hosting the show cracked a joke: "Oh, that issue's been clarified" ("Oh, ese tema ya se ha aclarado"). The name stuck.

Is the Clarification limited to a partial loss of melanin?

No. The Clarification consists of a complete genetic reconfiguration affecting not only pigmentation but also phenotype. Victims retain all original cognitive faculties and personality traits. No alteration of brain function has ever been observed in a clarified individual. Some physiological discrepancies have been found, arousing scientific curiosity. Apart from those, victims of the Clarification are the same persons they were before the Clarification.

How is it possible?

We have yet to understand the cause of the Clarification or the physiological mechanisms that allowed it to perform the baffling, simultaneous, large-scale transformation. Scientists at the Suzanne Comhaire-Sylvain Foundation for Clarification Research are hard at work exploring a variety of promising approaches to answering the question. Prominent biomedical engineer Dr. Robert Martínez is convinced the cause may have been environmental, a hypothesis that is widely gaining acceptance.

What is the importance of the Clarification?

The Clarification grievously affected the economies, demographics, and national security of many First World countries, and threw the social and cultural establishment of both Haiti and the Dominican Republic into utter disarray. The speed with which these changes occurred, during Year One of the event, prevented gradual adjustment and threatened to tear the social fabric of both countries. This period of confusion and slow adaptation to fast changes is known today as "Clarification Shift." The importance of the Clarification is hardly local, and its consequences and ramifications are far from regional. After the Clarification nothing has been the same anywhere in the world. Perhaps one of the most enduring and far-reaching results of the Clarification is the final disintegration of Western moral paradigms and the bankruptcy of its cultural leadership.

Who can testify?

Clarified subjects are our top priority. Preference is also given to non-clarified Haitian and Dominican nationals directly or indirectly affected by the event. Foreign nationals living anywhere in La Hispaniola through the first five years of the Clarification are strongly encouraged to testify.

Can children testify?

Yes! Children ages seven and up can testify. They must be accompanied by a parent or guardian.

How much do you pay per testimonial?

The Clarification Oral History Project does not pay its contributors. In preliminary interviews that extend beyond noon, lunch is served free of charge. Interviewees who get callbacks and complete all five recording stages become eligible for grants and academic endowments awarded by the SCSFCR.

How can I testify?

Visit us at the COHP office nearest you from 9 a.m. to 12 p.m., or from 2 p.m. to 7 p.m. during the workweek. Drop by on Saturdays between 11 a.m. and 4 p.m. You will need to fill out a form and sign a release. If you can't read and write, please inform the personnel so that they can help you.

After that, a program undersecretary will evaluate the relevance of your purported testimony and proceed to record your story in a soundproof booth. Depending on the content (and often on the form) of your narration, you will be asked—or not—to appear for further recording sessions, usually no more than five.

You can also contact us for an appointment. Fill out the form, and in the appropriate box explain as best as you can, in the language in which you feel most comfortable, the relevance of your testimony. We will get back to you as soon as we can with further instructions. Depending on the relevance of their testimony, we will visit witnesses and victims with limited mobility at their homes.

What should I bring for my session?

Bring as many pictures as you can, if you can. They don't have to be printed out, digital snapshots in your phone will do. If you can support your claims with evidence, bring the evidence. These might include contracts, ID cards, receipts for enrollment in school or university, driver licenses, videos, letters of employment, severance checks, emails. If you can't get a hold of any of these, do not worry. We are more concerned that your story be consistent, relevant, and coherent, than that it be supported by a paper trail.

I've been clarified. How can I prove it?

Perfect, native command of Haitian Creole or Spanish is your best calling card. Unclarified relatives (emigrés outside the island) might also serve the purpose by verifying your identity. Family members do not recognize each other by skin color alone, but by a shared life history that can be invoked to confirm who's who.

Contrary to popular belief, clarified individuals do retain a semblance of their former selves, and we have today facial recognition software able to determine significant correlations between former self and clarified self. So, again, pictures, birth certificates, ID cards, driver's licenses, and passports are useful for establishing identity.

What's your workload?

Our workload is enormous and our resources minimal. We already have hundreds of oral histories to process, each varying in length from half an hour to sixty-five hours, and it's only the beginning. We depend on the goodwill and loyal sacrifice of many volunteers, a force that ebbs and flows like the tides.

We are always in dire need of translators, transcribers, interviewers, and office staff. Translation and transcription happen on a merit-based system that moves testimonies up and down a priority list. Volunteers, managerial staff, registered scholars, and the COHP board of directors vote online to move the most relevant stories up the priority pipeline.

How can I help?

We're looking for volunteers highly proficient in Haitian Creole, Spanish, and English. They must be familiar with the use of personal computers and popular word-processing programs. All volunteers must sign up for a minimum of two shifts a week (ten hours), and will be assigned to different offices according to need. We do try to staff our offices with volunteers that live nearby. We're constantly recruiting for the following positions:

- *Interviewers.* These are personable, charismatic, deeply sympathetic individuals in charge of conducting the interviews and recording the testimonies of witnesses and victims. They must be highly proficient in the language of the storytellers.
- *Translators.* We seek meticulous and careful polyglots to translate all testimonies into English, Haitian Creole, and Spanish.
- *Transcribers.* Sometimes interviewers transcribe their own interviews, but we proudly maintain a dedicated force of accurate transcribers with sharp ears.
- *Coordinators.* These are the people responsible for the good governance of our offices. They answer emails, schedule appointments, assign shifts, evaluate testimonial relevance, and much more.
- *Scouts.* Are you hyperkinetic? Do you enjoy being constantly on the move? Then you would make a wonderful scout. Scouts comb the Dominican and Haitian countryside

hunting for stories, anecdotes, and the odd gifted story-teller. Some of our most important oral histories have been gleaned by scouts venturing deep into the mountains.

Which one are you? Let's find out.

You can also help by encouraging others to testify. If you know people with great stories of the Clarification, direct them to our web-site, tell them to come (maybe come with them), or help them make an appointment with us online.

Who or what is "the Exception"?

"The Exception" is the name given to Sylvie Petit-D'Or, a girl of twelve at the time of the Clarification, and the only Haitian meeting all requirements for clarification who did not clarify. Sylvie's testi-monies are especially important, as they provide a unique point of view of the social repercussions of the event. Needless to say, she was subjected to a battery of experiments as soon as she was discov-ered. One of the first international successes of the Suzanne Com-haire-Sylvain Foundation for Clarification Research was her rescue from the lab of the Franco-American team studying her immunity.

The Clarification: An In-Depth Look

In the wee hours of January 12, 2016, every Haitian and Domini-can of Haitian ancestry up to the third generation, male and female, young and old, living at the time anywhere on the island of La Hispaniola and its adjacent islets, keys, and atolls, changed into a fair-haired, fair-skinned Caucasian. Even those who were white[1] to begin with assumed the remaining characteristics of the Caucasoid group; thus, black-haired white and light-skinned individuals meet-ing the aforementioned requirements woke up that morning own-ers of chestnut blond, raspberry blond, blond, sandy blond, golden blond, light blond, white blond, and platinum blond, lank to wavy

---

1. While "whiteness" in most developed countries is a rigid category, in the Caribbean—and especially in La Hispaniola—it is a fluid, relaxed notion where classic, First World expectations of whiteness coexist with local interpretations that would never meet our former colonizers' stringent criteria.

manes[2] (if they had manes in the first place—bald subjects remained bald).[3] This multitudinous transformation has come to be known as the *Clarification*—its victims, for the sake of clarity and brevity, are generally referred to as the *clarified*.[4]

A period of turmoil followed the Clarification, as the island of La Hispaniola, the rest of the Caribbean, and the Western countries invested in the region coped with the unprecedented disaster and its unforeseen social, economic, cultural, and moral consequences.[5] The Clarification Oral History Project attempts to chronicle these and further stages of the Clarification through the collection of personal testimonies.

Nature of the Transformation

The Clarification is not a partial loss of melanin. It is not vitiligo, at least not in its classic presentation.[6] It is not environmental albinism, as some have posited. The Clarification, in sum, is not a skin condition. The Clarification is a complete chromosomal reconfiguration affecting not only melanin accumulation, but the shape of soft tis-

---

2. The importance of hair in the Caribbean can hardly be overstated, hence a multitude of books on the topic of hair sprung almost immediately after the event. For a great ethnographical study of segregation by hair in clarified communities, read Vivian du Maurier's *Now That We Have Good Hair: New Standards of the Clarified* (Durham: Duke University Press, 2017). Prof. du Maurier has identified upward of thirty meaningful blond categories. See also Lena Burgos's *The Good, the Bad, and the Clarified: Hair in the New Caribbean* (New York: CUNY Dominican Studies Institute, 2018) for a meticulous look into the sociolinguistic adaptations that arose in both sides of La Hispaniola to cope with the miraculous metamorphosis.

3. Male baldness patterns, however, have been found to translate on the clarified from Negroid to Caucasoid. See Sherwin Jacquelin, *When It All Falls Out: Divergences in Androgenetic Alopecia* (New York: Touchstone, 2018).

4. We follow this convention in the rest of this short article and elsewhere.

5. The bibliography concerning this topic is immense. We are currently working on providing a complete list of references. Check our website for a link to this work in progress.

6. Molecular biologist and geneticist Palmira Traoré—whose magnificent testimony was one of the first to grace our oral history records—has presented substantial evidence that supports the possibility that the Clarification is in fact a robust form of vitiligo. See "Protein Scaffolding in RNA Selective Mutation: The Clarification and Oxidative Stress in Segmental and Non-Segmental Vitiligo," *The Lancet*, vol. 537, no. 20032 (May 14, 2019): 1360–1385.

sues, fat distribution, muscle layering, and facial bone structures. As such, the event thoroughly refashioned the bodies of its victims to conform precisely to the biological taxon of the so-called Caucasian race.

"What we're looking at is an alteration of single base units in DNA over a wide array of genes," avers François Malespin, director of the Caribbean Genome Project of the Universidad Autónoma de Santo Domingo. "A mutation in the strict sense, yes, but one that has proven to be unreasonably selective and inexplicably fast-acting."[7] In addition to alteration, Malespin has detected deletion, insertion, and rearrangement of larger sections of genes or chromosomes.

Specifically, the mutation zeroed in on the genes that manufacture the proteins controlling the growth and shape—along the x, y, and z axes—of all bones of the viscerocranium, neurocranium, maxilla, mandible, nasal bone, and zygomatic bone; the distribution of truncal-abdominal fat and visceral fat; and the production and accumulation of melanocytes. The genetic expression of the new values provided by the mutation, in all victims, is the Caucasian phenotype. No pertinent genes are left unmodified, and all genes find expression. This exactitude is nothing short of miraculous. "It's as if someone had moved the sliders and turned the knobs precisely to produce white folk," Malespin has famously said. African American author Ta-Nehisi Coates has put it differently: "Saying that this thing, whatever it was, 'moved the sliders and turned the knobs precisely' to *suppress* black folk, would be more to the point."[8]

The Affected

The Clarification was *unreasonably selective*, this being one of its two most confounding aspects according to scientific consensus.[9] With

---

7. These are arguably the two most crucial concepts in Clarification research. More on them further on.

8. "A Miracle for Who?" *The Atlantic*, September 30, 2020.

9. The fact that the mutation itself transformed black people into white people is not mysterious at all, because tweaking the genes that it did, in the way that it did, will have exactly the consequences we see in the clarified. Victims who had their genome mapped before clarification are especially valuable, as they provide an important basis for comparison. The study of clarified DNA is, in other words, a well-trodden path offering few mysteries. Funding—and thus research—currently focuses on identifying the mutation agent and describing its

this concept, scientists attempt to describe the fact that the Clarification seems to have moved through the population sparing or affecting individuals according to nonmetabolic, nongenetic, nonbiological, nonenergetic criteria. Regardless of shared genetic uniformity, only Haitians and Dominicans of Haitian ancestry up to the third generation, living anywhere at the time in the island of La Hispaniola or in any of its outlying islets and keys—or at sea anywhere within its territorial waters—were affected by the Clarification. Dominican citizens sharing the same Negroid genetic makeup as their Haitian door-to-door neighbors in the populous shantytowns of Santo Domingo did not clarify. Neither did Dominicans descended from Haitians four generations back: the mutational rule rigorously stopped at the third generation. Thus, most victims now belong to families composed of clarified and non-clarified members, as some of them were either not present during the clarification—having migrated—or belong to a generation beyond the third . . . How is this possible?

"Whatever the mutation agent was," renowned Clarification geneticist Ninoska Jáquez-Marchena once said in an oft-anthologized interview, "it was the best census taker in the history of humankind."[10] Researchers are dumbfounded by the mutagen's apparent ability to discriminate on the basis of man-made (national) constructs devoid of biochemical tags. Needless to say, very little headway has been achieved in this field.

Simultaneity and Epicenter

As if that wasn't bad enough, the Clarification was *inexplicably fast-acting,* which is the second most frustrating attribute of the mysterious event. In less than hour, all subjects meeting the parameters of the unknown mutagen's rule were clarified; that's 14.32 million people over 76,192 square kilometers, hitting a success rate of

---

mechanism (the first step in the development of a cure or, as the more conspiratorially minded scientists fear, a weaponization), and on the social and cultural aftershocks of the Clarification.

10. Benjamín Torres Gotay, "Reasonably Democratic and Excruciatingly Slow: Inside Doctor Jáquez-Marchena's Lab," *The New York Times,* February 7, 2021.

99.99 percent,[11] all of which points to an agent of mind-boggling capabilities.

The staggering speed of the phenomenon gave an initial impression of simultaneity, further compounding the problem, but later observations dispelled that notion. By carefully scrutinizing oral testimonies, experts at the Suzanne Comhaire-Sylvain Foundation for Clarification Research discovered regular discrepancies per square kilometer in individual reporting of times of final transformation. It began to be suspected that simultaneity was only a local mirage restricted to the area affected in each out-of-phase segment. When enough testimonies (covering the whole area of La Hispaniola) had been collected, a learning macro was let loose on the data to dig up the relationship between the earliest time recorded and the latest. The algorithm returned a surprising result: the Clarification radiated in concentric intervals that grew exponentially from an epicenter located halfway between the towns of Petit-Goâve and Léogâne.

The Clarification's epicenter—at least as officially measured by the SCSFCR's team—misses the epicenter of the 2012 earthquake by less than half a kilometer. Independent specialists armed with different computer models argue that both epicenters align perfectly.[12] Although the Foundation remains skeptical, it maintains fully staffed field-research headquarters in the small village of Mayombe, straddling the epicenters of both natural disasters.

According to many testimonies, individual transformations took approximately four to five seconds to complete. Many report having sneezed, coughed, vomited, or briefly choked. Those who were awake agree to have changed "in the blink of an eye." By the time the last victim clarified,[13] the first had already been a white person for close to an hour.[14]

11. More about the missing 0.01 percent (a.k.a. The Exception) will appear in the upcoming collection of oral testimonies titled *On the Issue of Our Clarification*.

12. Jerome Stuart, "Clarification Propagation and Earthquake Aftershocks: Parallel Manifestations of the Sigmoid Curve Under a Consolidated Equation," *Mathematics of Computation*, vol. 110, no. 2 (June 2016): 2305–2339.

13. Marceline De los Santos, at the front desk of the Riu Melao Hotel in Cabo Engaño, Punta Cana.

14. Kervens Jean-Destin, a farmer brewing his morning coffee in Mayombe, Haiti.

Causes

In the race to identify the mutagen responsible for the Clarification, the international scientific community has posited innumerable hypotheses naming equally innumerable culprits: pollutants, spores, cosmic rays, gamma rays, solar flares, food poisoning, allergens, unknown gaseous compounds leaking from the Enriquillo-Plaintain Garden Fault Zone, rock ash, drainage from gold cyanidation sluiced into rivers by mining companies, Agent Orange, mustard gas, mutated forms of the *Mycobacterium leprae* and the *Mycobacterium lepromatosis*, bilharzia, toxoplasmosis, dengue, Zika, chikungunya, lead poisoning, asbestos poisoning, and mercury poisoning, among many others.

Less scientifically minded approaches variously blame the Rapture, sin, witchcraft, Santeria, voodoo, terrorists, big Pharma, Barack Obama, the Knights Templar, the Illuminati, Dutty Boukman's curse, the Antichrist, Evangelism, Satanism, Adventism, Pentecostalism, the CIA, the Pentagon, Al Qaeda, NASA, and Rosie O'Donnell.[15]

Put plainly, no single line of research has yielded evidence to support any of the theories presented over the years. This state of affairs does not seem like it will change any time soon.

Sociopolitical Consequences

To say that the Clarification had significant sociopolitical repercussions spanning the globe would be an understatement. However, by far the largest, most brutal impact has been sustained by the Western world.

With the Clarification, dominant economic structures crumbled, and the US, Canada, and France—the so-called Imperial Trident[16] that historically has benefited the most from Haiti's prostration—immediately sank into woeful recession, dragging the EU with it.

---

15. Roy Mitchum, *The Perfect Alibi: Rosie O'Donnell and the Quest for Racial Supremacy* (Miami: JustSaying Press, 2022). Admittedly bonkers, Mitchum is a charismatic orator. His theories have been espoused by thousands of followers, and his YouTube channel has a million-plus subscribers.

16. Ricardo Seitenfus, *Haiti: Dilemmas e fracassos internacionais* (Ijuí: Editora Unijuí, 2014).

The "erasure of observable racial compartments"[17] made it impossible to preserve an economic system based on the dehumanization of specific phenotypes that ease the subjugation of their bearers. Liberty and equality, the central tenets of political organization in Western societies, were finally laid to rest as nothing more than the cognitively dissonant propaganda that masked the real motor of human progress: carefully maintained inequality and finely tuned bondage. For some, this was revealed by the Clarification; for others, finally and definitely confirmed by it.[18]

Among the first contemptible actions perpetrated against the clarified by the developed world was the kidnapping of hundreds of poor clarified children. In the chaos that followed the transformation, various international organizations and private agents absconded with children found wandering in the streets, unrecognized by their parents and unable to recognize their parents themselves. These children were immediately offered in adoption to families all over the US, Europe, and Canada, and were never seen again. Some of the organizations that have gone to trial over this abominable crime have defended their actions saying they had engaged in a "rescue mission" that saved "countless children's lives" by retrieving them from a country plagued by "awful living conditions." In an speech before the UN, clarified Haitian journalist and novelist Deisy Toussaint reminded the Assembly that those children had been living in Haiti all their lives "and the world had not cared whether the living conditions were awful or not."[19]

By the end of Year One, life in Haiti improved. The US and EU's lobbyists stationed in Port-au-Prince mysteriously refrained from arguing against raising the minimum wage in Haiti, and workers in the Free Trade Zones had a respite. Other industries followed. There

---

17. Magdalene Jefferson-Colón, "Leveling the Field: Visual Blockages to Empathy and the Case of the Clarified," *The Neurological Insider*, vol. 12, no. 45 (March 2020): 25–47.

18. The Black Lives Matter movement has issued a memorable statement (now part of many a school curriculum) that dissects with acerbic wit the cynicism and proffered innocence of "the surprised." It is to be hoped that "it won't take another cataclysm for the dominant segments of a society to give the downtrodden the benefit of the doubt when they speak up" ("You Were Saying?: A Commentary on the Clarification," *The Chicago Tribune*, November 2, 2017.).

19. "Robbed of Our Children, Robbed of Our Future," *Aftershocks of the Clarification*, speech before the General Assembly, United Nations, March 23, 2019.

was an influx of tourism, and visa requirements for Haitian nationals were relaxed all around the world.

With blackness eradicated and the clarified now graced with the privilege of being white—considered a myth by many whites—it became next to impossible for First World countries to secure labor at the old prices and, more importantly, to show the financial determination to procure it, finding in whiteness an impassable moral blockage to exploitation, and again revealing the prejudices—conscious or not—favoring members of the in-group. By uncovering them, the Clarification accentuated these contradictions to the point of total moral collapse.

In the Dominican Republic and Haiti economic readjustment was compounded by sociocultural havoc, as the most vulnerable groups in both countries suddenly acquired the appearance of what centuries of colonial violence had deemed the highest beauty standard and the ultimate badge of authority and power. Many of the testimonies already gathered by the writer of this article and by the Clarification Oral History Project attest to the tragicomedy and irony inherent in this reversal.

Social norms were destabilized. Non-clarified Dominican overseers in the cane fields and other plantations had a difficult time giving orders to their clarified, Nordic-God workers. The same happened to housewives and their clarified maids, bosses and their clarified employees, crime lords and their clarified thugs.

But even as the US and Europe were reluctant to take advantage of the economic vulnerability of most of the clarified, and non-clarified Dominicans found it hard to order white people around, non-clarified individuals in La Hispaniola and the rest of the Caribbean moved to take advantage of the clarified in a different way. During Year One, marriages between clarified and non-clarified spiked. Pregnancies of Dominican women by Haitian men, and vice versa, hit an all-time high. It was surmised by a small number of pioneers, before any evidence was available, that the Caucasoid look was heritable, so at first the trend shows in the graph as a horizontal line slightly curving upward. When the evidence finally arrived, in the form of mixed, light-skinned, blond, blue-eyed babies, the horizontal line becomes a vertical line shooting skyward.

The *bateyes,* the dismal living quarters that traditionally housed Haitian sugar cane workers and their families, emptied by the beginning of Year Two. Men and women from all over La Hispaniola, and from other islands in the Caribbean, traveled to distant sugar cane fields in search of poor clarified brides and grooms. Later, they would go directly to Haiti. In cities all across the island a similar situation arose, compounding the already hectic traffic.

Also by Year Two, the Dominican Republic exonerated Haitian nationals of all traveling restrictions and granted Dominican citizenship to all undocumented Haitian migrants and to all descendants of undocumented Haitian migrants.[20] By Year Three, it created several incentives for migration, including giving away land for cultivation. By the beginning of Year Four, a wall had been constructed along the Dominican-Haitian border . . . by Haiti.

These are only a few examples.[21] Studies of the changes and shifts ushered by the Clarification in the economic, social, and cultural landscape of the Western world are by far the most insightful and correspond to the most advanced field in Clarification research.

Sylvie Petit-D'Or: "The Exception"

To date, the only known person excepted by the mutagen despite meeting all requirements for clarification is a twenty-eight-year-old computer scientist named Sylvie Petit-D'Or. Born in the commune of Boucan-Carré in the Mirebalais Arrondissement, Dr. Petit-D'Or was twelve years old at the time of the Clarification and is probably the most studied human subject in the history of the field.

The COHP preserves her oral testimony and treasures the opportunity to soon share it, as it provides a unique perspective on the turmoil during and immediately following the Clarification. Many authorized and unauthorized biographies have been written about Dr. Petit-D'Or,[22] and the results of a year and a half of illegal testing and experimenting have been recovered and released to the public

---

20. The Dominican government had stripped the latter of Dominican citizenship with the infamous and onerous *Sentencia 168/13* issued by the Constitutional Tribunal, effectively annulled by the end of Year One.

21. Non-clarified migrant communities added to the already combustible mix, turning this tragedy into a deeper comedy of errors. For a great look at the intersections between the island's clarified and the non-clarified diaspora, read Ivolia Dufresne's *White People Are Cooking My Favorite Foods* (New York: Caribooks, 2023).

22. Yet only one counts with her endorsement, albeit lukewarm: Pedro Cabiya's *The Only Exception* (Santo Domingo-Barcelona: Zemí Book Editores, 2025).

. . . with Petit-D'Or's generous consent. But when the transcription of her interviews is finished, we will be able to read the story—told in her own words, with her own voice—of her humble beginnings in a small hut near a brook, her years as a street urchin in Santo Domingo, her captivity in a French lab, her spectacular escape, and what it finally took to leave her ordeal behind and move on. In many ways, the story of the Exception is what gives the Clarification a frame of reference, a context, a tether.

Conclusion: The Role of Oral History

After the initial pandemonium cooled—halfway through Year Two—and the new force represented by the clarified sought a point of equilibrium, new social dynamics flipped dominant paradigms by curtailing First World deniability and exceptionalism.

In La Hispaniola, as in the rest of the Caribbean, skin color and its multiple gradations served as goalposts for deeply pigmentocratic societies. The Clarification eradicated these references and thus neutralized traditional stratification by bringing it out in the open; dissolved calcified colonial legacies by uncovering them and making them visible; and heralded a period of brutal socioeconomic upheaval. The oral histories we aim to preserve record these processes.

Curanderas in the Ceiling

ALEX TEMBLADOR

There are fish in the ceiling. Giant orange and white clown fish swimming above my head, like sharks circling prey. A clear layer of glass and eight feet of air separates me and the fish. I lie on the operating table. Awake.

My mother is holding my left hand so tightly, I fear she might crush it to dust and to dust it will return. That's in the Bible—somewhere. In Spanish it'd be: *De polvo a polvo.* I have lost all feeling in my hand. But all I can focus on are the clown fish that the hospital has placed in the ceiling above me. When the nurse wheeled me into the room earlier, I noticed blue fish swimming in the floor.

I wish the fish would stop moving. With the pain medicine and the fish, I'm a little nauseous. And I wish the lady that is here with my mother would be still too. Doña Maria. She who pulled me through the globs of blood that came from my mother's uterus. She cleaned out the goop, as it made its way into my mouth, with her pointer finger that had long ago lost its nail when she was hammering a makeshift cross together and it had never regrown. Doña, who is now peering over the doctor's shoulder into my vagina, down a concave of muscles toward my cervix at the white circle that has appeared from the vinegar solution the gynecologist applied moments before.

The solution causes a slight burning and I squirm a bit in discomfort. My mother is still crushing my hand but now she has begun to ask *los Santos* for help, followed by more praying to Jesus, and Mary, and finally straight to *Dios,* all in Spanish so that the *güera* nurse with blond hair who is preparing the station for the surgery can't help but glance at my mother. The muscles in the nurse's face twitch as if she is trying to figure out whether to laugh or to look at me with pity for the embarrassment I am suffering on the day of my surgery.

If only it was Mamá who was the only other person in the room with me. But she insisted Doña Maria accompany her. Actually, Mamá didn't even want me to come to the gynecologist, even if she is a Mexican woman. Who ever heard of a woman needing to peer into the parts of another woman that *Dios* Himself does not shine a light upon and never shall? The only time someone should look down *there* is when a child is being pulled from the darkness to the world. Mamá didn't even know I was coming to these women doctors. And why do I need to even go to a woman doctor? she had asked. Then realized *why,* and scolded me. *¿Mi hijita una ramera? Sleeping around and giving you diseases. What Mexican man will want to marry you now?* I tried to explain that it was only with one guy, leaving out the part that he wasn't even *Mexicano,* he's a *güero,* a white guy, but she wouldn't listen to me.

Earlier, I thought Mamá would feel better and send Doña home when she saw that the doctor was a Mexican woman, Dr. Ramirez. But she didn't. Especially not after Mamá tried to speak Spanish to her.

Oh good. A Mexicana. You understand then. Please tell me what my child says is not true. You understand there are better ways to take care of the malo in her, my mother had said to the doctor as the doctor put on surgical gloves.

The doctor gave my mother an odd look and then looked at me. "Miss Gonzalez, please tell your mother that I do not speak Spanish, but if she would like an interpreter, the office is required to provide one."

My mother looked at the doctor then back at me. I translated. My mother's jaw dropped. *Your doctor doesn't speak Spanish? But she's Mexicana!*

Mom, I said, *not all Mexicans can speak Spanish.*

She shook her head and looked at Doña Maria who had replied, *Then she is no Mexicana. These doctors. See, this medicine makes our women forget who they are, forget their language!*

I looked at the doctor. "So an interpreter or not?" the doctor asked.

I shook my head no.

Mamá was even happier that she had brought Doña Maria. Especially since I had a Mexican doctor who couldn't speak Spanish—Mamá said something wasn't right about that. Maybe Doña could fix the doctor's tongue so she could speak her native language again. But first and foremost, Doña must take away the *malo* that has found its way into my body, she must. Mamá does not believe there are "abnormal cells on my cervix" as I have explained. She does not believe that after sleeping with the first and only guy I had ever slept with that I contracted HPV. "HPV—*a la caca!*" She yelled at me. She does not believe it can give me cancer if it is not taken out immediately since it has developed to an intermediate stage that is worse than mild, and barely less than cancer. She only believes that someone has placed this harm on me or that some evil spirit has done this to me, perhaps *el Diablo* himself!

The doctor peers over the cloth that has been placed over the top of my legs. She did not understand why I needed two women in the room, and she did not understand when I said one of the women was not related to me at all, that she was a *curandera*, a Mexican healer, and that my mother insisted she come along. She did not understand that it was a compromise between Mamá and Papá. That Papá did not believe at all in the *curandera*'s healing powers, that he thought they were all *brujas,* and to only trust the white American doctors. But Mamá had found the hottest chilies and had placed them in every one of my father's meals until he relented and allowed the *curandera* to come along. The doctor did not understand any of this. She didn't even know what a *curandera* was! Maybe it's because she is an atheist. Maybe because she really isn't Mexican like Mamá says.

This morning when the doctor was going over the procedure and having me sign forms she said, "Miss Gonzalez, you are twenty years old, not a minor anymore, you did not even have to tell your parents much less allow someone like *this* in the examination room."

The connotation of the word *this* indicated that she thought nothing of *curanderas.* It was the way she said *this* that made me insist on Doña's attendance, even though I truly did not want her there.

"But the Equality and Accommodation of Religions, Beliefs, and Practices Act allows for Doña Maria to accompany me," I had said to the doctor.

"I know what the EARBPA says and I know we have to accommodate your belief system; however, the Medical Emergency Veto Act allows for me to veto such accommodation requests under EARBPA and I do not feel comfortable to do my duty with this Doña character present." She pronounced *Doña* as "Donna."

Poor doctor didn't know she was dealing with a pre-law student with a focus in post-modern laws of equality. "The MEVA only pertains to an emergency and I don't think the state or the courts would consider this an emergency surgery. If you don't let Doña Maria in the operating room, you will be violating EARBPA and even the Protection of Mexicans from Discrimination Act and that's grounds for a lawsuit."

It was then that the doctor had agreed. I heard her say to another doctor: "We really need to make sure EARBPA is repealed this year."

How could I explain that this woman, this *curandera*, had cured me of numerous coughs when I was younger with some *te con canela*, with a little drop of whiskey and honey? That Doña Maria had brought my brother back from the brink of death when he had become so depressed he had stopped eating for three days and would not leave his bed. She cleansed him of all the bad spirits that had burrowed their way into him. She said he had *susto*, his soul had wondered halfway to the other side, but she grabbed it in the fog and forced it back into his body. This was before Papá had become manager at the factory, before we had money and good insurance to pay for a *güera* doctor, and all we had was Doña Maria. When I had begun to attend Arizona State University, most of my friends who were *güeras* had told me how important it was to go to the health care clinic on campus to get my first pap smear and to get on birth control, especially since it was free and one could never be too safe.

Doña Maria moves away from behind the doctor's shoulder now and is by my mother's side. Her hair is wild, sticking up on the top and slicked straight down in the back.

This is wrong, she tells my mother in Spanish. *This doctor knows nothing. She needs comfort, teas, una limpia, and a new diet, not a piece of metal shoved inside her!*

Mom looks so confused. Papá told her to let the doctors do what they know how to do. To make sure Doña Maria doesn't get in the way. He reminded her who the man of the house was. To which she replied with, "*Pah! Hombre de la casa el dije!*" Despite her sarcastic remark she did not wish to displease Papá.

Please Doña Maria, help my child. Do una limpia while the doctor does his procedure, yes? That can help, no? my mother asks. Doña Maria's face scrunches in anger and the crease between her eyebrows speaks of disappointment, not at my mother, but at me.

Yes, I will, Doña Maria replies. Then she looks at me. *You will regret this. I could have done all this without the pain and the cost. Remember that.* I look away a little ashamed for not having enough faith in God, in her, whom I've always had faith in before. But not now. The thought of getting cancer or losing the ability to have children concerns me too much. And besides, what will my friends say if I tell them I didn't go through with the surgery?

I look down the length of my body again. The doctor has turned to the blond nurse, asking her for something. The nurse looks at the silver table in front of her and grabs a syringe. Suddenly, I feel cold and my body begins to shake a little. Doña Maria has pulled out a stick of something and a lighter from the big bag that hangs over her shoulder. She pulls a match out to light the stick when the doctor notices.

"What is she doing? You can't light that in here! This is a sterile environment," the doctor says to Doña and then looks at me, because I told her that Doña cannot speak English. I translate for the doctor but before Doña can respond my mother interrupts.

"It's okay. She help, yes? It's fine."

The doctor asks me, "What is she trying to do with that?"

"A cleansing," I respond. "It's to push evil spirits away, to cleanse my soul. I'm sorry. Please, she won't get in the way. I promise."

The doctor raises her hand to push her hair back, and then stops, remembering that she has on plastic gloves that have been in my vagina for the last twenty minutes preparing for the procedure.

"Damn laws," she mutters and I know she has given in once more.

I nod vigorously, then cringe when I feel my vagina muscles contract around the metal speculum. Before I can tell Doña she can go ahead, Mamá does. I drop my head backward onto the table. Tears come to my eyes but I swallow them down. I look at the ceiling again.

"Miss Gonzalez, I am about to administer the anesthesia around your cervix. You will probably feel a few pinches." I probably won't feel anything. Didn't they already give me something for this? I can't remember. They gave me so much medicine earlier. For my heart. For my pain. For my bladder.

I shut my eyes tight. "Okay." Mamá squeezes my hand, a signal that she cannot see the needle anymore and that I am about to feel the pinch. I can smell whatever Doña Maria is burning—sage. It reminds me of the many times my mother took me to get cleansings. When I was thirteen and Mamá found me and my cousins looking at a men's magazine with half-naked male athletes in their tighty-whities. She said I needed my soul cleansed for looking at such things.

I feel the pinch and my fingers convulse around Mamá's hands. And another one, and another one. Until I only feel a pressure on the next one. And then nothing. I relax some, until I see Doña Maria above me making the sign of the cross over my body. She pulls a clear bottle out, dips her fingers in it, and then makes the cross over my forehead. Lukewarm holy water. She puts the vial back and pulls out some more sage and begins saying Hail Marys and Our Fathers over my body, flicking the sage in rhythm, sweeping the bad spirits away. She finally finishes. I lift my head up slowly. The doctor and the nurse are frozen in position. The doctor has her hand held out to the nurse, waiting for some instrument, and the nurse stands inches away, hand held out, but not far enough.

Doña Maria finally notices them. She makes a "humph" sound. It breaks the frozen state of the doctor and the nurse.

"Uh, nurse?" the doctor says. Nurse rushes to the doctor and hands her the tool. The doctor goes back inside me.

"Can you feel that?"

"No," I reply.

"That?" she asks.

"No."

"That?"

"No."

"Okay," she says. "We are ready to remove the cells. Are you ready?"

Of course I'm not freaking ready. She's about to take an instrument and cut off a sliver of tissue from my cervix. Even though I have the anesthesia, she said I may feel some discomfort, a little bit of pain.

But I nod yes, although "no" is stuck in my throat like the thick *molé* sauce Mamá makes. The nurse and the doctor begin preparing, and I look back at the fishes before Mamá interrupts my gaze.

Mija, Doña says we must pray, yes?

I nod, because I am past the point of wishing my mother and her *curandera* would act normal. My mother lets go of my hand and joins Doña Maria, who has already knelt beside the table. Doña pulls out a few plastic statues from her bag and places them beside me. Our Lady of Guadalupe, Our Lady of Lourdes, Saint Bertha, patron saints of healing—creating a mini altar of safety, good intentions, and love.

The doctor and the nurse are moving around. I hear instruments clacking against the metal table. The doctor and nurse are speaking quietly to each other. I am not looking at them, but I hear their conversation pause when Mamá and Doña began praying aloud. Their voices come together and find a rhythm. I close my eyes. Regardless of the weirdness of the whole fiasco, their voices calm me. My mother's voice rises higher. She has prayed over me many times in my life. When I had the fever and chills; when she thought I was sleeping but I wasn't and she would pray that I would have happy dreams; when I came home from the college one day, crying my eyes out, because my boyfriend had broken up with me and I found out he was seeing some *güera* on the cheerleading squad with big boobs and a big butt and fiery red hair.

I think of my ex and his new white girlfriend—*Ashley.* He used to say I was the prettiest Latina in the world, even though I told him that I prefer *Mexican.* Not *Latina.* He'd just laughed and said—"same thing."

He didn't respond much when I called him crying after I found out about the HPV.

"You gave me an STD?" His voice rose on the phone.

"No! You gave it to me. Boys carry the virus." He argued with me, saying he hadn't ever had an STD, and I probably got it from someone else. I wanted to argue that I had never been with anyone else, but I knew he wouldn't believe me because I had implied that I had been with a few other guys before him, to try to make myself seem experienced.

The rest of our conversation didn't go very well. I told him to be safe, that he might pass it on to someone else, but he only replied with "uh-huh"s so I wasn't sure if he was really listening. Then he ended the conversation by bringing *her* name up: "Look I got to go. Got to pick Ashley up from practice. You take care and all."

The click of the phone made my stomach clench.

The doctor interrupts my thoughts. She has to speak over my mother's and Doña's voices. "I'm about to shave the infected cells. From there, I will staunch the bleeding with this instrument here."

Mamá begins to cry. She sees the doctor being handed a big scary rod instrument. She doesn't stop praying though. She just cries and prays, cries and prays. Next to her, Doña seems to have gone into a trance. Her lips are moving, and she is making weird noises that sound like a chupacabra. *Coo-cooey! Coo-cooey!* Suddenly, she jumps up, much quicker than a woman of seventy. Which causes me to jump and the doctor to curse.

"You can't move, Miss Gonzalez! Get that woman to stand still!" The doctor yells, her voice reverberating against the stark walls.

I repeat what the doctor says in Spanish to Doña, a bit breathlessly. It has just hit me that other parts of me could have been cut off accidently, thanks to Doña. But she doesn't seem to be listening. She has pulled out an egg from her bag and is rubbing it over my forehead. She places her hand on my chest so I can't lean my head up and I am forced to look up at the fishes again. I begin to count them. One, two, four, seven.

"Miss Gonzalez?" the doctor says.

"Miss Gonzalez!" the doctor says more forcefully. My head whips up. I'm feeling a bit woozy and queasy.

"Yes. Sorry, what?"

The doctor's eyebrows are pinched in frustration. "You cannot move. Do you understand me? I don't care if that woman is the Dalai Lama or Jesus Christ Himself, you make sure she doesn't do anything crazy like that again. I'm not going to lose my license because I accidentally shaved off too much!"

My mom stops praying and speaks up before I can. "Everything good, yes? No problems, yes? Calm, yes?"

"Yes, it's fine. Sorry. Just do it already," I say to the doctor, not caring if I am polite anymore. I allow my body to fall backward toward the table again, too tired to do anything else. The conversation between the doctor and me has not deterred Doña, and she continues to administer the cleansing.

I hear the doctor say, "Okay, let's try this again. Be very still." I nod, even though she isn't looking at me but lost beneath the white cover.

Doña is muttering over me. I look at the fishes, trying to not think about anything. Trying to tune out the noise, the *loco* in the room. Waiting for the doctor to start. There is one little fish among the larger clown fish. It darts in and out between the others.

Chingao! ¡Hijo de su madre! I lose my breath and it feels like my entire lower body has contracted and for a second I am nervous that I will have a bowel movement in front of everyone. I can feel it, a slight burning feeling in the lower regions of my abdomen. Cuss words begin flying in my mind as I grip the sides of the table, while Doña is rubbing the egg over my stomach and chanting, and my mother is still on the ground crying and praying. *¡Hijole ¡A dios Mio! ¡Ay wei!*

"Okay. Now I'm going to cauterize the bleeding. Nurse."

I begin breathing like a woman in labor: quick in, quick out. I want to cry out, but I don't. I am scared what it might do to my mother and the doctor who is holding tools that burn human flesh. I look up. The small fish is looking at me. He has swum to the bottom of the ceiling; his nose must almost be touching the glass.

Suddenly, I feel pressure followed by the smell of burning flesh. I gulp down the bile that has risen in my throat no sooner than Doña Maria finishes with the egg and begins yelling at me.

What's that? What is that smell? Hija are they burning you? she asks in Spanish.

To stop blood, I manage to reply.

Her hands fly to her head. *Ay! Monsters! And you allow this!* She is pointing at me now. *Burning you.*

I hear the doctor speak up. "Is there a problem, Miss Gonzalez?"

Doña then turns to the doctor, who is pulling the instrument out with part of my blood on the tip of it and drops it in a bag the nurse is holding. Doña's finger is pointing now at her. *I curse you and all these doctors. Hurting women with your medicines, your burning instruments. You will burn in hell with the devil. White man's whore! Manditos!* And then she spat on the ground. Twice. To seal the curse.

I hear Mamá gasp as Doña Maria claps twice and disappears leaving behind *las estatuas* on the bed.

Mamá begins speaking to the doctors. "Everything okay. She say thank you. All good, yes?"

"Where did she go? Where is she?" the doctor is asking.

"She was just right there!" the nurse says shakily.

I look up at the ceiling and suddenly, the small fish is replaced by a small Doña Maria, swimming, looking down at me. Her skin is orange like the small little fish. But it is her all right.

I can't stop looking up at Doña. No one else has noticed her above us.

My mother says, "She go. She have leave. Say thank you."

"You didn't say she was a witch, Ms. Gonzalez. They don't fall under the EARBPA act, and the Equality for Dark Forces Act does not apply here," the doctor says.

Suddenly, the nurse throws her hands in the air, palms out toward me with her head thrown back. A string of unintelligible words comes from her mouth at a high level. A Pentecostal. I have seen this on TV, speaking in tongues. They do this now, in public. I hear they can't control it.

I want to say something, but in that moment, I can feel the blood rushing from my head, my vision blurs and begins to fade. I can hear the nurse speaking in tongues, Mamá crying, and the doctor yelling at someone. I can feel my head falling backward toward the table, until the last thing I see is Doña Maria, her cheeks puffed out like the clown fish, holding in her breath and flopping her arms as she pushes herself closer to the glass barrier so that I can see the look of disappointment on her face.

◆

A week later I return to the doctor's office for my after-exam check-up. I am wearing a pad to help the bleeding. Mamá insists on driving me. When I complain about the pad, my mother replies, *Aren't you comfortable with those now?* I reply yes, forgetting that my mother does not know about the tampons I usually wear. She says tampons are bad for women, that they keep all the bad blood inside.

There are no fish in the ceiling of the patient room in which I wait. When I see the doctor, she asks basic questions as she is checking my cervix. How are you feeling? How is the bleeding? Any side effects? I answer quickly, but I want to know about the results. I want to know if they got all the bad cells out, if I will be okay. She comments that I am healing quite well.

After I'm dressed I feel the need to say, "Sorry about all the craziness last week."

"Craziness?"

"Yes, you know, the surgery and everything?"

I notice a wrinkle in the middle of her forehead that doesn't seem to go with the smile she gives me. Then she says, "So anyway, your results. They came back clear of all abnormal cells."

"Wait—what?"

"Abnormal cells. The lab couldn't find any."

"I don't get it. Nothing? They weren't any? How is that possible?"

The doctor shrugs. "That happens sometimes. Your body must have fought it off before the procedure." I am stunned. Not sure how to respond, how to feel.

"Does that usually happen? I mean that sounds rare?"

She laughs. "It happens more often than you think. So here is a copy for you. And I set up an appointment six months from now, if you don't have any more questions?"

"No, uh . . . thank you." I stand up when she asks one more question.

"So was it worth it?"

"Was what worth it?"

"The surgery?"

Once I leave the doctor's office and meet Mamá outside in the foyer and tell her the news, she will probably rejoice and start crying out thanks to God, in front of everyone. Then she will call Doña Maria and discuss the miracle. Even though I will explain that the doctor said it isn't rare, that this occurs to girls without *curanderas,* she will not believe me. And Doña will insist that I drink some tea and get a cleansing once a week for three weeks to make sure the *malo* doesn't return. Then Mamá will beam and gloat at Papá at dinner, saying: *See Chelo? I told you Doña Maria would cure our hija.* And no matter how much Papá tells Mamá that it was science, and that Doña is just a crazy lady getting money from poor Mexicans, that those ceremonies she does in the back of her house far from the world, well, they don't make her a saint or healer . . . but no matter what he says—Mamá won't listen. And I'll keep having dreams of Doña as a clown fish.

I respond by waving the test results in my hand at the doctor before walking out.

Dream Rider

DANIEL PARADA

DREAM RIDER

DANIEL PARADA

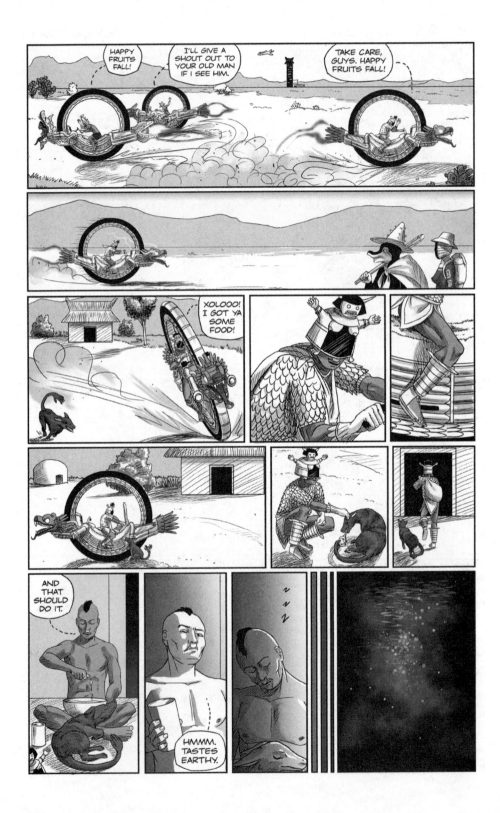

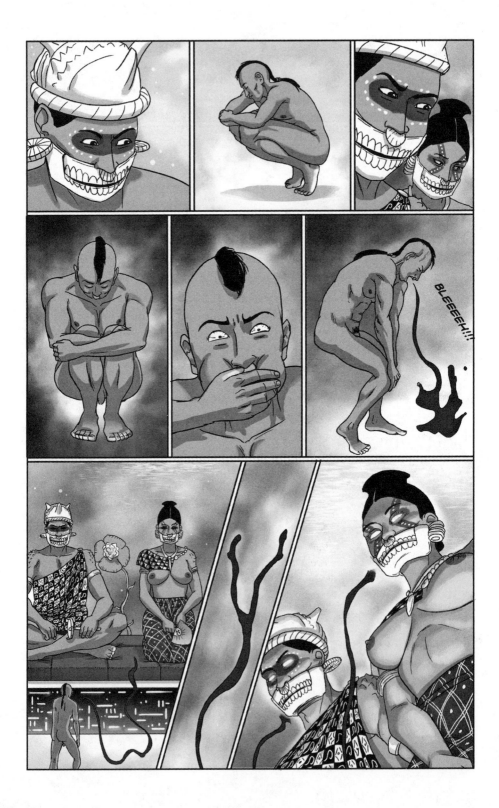

BLEEEH!!!

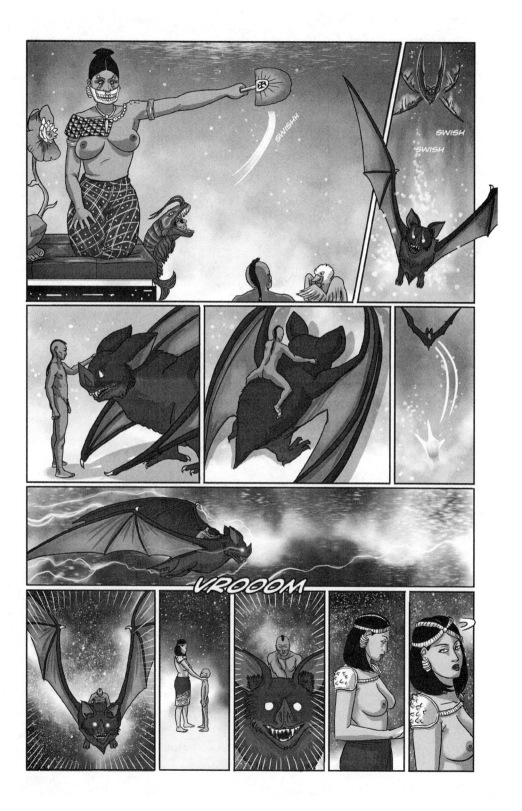

SWISHH

SWISH

SWISH

VROOOM

Spooky Action at a Distance

LAURA VILLAREAL

I can hear a black hole bend light outside my window.
    It sounds like a splitting seam or the space

between my fingers. I tried to sew my fingers together.
    Even bound them in leather & twine. But no matter
how I tethered them, they ripped & re-created s p a c e.

I bustle down the icy cobblestone, yelling:
    "I'm running a sale! Thimbles, needles, & buttons

    only 50 cents.
    I have a free class on cross-stitching
        galaxies every orbit of Charon."

        I've seen 10,555 moonrises & like every particle on Pluto
                I wait for entanglement to occur,
for my partner particle to spin & my own spin
to be determined by what particles call "spooky action at a distance."

    How many half-lives must I wait
    to find momentum?
    & what about on Earth,

people gushed about Pluto's heart
until they knew it was broken.

What is it about distance & separation
that causes universal unease?

I toss & turn
a ball of yarn in my hand, thinking of Pluto,
Earth & my partner particle probably light years away.

I mumble:
"I wish I could collapse into myself
like a black hole, then at least my gravity would matter."

Just as my wish enters the ether, I feel myself begin to vibrate,
begin to know my spin—
a tingling of recognition,
but then the feeling stops.
It stops & fades gently like
two ends of newly cut red string.

BlindVision

GRISEL Y. ACOSTA

They look like glasses to block the sun, the kind you get at the doctor, except for the flicker of light at the center of each lens, like a blue, green, or red signal, slowly dying, somehow lingering.

On a train it is peaceful, rows of bodies along opposite walls, seated, facing each other, but not seeing or interacting. All they see is the BlindVision. No bumping, no talking, a quiet ride.

It appears more chaotic in the streets. An expansion of the Blind-Vision includes SoniCo—Sonic Coordinates, or suits that move bodies to destinations without abandoning the BlindVision. The trajectory is set in advance. The idea is to continue being productive without ever feeling it, staying completely blind to anything uncomfortable. The lenses and earphones are left on throughout the length of an action or comedic film programme. While they watch, their bodies are placed on-course and driven. The technology originated in Japan. A forced inner-ear imbalance pushes their limbs toward, into, through their trajectories. SoniCo gave folks dizzy spells at first. Simple music or other logic-centered sound reduces that feeling. BlindVision, the pleasant film, makes them unaware of any unusual movements. Motion Sensor Surround System insures against collisions in the streets. Hundreds of bodies jolt, jump, twist and turn, speed past, run, skip, and come just-this-close, each movement made according to what the BlindVision demands. Reports show less than 0.01 percent collision. If the streets are especially crowded, the required movement might make them feel sore, but this is rare. Usually, they feel nothing at all. It's quite healthy, actually.

The film programme plays, the sound programme plays, and when it is over, they are at work or done with daily exercise or finished shopping. The latest marketplaces have items with set coordinates. BlindVision paid for this service. Many decide to have daily trajectories on file for easy access. They can plan set activities for months in advance. Some use BlindVision for recreation, too. After using BlindVision regularly, the moments without it seem . . . difficult.

More expensive versions deliver NanoBeautie. It was a way to sell something as cool. Models were the first to use it and once women saw the possibilities in beauty, it sold fast. As you watch the programme, tiny molecules enter the surface of the eye and regroup within the iris cells to form spectacular colors, lighted swirls of ultraviolet, copper, and infrared. Or, with the NaNose Cup the beauty minerals are breathed in. They connect to muscular and joint tissue and influence the bodies toward machine-like movement. Instead of jerking around in the SoniCo suits, these BlindVision users glide like liquid in their trajectories. They look like mechanized ballet dancers on the street for anyone still not wearing BlindVision. Earlier versions of NanoBeautie dried out, corroded the bodies. They had to drink oil, change their diet. The newer versions are said to be better, but there is legal controversy. With or without NanoBeautie, BlindVision is popular. Millions cannot imagine getting through the day without it. Facing mindless tasks, like taking the train, is easier with BlindVision.

This is what David uses his BlindVision for the most. He likes to believe he doesn't rely on it like all the others. Sure, he is in love with the purple-eyed siren who is a BlindVision addict—she moves like a doll in a jewel box—but he isn't her. He still faces the people at the grocery store, usually. One or two programme days doesn't count, right?

Today he arrives at the Spiralipo Oil and Preservative offices especially sore. He asks himself if he set the BVSpeed to *workout* or *stroll*. A view of the cloud in his desk computer shows *workout*. Okay. But he doesn't remember that. He doesn't remember much. Mirrors show an unknown man, aging, brownish-grey hair unkempt. David questions time. He looks at the date and it says "Monday."

He says to Fred, in the cubicle next to him, "I could've sworn it was Wednesday."

Fred, bespectacled and pudgy, doesn't look up from his screen and mumbles, "Uhhhhmmm."

David looks at the entire office from above his cubicle and sees the rows and columns of BlindVision light signals. Simple tasks at work can be programmed, too.

David reaches over and shakes Fred and says, "Look at my programme." David sends his BVCloud to Fred's BVCloud.

"Why?"

David repeats, "I could've sworn it was Wednesday. Open my data, man."

"Oh, sure, okay."

Everyone knows the schpiel. *If BlindVision causes any disorientation of time, physicality, or psychology, discontinue use and immediately contact the BlindVision Programming Headquarters for free product replacement and health care, if necessary.* Usually this just means there is a glitch in the programme. It is easier to give it to Fred, a whiz with such things, than to deal with the BlindVision people. David daydreams of creating a programme to deal with the BlindVision Programming people.

"I can't find anything wrong," Fred says.

"No? Then why am I so tired? Why do I think it's Wednesday? Am I gonna have to call BV?" David whines. "You know what a pain that is."

"Let me try something else." Fred punches in a few keys. "Well, I'm not sure about the Wednesday part but I think it's natural for you to feel tired if you've logged in over forty miles over the past two days."

"What?"

"It says here you've walked over forty miles within the past two days."

"What? That can't be right." David stretches over the cubicle top to look at the computer screen more closely, nearly teetering over the weak structure.

"I didn't notice it at first because the mileage is categorized under Shopping and Recreation."

"I didn't programme this weekend."

"The heavy programming explains why you're tired and it might explain your time disorientation."

"But I didn't programme this weekend."

Fred returns David's cloud data and goes back to work. David decides he'll deal with his programming flaw after work.

◆

David rings Lucent's bell. Lucent's bell sends a signal to her Blind-Vision. Her BlindVision calmly interrupts her recreational violence film programme with a female voice that says, "You have a visitor. Blink for reality." Lucent blinks, takes off her BlindVision, and answers the door.

"You look like hell," she says to David.

"My programme is flawed. I had to walk here without a programme."

"Shit, are all of them flawed? Is there going to be a recall?"

"No, no, I just didn't want to risk it."

"So, how are the masses, then?" Lucent looks out the window and stares below at the swarm of people swerving out of each other's way without seeing each other. She reaches for her BlindVision but then remembers David is there.

"Scary," he answers. "Those beady BlindVision eyes creep me out. Maybe I should just go natural."

"Ha!" She laughs as if a child were claiming it could resist candy.

"Will you have someone check my programme? It says I logged over forty miles this weekend. I don't know where I've been!"

"What? That's impossible."

"Do you understand now?"

"Okay, okay, don't worry."

She presses a green button on the Videogram and a bright white dot in the middle of the room becomes the face of a man.

"Helmut," she says.

"Ah, lovely Lucent."

Behind Helmut, rows of bodies are reclined. They have BlindVision and smiles on their faces.

"What is that? A Pleasure Party?"

"What else?"

"Send me the programme?"

"Of course. Is that all?"

"No. My friend . . ." she gestures behind her. David waves. " . . . has a corrupted programme."

"He should send it to BlindVision," Helmut says dryly.

"I *am* sending it," David interrupts, fully aware of Videospies. "She just thought you might narrow the issue."

"I'll be there at ten." The Videogram signs off. Lucent turns toward David.

"Well, since we're both awake . . ." She floats toward David, a Zamboni on ice, her vinyl-like crown of black hair framing a smooth face, smooth like moulded silver, and the silver framing her lit eyes, purple fire that spins in halos around black holes. She drops her red satin robe to reveal her hard silver-white body, perfect like a bumper on a Ford line, and David holds it, cradles it in his arms, the way a boy ages ago cradled the only metal toy he owned. Everything about her is NanoBeautie, from her whitened skin, which was once a deep brown, to her mirror-shine hair, which used to have curl. David knows it is wrong—he knew her before, when things were different, when she was herself—but something doesn't allow him to tell her to stop. It's as if a metal in him were drawn to the metal in her, as if they formed a magnet that distorted light waves, as if he could barely see what existed before.

Helmut arrives at ten. He programmed it. David and Lucent forget because they took a nap when they were awake. Lucent puts on her robe, answers the door. Helmut smiles at both of them, opens up a cloud and searches for David's data on Lucent's computer, and begins to whistle. David puts his pants on, touches the screen on his wrist, sends a credit programme from his cloud to Helmut.

"Thank you," he says, "for being discreet, too," Helmut says without moving his eyes from the screen.

"Sure," David says to the back of Helmut's head.

"Oh, no one will bother us," Lucent whines. She feels guilty about her naive Videogram talk. "We're just junkies," she continues, laughing, then coughing. She hacks up NanoBeautie granules with blood.

"Have you had oil today?" David asks.

"I always forget," Lucent says as she tries to blow off the question.

David walks to the kitchen cabinet. He grabs a bottle of vOILa, opens it, and repeats the commercial as he hands it to Lucent: "Stay smooth."

"Aw, I get bored with the flavors."

"I have a programme for that!" Helmut yells.

"Leave it; I'll owe you," David answers back.

"No problem."

Lucent drinks from the bottle. Helmut motions to David to come closer and then whispers, "You have problems."

"I have problems?"

"Your programme has been intercepted."

"What does that mean?"

"Someone else has been programming you."

"Who?"

"I don't know."

"It doesn't say there?"

"They don't leave a signature!" Helmut laughs.

"What are they programming?"

"That was the hardest part, to map your interception. You have been walking roughly ten miles out of the city perimeter, two times every weekend for the past year."

"A year!" David is sweating.

"Yes."

"Why did I only notice it now?"

"You're old. You can't compensate this new programme at maximum capacity anymore."

"Thanks, asshole. Where have I been going?"

"Here are the coordinates."

David looks at the printout. "I don't know this place. Who is doing this?"

"I don't know."

"I should report this, no?"

"David, listen. This is serious. Someone . . . who knows how to do this . . . is not an amateur. It is a miracle I was able to map this. We could both be in trouble."

"But . . . am I the only person . . ." David pauses. "What if this is being done . . . done to . . ." David points out the window.

"It is. It has been. Are you shocked? Honestly?"

"But I don't even use BlindVision that much . . ."

Helmut smiles flat, then says, "I'm leaving." Helmut taps Lucent on the knee. She is already on BlindVision. "Tell her I've left. I left something special for both of you in her cloud. No charge, okay?"

"Thank you," David mutters, but Helmut is gone.

David doesn't use a programme in the morning. He doesn't go to work. His office computer calls him and BlindVision Central to see if there is a flaw in his programme, but David cannot be reached. He is offline. And he is walking, roughly, ten miles outside of the city perimeter. David is surprised at how his limbs are used to the walk, but without the BlindVision, he notices his body perspire and this wet, itchy feeling is uncomfortable. He sees and hears all sorts of things he had forgotten, like wild grass on the side of the road, and screeching of grasshoppers and crickets. Every now and then, he checks the coordinates that Helmut gave him and he wonders if he is actually reading the map right. He remembers reading maps as a child, which then takes him to when he and Lucent were kids, in school together. Back then she was Lucinda Vargas. He didn't change his name, David, but he remembers having difficulties, too, applications for college that weren't looked at because of his last name, Rodriguez. Lucinda worked for a women's clinic that drew such rage, she had to change her name. One stalker found her and was so violent, well, the trial awarded her some money. She used most of it on BlindVision programmes to deal with depression. Everyone was angry then. What happened to that anger? Very few people are angry now. He realizes that he is lost in his own thoughts for the first time in years, which seems like getting lost in BlindVision, but not exactly like BlindVision. Something is different about this kind of lost.

The paved road stops, but he can see now where he is going. There is a structure in the distance, a grey building, long and wide, not exactly tall, but spread out over a great deal of land. That has to be it. His shoes are not suited for unpaved territory, but he can't stop now. He has to see where he has been going for the past year. The walk, in total, takes about three and a half hours. When he arrives at the building, he cannot see it from end to end, it is so large, but somehow a door appears. He wonders if the door would have appeared at any section of the building he first arrived at. Inside, there are no walls and there is a large metallic taste in the air, and a static, dry energy that surrounds him, but the sound, that strange jarring hum coming from rows and rows of machines he doesn't understand, is what is most disconcerting to David. He doesn't feel comfortable at all and turns around to leave, but he cannot find the door to exit. Overwhelmed, he crouches down and covers his ears. His skin becomes wet with sweat. He feels the veins in his arms swell and despite the pain, draws his arms around his head even tighter. The sound, the sensation in the air, the vibrations of the machines, all of it is strange and puts a weight on him that he doesn't understand. David looks around, up from the ground, and he sees a figure approaching, walking toward him, in the distance, a very blurry figure. His eyes shut before the figure comes into focus. Then, nothing.

When David wakes up, he is in a medical office, but somehow he knows that he is in the same place—perhaps that metallic smell—and he knows the person looking at him isn't a doctor. It is the person who was walking toward him.

"Hello, David. Sorry about the atmosphere. Very few of us are used to it," the person says. "Once you're around the machines more often, you get used to it." David's eyes focus and he sees a woman. Her look is collected, impressive, but not like Lucent. This woman is aware of everything. Lucent is aware, too, but has chosen to retreat. This woman is aware and is in control of . . . of what, David wonders . . . of people like Lucent . . . and David. David lifts his head up from the medical bench, turns over on his side, and vomits onto the floor. The woman presses a button and an attendant comes in to clean up the mess. She gives David a paper cup of water. He drinks it. His eyes are red and his breathing is heavy, but he tries to take in air in a rhythm that begins to calm him.

"David, I will get to the point. You know you've been coming here for a year. I'm a little surprised that your body is somehow not used to being here, but we are still studying the effects of withdrawal from BlindVision. We'd hoped that your trips would orient you to the space, and you *have* had a less jarring reaction than the others, given the fact that you participate less, but regardless of that, you are here and that is good. Most RL candidates pass out before reaching the building. A few, like you, are able to enter. Do you feel better? Are you ready to continue?"

David looks at this person, his breathing now steady, his eyes still red, a crease of concern beginning to form over his brow. He says, "Where am I? What do you expect of me? Who are the others you mention? I don't understand anything you've said."

"You notice when things are wrong, David. Most BlindVision users don't notice much beyond their programme. You avoid using it, at times. Most BlindVision users are addicted and have accepted addiction. You have been selected to be in Real Life, to see beyond the programme, to actually see the larger structure and work with others without avoiding contact. Your training begins today. Your desire to go offline and come here confirm your desire for something different. Are you ready to start?"

"Are you human?"

"Of course."

"Will I see my friends ever again?"

"Those weren't your friends. They were people you interacted with in between BlindVision."

"But Lucent . . ."

"Lucent is a hunk of metal now, you know that."

David cringed. "What would I do here? Where *is* here?"

"You know we're outside the city. Regarding what you'll do, it depends; there are a variety of tasks a chosen few of us take on . . ."

"A chosen few . . . you said that before. . . . what about . . ." David gestured toward the door, "why have we done this thing to everyone out there?"

"They agreed to it."

"They became *addicted* . . . meanwhile a chosen few of us could see the bigger picture, and now we just use them? What exactly are we doing? I don't know . . ."

"Yes, you do. You walked here. Do you know how many people we've tried to reach? Most are too unhealthy to make it. Others cannot leave their world. Will you be one of those?"

"Look, you're telling me right now that I have to leave everyone, without a goodbye. You're telling me I'm better than them, because I left, because I was capable of leaving. And you're telling me all this while I'm disoriented, which I think is manipulative. How can I possibly trust you? I need you to tell me what are we actually doing? What is this place and what do you expect of me? And why does all this exist to begin with? How can I leave that," he points outside the building, "without understanding anything?"

"David, if you look in your heart," she comes close to him, to his face, "you'll know exactly what I'm asking you to do. They work, we decide their work. They escape, we plan. They make no decisions, we make all decisions. Do you want to continue to let your body and spirit wither in that world, or do you want to be part of a world that is real? I'll remind you, your body made its choice long before your mind did. I suggest you listen to it."

David takes a deep breath. "I need a minute, outside, if possible."

She sighs, as if she's heard those words before. "Wear these." She hands him earplugs. "You're making the wrong decision. Maybe you're more addicted than we thought. "

"I haven't made a decision."

"Sure."

"What is your name?"

"Sone."

David nods and walks toward a door that Sone points to. He is immediately outside. He still does not understand the way the building works. He wonders exactly how much technology has advanced during the BlindVision years. He wonders how many people actually have access to that technology. David leans against the façade of the grey structure, which is completely smooth save for nearly imperceptible ridged horizontal waves toward the top, which David leans back to squint at. He moves his eyes back down toward the direction of City Center, thinks of Lucent/Lucinda as a child, brown, smiling in waves at the beach, a beach he cannot remember the name of. David thinks of ocean waves, light waves, sound waves, and the current of waves, how they control where everything goes. And then he thinks he remembers something: Lucinda reaching toward him, underwater, when he was caught in an undertow. Didn't she reach for him? Didn't she pull him up? BlindVision makes faint memories seem false, unreal. Yet, he feels the pull of the memory. His legs begin to move . . . away from the building, away from the overwhelming sound, away from answers he knows he will not like. He walks toward the Blind, toward Lucinda, who he knows is almost dead, like he will be if he uses again, toward an unreality he knows he will also not like, but he walks toward it, completely aware of his choice.

PART IV

When Dreams Awaken

The Chupacabra Next Door

ROXANNE OCASIO

There was one absolute law in Maryssa's neighborhood: come home before the streetlights turn on. And every child obeyed that law, until they thought themselves too old—or became too stupid—to follow it. They risked the punishment of mothers or grandmothers or occasionally fathers if they didn't return home at the appropriate hour and ignored the third-hand stories of Puerto Ricans fleeing as far north as Ohio to escape chupacabras. Bad things always seemed to happen after dark in Lorain.

Maryssa found herself in the midst of one such rebellious group, waiting for sunset. She nearly walked into Juan Carlos and Ben as they high-fived right in front of her face. "Take it easy, blanquito," Juan said in farewell.

Ben nodded. He was their neighbor, though Maryssa didn't know him well, so she was surprised when he started walking in the other direction with her sister, Jazmine. Maryssa considered going with them. She had a book report to finish, two different sketches of dragons she'd done during lunch that were begging for color, and a stack of quinceañera invitations to address to distant relatives. And she would rather be home, wrapped in a blanket with a cup of Abuela's hot chocolate than roaming the neighborhood with kids she barely knew.

But then she remembered why she had to stay.

"You scared, Prissy Rissie?" Juan tapped the flat brim of his baseball hat, flashing a crooked grin. "You 'bout to go home with the blanquito too?"

"I'm not scared." Maryssa fiddled with the crucifix around her neck. Juan always challenged her bravery, ever since they were in diapers. He was the only one she'd known long enough to feel the need to prove herself. "And you know Ben ain't blanquito, right? He's just light-skinned. Not all Puerto Ricans are tan, Juancito."

"Don't call me that!"

A car swished past and parked alongside the curb. Grandparents left their porches and went inside. Younger children raced past, giggling. Maryssa and Juan lost interest in trading invectives and turned with the others to watch the gray-violet sky grow darker. Streetlights popped on, tracing a line down one side of the road and then the other. They waited for shadows to crawl out and choke them, or for some kind of illicit activity to take place on the corner.

Nothing happened.

As they continued down the sidewalk, Juan launched into an epic tale of the fight he had gotten into on the bus. The names and places meant little to Maryssa, who attended a private school across town, and homework beckoned over the lure of being out after the streetlights turned on. She decided to slip away, but Juan noticed. "Prissy Ris—Dios mio, what's that?"

A creature had appeared at the end of the block.

It had silvery scales all over its body that reflected the nearest streetlight. Bony wings flapped behind its back, and a thin tail snapped against the sidewalk. Gray lips curved away from teeth that were sharper than those of the neighborhood dogs. Its nose was pointed, more like a snout. Ears perked up as the children began to whimper.

Chupacabra.

Juan shrieked the loudest of all. They scattered, jumping fences and trampling sparse gardens and weaving between cars parked on the street. Maryssa stood for a moment too long, frozen. Run. *Run.*

She sprinted after the others. The creature followed, wings beating loudly as she darted across backyards and stumbled over her own feet. Would that thing eat her? This was far worse than the dealers and pimps her grandmother warned her to avoid. Maryssa ran down an alley and slammed into the chain-link fence surrounding the local park.

Trapped.

The chupacabra blocked the entrance to the alley. She pressed her back against the fence, felt every individual link through her Lakeside Prep sweatshirt. The creature tilted its head, as if it could smell her fear. Maryssa swallowed, trying to summon courage instead. She opened her mouth to say something, to beg, but could only gasp for breath.

Then, it spoke: "Don't be afraid. I'm not going to hurt you."

Maryssa hooked her fingers through the fence and studied the monster. Its voice was deep, calm. "Those chupacabra stories are r-real?" she asked, finally finding her tongue.

"Yeah." It—he—pointed to the crucifix around her neck. "You're wearing a hunter's cross and you thought the viejitos made that shit up?"

"I-I just thought they told stories to keep us inside after dark." She sighed, loosening the knot in her chest. "So you eat goats, right?"

"No."

"No?"

"We drink the blood of evil men."

Maryssa almost laughed. "Wait, you're serious?"

"Where better than this place at night?" He extended his arms to indicate the neighborhood. The gesture was casual, almost human. "Which is why you need to go home, Maryssa."

She met his gaze. "How do you know my name?"

"Why should I tell you?"

"Because you're a freaking chupacabra and I'll tell everyone I saw you!"

"No one will believe you."

"Carajo, you're just as bad as Juancito."

He grimaced, his sharp teeth becoming less pointed. Blue eyes shimmered and faded to brown. Wings disappeared into his shoulder blades with a soft hiss. Dark hair grew onto his scalp. Gray scales melted into skin, the pale shade that had drawn criticism from Juan earlier. Clothes appeared when appropriate, much to her relief.

And the chupacabra became her neighbor, Ben.

"Well, I guess you're *really* not blanquito," Maryssa said.

"No." He sounded much more like a fifteen-year-old boy now. "I hate when he calls me that. Both my parents are from Puerto Rico. We're just light-skinned."

"And also chupacabras?"

"Yeah." Ben scratched his head. "I'm guessing your abuela didn't tell you that cross around your neck means your family used to hunt alongside us, fighting against evil."

She scoffed. "That only happens on TV. With white girls."

"Where do you think the idea came from?" He motioned for her to follow. "Come on, you should get home."

"Promise you won't eat me?"

Ben laughed softly. "No."

It wasn't until they turned back that Maryssa realized how far she had run. Nearly eight blocks, all the way to the park fence that separated one section of the city from another. She trailed behind Ben and examined him. No holes in his clothes, no silvery spots on his skin. Streetlights seemed to dim as they strolled beneath them. All the children had gone, leaving the occasional person smoking on a stoop. Ben made eye contact with anyone they passed, unafraid. This couldn't be the same quiet boy who lived beside her.

A dozen questions spiraled in her mind. Maryssa tried to find the most eloquently phrased, but instead asked, "So where did the clothes come from when you . . . did whatever it is that you did?"

"Transformed," he said. "They're sort of an illusion. I wouldn't get too close."

She stopped.

Ben grinned. "During the day I wear actual clothes."

Maryssa fell behind again, pulling up her hood to hide her face. "Does it hurt?"

"Nah. I'm more comfortable in that form. It's how I was born." He pinched his arm, and silver scales reappeared between his fingers. "Human skin itches."

"Do your parents . . . drink the blood of evil men too?"

"Well, yeah." Ben slowed his step, but so did she. "Sometimes we can get by on goats, but there aren't too many of those in Lorain. City ordinances and all that."

She twisted her mouth. "I thought you said you didn't eat goats."

"They work in an emergency. Goats are mean-spirited enough to count as sort of evil." They turned onto her street, and he cleared his throat. "You doing a science experiment or something?"

Maryssa jammed her hands into the front pocket of her sweatshirt, walking faster. She had said the same thing to her prep school classmates, the children who constantly asked her about any special holidays she celebrated or whether her parents had come from the island. *Say something in Spanish,* they commanded. *Cállate, puta.* She had nearly choked on her laughter when they oohed afterward. Was she making Ben feel that way? She chewed on the inside of her lip until she tore a hole in the soft flesh, tasting blood. The faint wail of a steel mill train sent a shiver through her body. Light peeked out from behind the blinds covering the front window of her beige two-story house. Someone was waiting for her, yet Maryssa lingered. "Do you have to drink it all the time?" she asked.

"No, it usually lasts for a while," he said. "If I go too long I get the fever, and that's just all bad. You go totally crazy. I eat food, too. Pizza and pastelillos are my favorite."

"Mine too." Maryssa brushed dark hair out of her face. "Do the people—do they die?"

"Yeah, but they're evil." Ben pointed to his eyes. "They change, like a sensor. Blue is the default. When they turn red—and only then—I'm able to drink. And only from the truly evil: people who have intentionally harmed another person, physically or spiritually, beyond what can be repaired. It's worked that way for centuries."

"Sorry, I'm asking too many questions." She placed her foot on the bottom step and turned. "Thanks for walking me home."

He nodded and exhaled, his skin transforming into scales. Shoulders slumped slightly, tail hung limp. Or did she imagine him that way? It was as if he mirrored what Maryssa felt inside her own heart: a sense of loneliness.

"Be careful out there," she added, "fighting evil and stuff."

He laughed and reached out to pat her arm. She cringed, instantly hating herself for it.

"Just don't tell anyone," he said, scowling. "I don't want to have to drink your blood over something dumb."

Ben flew away. Maryssa ran inside and let the door close softly against her back, then took the stairs two at a time without removing her shoes. She didn't think about being late, or hiding from her grandparents, or if her parents had come home from work.

Ben was a chupacabra.

And it was interesting and terrifying, to say the least.

She burst through the door of the room she shared with her sister, still attempting to calm her breath. Jazmine lay across her bed with her face in a library copy of *Wuthering Heights*. "You're so lucky Abuelo ate the last donut and made Abuela mad," she said, "otherwise you would've gotten whooped for sure. Why didn't you call?"

"You have the phone, remember?" Maryssa dropped onto the foot of her own bed. "And you came home without me. With Ben."

Jazmine set the book down. "He was asking about you, Ris. I think he might like you or something. Did you know he ain't actually white?"

Silver wings fluttered by their window, like the tail of a comet.

"I know," Maryssa said, and swallowed.

❖

Following her discovery, Maryssa began a new afternoon routine. For several weeks, she sat on the porch after homework to draw her graphic novel—though her grandmother preferred her to stay inside to avoid unnecessary trouble—and she stopped wandering around the neighborhood. But Ben and Juan Carlos walked by almost daily, even playing their pickup baseball games on the street in front of her house. Despite the warmer weather, Ben wore a hat and long sleeves, grinning at her from a makeshift second base. Why was he always around now? Maryssa's jaw clenched whenever he appeared, yet she kept drawing him into her tales of dragons and fairies and hunters of evil. His world—their world, a thought that tangled her fingers in the chain of her crucifix—drew her like ocean to shore. But she couldn't make herself rise from the porch, in direct defiance of her sanity and grandmother. Whispers of chupacabras in the neighborhood grew louder, but were quickly dismissed by viejitos who had, once, told those stories so eagerly.

Then, just before summer, Juan Carlos ran away. His family searched for him—they said the argument had been a misunderstanding—to no avail. The alliance of neighborhood children fell apart without Juan to protect them from older kids and gangs. A boy who lived three houses down sported a black eye and a sling, the result of an unfair fight. The girl across the street was forced to get a pixie haircut after someone had singed her long braid for fun. Worst of all, Ben didn't appear at random moments anymore. Others moved or were evicted or went to detention facilities. They were worlds away from Maryssa, though they lived on the same block.

One night, after the school year drew to a close, she decided to find Ben and ask him to help her find Juan Carlos. But her grandmother caught her, spanked her, and sent her to bed.

Another night, Maryssa waited until Jazmine fell asleep with a book and the television downstairs had been shut off. She listened for the sound of her grandparents snoring, watched her father leave for his once-a-week third shift at the steel mill, then dressed and crept downstairs. Was this really worth getting caught again, this time confined to her room for the remainder of the summer? Maryssa turned the knob slowly and pushed the door, letting it close on her fingers first to dampen the noise. She bounced on the balls of her feet across the porch, down the steps, and onto the sidewalk.

Ben sat on his stoop, his elbows on his knees.

Maryssa turned abruptly. "Why the hell are you sitting there like that?"

"Why the hell are you dancing across your porch like a ballerina?"

"Touché. Come on, let's go find Juan Carlos."

He shook his head.

"What, he didn't know you're a . . . ?" She gestured.

"It's more complicated than you think." Ben stood and transformed into his silvery skin, prompting her to look away. "Déjalo."

"But you told *me* about—you know."

"Because you're cute."

"That's dumb. And so not the real reason."

"Okay," he said, sniffing the air. "Because you don't let anyone push you around. I think you'd make a great hunting partner. It's in your blood. So how about it? I'll train you."

"For real?" Maryssa forced her gaze to meet his, still not believing the words coming from his mouth. "'Ta loco. My grandma would kick my ass if—"

"She wouldn't." His lips curled up in what appeared to be a smile, his tail striking the sidewalk. "My parents moved up here looking for the great hunting houses. That's the reason they're still visiting Ponce: they're trying to get the Council to accept human hunting partners again."

"We're not good enough for them?"

"Humans are kind of weak."

She balled up her fists. "How about I break your nose and show you how weak I am?"

"You wouldn't do that."

"Watch me."

"You're stubborn, you know that?" Ben laughed, a musical sound that dissolved the angry burn in her chest. "So will you do it? School's out now, so it's a perfect time to train. Oh, but you gotta wear sneakers, not chanclas."

Maryssa twisted her mouth. "If I say yes, can we look for Juan so the neighborhood kids stop getting beaten up?"

He sighed. "Fine. Come on."

They walked to the local park. Maryssa cringed when Ben lifted her by the armpits and flew over the chain-link fence. She stumbled when he released her, relieved to be let go. "Where do we start?" she asked.

"Run up the slide," he said, pointing with his claw to the plastic spiral.

Maryssa kicked off her flip-flops and ran. She had done this numerous times as a small child, when going to the park wasn't a euphemism for some kind of clandestine meeting. Her legs carried her up the winding slide with ease. "This is training?" she said, arms akimbo. "I've been doing that since I could walk."

He gestured as he spoke, his tail wagging. "Now, jump from there to the teeter-totter, use that as a springboard, and jump onto the swings so that you land standing on the swing. Don't sit on the swing. And don't fall off the teeter-totter."

She glared at him. "Seriously?"

And so every night, Ben trained Maryssa to be a hunter. They ran laps around the neighborhood to build up her endurance. She learned how to *really* fight—nothing like those private-school scuffles she had been in long ago—and was terrible at it. Ben encouraged her whenever she wanted to quit, being rather talkative for a mythical creature. He told her how the chupacabras had lived in peace among the Taínos, eventually blending into Puerto Rican society in an attempt to overthrow their European colonizers. A fascinating history that made Maryssa even more curious about her neighbor, the chupacabra. Yet during the time they spent together, she felt a weight on her shoulders that crept down into her stomach. What if Abuelo checked her bed and found her gone? What if Jazmine figured it out and resented her for not being included? Worse, what if she was a terrible hunter? She couldn't tell Ben these things; he was already critical of her fighting skills.

"Wanna go flying?" he asked her, on the hottest night of the summer.

Before she could answer, he looped his arms beneath her armpits and took off. Maryssa could see all of Lorain, aglow in streetlights.

Smoke from the steel mill curled into the cloudless sky, making her wonder if her dad could see her from where he worked. A police siren wailed nearby, then grew faint. Air danced on her cheeks and down her sweat-soaked shirt, refreshing her. She tossed her head back, gently hitting Ben's chest, and laughed. His touch no longer frightened her. High above the city, she felt as if she might really become a hunter one day.

When she remembered Ben was naked, her face burned.

They landed on the beach near Lake Erie. Maryssa could barely see, but Ben stopped every few minutes to pick up small seashells that dotted the shoreline. He handed them to her, careful not to scratch her palm with his claws. "The game was terrible," he said. "After Alvarez gave up that three-run homer, it was like they stopped trying."

"Abuelo was swearing at the TV." She pocketed the shells. "I finished that book you told me to read. The ending was a downer. I liked it, though. Very you."

He staggered. She glanced at him, but he shook his head. "I'm okay," he said.

"You don't look okay."

"I . . ." Ben swung out an arm to stop her. "Don't move."

She listened, but could only hear the lake lapping at her sneakers. They waited there for nearly a minute until the group of three appeared, using cell phones for light. Two girls and a boy, dressed in gang colors, and all much larger than Maryssa. The boy accidentally dropped a handful of dime bags and rolling papers onto the sand, then quickly scooped them up. They smelled like weed. Ben lowered his arm and backed away, growling softly.

The taller of the two girls grabbed Maryssa's wrist. "What are you looking at?" the taller girl asked them. "You 'bout to be sorry you came here."

Ben seized the tall girl's arm and flung her across the beach.

Maryssa met the shorter girl—who was still significantly taller than her—head on. She dodged and punched, then wrestled her opponent to the ground. A few blows to the stomach, one to the face. Exhaustion set in. She hadn't learned as much as she'd hoped; she was losing the fight. Shrieks echoed across the beach, entwining with Ben's low-pitched snarls. The others had likely seen him in the light. Maryssa took advantage of her opponent's wide-eyed reaction, shoving the heel of her hand into the girl's nose. She pushed the girl backward and finally pinned her. Ben landed beside them, teeth bared.

The girl passed out.

Ben helped Maryssa stand, then carried the unconscious girl away from the tide. "You did all right," he said, "only now you smell. Have we talked about chupacabras' sense of smell?"

"I sucked." Maryssa fell into step beside him as they resumed their stroll along the lake. She examined her scraped knuckles, then flexed her fingers. Pain shot through her arm. Drawing would be difficult for the next few days. "Where are the other two? Did you . . . Did you drink their blood?"

"Nope, they ran off." He pointed to his still-blue eyes. "They weren't evil, just mean."

"But don't you need to drink?" She dug her toe into the sand, discovering sore muscles in her leg. "You said you need to every once in a while."

"I'm fine, really. Want to train here for a bit?"

◆

No one questioned Maryssa's odd sleeping schedule during the summer break, but one afternoon Jazmine woke her up by shoving her out of bed. "Why the hell are you still asleep? We're going school shopping."

"Ben," Maryssa mumbled, without thinking.

"I knew it." Jazmine poked her in the ribs. "Just don't get pregnant."

And that was the end of it.

School resumed in early August; the big selling point of Lakeside Preparatory Academy was its extended school year. Maryssa marched off to ninth grade sporting her new trademark ponytail and a few oddly placed bandages. Ben continued training her, though he often insisted she take time off for homework and rest. She never expected to be so sore, to fall asleep during algebra and wake up in Jazmine's AP Chemistry class. Maryssa tried to focus on lessons, but instead found herself planning escape routes out of the room. Her grades slipped a bit. Abuela began making her a cup of hot chocolate every morning—the panacea of all Puerto Rican mothers—which drew complaints from Maryssa's younger brother. The disciplinary meeting came out of nowhere, though, when she'd been dragged into a fight involving total strangers.

Broken bones, none of which were hers, were a serious concern.

Her grandparents picked her up from school that day. Maryssa rubbed her bruised hands, sure she wouldn't be able to draw for a while. The ride home contained only one extra-long lecture about throwing away her future. When they arrived, Maryssa threw herself onto the porch steps. "¿M'ija, que te pasa?" her grandmother asked, sitting beside her. "Tell me what's wrong."

Maryssa's muscles throbbed, though not as much as they had after the fight at the lake. "Nothing."

Abuela stared at her.

"Nothing's wrong! I'm tired, okay? Déjame quieta."

"You don't tell me to leave you alone."

"I'm sorry." Maryssa rubbed her hands over her face. Should she finally confess? Abuela always had an answer for everything, maybe even this. "Fine. You know those stories about chupacabras that you told us?"

"You mean the neighbor?" Abuela put her hand to her heart. "Thank God. It's not drugs."

"You knew?" Maryssa faced her. "Why didn't you ever tell me they were real?"

"I did. You didn't listen." Her grandmother wrapped an arm around Maryssa's shoulders. "Nadie lo hace ya. That's why there are so many puertorriqueños in Lorain: it's as far north as we could get from the chupacabras and the politics. But people always have to start something, talking about fighting back." She clicked her tongue. "Déjalo. It's too dangerous."

◆

On a warm night in September, Maryssa found Ben hunched over the porch railing.

His silvery skin had paled to a nearly translucent shade of white. Sweat pooled in the creases on his brow and poured down his chest. Wings and tail drooped as if empty of bone and muscle. His strange blue eyes lost all of their color, becoming a sickly gray. How could this be the same person who had eaten dinner at her house twice this week? He was so thin. "I need to hunt tonight," he said, chest heaving. "Guess I've been slacking on the whole 'blood of evil men' thing. Will you come with me?"

"Y-yeah, but you don't look like you're in any shape to hunt."

"I got the fever."

"You said that chupacabras go crazy when they get the fever." She closed the gap between them. "Shouldn't we get your parents? Or maybe my abuela?"

"They're in Ponce again." He met her gaze. "I need *you*. You're my hunting partner."

Was this her fault? Not once in the last few months had Ben gone to hunt. As far as she knew, he'd spent all of his available time training her. Maryssa touched his arm. Scales blended one into another, a pleasant texture.

He was beautiful.

Ben handed her a small knife. "Take this. I probably won't have the strength to bite, so I'll need you to cut a slit for me."

Maryssa tucked the knife into the rear pocket of her jeans, but her stomach turned at the thought. He limped along beside her, and after a few blocks she yanked his arm and forced him to lean on her. She could feel his heart racing. The neighborhood was quiet, for once: no sirens, no car engines, no radios. They came to the chain-link fence that enclosed the park. The gate stood ajar, as if someone had entered recently. Ben rested against it, rattling the links. Maryssa withdrew the knife and flicked it open. "If I give you some of my blood," she said, hardly believing her own suggestion, "will it help? I don't think I'm evil, but I did get into a fight with—"

"No." Ben hobbled forward and pressed his hand to her cheek. "The cross protects you."

Maryssa fidgeted, unable to hide her blush. "Then come on, let's—"

"Once I drink, I wouldn't be able to stop." His hand slipped to the crook of her neck, fingers twisting in the chain as if to break it. "I'd drink until you were dead."

Her heart raced. It was the fever. He'd never suggest such a thing. Not him.

"Even then," he said, "the blood probably wouldn't do me any good, but . . ."

She swallowed.

His eyes flickered red. "It'd be better than nothing."

Maryssa aimed the knife toward his ribs.

"Well, blanquito, it took you long enough."

They turned toward the new voice, a familiar-looking boy in a flat-brimmed hat. He was flanked by two boys and a girl. A third boy, one that Maryssa knew lived around the corner, lay bruised and moaning on the grass beside the swing set.

"Juan Carlos?" She clutched the knife. "What are you doing here? Ben, what—"

"I told you," Ben growled, the words almost indistinguishable, "it's complicated."

Maryssa tossed a hand into the air, her jaw hanging. "Complicated how?"

Ben gave her a flat stare. "He's part of a group trying to wipe out all chupacabras."

"Well shit."

"Guess we didn't need éste." Juan kicked the injured boy onto his stomach. "And look, you brought Prissy Rissie with you. She actually trying to be a hunter?"

"Shut it, Juancito," she said.

"Don't call me that." Juan touched his hat. "My family didn't come all the way out here to live in shacks to have you damn monsters follow us. None of our families wanted that. We're starting a new alliance and we're gonna kill you all. And because of where we live, no one will notice. Y esta cabrona—"

Ben charged.

Maryssa jumped in after him. The girl came at her first, landed a solid blow to Maryssa's abdomen. She staggered, pain threatening to overwhelm her. Tears welled against her lashes. Was she not good enough to be a hunter after all? Ben's snarl brought her back. Maryssa planted her fist in the girl's stomach, kicked her opponent off balance, then shoved her to the ground. The impact from the punch burned her drawing hand. When the girl didn't move, Maryssa threw herself into the tangle of boys and chupacabra— though whether Ben actually needed the help, she couldn't be certain—and yanked Juan Carlos out by his collar. He launched a fist at her face, but she ducked under the punch and, remembering the knife, jabbed it up and into his stomach. Juan stumbled, then fell forward.

She was too stunned to retrieve her weapon.

Ben's eyes glowed in the darkness. He tore at the skin and muscle of the body beneath him until blood spurted in all directions, then he bent, snarling, and sank his teeth into the wound. It was far from a clean bite, like the movies portrayed. Maryssa crawled toward the fence and vomited, then forced herself to look back. The effects of the blood were immediate. His wings and tail snapped to attention, and his skin sparkled in the moonlight. Ben crawled over the dead boy and seized the next, who had just regained consciousness. There was pleading and praying in English and Spanish, then nothing. More ripped skin, another gush of blood. The girl awoke and scrambled to escape, but Ben's tail yanked her back. Maryssa vomited again, then wiped her mouth and crawled over to Juan. She pulled the knife out of his stomach, wiping the blade on damp grass.

Ben landed beside them, eyes still red. "Are you okay? Did he hurt you?"

"I'm fine," she said, though panic set in once more. "I might have stabbed him. Oops."

A smear of blood stained Ben's lips and chin, marring the shine of his scales. He buried his claws in Juan's side, holding him in place, and crouched to drink from the stab wound.

"You have to stop!" Maryssa pushed on Ben's shoulder. "It's Juan Carlos."

Ben's eyes flickered, red then blue, indecisive. "I can't."

"Yes, you can."

"No," he said, his deep voice strained. "The code. I can't defy the code—he hurt someone. He hurt you. His family wants mine dead."

"It's the fever, it's confusing you. He didn't hurt me beyond repair—look at me, I'm okay." She curled her fingers around the knife once more. Juan had passed out. "We can take him home, and maybe his family will keep him in line."

"His family wants me dead too."

"But he'll defend the neighborhood kids. He could change."

Ben growled. The muscles beneath her hand tensed, prepared to spring into action.

She yanked her collar and offered her neck. "Take mine."

"I'll kill you."

"Do it."

"No, I don't want to hurt you."

"Focus on that, Ben." Maryssa gripped his forearms. Fear dripped from her shoulders, pooled onto the grass around them. Did she really want this kind of life? Was she strong enough for this kind of life? When she considered going back to the pattern of school-draw-sleep, she shook her head. "You're strong. You *can* stop."

A cloud passed in front of the moon. He twitched violently in one direction, blanching, his breath caught in his throat. Maryssa reached for him, but he sank onto his haunches and pulled his claws from Juan's side. "I'm sorry," he said, eyes fading to blue. "I shouldn't have made you come."

"I'm admittedly a little freaked-out right now." She closed the knife and pocketed it, then stood. "We should take Juan home. His sister's a nurse."

They were silent a moment.

"Juan's right, you know." Ben scooped Juan into his arms, careful not to let his head droop. "They opposed us and then fled for a reason. I am a monster."

"No, you're not. You're complicated, yeah, but not a total monster." Maryssa stepped in front of him and gently cupped his face. "You're my partner. Next time, if I have to walk to the farms in Grafton and find you a goat, I will. Promise."

"I wouldn't make you walk." He smiled, transforming back into a human. "We'd fly, together."

An Adventure of Xuxa, La Ultima

REYES RAMIREZ

Xuxa, La Ultima, looks through her binoculars from a hill and sees a large, makeshift wall made of rotting wood, tin fencing, car doors, and other scrap material. There is a single guard holding an old rifle standing atop of it, clearly tired from vigilance and lack of sleep. Xuxa looks past her and notices some mid-size buildings, people coming in and out of them. *Small settlement, six to eight families, some crops, no livestock, not visible, anyway, minimal fortifications; could be overrun within minutes, easy, like this place never existed.*

❖

Upon finding any settlement of survivors in this wasteland, Xuxa, La Ultima, has to ask herself a grave question: *Do I let them know or do I let them burn?* It's a big question, absolutely, so Xuxa has this process, imperfect but available, where she is able to come to an answer.

First, La Ultima approaches their gates and asks to be accepted. If she's rejected, she lets Mil Fuegos's army of the undead, consisting of thousands of zombies, descend upon them. After all, how can she save any community if they won't even let her in? This has hap-

---

The Gabriel García Márquez quotes are from *Cien años de soledad* and "La soledad de America Latina," the dictionary entry for *Texas* is from Wikipedia and was translated by Reyes Ramirez, and the definitions of *estado* and *esclavo* are from the online Real Academia Española.

pened often. La Ultima moves on to the next settlement and only looks back to see the thick flames of a burning community dancing through the night sky.

If she's allowed in, La Ultima follows their orders. On her person, they will find: a handsome, pump-action shotgun (nicknamed la escupeta for how the short barrel spits out shot like an angry camel); fourteen cartridges (which look like burnt cicada shells); binoculars; a clean machete; cans of food (some expired, some not for human consumption); an extendable baton; a small vial of burnt sage on a string she wears around her neck; a full bottle of tequila (perhaps the last one since the agave died before any of this happened); a sewing kit; some torn books; and patches of leather (in order to repair the soles of her boots.) They ask her questions. She responds with half of her truths.

"Porfa, my name is [insert fake name here], and I'm tired of wandering," she says.

What she will not tell them, unless they pass her test, is that in a few days, Mil Fuegos and his army of zombies will arrive, knock down their walls, eat their people, raze their settlement, erase their history, and absorb their lives to increase the ranks of the undead army so that Mil Fuegos may continue his genocide upon the human race.

Upon being welcomed, Xuxa attempts to assimilate into their society. She takes notes. She evaluates these communities based on one question: Is this society looking to rebuild the earth with hope and love, creating a "new and sweeping utopia of life, where no one will be able to decide for others how they die, where love will prove true and happiness be possible, and where the races condemned to one hundred years of solitude will have, at last and forever, a second opportunity on earth"?

Usually when Xuxa is taken to meet a community's leader, a quick process follows where guards escort her to a stern yet concerned man who lays the ground rules for assimilation, tired yet tested clichés such as "If you don't work, you don't eat"; "Everyone contributes what they can"; "There are no free meals"; "This is not a democracy"; "Do as I say and I will reward you with stability"; etc., etc. If the society has *potential* to create a fair and just society, *though nothing is perfect,* Xuxa concedes, she will reveal more half-truths: "A man by the name of Mil Fuegos comes and you cannot stop him. He will kill you all. Do what you will with this information." Xuxa rarely finds out. She has never seen a community pack up and leave, which is the right answer. *You simply cannot defeat Mil Fuego's undead army; it numbers in the thousands, does not need rest, has no rules of occupation or engagement, and has no intention of leaving anything alive.* Xuxa can say all this, but can a society so selfish and self-centered as not to run away truly thrive? *This is what doomed us in the first place,* Xuxa believes. *Our inability to move on to save ourselves and not latch onto our ego or pride or traditions or history or delusions of self-worth.*

Right before Xuxa has escaped, prior to the arrival of Mil Fuegos's army, she saw communities anchor down (that is, if they believed her) and rev up the presence of armaments and patrols, all hands on deck to defend, etc., to stop the onslaught. It's never worked. La Ultima will look back in the night and there the flames will be.

La Ultima wasn't always this pessimistic. There was a point when she believed every community, ideology, and people had a right to exist, even in the face of the post-apocalypse. "We're better than all this," she'd say, looking at the moon and the stars, thinking past the ruins, the bones, the rotting meat, the dying people, the living dead. But then something happened. This is how Xuxa came to be La Ultima.

◆

Xuxa woke up shotgun ready in a car the color of an old turtle shell, stirred from sleep by a zombie trying to eat their way through the back passenger door, yawning and yawning over and over, black blood and old flesh smeared across the window, tearing away pieces of a face, exposing bone and molars. Xuxa imagined the life this one had before becoming this thing: perhaps a parent, perhaps a hunter, perhaps a member of a community destroyed long ago and now exiled into this horror of unliving. *What a fucking life. About time I got up anyway.* When she sat up, however, she saw that the zombie's torso was slathered in red paint, front and back. That's when she knew: Mil Fuegos's army was four, maybe five, days away. He has a system of sending out scout zombies like echolocation, measuring the time from when he sends out a scout to an area he suspects of holding a settlement to when he can find it. If he catches up to the scout, the less likely there is a settlement; if he can't catch up to it, then he surmises that it must've been captured or killed. *One or two times not being able to find it is a coincidence, three times is a certainty,* he'd say.

Xuxa put on her boots, shook her head violently to wake herself up, ate an apple she found from a tree nearby the night before, checking her map for possible areas nearby most likely to be fertile for settlements. The map is old, older than her, but it's not like anything could've changed since all this started. *He must be headed here,* she thought, looking at what appeared to be a suburban neighborhood. She saw a string of smoldering neighborhoods in this part of Texas, filled with charred corpses, half devoured, the rest perhaps joining Mil Fuegos's ranks. *Looking to clear these suburbs out, just as I suspected. About four miles ahead.* Xuxa then stared out the windshield at the road ahead with thick brown grass on both sides, so flat and dry in some areas that they wilted under their own weight, primed for a fire. Xuxa developed the skill to identify what can still get worse in the world, a dark art of the imagination.

Xuxa opened the car door opposite the one the zombie gnawed at, kicked the window, one, two, three times to break it, allowing the zombie to crawl in. Xuxa was already out the other door, walked around to where the zombie woke her, and waited. It turned around to exit back out the broken window, headfirst, to which Xuxa responded by slicing through its neck with her machete. Its head bounced pitifully and rested on the asphalt like a half-deflated ball. Then, another zombie stumbled up to the car from the grass. Then another, and another. Several zombies rose from the tall brown grass, rotten flowers unwilting. *Me breaking the glass must've alerted them. I should've fucking scouted better, but I was so tired. ¡No mames!* Xuxa, the person she is, knowing what she knows now, shouldn't have been this sloppy. Xuxa ran down the single road. Xuxa ran and ran. *It could take a few hours to get there. I have to warn them that he's coming.* Knowing what she knows now . . .

It's too late. They rose alongside the road she ran on in a perfect line, planted there deliberately. They snapped at her, snarling and crying, as though they needed to feast on Xuxa to suppress their agony. Xuxa followed the map from memory, hoping to reach the suburban enclave three miles down the road. The air she sucked in through her nose and blew out her mouth burned her lungs, throat, and nostrils. *Something is in the air. An untreated chemical spill?* Her head spun. A haze formed in front of her that her eyes had to fight through. Zombies kept rising, reaching out to her for a violent embrace. In her dazed running, Xuxa tripped over a hole. Many littered her path. *Is this all on purpose? Who is doing th—*A zombie had grabbed her ankle. Xuxa pulled out her retractable baton, extending it with a flick of her wrist, and bashed the zombie's head in with a flurry of swipes, the sound of dry leaves crunching underfoot. Xuxa rubbed her eyes and saw that the zombie was tied to a slab of buried concrete with a chain. *What is going on?* And then she heard it.

A car raced down the road toward Xuxa, headlights brighter than the sun. They saw her. She knew by the echoing cracks of gunfire piercing the earth around her with a whisper. Xuxa brought up her escupeta and fired at the vehicle, knocking out a headlight.

"She's armed! Flank her!"

Are they missing on purpose? Xuxa rose into a crouch and headed into the thick forest. There was so much gunfire and breaking shrubbery that Xuxa could barely hear men shouting orders, like ghosts speaking from another plane. She stumbled and couldn't move. A zombie held her in its arms, staring into her eyes, looking for something, mouth babbling like a baby. Xuxa looked back, the zombie's eyes fogged with pure whiteness. *Is this what everyone sees before they die?* The zombie's head explodes, a rosebud blooming into gore.

"On your fucking knees, now!"

A wall of flashlights shone in Xuxa's eyes, Xuxa herself not sure if she had already gone blind from looking into the ghoul's eyes for so long. She did as they said, crumbling to her knees.

"Hands behind your head!"

Xuxa did this. She felt someone approaching her, their energy harsh and angry. They put a bag over her head, Xuxa only seeing black. *Or is this what you see before death?*

"Is it one of ours?"

"I don't think so, sir."

"Take her alive! Can't afford to lose another right now."

Then, Xuxa couldn't think anymore.

❖

Zombies are razing the settlement. Xuxa is left alone in a small room by her mother, wearing her long black hair in a single braid, who leaves to do her part to fight them off. Xuxa can hear everything, the shooting, screams, the crying, the moans of the undead. She waits until there isn't anymore, for what seems like hours, just the crackling of fire and low moans. Xuxa's mother hasn't returned. Xuxa is scared. She steps outside and everything is in ruins: Mrs. Johnson's home burning, the community garden trampled, Dr. Lopez dragging himself to nowhere in particular.

Xuxa can't move. Dr. Lopez sees her and starts to claw his way to her. Xuxa still can't move. He is almost to her feet, wanting to devour Xuxa. Right before Dr. Lopez can reach her legs, a man reveals himself from the ether, taking off his hood, slathered in dead meat, with the rest of his body covered in dry leaves and hay. He steps on Dr. Lopez's head hard enough to crush it. Xuxa looks at the man. His eyes are calm, and he does not smile.

"Come, child, I will teach you to be invisible."

"What happened?"

"Justice, my child."

"Where's my mom?"

"That's two questions, babosa. There isn't any time for questions anymore."

"Help me."

"I will not help you. I will empower you to do all this," Mil Fuegos said.

❖

Xuxa came to, still only able to see blackness.

"She's awake," one voice said.

Another voice ordered, "Take her to my General."

"Yes, sir."

Sets of arms forced Xuxa to her feet, dragging her through opening and closing doors, outside and inside buildings, until they stop. The arms placed Xuxa into a chair.

"You can take the bag off now, soldier."

"Yes, my General."

The bag came off, and Xuxa saw an older white man in an ornate military uniform, speckled with medals and ribbons of varying colors and sizes, all shiny and bright, sitting behind a big oak desk, polished to perfection. The General inspected her, looked her up and down, never blinked. He opened his mouth to speak.

"At this point, you're already dead. We can do with you what we want. Shit, we could have killed you already. At this point, you're living on borrowed time. Listen carefully and consider what I am going to say to you. It's that or I have you killed now."

Xuxa looked back into his eyes, unafraid. Xuxa nodded only once.

"Good. We looked through your things. Found these notes," he said, throwing her notebook in front of her. "What are they for?"

"Journaling."

"Cute." The General snapped his fingers. Two guards came over. One restrained her while the other took her right arm and placed it on the desk. The General grabbed her pinky and pulled it back, far enough to strain her skin. "I think you know what's going to happen next unless you give me real answers," he said, looked directly into her brown eyes.

"I take notes on other communities I encounter," Xuxa responded, breathing in deeper through her nostrils.

"What for?"

"Whether I want to stay or not."

"Smart. Well, the way I see it, you've found the best one. This stronghold was established by me, the most stable, powerful, and growing settlement in the world. We're reestablishing a new world order. A white one, as originally intended until history was routed in the wrong direction. God made the world into shit on seeing how further and further away we strayed from His vision. You see, it's up to me to set history back on track for whites, for humans. God gave us a clean white slate, and we need to keep it that way. As far as I can tell, your kind are no different than those fuck-brains out there."

"What do you want?"

The General then lightened up. He leaned back in his chair and put his boots on the desk. "That's what I want to hear. Haw-blahs ess-pan-ole, right? It's in your notes. See, normally, when my men capture a spic like you, they either cave your head in and feed the dogs with your body, or assign you labor to do until you fucking die from it and post you up outside like all the other fuck-brains. Com-pren-day?"

Xuxa nodded.

"I need to hear a 'yes, sir,'" the General said. The soldier that held her finger stretched it farther back, almost to a breaking point.

"Yes, sir," Xuxa choked out.

"Good. Part of this new world for us is that we need a history before all this shit happened. The right history. You see, when we settled this area, we found a library nearby. Thing is, all the books we found were in all kinds of different languages. The last people here must've taken the books in English with them or whatever, but can you see my dilemma? None of us here speak that spic language. Don't need it for the new world we're building. How can you build a glorious future when you don't have the history to back it up? I could make it all up, but there's no need to. Whites built the civilization that held us for centuries before mongrels like you tore it all down. But I figured, God was testing me. I was right because here you are. God brought you to my feet to decode the books for me. That's what you're going to do. Translate the books into English, specifically the history books. They'll be brought to me for editing. Then that history will be the foundation that we base this new world."

He's a goddamn madman.

"Anyway," the General continued, "you can't escape. You saw how well we've got the surrounding area locked down. If you try to stall our plan with any shenanigans, we'll fuck you up. Understand?"

"Yes, sir," Xuxa said. *I need to buy some time for Mil Fuegos to come, at least. He'll ruin this place. Carajo, one tyrant for another.* The soldiers released Xuxa.

"Good. Set her up immediately. Paper, pens. No one fucks with her, is that clear? We need these books translated yesterday," the General said.

"Right away, my General."

"Don't feel bad, sweetheart," the General said, looking again into Xuxa's eyes. He reached into his desk and pulled out Xuxa's bottle of tequila, served two shots: one for himself, one for Xuxa. "Haven't had tequila since I was a young man, I tell you. Consider it an honor that you're helping the white world begin anew."

Xuxa knocked the shot back, never breaking eye contact with the General.

❖

Mil Fuegos rubs a stick into a tuft of dry grass, small strands of smoke rising.

"Mi nena, escucha," he says. "History has reached its ending point. There is no need to continue humanidad. According to los Aztecas, this is the fifth incarnation of reality. The previous four realities ended in horror: one with jaguars devouring every human, one with a mighty hurricane swallowing every person, one with fire raining down to consume all it touched, one with torrents of blood drowning the earth. The gods, in all their genius, ended our reality with the dead returning to feast on the living, our collective history catching up to confront us. You see, Xuxa, we were placed in this reality to carry out the will of the gods. That is why we leave nothing left. If it can be destroyed, we fulfill its fate. ¿Entiendes?"

"Si," Xuxa says.

They are both covered in dirt, blood, grass, and hay to mask themselves from the zombies devouring the bodies around them. One tears into the torso of a person like a generous gift, pulling out organs to stuff into their mouth. Other zombies converge upon the same body, fighting each other for flesh. Another zombie sits like a child, licking their fingers to soak up all the blood. Another zombie, all teeth missing, gobs on a sticky mass of crimson gore.

"Never feel bad for destroying a community. If it were meant to last, the gods would not have let us find them, mi nena."

Xuxa looks into his eyes. Mil Fuegos's fire starts.

❖

Xuxa sat in a classroom with four large tables, seats, a stack of blank paper, a cup filled with many different types of pens, and a pile of books in a corner that reached her knees. She'd never had access to so many books at once. Mil Fuegos had taught her how to read, but only let her choose from a specially curated list of texts that included religious materials, medical books, and weapons manuals. Whenever they encountered a library, Mil Fuegos set fire to it faster than anything else, the black smoke of burning ink staining the blue sky. A feeling of excitement overwhelmed her as she saw so many different covers for different stories by different people, even though they kept her handcuffs tight on her wrists. Many books were in Spanish, but some were in languages she didn't recognize; some used lines and circles, some looked similar to English and Spanish, even using the same alphabet, but the words were nothing she recognized. *How deep the world was before all this happened.*

"Hey, hurry up. Find a history book and get to work," her assigned guard said. A white woman, she had on desert camouflage pants, a beige shirt and hat, sunglasses, blond hair in a ponytail, black gloves, a belt with a walkie talkie and a spare magazine for her AR-15 that she held at the ready. *At least I can read and learn some things before Mil Fuegos arrives. It's just a matter of waiting.*

Xuxa picked up several books, carrying as many possible in her arms like a load of gold, and took them to a table. She read the titles of the books before her: *El manual de árboles locales, Ciencia de la tierra: octava edición, Las escrituras de Gabriel García Márquez, Enciclopedia mundial 1996: TUV, Atlas mundial 1983, Diccionario español, Obras completas de Frida Kahlo,* and *La historia de los estados unidos: 1751–1900.*

The Frida Kahlo book held gorgeous images of a woman who was a stag, portraits, and surreal paintings of pain. Xuxa nearly cried from their beauty. She then looked through the others, reading their table of contents, their first and last sentences. The Márquez one had several interesting titles in it. It began with a book: "Muchos años después, frente al pelotón de fusilamiento, el coronel Aureliano Buendía había de recordar aquella tarde remota en que su padre lo llevó a conocer el hielo." It ended with a speech: "Una nueva y arrasadora utopía de la vida, donde nadie pueda decidir por otros hasta la forma de morir, donde de veras sea cierto el amor y sea posible la felicidad, y donde las estirpes condenadas a cien años de soledad tengan por fin y para siempre una segunda oportunidad sobre la tierra."

Everything else seemed straightforward by their titles: the encyclopedias seemed to have short information blurbs about a topic, but only for the certain parts of the alphabet that the book held; the earth sciences book had a periodic table and an index; the atlas had large, colorful maps of places all over the world; the tree manual listed arboles like acacia, cypress, and yaupon. However, Xuxa kept running into a word she didn't recognize. *What the hell is* Texas? Xuxa had seen it many times in her travels, but never knew what it meant. Whenever she asked Mil Fuegos, he'd just say: *Puros mentiras. No gastas su tiempo con eso.*

Xuxa looked in the TUV encyclopedia, searched the T's, and found *Texas*:

> Texas es el segundo estado más grande en los Estados Unidos por área y población. México controló el territorio hasta 1836 cuando Texas ganó su independencia. La anexión del estado desencadenó una cadena de eventos que llevaron a la Guerra México-Americana en 1846. Un estado esclavo antes de la Guerra Civil Americana, Texas declaró su separación de los EE. UU. A principios de 1861, y se unió oficialmente a los Estados Confederados de América en marzo 2 del mismo año. Después de la Guerra Civil y la restauración de su representación en el gobierno federal, Texas entró en un largo período de estancamiento económico.

Xuxa then looked up the word *estado esclavo* in the diccionario as she wasn't sure what that meant either. She only found *estado* and *esclavo.* For *estado,* she read: "País soberano, reconocido como tal en el orden internacional, asentado en un territorio determinado y dotado de órganos de gobierno propios." For *esclavo,* she read: "Uno que carece de libertad por estar bajo el dominio de otra." *One who lacks freedom because they are under the dominion of another. A nation with a government built to take away the freedom of others? People killed to have something like this in the world?*

"Hey, what the fuck are you doing?" the guard said. "You haven't written shit!" Xuxa then went blind-white for a moment, a sharp pain pulsing from the back of her head. The guard had hit her with the butt of her AR-15. "My General was very clear with his orders. Translate the history books! That's it. Can your spic brain handle that? Which one is the history book?" Xuxa pointed to the American history book. "I better see you reading from this book then, and actually fucking writing. You hear me?"

"I need some of the other books to look words up," Xuxa said.

"Fine. Let's see, this one doesn't seem to be of any use to us," the guard said, picking up the Frida Kahlo book. She then threw the book to the ground and fired rounds into it, shredding the pages into slivers of colors. Xuxa's ears rang while she hid the Márquez book under another. *What you love most, they will kill first.* The guard's walkie-talkie spoke.

"Shots fired. What was that?"

"It was me, just teaching the spic a lesson," the guard responded into the machine. Xuxa still didn't understand what that word meant, *spic,* but they kept calling her that.

"Be careful. My General was very clear on not hurting her."

"Yes, sir." The guard put away her walkie talkie. "You, get to fucking work before your luck runs out."

Xuxa complied. She translated as much of the American history book as she could, discovering new, horrible things about the world before: slavery, racism, civil war, the Holocaust, assassinations, etc. *Nations were built to empower one set of people, then disempower others. Are we doomed to repeat all this?*

At the end of the day, the guard looked at all the writing Xuxa had done and took all the pages, placed them in a folder, and asked Xuxa to step over the handcuffs so that her hands were behind her back. Xuxa was escorted to her cell, but not before witnessing the society the General had built. In a way, it was perfect, the suburban homes painted with fresh coats of white paint, green grass, clean streets, denizens walking around unworried and with clean clothes. In the distance, she saw the giant wall looming. Xuxa couldn't see anyone who looked like herself, however, everyone white-skinned. *Of course. Just like in the books.* There were even crops in the far corner, guards with guns patrolling it with non-white people working the dirt.

The guard took Xuxa to a wall, one that wasn't as large as the outer wall, where there was a small opening, filled with guards and weapons, something that the area she had just walked through lacked. Barbed wire lined the top of this smaller wall, and guards were stationed at intervals along it. Another guard confronted Xuxa and her escort.

"Oh, is this the special spic?" the other guard laughed, grabbing Xuxa by the chin and shaking her head. Xuxa put her body's weight on her left leg, then kicked with all her strength with her right leg, driving her foot into the belly of the guard, sending him flying back. All of the guns turned on Xuxa.

"Don't shoot! My General has very specific orders to not shoot this one!"

The guns lowered. The kicked guard rose to his feet and slapped Xuxa.

"Bitch! Get her the fuck out of my sight!"

Xuxa, bleeding from the mouth, was then shoved past the wall where a woman seemed to have been waiting for her. She wore a shawl and had bright brown eyes, a little older in age and darker-skinned than Xuxa. The guard took off Xuxa's handcuffs and pushed her toward the other woman.

"She is to report to this station tomorrow morning at dawn. You understand?"

"Yes, ma'am."

"She's even a minute late, you're fucking dead."

"Yes, ma'am," the woman responded. The wall door was closed behind them. "Come on. I'm supposed to show you where you sleep."

"Who are you?"

"I'm Tierra, your escort."

"Tierra? Like Earth?"

"Ha. Yes. Like Earth. You are Xuxa, correct? You kicking that guard was hilarious. I like you already. But you need to be careful from here on out. I'm now liable for your actions."

Xuxa saw the community before her. It was squalid, the homes made of spare wood and sheet metal. No grass grew, just dirt and dust. *It looks like the bastards just tore down the homes here. Why? Out of spite?* Then Xuxa saw that the denizens looked more like herself, darker-skinned then those on the other side of the wall, brown and black and varying shades of both. There were no children or older people. Then, on one of the walls, bodies hung from nooses, knives stuck in their bodies with signs reading *Can't escape, Don't try, Failure.* Xuxa looked but didn't say anything. *I can see why Mil Fuegos wants what he wants.*

"Just ignore that. Those are people who tried to escape, but I heard it's awful out there. Got the place rigged to make it impossible to make it far."

"Yeah, I saw." Xuxa remembered the blurring of her senses, the zombies chained to their stations. "Is this how the General has all of you living? Whites on one side, not white on this side?"

"Yes."

"I've read this in the history books . . ."

"History repeats itself, yes. I know."

"How do you . . ."

"I used to be a history teacher, before all this."

"How old are you?"

"That's rude. Come on already, let me take you to your space and get you some food. We can talk more then."

Along the way, Xuxa saw people lying on the floor from hunger and exhaustion. But she also saw people crafting furniture, singing, playing games she didn't understand. *The General is simply recreating history. I cannot let him. What knowledge is worth learning that is based on the suffering of others? Is it truly knowledge if it is not accessible to others? This nightmare stops here.*

Tierra led Xuxa to a small hut with a single candle burning, a yellow glow in the darkness. Xuxa sat on the floor in front of a small table while Tierra served herself and Xuxa corn mush and water.

"I'm sharing some of my rations with you, so you enjoy every bite and sip of that for me," Tierra said.

"Thank you. What does *spic* mean?" Xuxa asked. Tierra choked on her water.

"Is that what they've been calling you? Damn. It's all right, they call me worse."

"I assumed it was bad. But what is it?"

"Let's just say it's not a nice word for people who look like you. A very bad word."

"Of course. Listen, Tierra, we've got to get out of here. Fast."

"Go figure. You listen, Xuxa. We've tried that. We've tried to escape, but things only get worse from there. You saw. We all love each other here too much to make it worse for others. Understand? If you try anything, they'll hurt us. You are part of something bigger now, so try and get used to that."

Xuxa wasn't used to this, her actions accountable to others. *Is this what a community is like?* Xuxa told Tierra everything: her orders from the General, what she read, Mil Fuegos's pelagic-sized army of the undead, and how close he was, perhaps only two days away.

"Holy shit. How do you know this person?"

"He raised me, taught me everything I know. Now I wander. His name, it means . . ."

"One thousand fires," Tierra said.

"You speak Spanish?"

"Si."

"But the General said that I was the first person to speak Spanish he found."

"The General is a piece of shit, but he isn't dumb. He killed everyone he caught speaking it. Some of us stopped because of that. He said that to you so you wouldn't know anything. Now that he's found all these books, he needs Spanish speakers. He's going to kill you after you translate the books, you know. In fact, he's probably going to kill me too after spending time with you."

"So you'll help me? When Mil Fuegos's army arrives, we need to blow open a hole in the wall to make sure we get out of here. You and everyone can escape through the opening as the soldiers deal with the undead."

"Blow open a hole in the wall? What the hell are you talking about?"

"An explosive. We can make one and blow a big fucking hole in the wall. That way, we can be sure this place is fucked."

"How do we make an explosive?"

"I saw they have green grass and crops on the other side. That means you use fertilizer, right? They also have cars, which means gasoline, si? Mix them and boom." Xuxa remembered all the times Mil Fuegos taught her to make explosives of various kinds using different chemicals and detonators. *Piénsalo como haciendo un pastelito,* he once said, pouring gasolina into a trough of fertilizer to blow open a gate.

"Yeah, but how do we get the mixture right?"

"I've got that part down." Xuxa wrote down the ingredients for a fertilizer-based explosive on a piece of paper with a pen she took from the room.

"It's gonna take a minute to make this."

"We have a day," Xuxa assured.

"All right. I guess some chance is better than none. Get some sleep. I'll get this out to the right people."

"The guards will be focused on Mil Fuegos's army, so I wouldn't worry too much about fighting. But you may have to procure your own weapons for the outside."

"We'll see."

◆

In the darkness of a night, Mil Fuegos shoots an arrow from his bow into a person serving as a lookout on their community's wall, collapsing like a song note. He then lights his next arrow on fire, Xuxa handing him a match and oil rag, and releases it into the wall so it sticks there. Mil Fuegos runs, and Xuxa follows. The vanguard of his undead army staggers to the wall in minutes, attracted by the light, banging on it, causing it to waver. Xuxa can hear the clamoring of people, shouting to get organized and mount a defense. But it's too late.

Xuxa hands over fireworks to Mil Fuegos, who lights and fires them into the air, an artificial constellation for his army of zombies to follow. Their moans echo throughout the night like ocean waves pulled by the moon's glow. Mil Fuegos unravels the rope around his waist and ties a grappling hook to it, throwing it over another section of the wall. He and Xuxa climb it to the top. Everyone is distracted by the horde smashing through the front gates, so Mil Fuegos and Xuxa assemble Molotov cocktails to throw at homes and people: sealed bottles of gasoline opened, oil rags stuffed in, ends lit, then thrown. There's so much light in this world, Xuxa thinks.

Someone sees them, points at them. Mil Fuegos promptly fires an arrow into his heart, pinpoint precision. Finally, Mil Fuegos fires an arrow with dynamite at the gate to weaken it. It explodes. The zombies enter in gushes, like blood exiting a deep wound. Mil Fuegos and Xuxa fire arrows at the legs of fleeing people, forcing them to fall and cry at their impending doom. They are immediately devoured. Some zombies tear first at their bellies and pull out gobs of organs. Others bite off fingers from hands. Still others ravage the faces as mouths scream until they can scream no longer. Mil Fuegos gasps at the beauty of his phantasmagoria, nose pointed upward toward the sky and nostrils expanding to profoundly take it all in. Xuxa watches neither in pleasure or horror. It only took an hour.

Mil Fuegos and Xuxa begin a sweep and find cans of food. They sit down to eat as the flames and zombies continue their work. With a spoonful of beans near his mouth, Mil Fuegos notices a family trying to escape. He points at them with his spoon.

"Termínalos, Xuxa." Xuxa nods and follows them.

She catches up to them and fires an arrow into the back of the patriarch, who falls like a tree. The mother and daughter turn and weep, begging Xuxa for mercy. Xuxa looks at them, emotionless. She doesn't want to do this, their cries pulling the tears from her own eyes.

"Ya sabía," Mil Fuegos says, walking in from behind Xuxa. "You are going to have to get used to this, Xuxa. Remember, the gods would not have put them in our path if they didn't deserve this fate." He pulls out his club. The mother and daughter put their hands up in vain.

The mother and daughter look at Xuxa and scream her name as Mil Fuegos walks at them, raising his club in the air.

Xuxa. Xuxa!

❖

Xuxa woke up, sweating. Tierra was snapping her fingers and calling her name to awaken her. Tierra's eyes were bloodshot and bags hung under them, as though she hadn't slept all night.

"We're getting everything together."

"Ok. Muy bien," Xuxa said, still rusty from her sleep.

"Hurry and get up before you get me killed."

At the checkpoint, the guards put Xuxa in handcuffs and handed her off to a guard different than before.

"Special orders from my General. I'm to take her directly to him."

Handed off and escorted through the main area of the settlement, Xuxa memorized the way to where the General stayed. When they arrived, the guard knocked on a large door.

"Come in!" the General shouted. The guard opened the door and shoved Xuxa in, closing the door behind her. "Have a seat. I saw your translations from yesterday. Very direct. That's good. I've got some notes for you. Watch."

The General pulled out the same folder from yesterday and took out the papers within it. He began showing Xuxa his editing process.

For example, the paragraph about Texas history that Xuxa translated earlier read:

> Texas is the second-largest state in the United States by area and population. Mexico controlled the territory until 1836, when Texas won its independence. The annexation of the state set off a chain of events that ended in the Mexican-American War in 1846. A slave state before the American Civil War, Texas declared its separation from the US. At the beginning of 1861, Texas officially joined the Confederate States of America on March 2 of the same year. After the Civil War and the restoration of its representation in the federal government, Texas entered into a long period of economic stagnation.

The General changed it to:

> Texas was the greatest state in the United States. Mexico tyrannically controlled the territory through oppressive laws that robbed Texans of their rights until 1836, when Texas fought and unilaterally won its independence. The US annexed Texas and both triumphantly defeated Mexico in a war in 1846. A slave nation under God, the US and Texas enjoyed prosperity and entered a long period of economic growth.

The General made other sweeping changes. The preamble to the Constitution now read:

> We the White People of the United States, in Order to form a more perfect Union, establish Justice, insure domestic Tranquility, provide for the common defense, promote the general Welfare of Whiteness, uphold a Christian God, and secure the Blessings of Liberty to Whites and their Posterity, do ordain and establish this Constitution for the United States of America.

Xuxa could have laughed at all this if it wasn't so real. *Who's to say it wasn't really like this? What good is this history other than to avoid it? People like him only wish to hear the history they've written. What does he even need me for?*

"You see what I want? I want you to do all this because it's important that your kind accept this history the most. That this is how it's always been, and how it will always be. Got it?"

"Yes, sir."

"Good. Get back to work," the General said. However, his walkie-talkie garbled, then said in clear words:

"My General, permission to report."

"Go on."

"We've found something odd. One of the undead has been found with something strange."

"Oh yeah? Spit it out."

"It seems to have purposely been slathered with red paint."

"What? Why the hell do I care?"

"Sir, this is the second one we've found this month."

I killed the third one. He's coming tonight! I have to let Tierra know.

"Just keep your wits about you. You think the undead have formed their own country or something? Don't waste my time."

"Yes, my General."

"General, may I say something?" Xuxa asked.

"What the fuck do you want?"

"I can get this process done faster, I just need an assistant to help me look through the books. They just need to know the word *historia* and separate the books that have that from the others. That's all. Just give me Tierra since she knows me already."

"Fine. Just get to work. Everyone is being a pain in my ass today. Lucky I got this." The General pulled out Xuxa's bottle of tequila from his desk and waved it to mock her.

You will die soon enough, pendejo.

In the room full of books and blank paper, Xuxa, hands laid on the table before her in handcuffs, waited for Tierra to arrive. *Oh fuck, he's coming, he's coming, he's coming. We'll have to mix and detonate on-site for this to work fast enough. Let's hope her people can get the stuff quickly in time.* There was a knock on the door.

A guard brought Tierra blindfolded and in handcuffs at the end of a rifle. She looked angry. The guard removed the blindfold and handcuffs slowly, methodically. Tierra walked over calmly.

"Yes, ma'am? How can I help you?" she said, as though she didn't know Xuxa. The guard pulled up a chair at the front of the room and sat, AR-15 resting in her lap.

Through clenched teeth, Xuxa responded, "Sit down, please," setting a chair next to herself.

"What the fuck is going on?" Tierra asked.

"He's coming tonight!" Xuxa said, squeezing Tierra's thigh.

"¿Pues, que chingado vamos hacer aquí?" Tierra coughed.

"Hey, what's with all the whispering?" the guard piped in.

"Tenemos que hacer algo ahorita," Xuxa stressed.

"We need time. We have people getting your materials."

"All right, I'm coming over there!" the guard shouted, AR-15 at her shoulder.

"Nothing, nothing!" Tierra yelled back, hands up, palms facing the guard. Xuxa sat silently.

The guard shouted commands to Tierra, "On your knees! Hands behind your head! Now!" Xuxa noticed it was the white woman from yesterday. Tierra followed the commands, stared at Xuxa with wide eyes to compel her to do something. "You, spic! What is going on?" Her rifle was situated at the back of Tierra's head.

Xuxa weakly pointed to the stack of books in the far corner. The guard turns her head to see. "Th-the book. It—It's—"

Tierra turned around, grabbed the end of the rifle, and pushed away from herself. Xuxa stood and punched the guard in the throat. The rifle fired three rounds into a corner. Tierra wrestled the AR-15 from the guard's hands while Xuxa wrapped her handcuff chain around the neck of the guard, fell backward, and pulled tight, her knees in the guard's back. Xuxa pulled and pulled. The guard choked, spat blood, and tried to loosen the grip of the chain with her fingers, legs flailed like the tail of a breathless fish. Tierra pointed the rifle at the guard but let Xuxa finish what she started. Xuxa pulled until the flailing weakened, spasmed, then stopped, before she let go. Xuxa lifted her arms and kicked the guard off herself, spitting at her body immediately afterward. The radio talked.

"Shots fired. What's going on in there?"

"What the fuck was that?" Xuxa asked as she caught her breath.

"I had to do something! I had no other choice! The bitch was gonna shoot me!"

"Give me the walkie-talkie!" Tierra wrangled the walkie-talkie from the dead guard's belt and threw it to Xuxa.

"I repeat, shots fired. Is everything okay?" the radio asked. Xuxa breathed in deeply and did her best imitation of the guard, rubbing the speaker of the walkie-talkie. "Had to teach the spic another lesson."

"Okay. Be sure to turn in your talkie for repair."

"Yes, sir."

The radio stopped speaking.

Xuxa and Tierra looked at each other, surprised they had fooled the soldiers.

Tierra broke the silence. "What now?"

"How long 'til we get the gas and fertilizer? We'll have to mix and detonate on-site. It'll have to be quick and rough."

"I don't know! You said we had 24 hours!"

"I said we had a day! Never mind. We'll have to wait until Mil Fuegos makes his move. The guards will be occupied."

"Are you sure?"

"We don't have any other option. We'll have to sit by the radio and listen and move fast." Xuxa searched the guard's body and found a pistol, a spare magazine for the AR-15, and the keys for her handcuffs, which Tierra removed. Tierra handed the rifle over, but Xuxa insisted Tierra take the pistol. They both sat and waited.

"I can't believe it. This is going to end," Tierra laughed, almost crying.

"I hope so."

"No. It must end, Xuxa. It must," Tierra pleaded, looking deeply into Xuxa's eyes.

Xuxa picked up a book and weighed it in her hands. "Did you know that some people die making sure certain ideas don't take hold, Tierra?"

"Yes. I know."

"I promise you, nothing of that mad man's ideas will leave here tonight. Even if I have to die," Xuxa said. She looked at the book in her hand and saw it was the Márquez book, the one she made sure to hide. *Una nueva y arrasadora utopía de la vida, donde nadie pueda decidir por otros hasta la forma de morir . . .* Xuxa ripped the book in half by the spine, since it was so big, and secured both halves in her waistband to take with her. They waited and listened for hours. The radio shouted.

"Alert! An arrow has been shot at the main gate. It seems to be on fire. Investigating."

"There he is," Xuxa said. She rose to her feet and readied her rifle.

When they left the building, Xuxa could already hear the familiar moans of Mil Fuegos's army. Xuxa and Tierra hid and watched as soldiers ran to the front gate, rounds firing. *There's no coordination among the volleys. Mil Fuegos has only sent his vanguard. We have little time to spare.* "Let's go," Xuxa said.

They ran to the inner wall that separated the white section from the non-white section. Xuxa aimed, fired, and killed the guards keeping the esclavos in, firing in a cadence so that each shot rang like a tolling bell.

Tierra opened the wall's door, entered, and everyone gathered around her.

"We need the gas and fertilizer now!"

"This way!" someone yelled. *Everyone seems to know what's going on. Is this what a good community is? But really, how many of those can there be left?*

The community led Xuxa and Tierra to the fertilizer and gas. *It still needs to be mixed.* Fireworks exploded in the night sky. *The next wave has begun!* The night moans deepened. Xuxa felt her breath get heavier.

"Let's take this to the back wall, before Mil Fuegos gets his army back there!" Xuxa yelled. They all ran together. *Am I part of something?*

Xuxa didn't waste any time as she mixed the gas and fertilizer in the exact proportions Mil Fuegos showed her. *Como un pastelito . . .* She then instructed everyone to stand far back, far, far back, pouring a trail of gasoline behind herself to light like a detonator.

"Everyone, get down!" Xuxa screamed as she lit the gas trail, flaring in a line, a shining path.

The explosion was grand. The air was knocked out of everyone's lungs. They recovered to see a hole in the wall, out into the black night.

"Come on, let's get out of here," Tierra said, grabbing Xuxa by the arm. Xuxa yanked herself from her grasp.

"You have to go, Tierra. Go as far away as you can. Forget this place," Xuxa pleaded. "I have to go back and make sure the General is dead. I promised." Tierra didn't waste time trying to change Xuxa's mind. She only looked into Xuxa's eyes for a single moment, long enough for the two of them to know what it meant: *Good luck.* She handed Xuxa the pistol and said, "I think you'll need this more than me." Tierra then turned around and headed out, the last time Xuxa would see her. *Start something new, something better.*

Xuxa picked up the last of the gas and fertilizer. She held the rifle in her right hand and her eyes looked forward. Xuxa ran toward the white section of the settlement, ready to blow it to hell. Her body shook with fatigue and extra weight. Soldiers held the line near the front gate, firing in more coordinated efforts. They used the front gate as a funnel to control the flow of Mil Fuegos's army. Xuxa saw the outer wall shaking. *It normally doesn't take this long for Mil Fuegos's army to break through.*

Xuxa stationed herself at the bottom of the shaking wall. *What comes up must come down.* She mixed the ingredients again, pouring them as though laying out a snake's large corpse. *Here I am, doing Mil Fuegos's dirty work. At what point do I get to make my own path?* Xuxa didn't have the gasoline to make a trail long enough to light it from a safe distance. *I have to*—Xuxa looked around, then up. There he was. Mil Fuegos looked down upon her from atop the wall, staring through her. He wore the head of a stag, the horns piercing upward toward the night sky, and a bulletproof vest, his face shrouded in a damp rag. Mil Fuegos picked up his bow and pulled an arrow from his quiver in a seamless motion. Xuxa ran as quickly as possible, for she knew what followed. She could see him in her mind's eye lighting the arrow on fire with an oil rag and match, aiming at the mixture, pulling the arrow back, and letting go. *Boom.* Xuxa fell forward and let the remnants of the blast wash over her body, her lungs unable to take in air for a moment.

Xuxa took a moment to breathe, her torso muscles aching from expansion, and rolled onto her back. She looked into the sky, coughing and sucking in as much air as her mouth could swallow. Mil Fuegos was gone. *Back to his chaos.* Zombies piled in through the new hole, hungry and desperate. A zombie approached Xuxa, but she mustered enough strength to kick it over, following that up with a stomp to its skull. She rose to her feet and ran. Soldiers began firing at her. Xuxa noticed that she had dropped her rifle in her sprint, only having a pistol. *This is more than enough to kill that pendejo.* Xuxa ran for cover. The shooting accelerated, and she saw that the zombies overran the soldiers from two sides now.

She lugged her body to the General's office, as though drunk. *Everything hurts.*

She approached the big door but didn't knock. He was there, sitting at his desk, drinking Xuxa's tequila.

"You're here," Xuxa said, surprised. "You know, other men like yourself try to make a run for it."

"Only defeated men run," he said, sniffing the tequila's aroma from the top of his glass. "You're a fool if you think I was the only one. A nation like this isn't simply alone. I exist because it works, because there's so many of us." The General leaned his head back to swallow the tequila shot. Xuxa shot him in the heart immediately. *Then it'll be my life's mission to kill the rest of your kind.*

She retrieved her bottle, now only half left, and searched his desk. The folder was there. Xuxa held the translated pages and dropped them outside a window. Some floated away into the ether. Other pages fell into flames, the burning edges crinkling like a dying spider.

Xuxa looked around. Every building in the settlement burned, homes collapsed under the heat, zombies devoured the bodies with large chomps and deep swallows. This was the highest number of undead Xuxa had seen. No one alive. Except for Mil Fuegos, who sat nearby with a stack of books, knees almost to his chest, reading one that seemed to have engrossed him as he rubbed his chin. He looked up, as though he felt Xuxa's eyes on him. He smiled and waved.

"I saw you blow that wall open! Just like I taught you! Don't you miss this, Xuxa?" he yelled, spinning in a circle, arms spread open like a dervish.

Xuxa stepped back, pistol at the ready. *He's coming.* Mil Fuegos leapt like the stag he wore, making his way into the General's office. Xuxa kept her pistol aimed at his face.

"¿Que haces aquí? Are you following me, nena?"

"I'm going to kill you."

"Ha. Going around thinking there's still something to be saved, thinking on your own and all that mierda," Mil Fuegos said, "Why, you must be the last real person alive, eh? Hope is a thing of the past. Créeme Xuxa, eres la ultima."

Xuxa squeezed the trigger. Mil Fuegos moved in time to dodge the bullet and wrestled the gun from her hand, pushing her backward. He aimed the pistol at her, hesitated to shoot.

"You saw what this place was. You'll join me again, soon enough. You simply aren't ready," he said, as though placing a curse. Mil Fuegos kept the pistol drawn at Xuxa while backing up toward the window he leaped in from. He fell backward, laughing.

There's the General's model for the world, then there's Mil Fuegos's. Men only live for the past. How do we begin the world anew for everyone? I don't know. I don't know. I don't know.

Xuxa escaped the settlement, witnessing once more the zombies devouring bodies, the wet chewing of flesh and wet sucking of bone, quietly piercing the skulls of any that approached her with a loose strand of rebar. Xuxa walked and walked, book in her belt. She picked up a shotgun off of a dead soldier along the way, her new escupeta, but didn't fire it out of fear of attracting the undead. She escaped the settlement and slowly made her way up a hill. Xuxa looked backward at the horizon, lit with a roaring fire. Tears leaked from Xuxa's eyes. Her tongue tasted salt.

I'll be ready for you one day, Mil Fuegos.

❖

Xuxa, La Ultima, approaches the tired guard holding the old rifle standing atop the makeshift wall. The old rifle points in her direction, slightly shaking, the barrel moving like a bird's eye.

"Who—who are you?"

"Porfa, my name is Alondra, and I'm tired of wandering," Xuxa says, laying down her escupeta and machete at her feet. "None of the undead are too close by. I escaped them about three miles back." The guard lowers their rifle and calls out to others, now stepping down to disappear behind the wall. The makeshift wall clumsily opens, the bottom scraping along the dirt. A woman with long black hair, dark skin, dressed in dirty jeans and a brown shirt runs out with a bottle of water, worry in her eyes.

She asks, out of breath, "Are you all right? How long have you been out there? Please come in, Alondra." Her voice reminds Xuxa of Tierra, whom she hadn't seen since that collapsing night years ago.

Why are they so welcoming? Perhaps they are naive, perhaps they've been wanderers too. Whatever the reason, Xuxa, La Ultima, has hope.

Night Flowers

STEPHANIE ADAMS-SANTOS

It is easier not to speak of how we got from there to here. It is easier not to speak. But the story is there even in silence.

It was a month that should have been winter. We should have been cozied before a hearth lit by a warm fire. Instead, the fire was everywhere. It raged behind us, inside of us. To escape it, we had to escape ourselves.

On a Tuesday, we left behind the burning casita. The car, the phone, the decency of a warm shower or even a simple bar of soap, a red lip, cafecitos at daybreak and sundown, leggings, aspirin, hours cozied in the glow of the television—these things too burned behind us. By Friday that week it was all undone . . .

I want to tell you more, but there's no point. The pendulum had simply swung. One day you are *there*, the next moment you are *here*. Things happen in between that we can't account for. We are creatures of strangely supple minds. We adapt.

One day, crawling over a stack of corpses, I found myself searching all the pockets. Most were empty, but here and there I would find something of use to me—a pocket knife or a rosary. Rosaries were useful to me for a while. I began to collect them. I liked to hear the twinkling of the little christs bumping against each other around my neck. But in time, I left them behind.

One by one the others lay down their things too. Antonia. Kika. Marisol. Gracielita. Li. Faustina. Yolanda. One by one they would sleep and not come up. My mother, my sisters, my aunts. Antonia. Kika. Marisol. Gracielita. Li. Faustina. Yolanda. My beginnings and my end.

Somewhere behind me, I swear to you, there is a path made of rosaries . . .

After everything, it was just the two of us. Mariano and I, as if alone in the bedroom again. We walked in silence.

Incomprehensible distance. It took a long time to move away from the putrid graveyard of the city and its endless sprawl. We walked and walked. Our feet destroyed and rebuilt themselves in thick, rubbery layers, over and over. We lived and died by our feet. Walking was as breathing. *To walk is to breathe.*

I looked down one day and noticed my feet were wide as hands, pads thick as a dog's. Deep down, I think, we were both hoping to find a city beyond all this. But we never spoke a word of our hopes.

After some time, the path became soft and the colors around us had changed. In this new place it was dense and green and quiet. We started speaking again. It didn't take long for Mariano to admonish me.

He pointed out that I had become hard and apart from him. He said my eyes looked like two clams that had dug themselves deep into a tunnel and only peered back at him through the darkness. He said that my mind was slow and loose as an empty net floating aimlessly in the sea. He said I was lost. He said it in more crude terms, but he was right.

I had become a full-time somnambulist. It didn't matter if I was awake or asleep. My eyes would disconnect from their sockets, it seemed, and travel on ahead of me. They turned grayer and grayer, like a fog. Like my eyes had been replaced with a shark's.

At the horizon's edge my gaze teetered and dropped like two leaded anchors. And I dragged along like an empty skiff, pulled toward some vague place of light.

Who knows how long I lived like this. I didn't count the days.

And then one morning I heard the singing of insects. Something living and warm had returned and had begun to swim among my primitive thoughts. My clam eyes crawled back to the front of my face. The fog lifted. Somewhere, a lizard flitted between shadows. Something stung me on the thigh and I bled. Even the constant presence of Mariano became as tolerable as anything else. I had life again, and wept with joy.

As a child I thought of the jungle as a place of horrors. When I was six I had been bit badly by an iguana and on another occasion had nearly lost an eye to a black, thorny branch as it whipped me across the face. Mosquitos had often feasted on my limbs and long after they'd gone I still felt their proboscides as phantom instruments of torture, harrowing my nerves. Everything stung in the jungle. My childhood impression had been one of punishment and torture.

But here it was, thick and undisturbed, almost lewd in its flowering. As we slowly made our way in, the plants seemed to bend a path for me and smile softly with velvet green light and gentle articulations. I felt a vague sense of home, dare I say contentment?

But by then I knew nothing could be trusted, and was wary. Mariano rejoiced. He said our tormented journey was at some kind of an end, that we had escaped death after all.

Just as stillness came to perch on the tip of my being like a hummingbird, just as I nearly pronounced its name into the world and into myself—it was then, of course, that death did in fact come. Not for me, but for him—though I suppose when death visits one, it visits all.

The following morning after our arrival in the jungle, not knowing any better, I rose early by myself and meditated on the scarred, lurid flower of a tree before cutting down its fruit. I went back and touched Mariano's shoulder lightly. *Plátanos,* I said.

A la.

Mariano was rigid and cold. It was as though my hand had been pierced by a thorn and retracted by its own accord. I compelled myself to tap him again, more playfully, as though it were only a joke. But once again I had the sensation of having touched something sharp and forbidden. And still he did not stir, not one little bit.

An excruciating needle of cold traveled from my fingertips to my neck and into my brain, where it fertilized the thought of a corpse. The word opened up, red and swollen like the plátano flower: *corpse*—then a weight fell down through the whole length of my body to the very bottoms of my feet, where it stayed, tingling in the soles like thick slabs of meat. A flat light fell through the leaves, the same matte finish of a napkin.

Staring off into nothing, I buffered myself against these thoughts and arranged the uneaten plátanos on a broad leaf just in case he woke. I wouldn't dare have breakfast without him. In retrospect, it had not ever occurred to me that I could leave Mariano's side while he was alive, so neither did it occur to me then that I could leave his corpse.

Over and over, like the surf swallowing and spitting up one's feet at the edge of the sea, burying them each time more deeply in the sand, the truth of his death persisted, a cold call-and-response: *had he really died*, yes he had, *had he,* yes he had. Over and over.

Had he really died? Yes, he had. He had.

Ay, Mariano. How could that imponderable life simply stop before the end of its sentence? I had never imagined such a banal possibility for my uncle as death. Though I had witnessed the unspeakable horrors of the cities, all that stinking and screaming and then the putrefied silence that came afterward, the disease, the walking over Them with our scarves pressed against our noses and mouths, gagging . . . I had never thought, not once, that *he* of all people was capable of leaving his body on the earth to rot.

I pissed once several dozen yards away and ate half of a plátano with guilt before retching it up, but otherwise I remained there the whole day beside him, eyes dug back into their tunnels of dark.

At last the moon came and laid her gray-green mantle over us like the thin sábana my mother used to slide over me at night. I shivered slightly, feeling the phantom weight of plátano still undigested in my gut, and could taste it still in my teeth, and the whole impenetrable scene soaked freshly into my eyes but this time with a shade of green.

Once again the fact of the matter was made plain. Plain as a hammer shunting a nail into its hole: *my uncle is dead.*

I noticed that the air had begun to feel inadequate, as though it were secretly pouring its substance into some other place. I feared that soon it would be completely and unbearably empty, not just of oxygen but of *ether*—or something else I couldn't explain, something vital.

I decided to hum a song to fill up the space. I wondered what to sing. Something stirred in my memory, some vague and clunky shape of a tune, like an animal or a drunk clambering through the streets at night. It had been too long since I last sang. I couldn't recall anything more than a few disconnected fragments from my childhood. Lacking the vital energy to create something new, I lay down near Mariano's body the way he always liked, facing him, and pretended we were both asleep like I had done since I was small.

A dark monolith, horizontal, extending its weight over my eyes, over my . . .

There was a noise. My eyes fluttered out of unconsciousness.

The noise was soft and penetrating, like somebody breathing just beside you, the kind of noise that only ghosts can make. I'm not one to be easily spooked, but fear crept into me and I convinced myself I could see the slightest movements of air passing through Mariano's lips.

Surely he was dead. Or wasn't he? What an awful thought I had— that his corpse could animate and clutch me in a putrid embrace. Or was the breathing only in my mind?

Still, as darkness came, I couldn't leave him. I tossed and turned, sometimes gazing into his dead face, other times into the black jungle that surrounded us. My neck felt ice-cold, and in that frigid paralysis, my mind sunk down and down until I slept again. Though it must have only been the sleep of a cat, for some slight tremor of the earth made me bolt awake and I turned to find that Mariano's dead eyes were wide open.

They glistened slightly, full of an old, stony luster. His mouth, too, was cracked open. I was certain his face had not been so before, but in the vicinity of sleep one begins to doubt the shape and size of what is true. My perceptions began to shroud themselves in possibility. I swore I could remember pulling down the lids over his eyes that morning. I remembered lifting up the stiff jaw to stop his corpse from ogling.

Now I caught myself staring into the occult shade that his body threw upon the ground.

Something . . . something was there.

I stared at the ground beside his body with the same expectation as one waiting for the sound of a knock at a door.

A door: I remembered suddenly my old house. And behind that memory, there was something else. Something even older.

And then the soil quivered and it came. It was one of those fearful vines you sometimes hear about. They needle their way up from deep in the earth, attracted to the pheromones of death.

I heard the light crumbling of earth as the vine slid out, black-green and gleaming. Its blind snout moved back and forth, exploring the air, feeling its way toward the tender opening of my uncle's mouth. It lifted itself like a serpent and swayed in the vicinity of his eyes for a long time as though sniffing something out.

After a while, it probed resolutely at the inner corner of his left eye and penetrated his face.

Though he was quite dead—now I was sure of it—a pale band of tears fell down from Mariano's eye and trickled silently across the arch of his nose until it disappeared into the crease of his other eye. From where I watched, it all seemed interminably far away.

I thought his tears looked just like a waterfall. The way waterfalls look from a distance: pale silk against the darkness.

In fact, the whole scene had the aura of water—the rivulet of tears, the color and scent of the light, even the vine glistened like river water over stones as it made passage out of the earth and into Mariano's skull.

The vine not only went in, but came back out. Mariano's tongue waggled and lifted in his open mouth, pushing between his teeth like it was trying to kiss. It was so startling I made a small cry, but it was only the vine, which had bore its way down through the eye and the soft tissues of the brain and down through the back of the palate until it found its way out again through the mouth.

It bore its way out from the tip of the tongue and, without pause, circled up and into the nostril, stringing up Mariano's tongue like a crude clay bead on a chain.

On and on this went, the vine winding itself in and around my uncle's skull all through the night.

❖

A locust's scream signaled the morning.

I looked for Mariano but he was gone. Just a thick nest of vines clustered with yellow-tipped buds burgeoning from the neck of a corpse.

In the glow of those impending blooms I felt a strange impression. A fire lit, up and down my limbs, soft as the velvet light of a star.

I knelt beside the monstrosity and prayed, though to whom or for what I couldn't say.

As if in response, the flowers opened. In them I could smell the heavy cologne that Mariano had worn when I was a girl—a scent that once upon a time had lingered in the bedroom like an unclean spirit, trapped between this world and the next.

A wind came into the clearing and stirred up the yellow heads. They shook against each other in the breeze with a violence I admired. I heard in them the peal of tiny bells.

I felt dizzy and nearly wretched. I tried to come up from my knees, but bloodless from the thighs down I tumbled backward over the dead stumps of my legs, ruining the pretty display of plátanos. Their flesh-scent, crushed against my thigh, reminded me of hunger.

And who can deny hunger, which speaks through us and past us, a music from beyond?

I left no flowers for my uncle, as he had his own.

❖

Since the night I left Mariano, I have made this jungle my home.

Whatever it was we were searching for before—I no longer want it. Unbothered by any more of my species, I spend my days dreaming into the swirling atmospheres of this new world, hunting the flesh of the plátano. I lose myself in the labyrinth of the jungle. I am utterly, resplendently alone.

I know the blind vines are always there, tremoring underground, patiently waiting for a host to take their flowers. I find them sometimes. The night flowers, blooming in the dark. Sometimes the scent of them opens me up like a knife with its edge. Other times the alkaloids are soft and mesmerizing, smelling of my mother's hair when I was young enough to sleep in it.

On nights when the moon is hidden behind the mists and the whole planet is muffled and secretive, I can hear the downy tufts of voices carried in the wind like dandelion seed. I know their source.

It is they, after all, the night-flowering vines, who cloistered up their seeds from the mutant gases and rains of those terrible years and buried themselves alive in the darkness of the planet. I would guess that they inherited not only the fertile ruins of our kind, but the remnants of stranger kingdoms as well.

Alive under the surface of everything, sheltered from the stars, they evolved the blind vision that sees by a light neither you nor I can fathom.

When I think of them, a smile creeps over my lips.

I can see them now, long ago, in the ground beneath me.

Long ago, it was them I had prayed to, clutching the string of pink plastic beads in my bedroom and murmuring *por favor por favor por favor* as Mariano's voice slurred outside my door.

They were the ones who listened while everything else screeched for salvation. Under the earth they fed on the slow, holy substance that can only be eaten in such total darkness.

They took it all into themselves. They turned nothing away that came to them, vibrating under the earth like the silent children of locusts.

There is nothing they did not taste. Not one sorrow escaped them.

Alma y Corazón

JULIA RIOS

The world was ending and the love was gone. Alma could see the signs, the shifting shadows of demons tearing at the thin wall between their dimension and hers. She needed to fight, to preserve the border, but they wouldn't let her. In this place with its bland colors and fluorescent lights, they all thought she was crazy.

"You should rest," the nurse said. "Here, take your pills."

Alma turned her head, pushing away. "I have to tell Corazón. We have to fix it."

The nurse caught her by the chin and forced the pills into her mouth, watching to make sure she swallowed. "Shh, it's okay. There's no need to get worked up."

Alma was dizzy. The lights were too bright, and the clock on the wall above her bed kept ticking in that particular way, like waiting, like breathing. The clock *was* breathing. It contained all of the universe inside it and she needed to stay awake to watch it or everything would fly apart. All the demons would come through. All the world would come undone. She needed Corazón.

"Tell her," Alma said, her voice already beginning to slur from the sedative. "Tell her we need to take up the silver sword again."

❖

When they were twelve, and the man had asked if they wanted to save the world, it had sounded like an adventure. Corazón didn't

278

know—couldn't know—how the squelch of the sacred blade slicing demon flesh would stick in her ears for days, how the shrieks of the damned would haunt Alma's dreams, how incredibly gruesome a task saving the world would turn out to be.

Corazón faced it with fierce courage and pragmatic stoicism, but Alma had always been sensitive. She couldn't let go of the horror. At night, her dreams were full of monsters, and none so monstrous as herself. She screamed in her sleep. As time passed, the memories didn't fade for her. They grew stronger until they took over everything, and she begged Corazón to help her fight things Corazón couldn't see.

It had been a month since Alma went away. Corazón only visited once. The nurses escorted her through the series of locked wards into a room with no door, where everyone listened to their conversation.

"They don't believe me. Tell them, Corazón. Tell them the truth."

Corazón held Alma's hand, touching palms, and matching scar to scar so they made a cross that no one could see, but both sisters could feel. She looked into Alma's eyes, knowing her sister would understand her soul, and the furious fire that burned in her heart. But she couldn't say what Alma wanted to hear. Not in front of everyone here. She left without saying another word. She didn't come back.

Her parents made Corazón see a counselor who asked her how she felt, and how she was doing in school, and if she believed in demons. Corazón lied because she was not going to that place.

"My sister is crazy," she said. "It sucks, yeah, but there's nothing I can do about it."

"Your sister is ill," said the counselor. "*Crazy* is a derogative term. It's natural that you might be experiencing some anger. I can help you process it if you let me."

"I don't need a counselor," Corazón said. For three long sessions she sat on the soft beige sofa, impassive as stone.

In the end, the counselor told Mr. and Mrs. de León that Corazón was strong, and unwilling to accept help. "She'll work through it on her own, I think. If she changes her mind, you know where to find me."

Corazón walked out of the office that day with fire in her chest that was part triumph, where before it had been all rage. She would guard her freedom with everything she had, because one of them should be free to help the other. This she promised herself.

Each night she prayed to God, asking Him to show her how to save her sister from the demons who still tormented her.

◆

Some days Alma felt more at peace than others. On those days, the world around her felt a little clearer, more in focus. The demons weren't as loud. She'd dreamt the angel last night, the terrible and beautiful man who had come to them three years ago. He was not soft, but he was gentle and strong. He'd told her Corazón would help. Alma knew that Corazón believed, even if she wouldn't answer her phone.

Mamá picked up on the first ring. "Baby, it's so good to hear from you. Are you okay?"

"I miss Corazón."

"Corazón misses you, too." Mamá's voice was full of warmth and sadness. "She's very busy getting ready for her quinceañera right now. She wishes it could be yours, too. I'm sure she'll talk to you soon." Then she passed the phone to Papá, who said they'd come visit later in the week.

Alma wiped her sweaty palms on her pajama pants, and swallowed her disappointment when she hung up. Once upon a time she had dreamed of a big quinceañera, of matching gowns, of dancing. Now that seemed so far away and childish. There were so many other more important things to do. The angel would find her sister and he'd show her the way.

◆

Corazón tried on dresses with Sunshine at Maria's Formals. Other girls wore colors, but Corazón was set on white. "It's like a wedding," said Sunshine. "Like you're a bride!"

"A bride of Christ is a nun," said Corazón. But secretly, she was pleased. Brides were sort of like superheroes. They had special outfits, and everyone thought they were important. They had power.

Corazón wanted miles of tulle with sequins and rhinestones, and a matching tiara to crown her black hair. She wanted to be a living star. She went through all the different whites and settled on the starkest, snowiest one she could find, to better stand out against her brown skin. No subtle ivory for Corazón. She would not blend into anyone's background.

Sunshine picked her way through a rack of pastels, sighing every third or fourth time she swept a hanger aside. "I want something brighter than these."

Corazón's phone buzzed, and the display showed the number from the hospital. She pressed *ignore*. She'd listen to her voicemail later, when she was alone. God had sent her a sign at school today. They would be called to fight again soon, and when they won, Alma would be better. For now, she envisioned her guilt squashed under folds of righteous white satin.

"There's a whole section of bright dresses in the back," she told Sunshine. "We can get you yellow to match your name."

Sunshine glared. "Very funny. I want pink."

Corazón laughed. "You're going to make Eduardo have a pink vest with his suit? I have to see this."

"I thought *you* were taking Eduardo, you know, since he's your cousin," Sunshine said. She didn't say, "And you don't have a boy-friend," but Corazón still winced.

"No. I have a better plan," said Corazón.

"Who's your escort?" Sunshine asked.

"There's a new kid in my English class. Today was his first day."

"Gabriel?" Sunshine scrunched up her nose in disapproval. "I heard he had to leave his last school 'cause he knocked up a gringa."

"You shouldn't believe gossip," said Corazón. Her hands clenched around the skirts of her dress so hard the rhinestones dented her fingertips. "Besides, I know you want to go with Eduardo. He's your chambelan, and Ricky is going with Karla. We'll all have real dates this way."

"Karla will want blue," said Sunshine.

Corazón's smile was more relief than excitement about dress shopping, but it was real all the same. "I think we can do a bunch of different colors for the damas. Let's go look at the bright ones."

❖

Alma dreamed the angel again that night, with his fiery, no-colored eyes. The time was getting closer. Dr. Sandoval didn't believe her, of course. In group therapy, he told her to work on staying rooted in reality.

"There are no demons here, Alma," he said, gentle and condescending. He thought she was delusional like Letitia, who claimed Angelina Jolie was her mother.

"They're here," said Alma. "They're everywhere. You have to let me out. I have to save the world. I have to." But then things got a little mixed-up again in her head. The grand clarity that always courted her was there, and she needed to catch it. "If there is a clock and it breathes, if there is water and it breathes, if I breathe then my breath can fight them? The demons are coming, and I have to breathe to pray," she said. All the words spiraled out of her like thread unwinding from a spool.

"Alma, you're slipping away again. We need you to come back to the real world," Dr. Sandoval said.

"You don't understand. Breath is life and love and demons are death so we all have to breathe. This is *important!*" Alma said. She could hear her tone rising as if from a distance, like she was outside of her body, listening to a radio version of herself.

"We all are breathing, Alma," said Dr. Sandoval. "But there is nothing magical about that. It's natural. You aren't doing magic. Come back to reality. Focus on being here, please."

"You don't understand!" Alma cried. She whispered it next, again and again, and then began blowing out breaths in patterns of five, because stars had five points and maybe that was the key.

Dr. Sandoval made everyone in the group say demons weren't real, and then the nurse brought pills that made Alma too tired to talk anymore.

They wheeled her back to her room because she was too dizzy to stand. She clutched the Bible as she drifted off, shutting her eyes against the evil snaking hands of the clock.

❖

Gabriel came after Sunday Mass to help Corazón with her surprise dance. He exchanged pleasantries with her parents like an old-fashioned gentleman, and then Corazón led him into the empty garage. Papá had moved both cars to the street just for this.

Glossy dark curls framed Gabriel's face, which was younger and smoother than it had been the first time. It glowed golden under the brown, like he'd used a shimmer powder, only beneath the skin instead of on top. He was the most beautiful boy Corazón had ever seen, but she knew this image was a lie. He was the man from before, with the same molten eyes that were at once no color and every color. He was an angel.

Corazón allowed him to kiss her hand and bow (this was the start of the dance), partly because she wanted to see if the touch of his lips against her skin would feel like sacred fire. It didn't. It just felt warm and soft, like a boy. She stepped back and held up a hand before he could twirl her around.

"What's wrong?" he asked.

"We're alone now," said Corazón. "You don't have to pretend here."

"Pretend what?"

Corazón turned away. She counted the rakes and shovels leaning against the wall (five all told, but two were broken). She took a deep breath. "I know what you are and why you're here. Just ask me already."

The air stilled. Corazón waited for a reply, not daring to move. This was it. Her call. Her *second* call.

Gabriel placed one hand on her shoulder, gentle as a dove's wing. "Please, Corazón, today I am only here to practice with you. All of that is over."

Corazón shook her head. "Alma told me you would come. God sends her visions. I'm ready to fight."

Gabriel trailed a finger down the side of Corazón's face. "You misunderstand, My Lady." The words were a soft flutter, neither English, nor Spanish; perhaps not any human language at all.

"Why would you come if not for that?" Corazón asked. She did not turn around, but crossed her arms over her chest and stared even harder at the rakes, willing her eyes to stay dry.

Gabriel hummed as if he was weighing his words. When at last he spoke, his voice was reverent.

"To dance with you, Lady. Will you do me the honor?"

Corazón melted inside. Part of her wanted to pretend this was just a dance with a beautiful boy. Someone who could love her. But angels did not fall in love, and even if they could, it wouldn't be right. Not when the reason for his visit was to give her a divine mission. She turned to face him, her heart pounding so hard she could feel it in her throat.

"And Alma? Should I just forget about her? She said you would help us fight."

Gabriel sighed. "I will help you if I can, Lady, but this is not the time for fighting. You must both remember to live." He held out his hand again, inviting her to take it.

He was waiting for the true call, Corazón told herself. He said this was not the time, but they *would* take up arms when the time was right. They must.

In the meantime, she took his hand and curtseyed.

◆

Alma was drowning in a sea of lost souls. They whirled around her, arms outstretched, writhing in agony, imploring her to save them. Some had the faces of people she loved, others of demons she'd killed. The atmosphere reeked of desperation and rot. The walls dripped blood.

"I have to save them." Alma said the words again and again like a prayer. The anguished crowd tugged and buffeted her so forcefully that she didn't notice the nurses leading her to Dr. Sandoval's office.

"How do I help? Show me how to help!" she cried.

"Who are you trying to help?" Dr. Sandoval asked. His voice cut through the moaning with disorienting clarity.

"The damned," Alma whispered. "So much blood. I have to save them. Love, breath, blood, life. I have to help them."

"Dreams," said Dr. Sandoval. "Nothing more. These troubling visions you have are not real."

But the lost souls still churned around her. Alma paced the room. She smeared her hands along the wallpaper, trying to wipe away the stains.

"Alma," Dr. Sandoval's voice called.

"*Alma, Alma,*" the chorus of the damned echoed.

Her stomach heaved. Even with her eyes closed, she saw them, begging her, blaming her, trying to pull her into Hell. She made the sign of the cross and whimpered. "I'm sorry. I'm so sorry."

"Alma, come back to reality, please. You are on Earth at Stanhope Hospital. There is no one in danger. You are safe. You do not need to save anyone."

Dr. Sandoval's voice was clear, but distant, and some part of Alma wanted to believe it, but she knew, she *knew* it wasn't true. She could feel the signs and symbols. She could *feel* them pulsing through her with every heartbeat. Like blood, like life. "Blood, life, blood is life, breath is life," she said. "It all means so much and I have to live. The angel said I have to live. I will give my blood and my breath. And love and Stanhope Hospital, the clock, the existence of time. I have to, I have to."

Again the words tumbling out, a sacred thread unwinding. Dr. Sandoval was asking her to calm down, but Alma was sure it all meant everything, if she could only understand. If she could make everyone understand. *Corazón will come,* she thought. *Corazón believes.*

❖

"We'd hoped that Alma could come today, baby. I'm sorry. Dr. Sandoval says she's been having a bad week. They can't let us take her, even for an afternoon. She needs to stay where people know how to help her." Mamá placed her hands over Corazón's, which were busy shredding a paper napkin. Her cereal was soggy because she'd left it too long, staring into space and brooding. She knew how to help her sister. She wanted to be done with the waiting.

"She should have a tiara, too," Corazón said.

"When she's well again," said Mamá. "We will give her a Sweet Sixteen, maybe. Like Inez had. It will be the same as a quince."

"It won't," said Corazón. She pushed the cereal away, forceful enough that milk sloshed over the side of the bowl and onto the glass tabletop.

Mamá didn't yell. She wasn't that kind of person. She just looked at Corazón, her eyes full of sadness. "It will be better, then. We'll make sure of it."

Corazón couldn't stand the pity. Everyone these days pitied her, even Sunshine, who was usually so good at being shallow. Yesterday she'd asked about Alma, tentative and tender the way people were at funerals. Corazón had told her to shut up. She didn't want to yell at Mamá, though; Mamá didn't deserve that.

"I have to get ready," she said instead.

❖

The world was soaked in blood. Blood and bones and flayed, writhing flesh. Alma spit out the pills when the nurse wasn't looking. She refused to ignore this truth.

On the wall, the clock hissed and growled. Demons seethed all around, snatching the lost souls, and rending them limb from limb, crowning each other with viscera and bones, transforming pain into evil triumph. The air thrummed with their unholy energy. They would break forth from their prison and swarm the earth if the sisters didn't stop them.

Why didn't Corazón come?

❖

The reception was at the casino hotel fifteen miles out of town. Corazón and her damas and chambelanes piled into a super-stretch SUV limousine for the ride from the church. It was big enough to fit twenty people easily, so the sixteen had plenty of room to stretch out, even with the canes the boys carried.

As soon as the doors closed, Karla and Ricky started making out like they always did whenever they got away from their parents. Everyone else chattered nonstop, exclaiming over the drinks (soda only, Eduardo noted) and the little crystal dishes of mints (the good buttery kind, reported Inez).

Corazón clutched her bouquet, brimming with anticipation. Soon she would be called to God's work. Beside her, Gabriel was tense, too.

In her mind, Corazón replayed the conversation they'd had in the garage, the reason he'd said he was there. *"To dance with you, My Lady."* She understood now what he meant. Wasn't fighting for the Lord the most powerful kind of dance? There was a rhythm to stabbing and dodging, to praying and consecrating, to imposing harmony over despair. Corazón ached to begin.

The event coordinator was standing outside to greet the limo. She lined them up and led them inside, Corazón and Gabriel at the back of the group. Gabriel tapped his cane against the marble floor in a jittery staccato as they walked. He did not speak, but watched intently as the MC announced all the other couples and ushered them into the ballroom.

The damas and chambelanes stood facing each other in a rainbow of formal attire. Overhead they extended flowers and canes to form a long arch. Gabriel offered his arm to Corazón, and walked with her down the center to the throne at the front of the room. When she sat, he stepped aside.

The padrinos came and crowned her, Tía Lupe placed the tiara on her head, and Tío Mario handed her the scepter. It was silver, with a double heart at the top, because that was so obviously perfect for Corazón. She had seen scepters with other designs, ones that had stars like magic wands, or crowns to match the tiara. But for Corazón, there could only ever be one choice. The scepter was a symbol of authority and responsibility, a signal that Corazón was starting adulthood. When she gripped the silver in her hand, she felt powerful. She felt ready.

The first waltz and the choreographed dances with the court passed in a blur. There was a dinner period, but Corazón didn't have any appetite. Everyone assumed it was because she was too excited, except Mamá who worried it was because she was still upset about Alma.

"Baby, don't you want to eat? ¿No quieres comer? Even a little?"

"I'm okay, just not hungry."

Dessert passed, and with it the toasts. Corazón didn't hear any of them.

Finally, it was time for the surprise dance. Gabriel rose and extended his hand, and Corazón walked with him to the center of the room. He touched his lips to her knuckles, then stepped back and bowed, just like they'd practiced. The music swelled and the lights dimmed. Corazón felt tingly all over, just like the first time Gabriel had come to issue God's call.

They floated through the room, dipping and twirling in synchronized perfection. The DJ started a fog machine so everything clouded into a surreal mist, and a cheer rose from the dining tables.

Then it was over.

The song ended, and everyone clapped, but Corazón felt hollow and wrong. She grasped Gabriel's hand, clinging uncertainly as the dance floor filled to capacity.

"What is it?" Gabriel whispered, his warm breath tickling her ear.

"I thought we would go to where we were called during the dance. We should be fighting the demons now."

Gabriel sighed. "Oh, Lady," he said. He sounded more sad and weary even than Mamá that morning.

❖

It was their quince today. Alma's skin tingled with shock at the realization. She had forgotten their birthday. She kept losing track of time; it felt like she was always half asleep.

She shook her head at the growling clock. "You be quiet now. Today is special. Corazón will come with the angel. I can feel it."

The nurse called from her station down the hall. "Alma? Are you okay in there?"

"Shh," Alma told the clock again, but it didn't listen. "¡Cállate!"

"Alma, honey, just calm down," the nurse said. "I'm going to bring your meds."

"No, no meds!" Alma shouted, but it was useless. The nurse would put her to sleep and leave her powerless to fight. Corazón would help her, though. They would take up the silver swords and save the world again. There was too much agony. They wouldn't allow it to get any worse. Not today.

❖

Gabriel led Corazón outside, not just out of the ballroom, but out of the hotel entirely. In the late afternoon, the parking lot was quiet. No one would hear them talking there.

Gabriel took both of Corazón's hands, touching scepter to cane, and fingers to fingers. His strange eyes searched her ordinary brown ones, pleading and commanding at the same time. "Lady, you have to let go. Your work is done. You must live now, and enjoy your life."

"But Alma sees them. God sends her visions. There are monsters, and the world is in danger. She needs me to stop them so she can be better."

Gabriel's gaze did not waver. He kept looking into her eyes steady and unblinking. "There are no monsters here, Lady. Not now. This world is in no danger. You did save it. Together you both saved it, and you sealed that crack with your pledge and your blood so those demons cannot pass that way again."

Corazón trembled, half in anger, half in fear. "Alma doesn't lie. She always tells the truth. She says we have to fight, so we have to fight! You *said* you would help us."

"The time to fight with swords is over, Lady. Now it is time to live. To love. You cannot kill monsters that do not exist. You can only move on, and be a voice of reason, once she is open to listening."

The sun was sinking behind the mountain, and the sky was a wash of peach, pink, and purple. Corazón ached at the beauty of it, and railed at the unfairness that would have her here and her sister in a hospital, scared and alone.

"Why would you come here if not to bring me back to fight again?" she demanded.

Gabriel glowed even more golden in this light than he did under full sun. "To comfort you, Lady, and to show you His will. I am His messenger."

"How can I be comforted when my sister is in torment? If He knew from the start that this would happen, that Alma would break, why did He ask it of us? How is that just? How is that merciful?"

The words came hot and fast. Corazón felt stupid in her giant white dress, frivolous and overwrought. How had she thought this would give her power? She wanted to dash the heart scepter against the pavement until it bent and crumpled.

The angel's hands were still on hers, though, and they would not let her go. It wasn't a violent grip, but a compulsion. Corazón would stay put until Gabriel decided otherwise. He no longer looked like a beautiful boy. He had changed both instantly and gradually, and now he was barely a person at all.

Corazón's eyes did not know where to look, or how to translate what she saw into a comprehensible shape. This was awe, she thought. The realization sat quietly in the back of her mind, crowded from the foreground by the waves of ecstatic attention an unmasked angel commanded. When the angel spoke, she felt the words everywhere: in the air, and on her own tongue, and in her very soul.

"She would always have broken, whether or not she chose to take up arms and fight for His glory. It is His will that you must make peace in your own heart. Make room for love. You must honor your shared past, and remember that it truly is past. Accept that your sister's demons are hers alone. You cannot vanquish them for her, Lady. I'm sorry."

Corazón stared into the center of the angel, fierce and determined. "So it's God's will that I have to stand by and watch her suffer? I can't do nothing. I won't."

"You might help her find the strength to face those demons, if you have a will to try. You must both remember to live." The angel shimmered regret and approval and awful, bright love. "I will not return. Goodbye, Lady."

And then Corazón was alone in a hotel parking lot, staring at empty space. Above her was the deep blue of early evening sky, and below her, sun-baked asphalt, full of meandering cracks. Gabriel's cane lay at her feet, the sole reminder that he had been there. When

Corazón bent to pick it up, she saw that it had changed into a silver scepter with a soaring dove on top: the symbol of the soul. A gift for Alma, she thought, feeling older than she had ever known it was possible to feel.

She stood slowly, just as Sunshine came out the side door in her bright pink dress, a champagne flute full of fruit punch in her hand. "There you are, Princesa," she said. "You're missing your royal festival. Come back in and have some fun. Eduardo is doing The Robot!"

◆

Alma tossed and turned in her bed, tangling the sheets around her legs. The demons around her soared and swirled, but the angel was there again, too, all gold and silver and no color and every color.

"Rest, My Lady," the angel said. "I have been to Corazón. She will come to you. You must listen to her. Remember to live."

"I will give my blood and my life," Alma said. "Show me the way."

"Rest," the angel repeated. "Remember to live."

Then the angel vanished and all that was left was the clock, the bed, the concept of time, Stanhope Hospital, a puzzle of fragments that Alma *knew* had meaning, *the* meaning, the key to saving everything.

Corazón would come, the angel had said. Corazón would know what to do.

◆

Corazón agreed to visit the next week. She felt bad for waiting, but it was too hard to come to terms with what the angel had said any sooner. Too hard to face Alma, to put aside her anger at Him for this great injustice. She carried no sword, but a silver scepter. Alma could not keep it in the hospital, she knew, but maybe they would let Corazón at least show it to her twin. She'd told her parents she'd bought it online. She would tell Alma the truth.

This time before they led her family through the locked doors to Alma's ward, Corazón asked if they could have privacy. "I just want to talk to Alma for a few minutes alone if that's okay?"

"Oh honey, sure," said Mamá. "We'll ask the nurse."

Corazón expected a challenge, but it was easy. They had some small lounges just for this kind of thing, with doors that closed.

There was a window so people could see in, and they had to ask some other patients to move their boardgame out of the lounge, but no one made a fuss at any point. The sisters were alone before Corazón had even had time to compose her thoughts about what to say.

"Alma," she said after a long silent hug. "I missed you."

"The angel said he would come to you. He said you would come to me."

"The angel did come," Corazón said. "He left this for you." She showed Alma the scepter with the soaring dove. "I have a heart one. Yours is the soul."

"It's not the sword, the silver blade. Why? Have you found the way to fight? I give my blood and my life."

Corazón shook her head. "We've gotten it wrong, Alma," she said. "The angel told me we're done. There is no more fight. Not here. Not now."

"But the demons," Alma said. "You have to believe. No one believes. You *know*, Corazón. You *saw!* They're here, too. They're everywhere. We have to. I know how to breathe if I can breathe just right. You have to help me fight!"

Corazón touched her palm to Alma's, scar to scar. "We did pledge our blood and our lives. I do remember. But it's done, Alma. The demons you think you see now are lies. You must remember to live in the world again."

"How can you not believe, when they're all around?" Alma demanded. "And the clock!"

"What about the clock?" Corazón asked, confused.

"The clock is evil! Listen to it breathing! And Stanhope Hospital. The concept of time. It's all connected. It's breathing! We have to stop it! It's alive and it's wrong!"

Corazón shook her head, blinking away tears. "It's not alive, Alma. It's just a clock. Nothing here is evil. You have to try to remember what's real."

"We have to breathe. Give blood and breath and life," said Alma. "You have to help me stop them."

Corazón squeezed Alma's hands, but she would not agree. "Alma, be here with me. We're in Stanhope Hospital. The clock isn't alive. There are no demons. You are safe. You can rest now."

"I have to remember to live," said Alma. "The angel said that."

"Yes," Corazón agreed. "Live. And find peace."

"I can't be at peace," Alma said. "How, when the world is ending?"

Corazón wanted to cry, to shout, but she understood now in a way that she hadn't before what the angel had been trying to say. She needed to be strong for her sister. And strength didn't always mean roaring ferociously. Sometimes it meant being quietly assertive.

"The world isn't ending," she said. "I'm so sorry I didn't come sooner. I'll come more often from now on. And I'll answer when you call."

"But the clock . . ."

"It's just a clock."

"Just a clock," said Alma. "It's just a clock? It's not breathing?"

"No," said Corazón.

"I have to remember to be in the world," said Alma.

"Here with me," Corazón said, squeezing Alma's hands.

"I'll try," Alma whispered.

"It's so good to have you back," Corazón said. She hugged her sister tight, relishing the feel of her familiar warmth. "That's why the angel came to me. To send me here to you."

"To breathe with me? Breath is life. Love is the fight," said Alma. "Love is the fight, right? We will fight them that way?"

"Don't talk like that, Alma. I worry you're drifting away again," said Corazón. "Stay here in this world. I'll call Mamá in, okay?"

The rest of the visit seemed to take forever, but when they were ready to leave, it turned out only an hour had passed.

"We'll come again soon," Mamá said to Alma.

"Tomorrow," Corazón promised. "I'll come every day."

The sun outside felt too bright, too cheery, Corazón thought.

Mamá patted her on the shoulder. "It's hard seeing her so lost, I know."

Corazón sighed. "Yes. It is hard. But that's no reason not to come."

"My brave Corazón," Mamá said. "Such love in you. Does a mother proud."

Corazón's fist clenched around the silver scepter she was keeping safe until Alma could come home. "Love is the fight," she said.

Ella

FREDERICK LUIS ALDAMA, FERNANDO DE PEÑA,
AND RODRIGO VARGAS

Ella

Frederick Luis Aldama
Fernando de Peña
Rodrigo Vargas

I wake.

I'm not in my bunk--one of hundreds that run up and down like a newspaper column in an abandoned structure; they say they used to build airplanes here--we call them nadvas today. They keep all of us chicas here; we work in the maquilas until we turn 21, anyway. Then they throw us to the wind where we must kill for comida and shelter. We're tattooed. We're chipped. They keep track when I wake. I'm unattached. I can't move. I have only images and thoughts to assemble into nightmares: blood, severed heads. . .

They keep me company.

We had to disconnect her brain. Diseased, her body betrayed her.

Her brain's fed within a thick, wispy pink, oily blue fluid. They promise: Sentience can exist and grow within this gelatinous substance that flickers with OI pulsations.

Months pass.

Are you sure it will work?

I wake. I roll over. I'm connected. I'm tentacled. More braceros than legs. I'm dizzy. The familiar siren roars. I climb down from my bunk. I line up ready for another day at the maquila.

Two-Bullet Cowgirl Blues

STEVE CASTRO

The hoarse throat made the cowhand's speech rougher
than the patrons at the tavern she frequented as a child.

She arose early enough to wring the rooster's neck while it slept.
There's no need in waking the neighbors anymore.
She then set about making her breakfast: buttermilk biscuits
from scratch on a cast iron wood stove
washed down with coffee, dark and strong like her papa.

Her mama died in a saloon fire, sparked by a broken neck.
Mama was racing down those infernal stairs
while holding the right hand of her young'un.

The cowhand walked with a limp, but she was a gifted gunslinger.
She once shot a fellow dead with the first bullet, then
brought him back to life with the second.

A Mirage

STEVE CASTRO

"Jaime!" I screamed his name for a full minute before he answered me.

"Sorry, I didn't hear you, Julio. How come you didn't use the intercom to reach me? Anyway, what's up?"

"The intercom isn't working properly. I need your help putting on my spacesuit."

"Protocol prohibits us from exiting this spaceship unless it's an emergency."

"I'm going out in search of a microwave."

"Are you insane, Julio? After budget cuts by the Central American Space Federation, if we installed a microwave in this spaceship, our sole engine would potentially lose so much power that we'd be stranded in space waiting to be rescued again. Plus, why are you eating mammoth tacos? That meat takes forever to heat up. If you ate cow-tongue tacos like a normal human, our stove oven would be able to heat them up in five seconds. Sometimes I wish we would never have cloned extinct animals."

"Jaime, you're a hypocrite. Didn't you tell me that dodo burritos were your favorite, and that your mistress loved goat-cheese empanadas. Those creatures would be extinct if it wasn't for Japanese and Canadian cloning technology."

Julio, your well-done mammoth taco is finished after a mere eight minutes, you ungrateful bastard, came the metallic voice reply from the stove oven.

As I started to walk toward the stove oven, I looked left, and from outside our ship's emergency door window, I swore I caught a glimpse of the microwave of my dreams passing me by.

The One

STEVE CASTRO

The fire was so massive and intense, its flames reached up to the heavens and incinerated the earth's moon. Food was so scarce in the blue planet after that apocalyptic scorching, the sole phoenix that rose from the soot and ashes became so hungry, it ate itself. That uroboric mythical creature was not alone in its plight. Behemoth clouds of smoke possessed the celeste sky, turning it charcoal. As for human survivors, an alien satellite homed in on a small child, all of his hairs singed from his body. He was walking alone, naked, but with a great fire in his eyes, which no galaxy had ever before seen or would ever see again.

Grave Talk

J. M. GUZMAN

Replacing my bones meant entering the paper heart of Teshani, the Shivering City. Nita was eating a lilac when she led me into its stretch of skin walls. Our descent into the ribs was without much security. No border scanners, no hassle. Only patient steps down viscous stairs. And Nita's black skin was the brightest thing in that nest.

We pared back curtains of woven paper.

Nita walked me the shorn way and the arrangements were the same as I recalled: large blue veins crisscrossed the dark walls. We slid past them, rounding each tunnel corner without so much as a pause. It wasn't necessary to infiltrate the tunnels given that we could just freely slip through Teshani's gates. The civil crest Nita affixed to my neck seasons ago was stamped and signed by envoys of Oshal the Iron Judge, more than enough to get me past security at the city's maw. The paper sash that cradled me was clearance for over a dozen zone cities. But Nita had a thing for theatrics. Undermining borders and their regulatory mechanisms was her greatest thrill in the world.

Making a point, as they say. And I was fine with it. Could empathize, even.

"I don't think we can make this quick."

Nita smiled at me. "Nothing is ever quick in Teshani. You should know that, but then it's been a long time since you've been here, hasn't it?"

"That's not funny," I said. We crossed one of the broken railroad tracks enchained by white moss, our bodies amber-lit by wax candles. There were violet hearts encased in the calcified ceiling, oozing black oil, pulsating irregularly. Engineering the city with their tenuous hold.

Moths, with their old dust wings, chased our bodies. My backpack creased the skin by my shoulders, shovel handle poking out.

"It is a little, stranger. Eres una niña nueva aquí, fresh like a little planner spit out of Yawali. I think we can all tell you're not from here anymore," Nita said, chewing on the lilac now.

"I guess. That's part fair. I almost forgot the tech restrictions of this zone."

"Yeah, well, the corrosion would remind you, right?" Nita said. She broke the neck of a stem. "Did you bring your shovel? The surgeon and I will have to dig you out."

I smiled. "Always."

Nita didn't ask which question I was answering. Instead, she said, "Then I guess you're not entirely a stranger, Alejandra. Teshani may be home for you yet."

And as she ate another flower, as blood filled her mouth with each chewed petal, Nita shut me off again. I couldn't feel anything. Our emotions were swapped in the dark, just like that. She thought she was doing a good thing, believed she was helping me. But it was like being forced into a mask.

Nita never asked me if I wanted to stop hurting. She just made it end. And I continued walking through the flesh corridor, trying to remember how to feel, slipping into Nita's cold skin.

❖

There were dead trains around us, black metal bodies scarred and bleeding wires that had long lost their color. But it didn't remind me of a grave. No. It was something like a garden of scattered iron that we picked over, a resting ground for engines to rise again. And Nita's naked hands reflected back a smattering of numbers, a little bit of proof that the indigo pull of mothlight tracked us in the darkness. Teshani marking our skin for a vigil.

"The doctor who's going to change out your bones, Kaled, refused at first. Said if the new bones reject you, you'd just become a regulator. Complained about not wanting to be complicit. But I made him promise to help me, to help you."

"I'm sorry you had to do that," I said. Guilty, confused. "Thank you. Por todo."

"It's okay. I just want you to know that I'm really trying to help you."

"I can see that."

The air trembled and there was a gap in our conversation. Perhaps I was silent because I was afraid of the body we would confront at the tunnel crossroads, perhaps it was the fact that I had been numbed. Maybe it was the knowledge that the city played voyeur, watching us through insect eyes. Truthfully, I wasn't sure why we could never speak to each other the way we needed to.

"Oh. Have you seen the ghosts?"

"No," I said.

"They stand sentinel outside the maw of Teshani. Ghostmaker security is just the type that don't show its face until you're out a throat. Reminds me of you."

"Are they holograms? The ghosts," I asked, ignoring the parts of her sentences I didn't want to interrogate.

"A few of them are," Nita replied. It was her attempt at small talk. So I brought it back.

"Some of us just can't let go of this city, I guess."

Nita stared at me. "What do you mean?"

A second heartbeat snuck into my ears like the knocking on a door. We were footfalls away from the body in the pillar, the one that would take us into Teshani's holds, the system that would give us a coin to sacrifice to the city if we were worthy.

We were about to be tested.

"Having ghosts as border guards is just a haunting," I said. "Calling back to the days where men with guns would shoot at the wrong ones. But I get it. I can't forget things either. I stayed feeling some kind of way, pero no lo ves."

"But I do."

"You do what?"

"I get you better now," Nita said.

"I'm not sure you do. Nunca hablas conmigo. And maybe it's my fault, maybe we just avoid what really needs talking about, but when you dropped me from your life, it made me realize how little I mattered and how much I'd be stuck here. So, these ghosts you say guard Teshani? I'm probably something like them. I'm stuck here, even when I'm gone, even in my head."

Nita opened her mouth and then shut it. The heartbeat grew louder. Gunshot patter closed out by a crash. And then the sound of an alternator dying, a heart winding down, and silence.

We stopped at the tunnel crossroads, staring into the shattered body of a reverend regulator—human, once. And after? Never alone. Its face was degloved, skin interlaced with metal. The torso was part glass, fulgurations cracking inside its mirror chest like a storm captured in a jar.

Nita was sweating and forcing a smile. Her cheek twitched in the cold.

"Do you remember?"

"Yeah," I said. There were coins slotted onto a stretch of red skin across the reverend regulator's face. Once, a cheek was there, an eye. I went to pull a coin out of its skull, bracing myself for rejection. A scream. My skin, flayed.

There was nothing. It slid out, silver in my palm. Nita did the same and then she staggered into a set of frosted rails, labored breathing and wet eyes. I stared as she shook in the dark. The reverend regulator's one damaged eye caught us as it checked its periphery. Judging. Such a whole thing, now part graveship, now given the religious afterglow it was promised. A purpose.

Nita's breathing quickened. I felt . . . nothing. She was straggling, entombed in my feeling, but I knew that when I was graved, she would move on, she would be just fine. Her pain was too temporary. Was I awful for thinking that made it mean less?

"Hey," I said. "Are you okay?"

The stupidest question, a burgeoning insult. In that helpless moment, for just a heartbeat, I hated myself.

"Do you always feel this way?" Nita asked this trembling. Her black skin was spotting white, milk circles collecting on her forehead. When Nita had swapped our emotions, she had also stolen my sickness. An attempt to be there for me, to make amends. Being a friend, maybe a lover. But I could feel Nita's numbness blooming in my chest, a flower raising itself. It killed away my pain, the only thing that made me feel alive. And Nita asked, "Do you always feel so . . . hurt?"

"I'm sorry," I said, and I didn't even know why I was apologizing. For feeling too much, maybe.

But Nita gathered herself silently and took the left path. The coin said so, of course.

I followed, numbed into frostbite. And I resented Nita in that moment, for stealing what she did to me, for leaving me hollow without a choice.

◆

We were climbing out of the tunnel mouth. There was no light at the crown, only strained dark bordering on gray. With each stair we took, my boots grew muddier with thick bile. The teeth in the chunks were marked black and they cracked underneath my heel. Their enamel had been worn down by the world.

"I was really surprised when you came to Yawali. When you told me you'd help me out, that you knew a surgeon. I thought me slinking back home was the end of us."

"I know," Nita said.

"I tried to hate you for a long time, you know. Back when you just left me here in your streets. I had to learn how to be mad and even then I couldn't do it for very long. Mostly? I was just sad."

"I don't know what to say."

"There's always something to say."

Then there was a crunching pause, an implicating silence.

When we emptied ourselves into the murmuring scrapyard, I licked a piece of silver and tipped it to the sky. It fell, a burning offering for the night.

Teshani's gravel skin encroached on the coin, devoured it. Assimilated the edges and symbol of Paper Queen Melucria. There was just a grave again, breathing.

Nita simply placed her silver coin on the rusted ground, waiting for the city to swallow it whole. In turn, my tongue gathered the taste of salt.

And around us, there were swappers nested in the dirt, pulling the wires of crying robots into their blistered chests. Exchanging their pain for a codebase of different feeling. Ignoring us. The walls were an amalgam of dead iron faces, lost limbs, dented torsos. The desperate song of brass teeth stripping wire carried itself into my ears.

Nita was still trembling. Still silent.

Teshani, in its own way, responded by welcoming us with apple-scented smoke. It rose from the ground, wisps contorting into a saffron haze. And we walked through the smoke until we were another set in the slew of brown faces mingling with the smog.

◆

Nita and I were back to pretending there wasn't unfinished pain between us.

The surgeon was in that small slice of ghostmaker territory lined by empty jars. It had a name, invocation dark, but I tried to keep it nestled. In fact, at first brush with those chalk-stained streets, I almost recoiled. It was all happening too fast. There was no sky, only a ceiling of old flesh pocked white.

And Cathedral Amal was the name for that sector of the city which waited for us. It was a place that curved my descriptions and resurrected my haunts. It was the most potent reminder that Teshani was built on the remains of a dead graveship. Ghostmaker territory indeed.

And I was fidgeting, deep chest anxiety racking my body, tidal wave tilt disorienting me. A slip into feeling again, a moment where Nita took off my skin. I exhaled. Naturally, Nita started laughing. I think it was her reflexive response to discomfort. Laugh the hurt away, the awkwardness, our bridgeless silence.

"Scared?"

"I mean, yeah. But not for the reasons you think," I replied.

In that moment, framed by burning streetlights that cracked the murk, I saw her in earnest: Nita Collado, Aerai born, not a Paper Eater or a Ghostmaker so much as a tactician in the deep. A Cauldron. Her hair was in twists, splaying out onto her sigil-covered face. The milk spots were gone from her forehead and were growing on my face instead. Raw-throat red words mapped her cheeks, encircling her brown eyes. Some of those segmented phrases were incantations against possession doubling as iconizations from the governmental folds of Teshani's center. Words that proved Nita was a foreigner, but a foreigner with power. Fact is there was no way to be anything but a stranger in a city built by strangers. Nita simply held a throne with all the guns and pain-stealing magic that conferred. And she seemed better, trembling gone, smirk in her eyes drawn. As my feeling reentered my flesh, as Nita's drug magic dulled in the push-pull of swapping, she asked, "What do you mean?"

"I'm not scared of this city or anything like that. I'm not a fucking Solaki commissioner. And no, I'm not even scared of you."

"Okay, I know that," she said, walking leisurely. There was an edge to her voice. "What is it, then?"

I stopped walking. "What if my body rejects the bones?"

And Nita kissed me in response. Held my hands. It was sudden, no foreshadowing, a foreign gesture. The reopening of a comforting memory and stranger because of it. It felt like the beginning of another lie. "It will be okay, Alejandra," she told me.

Around us, Teshani's walkers flitted about. I was so stuck inside myself I almost didn't notice their presence. They were mostly black-skinned, some with honey crests from the city-state Jaw and others with pale tattoos from Horn. So many migrants forced to signal their passage. Teachers, children, workers. Economists and surveyors. Briefly, the sound of dead trains screeching underground stirred something in my chest. "Will it?"

❖

There are some that say the journey matters more than the destination but I can't buy that. A journey can dispose of you. It can leave you battered.

But a destination, right? That's what we have. But that carries an assumption, too. The expectation that something will be *reached*.

But my death is promised, isn't it? Catacombs are supposed to keep in the dark.

❖

The drone choir, first. Each metal bird swooped low, splitting the air with spilled colors. More smoke, bioweapons like Nisipa and Cuco but more overt, less about monsters and more about neurochemical warfare. As my body was smoked out, I felt warm. Most of the stragglers around us had respirators but the smoke logged them in just as they did me. Teshani was doing its headcount. And the streets were swept of glass by masked workers, another day ticking by.

Nita was dry-heaving again but she played it off, kept her face away from me, eyes on the insect-laced flesh that replaced the sky, the wine roses matting the skin ceiling, upside down blooming. But Nita couldn't hide her body's jolt. When we swapped feelings, a door was opened.

❖

As we reached the far side of Cathedral Amal, close to the oil river, I noticed the streets were webbed in paper. And then it rained ink, softly at first, until we were battered black. Teshani's lungs were bleeding. And the sage-colored fog, newly risen from the folds of the street, shrouded each tenement building with its bright murk. It enveloped even the holds of the nursing quarters.

But it wasn't reflective of the rest of the city, no. Teshani was half flesh, half tech. The reverse engineering was an attempt to address the deformities of inherited colonial infrastructure. Before the grave-ship died in this zone, its skin was stretching to terraform the encircling land.

And after? There was no funeral. It became this city, a solution, a great yearning ship resuscitated with Tawari mirror tech and Aerai papermaking at equal turns.

But the bared questions still stood.

What were the truth conditions for a city to be alive? The Bone Translators of the city argued that they were the only ones capable of ascertaining Teshani's intent. But what were translators who let no one check their work? What was a city impaled by neurotechnology and veined with rivulets of wiring? What was it if not a puppet? A dying patient?

And I was in my newfound numbness again, a state that waxed and waned. The factories around us whined and coughed out their tired red smoke. Metal lungs exhaled the longest, which reminded me of Nita shoving her hand through a watchman's clockwork throat.

It reminded me of the rope that had been straightened.

Kaled Anei, a surgeon so renowned he was shared among Cauldrons and Ghostmakers. Nita, deep threat Cauldron, one of the only bodies in the world that couldn't be replicated. Empathy spreader, ace gunwielder. And me?

Just a breadmaker. Someone who wasn't trying to grow, no ambition, just trying to fucking survive, because wasn't that enough? It was okay to not want to bloom, to simply want your bones to hold your skin up. It was natural to reorient growth, frame it as the road to deeper empathy rather than conquest. So I told myself, deep mantra, anxiety settler.

And I could see the jars lining the side street. They led to a charnel home advertising acceptance. That was it. Borough with no sky, inhalation ceiling. Kaled and his bonework like a premonition of required pain.

One threshold away from a changed life. Kaled was going to replace my bones and free me of the corrosion's bleaching sickness. That was the happy ending, right? So simple, *too* simple for it go right.

But Nita gripped my hand again. It helped me so much, gave courage to each step. For an exhale, I believed that I was enough for her.

For myself.

Then, Nita spoke, and reminded me of our rope: "How long have you been sick? I just want to know. How long have you been dying? Tell me," she said. Desperately. Nita did not look me in the eyes. "And why did you go back to Yawali? You knew crossing a border without me would give you the corrosion. You knew it could kill you. Why would you make a choice like that?"

Because I couldn't stay here, couldn't rely on you, I wanted to say. But I didn't.

And she was right. If it wasn't for her, I would have been buried bleached in Yawali. I would have never found a surgeon in time. But I couldn't tell her that, part of me couldn't accept that I only deserved to live because I knew someone with pull. Nita who decided to pick me up long after she put me down. Now, I owed her.

But it was my turn to be silent.

◆

Dripping black, we slipped into the charnel home that sold bones and comfort. It was pillared by wrapped sentinels, clothed all rust and khaki, hands on their guns and only eyes peeking out from their face coverings. Men. They stood next to the milk walls.

With Nita nodding her way through, we were led to the back by a soldier named Fareed. There was a door waiting for us, maplewood and locked.

Fareed did not take out a key. Instead, he slid a folded sheet of paper underneath the door.

It unlocked.

◆

We descended side by side down cleaved bone stairs. Fareed locked the door behind us.

There were voices now, unintelligible, rising and lowering, whispering occasionally from the bone walls.

◆

Why does a cauldron take and take, only to stir the pain it holds? Should a person like me, who spilled herself willingly into the pot, have been better prepared?

I simply was not able to weather the boil. When it mangled me, I came out forever raw.

"I'm here now," Nita murmured as we descended deeper. Not loud enough to be confident, to sound real.

"Should that mean something?"

That was a naked question, one that bared the knife of accusation. Once a person leaves without warning, can you ever trust them to stay?

Nita flinched. "I think so."

"That was fucked-up of me. I didn't mean it like that," I said, knowing that an apology undid nothing, recognizing that truth too deep. "But you left when I needed you most," I amended.

"I'm trying to make up for leaving. I'm trying to . . . I'm sorry, okay? I just couldn't handle how you were."

"Did you want me to be like Farah? She told Santi to do what she had to do. Did you want me to not be fucking crushed?"

"Farah cares in her way." Nita shook her head. We stopped at a stair now, blinking complications at each other.

"In a way that's indistinguishable from not caring. So no, not really," I said.

In that sequence, the stairs had no end. They were the length of our conversation, stretching into a conclusion.

"I didn't know what you were going through, not really. You never told me."

"But why did I have to? You knew I was going through something. You knew Santi almost died, that she was my best friend. You knew enough."

And nothing in response. So I continued:

"If you're just going to leave again, why come back?"

"I never said that," Nita responded.

"Okay."

"And you weren't just victim. I'm not saying I didn't fuck up but you had your part in it. Don't pretend this was all on me, like I didn't tell you I wanted you to do more and be more. Like you didn't yell and gnash and guilt me."

I blinked. "Well, now that the corrosion has hit me, I guess it all works out."

Nita did not say anything. For an instant, I regretted wielding the truth as a weapon. The loaded gun. The guilting accusation.

I was everything she said and worse.

◆

The neurobiology of Teshani has always been understudied. There was evidence for capacity and pattern eclipses ago. But that and the migration analyses claiming that the city was overstuffed with souls and brown bodies, immigration port of the world with the most lenient tech restriction, did not confront the true problem.

Teshani retained the neurobiology of the graveship and its penchant for identification. But it was also the regulators that turned this into exclusion. I had always felt the city's eyes on me. Not in some malevolent way, no. More of a self-assured smirk, reaffirmation that I would always be stranger to the flesh streets.

Until now.

I was a breadmaker heartbeats away from becoming part graveship.

And my family in Yawali did not have the means to help me.

Only the city of barter and immigrants could.

Nita knew this. When I reached the final stair and took in the room, I tried to ready myself. And I knew that Nita was sacrificing, that she was taking in my pain and wearing it in intervals, like a necklace. Suffering for me. Ever since we reunited and she inhaled some of my sickness, I never thanked her. Never acknowledged it. Just let it go.

And isn't that what you're supposed to do?

Move on, they say. Coffins are only a memory.

◆

Doctor Kaled Anei's choice of grave was ringed corrosion scanners and scattered teeth gathered in each corner. The room was white, pristine. Paper was implanted on the ceiling and the floor. A crinkling world with an antiseptic smell.

There was also a hole in the floor a little larger than my body. Kaled knelt in front of it, dark oil smattering his brown arms. Black bones were scattered around him. He was pulling them out of the hole.

Kaled coughed. He turned to Nita and I, tears splattering his face. He continued crying as he spoke. "Is this what you want?"

No introduction, no hello, no century-long complimentary wait. I hesitated. "Yes."

"This is a type of debt, you know? I will do a binding like the Ghostmakers do in Triulsi. And I don't want to."

"I know," I said. I couldn't tell if his tears were untouched or simply a by-product of Nita's flowering. The catalyst didn't change the fact he was crying, so I'm not sure it mattered. And truthfully, I never knew when Nita stopped and we began.

"I am going to cage your shadow," the thin man said. "You will lose it."

"She knows," Nita responded.

Kaled bit his lip. "Then, Nita. I want you to bottle some of the pain and help me clear off her skin."

❖

"Hey, I love you," Nita whispered. "Never stopped."

I couldn't believe it but I tried. I went to reply but the anesthetic had destroyed my throat, rendered me tongueless. I feared that she mistook my silence for rejection.

"Don't worry. I'll make sure we raise you after we put you in the grave," Nita said.

But of course I worried.

It was my talent.

❖

There was no pain.

❖

My body was anchored to the paper floor and I was face-down. The skeleton inside me was distorting, trying to escape.

My skin: sliced open, parted like when scissors cut across fabric.

My insides: moss green, squirting black oil. Somehow, I knew this was a fact without seeing it. Nita pulled the skin of my back apart like opening a curtain. Kaled instructed her.

My bones: distorted, pulsating.

At what point did they stop becoming mine?

◆

A city can be one person, can be the corrosion brightening your skin and bones until you are bleached and dead. A city can be a doctor, the coffin that closes you from the world. A city can be my pain. Or it can be Nita, this long dream I'm not sure I can wake up from. A borough called Cathedral Amal splintered with memories, mirror to a grave.

But we know what a city is.

It will always be this fugue, a premonition of rejection. Waiting for the coin to finally drop.

PART V

Dreams Never Imagined

A Dangerous Wand

NICHOLAS BELARDES

Grandfather later told us Mr. Tiré was like a mirage—arms, legs, cheekbones, everything seemed warped by heat waves melting light and form as he walked through a desert sandstorm north of the village.

Luckily for the stranger, Grandfather had been returning on his motorcycle from the lagoon where he went twice a week to fish with his old friends who'd moved seaside. A recent purchase, the Indian Powerplus rumbled gracefully between Grandfather's legs. He cut a dark line through miles of faded road and sky as he spotted the man struggling through the wind.

Around ten years older than me, Mr. Tiré, twenty-six or there-abouts, wore the fine khaki attire of a well-funded explorer, and had draped around him an assortment of leather bags. Heaped upon those, three small baskets carried two bright-pink, five-toed worm lizards that could fit in the palm of a hand; a medium-sized, albeit plump, common chuckwalla; and a juvenile spinytail iguana.

Grandfather, recalling his story of their meeting, said he idled the engine and pushed his goggles to his forehead. He must have looked like a dirty old Jerusalem cricket when he heaved his canteen to the stranger. "Take it," he said. "That water skin beneath all your creatures looks smaller than a roadrunner bladder."

The wind was rust-colored and abrasive, yet the two men exchanged pleasantries and names as if frequenting a Mazatlán food seller. "I never turn away hospitality though I assure you I'm well stocked." Mr. Tiré took a shallow drink and handed back the container, examining the motorcycle. "That's a Big Twin," he added. "Rode one around Paris for a month during the war. A rather nasty lieutenant by the name of Hogsworth took away my privilege after I crashed into a fountain. Never quite got the hang of it. How do you like her?"

"She's fine," Grandfather said warily. "I'm sure you're needing a ride somewhere?"

"I'd be happy to stay a few nights in your village if I'm welcome," Mr. Tiré said. "Been traveling for miles and not used to walking by foot."

Grandfather admitted, as Mr. Tiré joined him on the motorcycle, that he expected to find a truck empty of gas somewhere down the crossroads from where they met. But Mr. Tiré said there wasn't one. Just he and the lizards.

Perplexed, Grandfather later told us: "How can a man walk through the desert and survive the heat with such a tiny water pouch and no stamina for such exercise?"

Grandfather said they then spoke of his motorcycle. He told Mr. Tiré how the bike survived a harrowing passage to central Baja from the fields of France after a deserter from the Battle of the Somme transported it via a South American merchant ship. The soldier had nearly wrecked it overboard while showing off during a squall.

"Did he really?" Mr. Tiré said. "Why would anyone perform such a dangerous stunt? Where was he traveling to?"

Grandfather yelled into the handkerchief covering his face: "The bike was taken north for three months on a ride through the mud roads of South and Central America. The soldier then boarded another ship. The second vessel took him from Manzanillo to Baja and then our village."

"And the soldier's name?" Mr. Tiré asked curiously. "He wasn't searching for trees, was he?"

Grandfather told us how odd the questions had been, that he told the man he was never given a name, though he described a scar that stretched white from beneath the soldier's right lid, deep across his nose to the edge of his mouth. "Do you know him?" Grandfather asked.

Mr. Tiré said he didn't, "But clearly the bike brought the man good fortune if he didn't crash overboard on the passage." Mr. Tiré then added in a peculiar manner: "Perhaps a spell had been cast to prevent him from drowning."

Grandfather told us he'd never heard such outlandish words. He'd known brujas and strange men who could raise water from the earth—but they were few and far between anymore. He wasn't sure he even believed in such things as he used to. And then things got stranger.

"I'm a magician," Mr. Tiré explained from the back of the motorcycle.

I was back in the village at this time trying to sell glass figurines of desert trees that I made from the sand of a nearby dune. I'd learned glassblowing from an elder who passed. Anyway, Grandfather explained everything about his ride with the stranger, including when Mr. Tiré remarked: "Un mago, un mágico, un encantador?" Grandfather later said the magician conveniently left out *brujo,* because as Mr. Tiré noted, "I am no witch doctor, nor do I want to be thought of as one."

When I saw the stranger he was so very pale and his pants were dirt-covered at the knees. I thought he may have been recently crawling. I assumed that's how he caught lizards, for he had no net or noose on the end of a stick. He must be very quick, I said to Grandfather.

"He's not from here." Grandfather said in our native tongue. He was making the obvious comment that we were a people less like those from the mainland or even from towns farther in the south where Spaniards' roots run deep and mix with those of the cities, or the transplants who come to Baja to fish the waters for tuna, marlin, and so forth, stealing the catches from the few remaining fishermen of the southern Baja tribes.

Grandfather wasn't the only one wary of this self-proclaimed magician. We'd been the victims of lighter-skinned peoples for generations. I don't just mean the salesmen and explorers, but pirates and smugglers. Ever since I was a little girl I can remember the government representatives who made their way here on horseback, who conscripted boys from the village, including my cousins who we never saw again. At least there was never much war around here, not in this strange place where desert trees bleed red and howls blow from the Cave of the Six Fingers across the milky nights.

When the magician came, villagers said he had to be from the city, a street performer like the boy Trico who our elders said came to us on a unicycle with constellations of beads in his spokes. Trico, one of our strangest visitors, pulled mysterious messages from thin air and from the ears of children that proclaimed, "majick is on the way," and "water awaits the thirsty." He rode out of the desert long before I was born, his tire hovering on sand, and his skin full and shiny like he'd never needed water in his life. He was carrying a pack of cards, and when he wasn't flipping those he was whirling four orange bowling pins end over end from one hand to the other in a great wheel of fire. They say he entertained and lived among us for weeks, happy to eat fresh pronghorn and drink the beer of cactus we call pulque in exchange for tricks on how to hawk fire like the spitting lizards that expectorate into the eyes of desert mice and birds.

They thought the magician a malabarista like Trico, that Mr. Tiré had been chased out of the streets of Mexico City for his cheap tricks and for stealing from the purses of the ladies who stopped to watch him. The villagers claimed that a young man like Mr. Tiré, no matter how well dressed, likely stuffed stolen belongings in his bags and lizard cages. Perhaps the chuckwalla with its angry eyes and tongue always flicking toward the unseen was an accomplice, stuffing rings in its fat belly. Perhaps Mr. Tiré had been nearly caught and so ran far away across the Sea of Cortés just like the war deserter whose motorcycle now belonged to Grandfather. Whenever I heard this part of the story from gossips in the short time before I was allowed to meet Mr. Tiré, I imagined him a giant, like the strange two-armed trees here that when five hundred years old tower above the sand like gods, bending whimsically toward the clouds ready to cast their spells on this place. Could this magician make himself instantly appear like such a gargantuan? I wanted to be a giant and run away too. I'd wanted my figurines, the glass ones that I create in the market, to take me around the world, away from the controlling hands of my grandparents, both of whom stole every coin I earned, then claimed I was too poor to ever do anyone any good. I wondered: if this magician could trick money from the souvenir sellers at the Teotihuacan marketplace, then he might grow a hundred feet tall, and swift as a jaguar, his boat-length strides take him up and down the Pyramid of the Moon before shrinking again and escaping into the night across the stepping stones of stars, and onto the surface of the sea like that mythical rider of unicycles, the young Trico, who I imagined in front of me reborn.

I finally saw the magician after he'd spent hours at one of the elders' houses. He was by himself, though not really—everyone watched him, including me. He set down his cages and bags at one of the tables. I was operating my forge at the edge of our market outside a tiny alley. I watched him greet the fruit seller. I watched him buy rabbit meat from my aunt's cousin. I watched the pink lizards. They were wormy with two mole-like front claws and no back legs. Each curled itself into knots. His spinytail iguana stared like I might have a handful of flies. Then I watched the magician start taking off coat after coat. Five in all by the end of it. Each was well-tailored, though dirty as the one before it, and he never seemed the bulkier or thinner for wearing them. I could only think that this was a trick of the eyes. Grandfather said he must be from one of the industry families whose silver mines dried up a decade ago but still thought themselves aristocrats, then eventually, when their mansions decayed, or the banks stole them, they turned to petty street crime.

Mr. Tiré nodded proudly to himself as his coats lay in one great pile, and said nothing as he came to where I had laid out some rather long and twisted lengths of glass that I made to represent the whimsical cirio trees that some call Boojum trees. My furnace was just a few feet away. It wasn't very large and had three openings on various tiers, with the largest hole bubbling as if filled with lava. He grinned then went and spoke quietly with Grandfather and the other elders. I could see how they whispered to him. The magician returned their soft words. They drank and sang around a crackling fire. I cleaned my workspace wondering how the magician knew some of our songs. Then I went to Grandfather to say goodnight. I overheard Mr. Tiré tell him that someone, a magician had been here generations ago, when no woman or man in this area had ever met an explorer, naturalist or missionary, and that Mr. Tiré had been trained by him in the arts of wand lore.

"By the way," the magician said to me from his place by the flames. I stood half asleep but then suddenly woke, thinking him a spirit that might start talking about the forging of stars. He continued: "My name is Salvador Tiré."

I quickly greeted him, and hid my racing heart, also kissing Grandfather, who told me I shouldn't be up so late, to make sure to give Grandmother any money I earned. I then went to Grandmother, who had heard us. She said in our native tongue that Mr. Tiré was a brujo, that he was here to melt the trees and consume both sand and animals and pull the water from below us and evaporate what was left into the sky.

I told her that he was certainly a mystery, but she didn't need to worry. "He seems harmless," I said. "He's just a lizard collector with odd thoughts about the world and a knowledge of our songs that he probably learned at the whale lagoons from Grandfather's hermit friends who live on the shore."

Grandfather told many of the villagers, including me, to leave Mr. Tiré alone, that he was indeed searching for certain legless and collared lizards, and would be inspecting the scent glands on the heads of pronghorn, though for what reason, Grandfather, nor any of the others knew. The magician also had a particular interest in plants. Grandfather said Mr. Tiré told him, "I hope you don't mind if I speak to them like long-lost relatives and friends."

It bewildered Grandmother when she heard all this, but most of all she was confounded that Mr. Tiré didn't do any magic, not right away, for wouldn't he want to prove to us what he said he was? Instead, he quietly kept to himself, purchasing a tent and then setting up camp on the outskirts of the village. There he placed his lizard cages on a long crate, and set next to those an oil lamp and a cot with netting on which he lay and read late into the night.

Like many of the others, Grandmother was quickly perturbed by Mr. Tiré's presence. The next day she came all the way to my glasswares table in the alley and said to me after spying the magician waking up late: "Séaran, you be careful around that brujo. He's not as lazy as you think. I've seen him pretend to sleep, lying with one eye open. Anyone who dreams in two worlds is dangerous."

I protested her observation of him but she said, "You're a young girl. A child. Barely sixteen. And him? He is no magician. If he was, where is his magic? He should be summoning spirits from the earth, or calling riches to pour from the heavens on us like hailstones. By the way, did you make any money today yet? Give it to me."

She wasn't alone in her thoughts. Other women made similar remarks. Our neighbor, Alazne, whose gray hair I'd braided before sunrise, said to me after I sold her one of my cirio tree pieces: "This brujo, I think, has no power other than to peer at lizards with some kind of mind's eye. Probably to make them dance when we're not looking. Do you see the way those pink ones climb his arms like little demons and whisper in his ears like they're answering hidden questions? Why don't they run away to burrow in the earth where they live in the mesquite roots? Why aren't they hiding in their tunnels? Ugly little things. Why does God make such creatures?"

She then spit: "I know why he wishes to do autopsies on each pronghorn hunted by the families here. He is deranged. Just like when he records every little detail and then hides that book of his and never speaks of it. He's scribbling nonsense. He has the desert madness."

I could only shake my head. I'd never met someone who studied the bits and pieces inside plants and animals, as well as their behaviors, nor someone who had the strange ability to communicate with something like a lizard. "Perhaps he is learning to tame the world," I said.

"Tame the world?" Alazne ground her teeth. "No one can tame a world. Did you hear what he told the men? He was in France, he said, learning about mustard gas. Do you know what that is? It's a poison cloud. Who studies such things? I'll tell you something else. He's brought that poison here," she snorted, "and it will choke us."

"Our desert plants, snakes, lizards, spiders, and scorpions are deadlier than any cloud," I said. But she ignored me and went on to shake her fist.

That night, Grandmother started complaining about something that I should have known was troubling her since she laid eyes on Mr. Tiré. "Everyone," she said, "knows I'm the most beautiful woman this village has seen since . . ." She gazed at me as if her beauty was something I didn't know. She took a breath before adding, "And he has yet to even give me one glance."

Grandfather walked into the room as she spoke and started laughing, saying she was always worrying about whether someone was in love with her, and that she missed her chance at true vanity by not moving to the city long ago to pose for advertisements, or to America where she could have auditioned for some of those moving pictures. "You need to realize," he said, "Mr. Tiré's seeming disregard for you is a sign of honor. He doesn't covet you the way that one traveler did who mysteriously disappeared."

I was listening, pretending to organize a box of figurines. You see, many of us know Grandfather likely buried that man out in the desert beneath one of the smaller Boojum trees. So it is always ear-catching to hear him mention the traveler.

Grandmother didn't take kindly to her husband's words. "You watch that brujo. He's more interested in our riches. A fraudulent man is like a thorn. Eventually, he will have to be pulled out. But not after causing a reddened, swollen infection."

Mr. Tiré eventually did make something unbelievable happen, but we didn't notice until the morning. It must have happened overnight when the moon disappears behind the gray night sands and the milk of the heavens is poured fullest. It was very early when I heard the startled voices and people running from their homes toward the edge of town. You would have thought that a chasm had opened, that we were all finally being swallowed by the Mother Spider inside the earth, that she'd had enough of her own mysteries and endless games of chance. But it was not that at all.

In fact, where once sand and dirt and shrubs hid a woodpecker family, and where the magician's tent had been, now stood a modest two-story home, and a hearty portion of a street as well, which was soon coated by a significant layer of dirt and sand. And not only that—outside his home stood one lone flickering electric streetlamp, though around here no one had anything more than candles and oil lamps, including one lamp in our home made from a four-hundred-year-old discarded conquistador helmet. Anyway, the magician's home was painted white and had a single turret with a half-circle window. Three chimneys protruded from the pitched roof and on the side of the home facing us I could see double-hung windows and one very large gothic-arched picture window in the second story.

Some of us laughed and danced in the street, giggling at this miracle. Surprisingly, it was Grandfather who cast the first accusation when the magician stepped outside his house.

"Mr. Tiré," Grandfather said, his eyes alight with the chocolate of desert twilight as he confronted the magician on the steps of this miraculously constructed home. "I thought at first you were a malabarista, then a fortune hunter or smuggler, then a friend. But now I realize you are a colonialist of the worst sort. You come to our village with your many coats, looking sickly as a starved calf. Your accent is from some faraway place. Not even a chilango, though you appear from . . ." His voice trailed as the spinytail iguana scurried over Mr. Tiré's shoulder from where it must have been clinging to his back. Grandfather continued: "You sing our songs then make no comment when someone speaks Cocopá and calls the sun, Inya. Then you build this, this monstrosity overnight? You are an imposter and trickster. What do you want from us? First you said you just needed rest, then you needed our lizards and to talk to plants. But this?"

It was then Mr. Tiré invited Grandfather inside. "Please. Have a drink with me. I have something to ask. But just you." He peered over Grandfather's shoulders. "None of the others, unless . . ."

"Unless what?" Grandfather asked.

"Nothing. Will you come in?"

Grandfather stepped inside. The door closed behind him.

A host of villagers crowded in the street and on the veranda surrounding the magician's house, trying to peer in the curtained windows, which the magician shut.

I had already left. I rearranged all the glass trees on my seller's table, and by that time was just firing up my furnace when I heard my name called. It was Grandfather hurriedly walking toward me. The magician, he said, had invited me into his house, and that I must come. "Mr. Tiré will not say another word to me unless I bring you."

"Me?" I said, a girl with a heart full of dreams.

I first stopped by our home to clean up, my insides uncomfortably twirling that young Mr. Tiré had requested my company. Of all the people in the village, he asked for me. I tried not to smile when I spotted Grandmother in the kitchen. All the wiser, she knew Grandfather was up to something, as she'd soon heard he'd gone inside the magically built home. "Isn't it enough," she said, now trying to shock me, "that the brujo's home has blocked our view of the hill where I lost my virginity? And now you want Séaran to go to his house like some kind of rabbit for his stew?"

"Would you stop it already?" Grandfather said. "Your granddaughter is not a rabbit. But this magician, this Mr. Tiré . . . he said he will not tell me what he will do for our family unless she is there. You see what he did overnight? I admit I called the man a colonialist. But then I went inside. You have to see the rooms, the bathing chambers. Three tubs! You can't imagine. And with clear, running water. I think he's going to make a home for us."

Grandmother wasn't concerned about a magic house as she pointed at me. "Do you really think she needs to be there for you to make a deal with the Devil? She needs to be selling her glass trinkets in the market. The travelers buy them . . ."

Finally, I spoke up. "Will you both leave me alone? I can take care of myself. Half the boys around here are snakes and you never seem to be worried about them. Now, you may not like it, but I am going. Grandfather will be there to see that I'm safe."

Not ten minutes later we entered the house that had appeared out of thin air.

Mr. Tiré scooted us through the foyer past entryways to two other rooms. He took us to the second floor, past a grand bathing chamber like I'd never seen. I couldn't imagine how water could be found to fill such palatial tubs. I counted three, each of polished travertine, and a chamber used for sweating surrounded by clear glass. We then entered an upstairs sitting room in the back of the house with a large rectangular window, the top of which held a row of delicate lattice-work. From here we not only had a perfect view of the hill where Grandmother lost her virginity, but a great swath of desert, and all of its many specimens of bushes and cacti and shrubs, and especially, as the magician pointed out, one of the bizarrely tilted cirio trees that grew like two furry green fingers from the desert. Because it wasn't yet midmorning, the sun lay like a golden egg between the twin trunks. Other smaller cirios, tilted this way and that, swirled their dual and sometimes singular spindly trunks toward the sky.

Right away, Grandfather realized something I didn't, perhaps out of paranoia, perhaps out of a general mistrust. "The cirio?" he said. "That large one. There isn't any other like it. You traveled from beyond the Sea of Cortés to build this magic home and view our prized specimen? Are you a logger? You can't make anything out of a cirio. Tell me you don't wish to destroy them? No tenemos ni un peso," Grandfather added, "pero somos milionarios. We won't let you cut down a single trunk."

"I have heard you and others call them cirios," said Mr. Tiré. "It's an old name given by Spaniards hundreds of years ago."

"We have another name that means 'tilted tree' in our language," Grandfather said defiantly. "But we don't always use it."

"Well, I don't call them that either," said the magician, whose eyes drifted to mine. "I know them merely as Boojum trees and I know of their anatomy. The epidermis is soft—supple, easily bruised. The flowers and seeds appear in summer and fall. And inside, oh, inside . . ."

"Boojum," Grandfather laughed. "That's a ridiculous name, one only naturalists like yourself have ever used."

"I'm no naturalist. I told you what I am."

I wondered then what Mr. Tiré really was too. A magician? A healer? A thief? I had never been this close to him. He smelled pleasant. A hint of smoke wafted invisibly from him like he'd been lazing by a hearth. I should add that he was more finely dressed than I'd ever seen him. He wore a notched lapel, double-breasted blue coat, vest, and a black tie. I wanted to touch his unshaven face to see if it felt rough like Grandfather's. Then I saw his gentle, brown eyes seemed to spark in me a kind of fire.

Mr. Tiré went on ignoring my stare: "A Boojum, I would have you know, means more than a tree. It is a danger. A warning. And, though you don't realize I am not the one to worry about, these very trees should be protected from others who might come and destroy them." He paused and nodded toward the window. "I admit, I do very much like that one. It stands taller than the rest and is nearly a thousand years old by my calculations."

"And so you would cut it down, steal it for what?" Grandfather said.

Mr. Tiré smiled. He seemed to know he'd gotten under Grandfather's skin, and didn't mind lingering on the idea of fear and betrayal. But then he said: "I don't want to cut one down. But I have bored into that tree. Last night as a matter of fact."

Grandfather looked horrified. "Why would you do such a thing?"

The magician raised an eyebrow. "For what's inside, of course. Tonight, come with me. I plan to take a better sample. One that I can use. Bring your granddaughter," he added as if I wasn't there.

"Why her?" Grandfather asked.

"I will explain tonight."

That night, after we had carefully avoided Grandmother's wrath, as Mr. Tiré led us into the desert by torchlight, he said: "You can always strike out alone and try to understand a country, but you're always a stranger and feel increasingly dislocated, don't you think?" He peered into the darkness, past the trill of crickets, then continued: "This bloody near-silent land is full of ghosts. I half expect to see deranged prophets dancing in the moonlight in self-mutilation."

I shivered at the images but still quietly followed, carrying a torch.

Soon we were at the great Boojum tree. Torchlight lit the bark and surrounding shrubs. Stars winked far above the upper spindly curve of the trunk.

The magician planted his torch near the tree's base sending a dozen scorpions scampering away. Then surprisingly from his cuffs flew the two pink two-legged lizards, which I imagined had been clinging to his forearms like bracelets. Each creature scampered toward dancing shadows in the sand and began eating any scorpion they could catch. I was horrified at the sight. I never ventured far at night, knowing that at any time I could be stung or bitten by something that would make my muscles stiffen. Out here one could get pricked on a cactus thorn so toxic that a hand or arm would turn red and bloated and cause a weeks-long madness.

"You know why so many gather here?" Mr. Tiré kicked a scorpion away from my foot. "These trees. They make a foul thing ripe for danger. I would not want to be stung by such a creature."

He then produced from a leather bag a cylindrical metal instrument that had a sharpened half-moon end. "Let me see your torch," he said to me, taking it and illuminating the soft tissue of the tree's outer layer until he found a spot to his liking about two-and-a-half feet from the desert floor. "Here," he said, returning the torch to me.

I felt a chill, like the scorpions and the lizards might be slithering around my legs in the dark. Why did I come out here? To prove I wasn't afraid? Grandfather was silent as well. I knew he thought the tree sacred, and that it was better to not offend it. I swatted a moth from my face, then several more as the magician suddenly pushed the instrument into the tree's flesh. The metal slid through the bark easier than I had imagined, as if its insides were some kind of paste.

"They say . . ." Mr. Tiré pressed his thumb along a sliding lever on the side of the mechanism and held it very still in the tree. Slowly, ever so slowly, and with a pained expression as if in great concentration, pulling the mechanism straight out, he added, "the Boojum has the hollow yet crunchy flavor of the will-o'-the-wisp."

"I wouldn't know," Grandfather finally spoke. "We've always forbidden anyone to eat them . . . Do you really have to be doing this?"

Finished with gathering his sample, Mr. Tiré closed the end of the mechanism and smiled, "There. Not so bad."

And then the strangest moment. A true horror of nature: innumerable spiders and scorpions began climbing the tree. Dozens, hundreds, scampering upward. Each creature crept into the flickering wound left by the magician's boring. Hundreds poured into the hole. It was a frightening sight. I couldn't help but think that we'd been seduced here by the power of magic.

"Perhaps we should retreat back to the house," Mr. Tiré said, noticing my fear. "Sometimes the natural world has an unnatural manner of healing, one that should only be witnessed by stars and night birds."

I was frightened, but not as much as one would expect, and not nearly as much as Grandfather.

"Agreed," Grandfather's voice shook. A flaming horror reflected in his torch-lit face as he seemed to realize that our desert, though we always knew it as strange, had somehow always been part of the darkness. "We should go," he added, "before the snakes come too."

We carried the torches back to the magician's house, sensing a slithering around us, listening to the creaking of elephant trees and the scuttling of other animals too, whose eyes reflected as if green with sparks. I was glad to finally return to the house, though when passing the lamppost, I saw its electric flickering had attracted a great many winged insects of all sizes—beetles, night flies, desert walking sticks, and feasting spiders, all covering the light post and bulb's glass casing like some macabre disease.

Inside the house we were taken to the kitchen. The magician poured dark-colored drinks that tasted of some kind of rum. "A strong elixir for the heart," he said.

Grandfather, still shaken by the strangeness of the Boojum tree, took a few sips, then said, "Why are we here at such an hour? What did we just witness?"

Mr. Tiré, bothered by Grandfather's impatience, turned his attention to me. "You have been very quiet this evening."

Grandfather interrupted. "She has nothing to say. I don't even know why I brought her." He shook his head at me. "Go home, Séaran. I'll find out what he wants. No more mysteries. Run along."

But I didn't move. Too curious, I felt a softness for Mr. Tiré. He wasn't so dangerous. In fact, here in the light, he was the most attractive man I'd ever seen.

The magician sipped his drink slowly, and for several seconds I wondered if he could read my thoughts. "You're a funny girl," he said. "I see you thinking. Always thinking. Watching."

"I'm not a girl," I said. I could tell by Grandfather's scowl that he was about to confirm the magician's statement. But Mr. Tiré was too quick:

"*Girl* is such an antiquated expression. You're a woman, though I'm hesitant to use such a word out of fear of offending your grandfather." He then changed the subject and motioned for us to follow. "Let me take you to another room. My intentions will be clearer then, for you will see," he said to Grandfather, "that I only want to marry the skills of this young lady to my desires."

I felt elated just then as if everything about life was suddenly beautiful and dark. I learned something, I felt I really did, that some are privileged by a kind of madness, and that this persuasive glimpse was a magnet, pulling me toward my interior. I wanted more. I didn't care if it meant insanity even though I still had no idea what his desires would mean for me.

"We will do no such thing," Grandfather started to say.

But this is where I stepped in again and took the magician's arm. "Lead the way," I said. Grandfather reached toward me but could do nothing to constrain my movements. I wondered if he'd grown weaker. Nevertheless, I didn't care. That feeling alone was freeing.

We walked down a hall, then several flights of stairs before we came to an open door and a familiar smell. In fact, everything about this place was familiar. Its dampness, its warmth—the unmistakable scent of beeswax and the smoldering of things.

"What is this?" Grandfather said.

This time I spoke first. "A furnace," I said, my eyes lit with wonder. "A glassblowing furnace."

"You are right there," said Mr. Tiré, who turned to Grandfather. "Séaran has a skill I most desire to make use of while here among the Boojums."

"What could you possibly want her to make?" Grandfather said. "Her skills are worthless. Hardly anyone buys her little glass trees."

It was then that Mr. Tiré took from his pocket a folded parchment that seemed to be quite old. He walked over to a table, unfolded and smoothed it out, saying as if we knew what he was talking about, "Proper dimensions for a Boojum *waxglass*." On the paper were the specifications for a rod that had molten shapes as whimsical as the Boojums themselves. He then added, "And if we're going to speak in generalities, a glass wand. Don't ever think they're all made out of wood. Shall we get started?"

"Boojum *waxglass*?" Grandfather said. "What could it possibly be used for?"

Mr. Tiré hesitantly took out of a coat pocket a wand not unlike the one on the diagram, only this rod was gold-tinged with tiny glass beetles along its curvature. Inside of its infundibular cavity a small amount of liquid seemed to boil and rotate on its own. "The wand you create," he said, "will be different from this one as it will have the extract from the Boojum tree inside of it along with a distillation of wiregrass, a form of King's Leaf, the likes of which have properties too numerous for me to explain at the moment. There will be other additions as well. The blood sap of the elephant tree, some of the beetles attracted to the lamppost outside, and the scent gland of a pronghorn. I found an especially impressive gland that I have boiling in this very room, just waiting for the additions. You see, though all wands are dangerous, this one will be especially so. That is . . ."

"That is, what?" Grandfather said. "Enough of this. We're going, and you're to leave our village now. Take your wand and your house with you."

"I don't want to leave," I said, having realized that once again I was being treated like a thing. I hated every moment of it. "Why do you think you can push me around in here of all places?" I yelled at Grandfather. "You witnessed the miracle of this place. Even the tree and the way every creature wanted to heal its wound was a miracle. Do you ever wonder why venom exists if it can't be used for something more than watching the world writhe in fear?" My every heart muscle hurt as Grandfather muttered and babbled and I interrupted again and told him to stop being ridiculous, that he was the one who brought me into this house to begin with. "You must live with what happens here," I demanded.

"She's quite right," said Mr. Tiré, just then aiming his wand at Grandfather. He flicked his wrist and Grandfather slipped into a chair, pulled by invisible bonds. The magician flicked his wrist again and Grandfather's arms were glued with some kind of jelly to the armrests. Once more and Grandfather's lips were literally melted shut. "Don't think," Mr. Tiré said, "that I'm leaving here without that wand. I have tried to teleport with the Boojum sample. It breaks down and turns to mush. I told you it was delicate. And, knowing what I know about these trees, I'm not about to bring a wandmaker here. Your granddaughter is my only hope."

I wasn't angry that Mr. Tiré used magic to subdue Grandfather. I only wished that I had that same power. It would be many years before I would realize that I never should have turned my back on my village the way I did, but it was too late. I was too proud and had finally seen a way for my own escape. That's why I turned to

Mr. Tiré and said, "If I do this for you, take me with you when you leave."

"Don't think I won't," Mr. Tiré said as I turned to the furnace and with a steady, full heart readied myself for what I was about to do.

On a hook was a length of iron blowpipe. I carefully coated the metal in a layer of beeswax. I held the blowpipe with the musty sleeve hanging next to it, and then through a hole in the furnace, dipped the end into the vat and twirled until I had a glowing yellow-orange glob that burned with the scent of honey. I was instantly covered in sweat and took a breath and then another, steadying myself. A few seconds later I puffed my cheeks out and blew. The glass expanded into a bubble that extended twelve or so inches. I made sure it was to specification in length, width, and diameter. I then whisked the glass into the next furnace, heating it slightly, and pulled it out again, prying on the sticky glass with an oversized pair of tweezers until barbs developed along its shaft that I stretched and pulled into shapes to resemble the convolutions of the Boojum tree. Satisfied, I stuffed the wand into the third opening. A small flash of smoke puffed toward me as water cooled the molten form. When I removed the glass I set it on the table upon a small pad to the horror of Grandfather's eyes.

◆

It had been nicknamed Malogrado Manor by resident magician-historian Santino Hernandez, for the deaths that happened there when a conflagration ripped through its halls and towers. Santino, only a child when the flames tragically came, hadn't mentioned the fires in any of his works, though Sir Robert LaFondier, the most highly regarded magician-historian anywhere, wrote extensively about the tragic blaze in his book *Five Famous Fires After the Exodus.* LaFondier included several testimonies in his chapter on the Malogrado fire, including one from the very young Santino Hernandez who claimed he'd seen a faerie laughing and running down Malogrado's halls with a candle from which shot a long red flame.

Santino sat across from Séaran de la Gaspar, now elderly, and whose black hair had long turned gray. Her eyes, once almond and inquisitive, had shrunk into the gaze of one worried that life is but a fleeting meteor. She rested against a high-backed chair. Santino's largest library drawing room was filled with shadows of books.

Hundreds in wooden bookcases shined with inlaid iron seals, in particular, the city of Wintershire, which was thought to no longer exist except in old seafaring maps, including a collection rescued from Verunfeld.

Séaran couldn't read any of the titles from where she sat but assumed at least a dozen were volumes of history in which Santino wrote his many counternarratives to the works of other magician-historians, including Sir Robert LaFondier, and one of the freshest young minds in a generation, Ornelle duBerg, whose first volume of history, *A Serendipitous Garden of Lies: The Winter Magician,* had been considered a literary-historical hybrid masterpiece. A member of the Society of Wands and Distinguished Luminaries, Santino was, at the least, well regarded.

Séaran watched the magician-historian tap a finger on a notepad and smile.

"I appreciate you telling me your story," he said. "I learned much about the Boojum *waxglass* from a Curator of Lost Wands. You knew Mr. Maximino Wagenblast? What was that he always said? *Know the first spell, know the wand, know the wizard.* Tragic, he's no longer with us."

"He lived about a mile from me in Hillside," she said. "His home was next to a lemon grove. He called it his Villa de Citron." She smiled as if remembering a happier time, then her voice trailed: "He had a mouse named Richard . . . but everyone's read about that."

"I'm looking forward to volume two of duBerg's work," Santino said. "Perhaps there will be more about this mouse." He then cleared his throat and scribbled on his notepad. "You know, I haven't been able to continue writing the history of this strange wand without your version of what happened in the Cucapá village all those years ago. I was so very lucky to find you, just as I was lucky to come across the wand from a Society magician."

"It's very difficult to remember."

"I know you're trying." He sipped a coffee. "You're not a teenager anymore. What are you now, eighty-seven?"

"When I stopped living?" She stared down at the pale blue of her skin. She still hadn't gotten used to being an apparition—if that's what she was, or partially so. Memories of her skin, warm with color and blood, were still vivid in her mind. "It's been some years since I turned . . ."

"Pardon me. I knew that. I meant no offense."

"It's no matter. I just wish . . ."

He cleared his throat. "You only made one such Boojum *waxglass*?"

"Only one."

"And you never knew magic before that?"

"Never. I was just a girl in a village, though I had a trade. As I told you, I was taught glassblowing from an elder who learned her trade in Mexico City."

"And after you made the wand that night, you left with Tiré?"

"I had to."

"You were forced?"

"Not exactly."

"Care to elaborate?"

"No one knows this story," she whispered.

He rattled his notes. "I realize this is difficult."

"I left with him willingly after we killed . . ."

Santino leaned forward in his chair. He was scribbling madly. "You killed who?"

"Not me. *We*. Mr. Tiré and I . . . I can never take full blame."

"Séaran, history needs to know what happened. Not only that, but this wand. Its history needs to be known."

"I know. I know. Mr. Tiré lost the wand," she said. "I'm surprised you have it back."

"Its loss is very well documented," he nodded. "Do you think it had to do with what happened the night you created it?"

She agreed: "It had everything to do with that night. You see, no matter who is at fault, the wand had to be created. Mr. Tiré had to do what he did to Grandfather. And I . . ." She hesitated. "Men just like women have flaws, and his was his obsession to create that wand in his grandiose home instead of using my forge, instead of boiling the extract for his wand in his tent, or in the alley where I worked. His privilege as a magician ruined him. He had access to too great of magic. And that is so very destructive."

"What was wrong with the home he built?" Santino asked. "He introduced civilization to your village in such a generous way . . . My notes suggest he was going to build more . . ."

"Generous? We were the bugs on the lamppost, hardly allowed on his porch, let alone inside. Did I not tell you of the bathworks? Why would he build those? It was his obsession but he was just as covered in dust as we were. I'm not to blame for that part. I was a young girl . . ." She watched the magician-historian write more notes and sip more coffee. It angered her how lifeless her skin had become. This. This was the result of the wand—to conquer death. It wasn't when Mr. Tiré died that she knew its power. It was after she herself had died several years ago when she realized she wasn't only a ghost, but something else, something unexplainable. She had been resurrected long before she died. It had been in her since creating the wand. And the sad part? She was to be locked forever in the body of an icily dead octogenarian.

"I had visions. I saw myself in his house that night," she went on, "before I even stepped foot there. I saw myself in the wand too. Then I became a part of its creation. Every glass Boojum tree I'd blown had already been in some ways representations of myself. And so, after I finished the wand, and Mr. Tiré said, 'Make another,' I did. I started the process all over again to make a second Boojum *waxglass*. Another representation of myself. That's when I saw the horror on Grandfather's face. Mr. Tiré—his back had been to us at the time. But Grandfather, he'd seen the first creation, and at the same time saw Grandmother come into the room. That was true fear."

"And what was that fear?" Santino asked.

"That she was going to try and stop me. That she might try and kill me, or Mr. Tiré. You have to understand, Santino. She'd lost her mind. She didn't understand what I was doing. And yet she accused me of madness. 'You're insane,' she said. 'You've become a demon of the night.'

"I was glassblowing when she reached for the wand, the one I'd already made. That's when I thought, what if she destroys it and the one I am trying to make? What if they can't be made again? That's when I lost all concentration. That's when I unwittingly sacrificed the partially made wand in my hand. That's why the molten hot glass leapt from my gloves into her heart, and is why the house caught fire—because as she fell, her clothes and the table soon burst into flames, and everything else with them."

"I understand such fires," Santino said. "Mr. Tiré's story, and yours, has been so difficult to track down. I'm glad you and he escaped. I'm sorry about your grandparents. Their loss is a shame." Santino held the Boojum *waxglass*. He turned the wand in his fingers.

"Have you used it?" she asked.

"Me? No. I won't." He held it up to the light so she could see how she'd put all of her best Boojum tree figurines into one beautiful glowing specimen—a wand. The glass swirled with liquid. Its innards bubbled. "So very unique," he said. "Who would ever think a first wand could be so elegant?"

"It's troubled," she said. "Something about it is not right."

"A curse from an old continent?" he asked himself. "To wield such a danger, one brushes with madness, and of course your resurrection came of its dark grace. It has power enough to summon, though I dare say I don't want to think about what or who this could bring back . . ."

She looked at him pitifully because he must have known his mistake.

"A couple more questions?" he begged.

She nodded.

"Is it true you destroyed the great Boojum tree?"

"Why not?" she rested her eyes on his. "It was never a tree of life. Though I buried my grandparents there as fuel in case something needed to grow from where the Boojum once towered."

His face grew very sad at this. "I had dreamed the tree was alive, that perhaps your part of the story wasn't true. My dream had been so vivid. I was hoping for an ancient tree that I could greet like an old friend . . . In final I must ask: What do you miss?"

Séaran carefully thought at this, wringing one cold hand against the other. "Being a teenager," she said. "Dreaming. Being in love. There was a boy in the village. He always tried to ride a unicycle that had been left at the village long ago but could never quite get the hang of it. I was teaching him glassblowing after the villager who taught me went to the other side. There was this innocence I had, these dreams I imagined. Do you know the moment you had your own? Do you know when they went away? We all want to take something back when we figure it out. Some think that has a pull on us like the moon over the oceans. I want to go back in time and escape gravity altogether and just float and dream in such tides. We're dreamers, you and I. We will always want for a better . . . something."

Madrina

SARA DANIELE RIVERA

PART I: GODMOTHER

16 October 3011

That night she woke in water, and it was daytime.

Late afternoon, she would guess. She was floating on her back, looking up at a reddening sun and cliffs lost under heaps of green. The wide, backlit glisten of a waterfall gashed out between leaf and rock, fractured into smaller falls. She couldn't see rainbows but imagined they parted white mist all around her.

The water that cradled her felt warm, thick, lotioned. She looked down and saw that the water was green, the gray green of a smoked emerald, a water tone she'd never seen before.

As far as she could tell, she was alone, alone with sun and cliff and this body, this new body. She examined it. Underwater, she ran her fingers over her new stomach, small but very round. The arms and legs were soft too. Her skin was dusky brown like a fig. The seam of a white shirt curled around the tops of her ribs and its light fabric billowed in the water, a cloud around her chest.

Beautiful. Divine. Where was she? She didn't care.

It always took a moment—sometimes up to an hour—for the madrina's memories to enter her mind after knocking around at the periphery like tentative guests. Today, the first thing to bubble up

339

was a word: *skydclan*. It meant family, or something like family. The madrina was lying in the water alone to avoid her skydclan, whoever they were. They were all gathered somewhere in a stone house in ambient light, celebrating, and she was expected there, expected to stand like a pillar in the center of a hive of children. The madrina wasn't avoiding the celebration out of malice or boredom. She was relishing a moment of privacy.

Body in water. Water on skin. No one else here. It had been months since the madrina had last seen this place empty. Maybe because summer was ending, and though the water retained warmth the air above felt like it had been blown off the height of a mountain. People stayed inside unless, like tonight, they went out to celebrate a feast day. Tonight they would light lanterns and float them downriver. Pinpoint lights like fireflies, LEDs. The madrina would meet her children, she decided, on their way to the river. She had time. She could rest a bit longer.

The visitor in the madrina's body had almost forgotten that she had a purpose. But how could she force herself to inventory every detail of their surroundings when all her madrina wanted was to close her eyes and rest? Silt shifted, clay-slime beneath their back. The sun descended incrementally. Now it crowned the shadow green.

"I'm in a warm spring," the visitor said out loud, testing the madrina's voice.

Saying things out loud had always helped her. That, and she always delighted in the sound of a new voice, its musculature and music. Every voice felt different from first vibration to final projection. This voice made her grin. So high, almost girl-like, and yet silver swirls of hair ferned out in the water. This woman was young and not young at once.

"That sounds right," said the madrina. "I still feel like if I wanted to do a flip, I could."

The visitor started. Water rippled away. It happened, sometimes, with a powerful personality. The madrina would speak too, using their joint voice, and it felt like talking to yourself but not knowing what your self was going to say. The visitor had experienced three such conversations before. The technology was designed to incite certain emotions: instead of fighting an invader, the madrina welcomed a visitor, and shared a story.

"What are the children celebrating?" asked the visitor.

"It's the festival of Halflight," said the madrina. "Our solstice. That's what you used to call it, mm? Or Samhain? Mmm. Isn't the water warm? I thought I'd be alone but here you are."

Time stamp: knowledge of the words solstice, Samhain. Places them in the past.

"I like being alone with you," said the visitor.

"Aren't you nice. You're like a relative, but not so looooud."

A twist of laughter in their mutual mouth. The madrina and visitor at once raised wet fingers to their lips and smeared water across them, moistening. It was unclear who directed the action.

"It's almost time for me to go," said the madrina. "The sun's almost gone." Shadow had fallen across the water, tumbled rock and tree.

"It's almost time for me to go too," said the visitor. "But I want to stay."

"This is your house too. Come back someday."

"What's your name?" asked the visitor.

"Avila."

"Lilet. I have this feeling, Avila. It's like I just adore you."

Avila laughed, and Lilet felt some pity in that laughter. She felt it deep in their mutual belly.

PART II: TRIGGER

30 October 3011

The M.A.D.R.I.N.A. Project Casebooks: Mimicry Anthropology through Direct Reallocation and Intertemporal-Substitution by Neural Affinity

Verbal Agreement 00:15–00:31—30 October 3011
Entry by Dr. Lilet DeEsparza, PhD

This is a free-flow journal entry requested by Dr. Nadya Shiburo. I've been asked to read aloud a transcript of a diary entry following the 13 MAY TRIGGER EVENT. MADRINA archives require documentation to account for the quick and full reinstation of our funding. I have stated for the record that my journals are personal rather than analytic in tone, so this account is recommended for grouping with other data of its kind concerning the TRIGGER EVENT.
BEGIN

When it began, the labs looked like they were sleeping. Bugs floated all viscous. People were quiet. The Bailey was turned off: safing, and dark. Safe mode never makes you feel safe.

Our Ayelids stayed on. As we walked around, we saw double dark: what was in front of us, and the eyelid overlay that narrated what was happening, what safe mode meant, the classification of the trigger event. One level above error: very mild.

It had been a couple years since the last trigger, long enough to make peace with it. Now here we all were, skirting corners, talking in whispers like rats, cradling our rats as if they were pets, laughing out of turn, lecturing ourselves and each other, anything, I think, to suppress that tiny part of ourselves that thought we might die, could die, would die, suspended and vacuumed in space. One night, the whole ship heaved, and we fell back against the walls. The ship made that awful breathing sound that it makes when we jump—only we couldn't be jumping.

A vision of our bodies blinking out. Our hearts clenched into nothing by cold. Those images you construct for yourself are powerful. Also, you grow up having to study them on the Bailey.

When the lights came back on it took us a few days to trust them. When everything began to hum and click and zoom around us like normal, we felt we should no longer be terrified. But we were. We didn't know what had happened. CC hadn't given the all-clear. In fact, for two days, they didn't say anything. The news stream on Ayelid reiterated old information.

Normal life on the Bailey was undercut then by a climate of secrecy. People (nanotech experts, communications experts) started getting called in to CC, one by one, and they'd come out looking so old and tired. If any of them broke their silence, I didn't hear about it.

Eventually they had to tell us. Each sector in turn: an attempt to contain and control the spread of panic. Mine was third.

We were gathered in the starfield room. They did this on purpose because no one could hear us, and only CC could let us out, and they wouldn't, not right away, not in the heat of it.

I remember only a few words of Captain Ruiz's monologue, the ones that became a refrain in my mind for the next month:

We are lost.

We've lost communication with Earth.

We've lost communication with Katla.

We experienced a safe mode malfunction that resulted in an accidental jump. CC tech was affected. If any believe they can help, we are assembling a team of specialists to continue researching, to determine our location, to come up with options. In the meantime, full ongoing project research allocation for this sector goes to the location-stamp technology of the MADRINA project, in case consciousness travel can give us the location of Earth.

I repeat: we've lost communication with Katla.

We've lost communication with Earth.

We don't know where we are.

It took only a minute for our audience to become a mob vibrating with its own anger and stress. The more passive people like me just went numb.

In the days to come, panic would ripple. It would generate grief cycles. You came out of that cycle determined to just work because you weren't dead yet, and every now and then, when you saw the brilliant minds who were working together threads of hope would ignite in you. How could humanity not find a solution? Someone would look out the window, find the right clue, and find out where we were. Of course they would.

Sure enough, people outside of the task force started making an avalanche of beamcoms to CC. I recognize the star system! I know where we are! But they were wrong every time.

After a while, CC didn't even bother to say anything. They went quiet. That quiet sliced and gored us. We didn't know what to do with so much uncertainty. We still don't.

END

PART III: MIDNIGHT

16 October 3011

Lilet's lips had started to go blue inside the chamber, so they pulled her out.

The air that greeted her felt like it came out of a tin can. The light that greeted her had been set to *sunset* and the liquid she woke in felt like cold mucous. The first thing she did was scratch her left arm. That was the only thing she knew for sure: her arm itched. Otherwise, she couldn't name anything in the room. Nothing in focus, not even the familiar text overlay from her Ayelid. It danced in her unfocused vision.

She started thrashing. She thrashed toward the light and a hundred pinpricks of pain rippled across her body as the TimeWires were torn out. Two sets of arms caught her, restrained her, and tried to extract the wires correctly.

By the time her own memories returned—not tepidly knocking at the door, but slammed back in from different angles—she was out of the TimePool, dripping on the composite floor. The arms that held her upright belonged to Nadya and Dabo, project head and chemist. Nadya's arms held her forcefully, Dabo's tenderly.

Dabo was removing the remaining wire from her forearms and clotting spots of blood with a cotton ball. When she saw him, and knew him, her body and breath gradually stilled.

"You look familiar," Lilet said.

"Once I went to nice restaurant on East Plankta Promenade," he said. "They served us prickly pear preserves. Bright green, globby, and lots of seeds."

"Is that what I look like right now?" she said, her voice weak but smiling.

"That's what you look like right now," Dabo said.

It was an old game of theirs. She'd tell him he looked like something normal, or bland, and he'd tell her she looked like something creative, specific, grotesque, because he knew that she loved the grotesque.

She eased her elbows away: she could stand on her own. She looked past Dabo at the TimePool, which the interns were already mopping, one of them gathering loose wires into her arms like a little silver bird's nest.

◆

A week after the TimePool incident, Dabo came to visit her in bed. Lilet could've transferred to her own bed, to theirs, at any point, but she *liked* this station bed. Bailey scientists and engineers had gotten good at creating basic materials from nothing, or close to nothing. Lilet slept in on one of their printed mattresses. Every point and angle of her body that made contact with the mattress hummed with satisfaction.

Or maybe she only told herself she was satisfied. She tried to convince herself that she liked being so immobile. She didn't talk to herself about the longing that had shattered across her heart since meeting Avila, about the strange sadness that choked her. It too touched every point of her body, sinking her deeper.

That week, Lilet mostly stayed in bed even though her hips groaned. She simply couldn't convince herself to wake up.

"Hi, corazón," Dabo said as he sat beside her one morning, greeting her in the language her mother had spoken. They always greeted each other this way. A tether to Earth and self.

"Titili," she said. Greeting the language his mother had spoken.

She looked down as he took her hand. It was the first time she realized that the colors she'd loved so much in Avila's world were the colors of their skin: hers a smoked emerald, a cold, rich green, Dabo's a deep forest black. A side effect of being born and raised on the Bailey.

"Say the word," he said. "And I turn this whole room into a game of pinball."

She laughed.

"You want to tell me about it today?" he asked.

"You've got study voice on," she said. "Like you can't help it."

"Ayla is very worried about you."

"Soffing named your Ayelid."

"I want to help."

There it came again: the shadow. Like the room of her mind had been set to *midnight*.

"Let me sleep, my butterfly," she said.

❖

Verbal Agreement 00:00–00:24—26 October 3011
Entry by Dr. Lilet DeEsparza, PhD

My name is Dr. Lilet DeEsparza. I am a participant in the MADRINA Project and this documentation pertains to a targeted TimePool study that took place October 16th, 3011, at 22:00 BAILEY TIME. Researchers are asked to bear in mind the parameters of the study, which equates neural flux following consciousness travel to the condition of sleep paralysis. This is my seventh TimePool trial. My personality type is INTP.

I remember a warm spring at the bottom of a waterfall. Type: 1067 A. Host was alone in the spring. Clothed. Garment type: Split, 24 X7, wait. Maybe she wasn't wearing—never mind. Skin palette: tumbleweed, oatgrass, midnight. Hair type: star streak, lemongrass. Language stamp: Nordic. My best time stamp: mid-23rd century. The host placed Samhain and LED lighting in the past. Society: agrarian. Unusually green. Request

to compare against other TimePool data in NORDIC countries as my spe-
cialty is LATINAMERICA.

If I were to describe my waking experience along the color chart, I'd say
that over the span of the past week I've felt turquoise and navy. I'm aware
that this is not typical of my assessments following a TimePool shift, but
is consistent with previous terminated participants. I feel like someone has
died.

PART IV: ANTHROPOLOGY

4 June 3015

Verbal Agreement 00:00–00:13—4 June 3015
Entrev. Coady Ka-Vera, Katla MCOMM, c/ Dr. Lilet DeEsparza,
PhD

INT: What does it mean to you to be here? To have set foot on land?

DES: It's almost . . . waking up, there's morning. And I've known mornings through TimeWire but it's very different to experience morning every day. You almost have too many options. The other day I went onto the Bailey and didn't leave until it was *spurod* out because I got overwhelmed by how many different places I could go. I think the human body and mind has only so much ability to internalize new sensory information. So I spend some time out, some time in . . .

I don't mean to diminish it. It means everything. It's land. For the first time I'm anchored to place. I'm just trying to express that it's as terrifying as it is euphoric.

Spurod?

Oh sorry. That means space-dark. Dark inside as outside, if you're in space.

I understand. My parents grew up on Noptera, the first ship, and talked to me a lot about their first year on Katla. It's longer than an Earth year, so you know, they had to get used to cycles.

That's what it is, cycles. Onboard the Bailey all we could do was mimic cyclical time. We were prepared, I guess, as much as we could be—obviously, there were so many medical professionals onboard, everywhere you turned there was another doctor speculating and publishing on what our bodies would do the second we were exposed to Katla. They prepared us for the fact that we'd probably be sick a lot, especially those of us raised on the ship, even with the precautionary treatments. We had never been exposed to changing weather. I've felt sick most of the time since I arrived and have been badly sick about four times now.

Since you mention doctors, something I was going to ask: things were structured a little differently on the Bailey because it was designed to service that transition from Earth to Katla. Nadya told me that you didn't really choose your professions. Can you tell me about that?

Honestly it was what I knew. It didn't feel rigid. Maybe it did for other kids. There was room on the Bailey for occupations outside of science, they just weren't the preference and there weren't many people available who could offer a high degree of training in those fields. And basically our operational web was a snapshot of what was live and available at the time we left Earth. So people could learn how to do things, how to play music, I guess. It was outdated information but the up-to-date information from Earth wasn't relevant to us anyway. Not aboard the Bailey, and not here on Katla. Once we got here, the only immediate reality had to be this one.

But cultural anthropology, my field, I got into it because I liked behavior. I liked biology too and anthropology became this synthesis of mind and body. For a long time though I actually thought I'd go into entomology because as a kid I *loved* bugs. I loved massive holos, filling my whole room with the insects of the Amazon and I'd play insects with my brother, tell him to pretend to be a helicopter damselfly. He'd try to act like that insect. At some point, I became more interested in the boy imitating the damselfly than the damselfly itself. I wanted to know why we do what we do. The educators aboard the Bailey were attuned to that shift.

And how did you get involved, then, in the MADRINA project?

It was initially a collaboration. The MADRINA collaborative grew out of the development of TimeWire, because it was important to the initial developers of TimeWire to keep consciousness travel ethical. It's an invasive technology, but also a technology with an extraordinary potential to change the narrative of the past, to give us insight into the past, particularly the undocumented past, which we determined, in the western colonial societies we were interested in, meant the matrilineal past.

When I first heard about this, I admit that I was hesitant. Isn't entering the mind of someone just another act of colonization? Someone other than the madrina is ultimately going to be writing her story.

It's a difficult ethical question. You're putting a lot of power in subjective hands. And I can't speak for the original collective or the entirety of their dialogue, but for me, as a participant and ultimately as a consciousness traveler . . . each trip was about listening. Honestly, when you go back, you don't have a lot of time, or it takes so much time to get your bearings that you're not going to bring back a revisionist history. You'd need a lot more information to really place that person's story in the constructs of their society. All you have time for is an impression. And, if you're lucky, a conversation. You get to know people in the past. People who are not known today, who were otherwise forgotten. It's like you're filling in a blank on this larger map of humanity. Maybe you're filling it in with something hazy and insubstantial, but at least it isn't blank anymore.

Why women?

The original collective was all women, born or identified. And yes. They were interested in women's stories and reconfiguring the world as matrilineal. But it was also that consciousness travelers match to women eight times out of ten. It's unclear how that matching happens. It seems to vary depending on how strictly gender roles were enforced or embedded in a certain culture at a certain time and how those roles were tied to biological sex. I've shared consciousness with a transwoman living in 2018, but I know people who have shared transgender consciousness in cultures and time periods when there was no societal language with which to identify what that meant. Which was fascinating. It meant that the MADRINA project could go beyond what the madrinas themselves were allowed, culturally, to be aware of. The point is to say that with MADRINA, we focused on women's stories, but "woman" means many things and we're still learning, across the entirety of history and time, what all the meanings are.

PART V: DWOONING

27 October 3011

Lilet walked down the hall in tinned darkness. All light was soft, peripheral, humming, beeping. An off-green glow from a lab to her left. An intermittent red alarm light to her right. All around her, rectangular space: the familiar blue-gray framework of the Bailey. Her Bailey. Her halls, the only ones she'd known.

Her station bed was located within the secure TimeWire zone. Her security clearance meant she could move freely after hours. Around-the-clock TimeWire security watched the outer perimeter, but Lilet slept in the inner sanctum as she healed, within the octagon of rooms that housed MADRINA and other ongoing TimeWire experiments. The TimePool slept in the center of the octagon, its waters turning and lapping at all times, so that as she neared the core (eight glass doors) she could see it, a black oval like a bathtub, four-foot-tall walls, and above it the faint cast of water-light, alternations in green. She could hear it too: a licking sound, cradling of a mother's womb. The doors parted for her and she stood alone beneath the dome.

Lilet breathed it in: the familiar encasement of metal and glass, cold air prickling her arms beneath the winglike material of the nightdress they'd given her. The room was always kept cold.

She didn't know if she could set the whole thing up herself. It would probably take most of the night. She would certainly get caught. She might get stuck in Avila's consciousness, might find halfway through that it was actually impossible to consciousness travel entirely on her own.

But Lilet would try. She was already wearing her TimeSuit underneath the nightdress. She slipped the dress off and it fluttered to the ground, and she moved toward the light feeling mothlike and new, like she'd found something she never expected to find. She'd been told she might find it, but hadn't known she would want the connection so badly: her own madrina. A woman of her bloodline.

◆

Tell me about this controversy. So many people went through the project— it was hard to retain people. I imagine there are different facets to that.

Yes, there are, but maybe not as many as you'd think. The screening process was intensive because you needed someone in an extremely stable mental state. The mental risks involved in consciousness travel were innumerable . . . disassociation, erroneous memory, depression, paranoia, PTSD in participants who traveled into women who lived in violent times and circumstances. We witnessed extreme, debilitating forms of homesickness, people who developed a crippling need for a place they'd never actually known.

You're also putting the body through a kind of trauma: keeping it at low temperature, penetrating the skin, keeping the body wet. If you ate in someone else's body, you sometimes felt, upon return, as if you'd eaten. And your mind would tell your body that it didn't want to eat again. Participants developed highly irregular patterns. For a while the average was three trips before we retired someone from the program. We retired at the earliest warning signs; we ran a full assessment on each participant after every trip. Not everyone wanted to quit and in some cases, that was another problem: addiction.

When I started traveling, I found that I was good at it. I could keep my body, my mind over *here,* and their body, their mind over *there.* My final assessments were free and clear. My team was astounded from the beginning, and then my ability became immensely valuable to them. Because I could start to recognize through-lines. I could compare trips to previous trips, from my own perspective. I could speak to trends and changes. And I liked learning. People are messy, complicated, emotional, but as an anthropologist I could approach that messiness in a methodological way.

Anyway. About the termination process.

My understanding is that immediate termination from the project happened if . . . the participant ended up in the mind of someone they knew?

Not someone they knew. I don't actually think anyone ended up *that* close in time, that they knew the person. No. What we encountered was that, because consciousness travel paired you with people who already shared strong mental affinity, you would, at some point, inevitably, end up in your own bloodline. In the consciousness of your own ancestor. People who encountered this knew it immediately, irrevocably, pit-of-the-stomach. They came out of that pool changed when it happened. We called it finding your own madrina. Keep in mind that the acronym means godmother.

Wow. That seems like a dwooning experience.

I don't . . .

Here on Katla, if the moon and sun are up at the same time, you get a bizarre light around them. It's purple. It kind of sparkles. And it's really unsettling for some people. They have an actual reaction to it. So something that gives you that unsettled feeling, all the way down to your bones, it's dawn-mooning, dwooning.

To my ear it's a slightly silly word.

We use a lot of words that I think will sound silly to you here.

Fair. So . . . once . . . dwooned . . . participants would snap. They had an insatiable need to go back. They'd try to break into TimeWire. They wanted their madrina's conversation, her guidance, they wanted to know their family secrets and truths. At that point, we couldn't risk it. People were not stable enough to travel again. Either they weren't stable enough or—like we found the one time we allowed a participant to go on one trip after the fact—the emotional tether was too strong. She'd pop right back in to that same person, that same body, the same location even. Her mind became too targeted.

Wouldn't that be useful? You said earlier that you never had enough time to really get a sense for context.

To be honest, no. It got too personal.

But you were the most stable of them all.

And so I tried to keep it a secret that I'd found her. Because I needed to see her again, and I knew I could handle a trip back. Or I thought I could.

PART VI: LIGHT

27 October 3011

"Welcome back. You missed the lanterns."

Avila carried an armful of damp, fern-like leaves that plastered against their joint forearms. The two of them, Avila and Lilet-in-Avila, walked in a loose pack of people. It seemed Lilet would always meet Avila at crepuscular times: she had arrived first at dusk, and now at dawn.

The forest path was mulch beneath them. Avila's skydclan—her people, her children, Lilet still didn't know exactly—circulated around them, playing, talking. The stone house that Lilet had seen before in Avila's memory stood ahead of them on the path now, embraced by trees that looked deciduous, that had a bluish tint to their leaves. Those leaves, the size of a large, splayed hand, hung low over the house and obscured its borders, framed its wooden front door.

"Shhhh," said Avila.

Lilet nodded lightly. She and Avila both knew that they couldn't speak with the same mouth in public. Lilet always remained cognizant of the rules of consciousness travel: Stay as inauspicious as possible. Do not endanger the madrina, do not make her appear insane, do not make her behave in a highly unconventional way for her circumstances. So Lilet took the opportunity to have Avila look around and study the people around her.

They all wore floor-length, skirted garments woven in jeweled earth tones. In place of shoes they wore the luminescent bioskins designed in the 2200s. Their feet shone in the dawn, but not a harsh light. They could see where they were going and their feet were encased in the most natural, hearty protection, not getting pricked by spines that came up through the forest floor. Most adults carried foliage, space baskets that compressed their bounty as well as regular woven baskets full of bulb vegetables.

Even though they weren't speaking, Lilet could sense Avila trying to soothe her confusion. Where on Earth were they?

A word cropped up in their consciousness: *heimagar.* Lilet felt the impressions of that word. Homeland, homeplace, heartplace.

Homeland, homeplace, heartplace. Lilet exchanged a word from her childhood: *hogar.*

"Old word," said Avila out loud.

Lilet could have asked the natural follow-up question (*how old*). She could have done many things in that forest, with those people, but she wouldn't that day.

She was yanked away from Avila just as they were about to enter the house.

Would there never be enough time, never, would there always be another house she barely missed? Before the world became a dark tunnel, Lilet noticed something familiar mounted to the left of the door: an intermittent red light. It looked like Bailey tech, like an alarm light from the ship. As Avila reached her hand out the door tech blinked green, just like it would on the Bailey. The kind of tech that knew you, that managed to feel personal.

❖

They hadn't even bothered to turn all the lights on when they pulled her out. To their credit, they were gentle, even if scared and angry.

Lilet emerged to find her team circulating around her in a dark flurry. Low glow of bioskins, glint of glass, shadow of their bodies all in motion, the misplaced *beep beeeeeeep* of the temperature gauge, water on the floor. Nadya's voice carried orders and the team fed her data: *We have three rent TimeWires. Bath volume low! She's breathing!*

Lilet *was* breathing. On the medical cot she'd been transferred to, lying on her back. Dabo's Ayelid was blinking green just above his eyes.

"I should have told you," she said.

He didn't look her in the eye.

But she motioned him close, and he bent down reluctantly. They gazed at each other, and his hand instinctively moved a slimy strand of her hair from her eyes.

"You can't tell anyone," she whispered. "What I have to tell you."

"What is it?"

But she swooned then, and his face blackened and closed. She didn't have a clear grasp on what she wanted to say anyway.

PART VII: LOCATION

27 October 3011

After being pulled from the TimePool, Lilet no longer stayed in the luxury of the station bed. She was moved to a holding cell in Bail-Jail (technically the Josiph Möller Detention Center), a place where the metal of the floor breathed cold up through her socks. It was a perfectly clean cube, her cell. Blue-tinged. Crisp corners. Stainless. The bed was a thick plate that *zooooohhhmed* out from the wall come nighttime. The back wall of the cube was a light-wall that emanated softly, a small comfort.

She got bored and anxious within an hour of being led to holding. Nadya had brought her here, saying nothing on that interminable walk, her arm looped through Lilet's as if they were intimate friends rather than captive and captor. Nadya said nothing until they were close and then she turned on Lilet, dwarfing her.

"Jesus Fucksaturn, Lilet," she said. "The Bailey is *lost* and we *needed* you."

"I know we're lost," said Lilet.

◆

MADRINA had resulted in a few positive location stamps. One of those had been Lilet's. She'd stamped them back to Lima, Perú, when she'd entered a woman who lived there in the 1940s, chosen off the street for her gleaming black hair to be the face of a shampoo ad. Lilet had entered her consciousness the moment she stood in front of her own ad, peeling off the back of a window at the neighborhood hair salon. The madrina had never seen herself photographed this way before. She stood there, looking at her own bare shoulders, the sleeves that barely cropped up, and suddenly she was arrested by dread, wondering what the men in her family would say, hoping that they wouldn't see it even though they walked by the salon every day.

Lilet remembered how enthusiastically they'd entered the Peruvian coordinates at CC. She also remembered the balloon deflation of the room when the coordinates blinked on a hovering black holo, the word *unknown* radiating around them. Only darkness. As she looked out at the gleaming black of space, Lilet remembered the madrina's hair.

◆

Dabo came by, three hours in. He found her sitting cross-legged perpendicular to the light-bars, braiding the sparse black of her own hair.

"Maybe I was entranced," she said, without looking up.

"Lilet," he lamented. "By what."

She looked up, smiled at his gentleness, wondering if her love for him was just her looking for a soft wing in a floating steel world. Grounding where there was no ground.

"The location stamps have all failed," she said. "We haven't been able to route back to Earth. We're too far. Butterfly. *Butterfly.* We can't flap our wings back home."

"You shouldn't be in here," he said. "Who do I talk to? Nadya?"

"It messes with my brain when they yank me out like that."

His hand hovered near the bars. She knew how desperately he wanted to reach through.

◆

"We have to shut down MADRINA, Lilet. CC gave us a time frame to find Earth and we're past it."

They sat in a white-walled room on either end of a long table. Behind Nadya's head, a depth-holo screen glistened. Lilet's Ayelid synced with it.

"There was more of a purpose to MADRINA, Nadya," Lilet said. She blinked, and the screen behind Nadya displayed it: a stillphoto of their original collective, smiling, ringing the TimePool. Nadya pursed her lips and Lilet blinked again, changing the image to a slideshow of the madrinas; they'd been able to find photo and video of some of the people they'd traveled into.

"It's become all about finding Earth," Lilet continued. "But that's not what it used to be. We didn't develop location stamping till midway through and now we're trying to invent as we go along."

"We did have a purpose," said Nadya, turning away from the screen. "Had. But hey you know what? I bet, at some point, we would've ended up in a woman right at the border. Someone living in one of those final foreclosed cities of Earth. Then we would've known our hell-history. We would've known exactly how much we wasted and destroyed and burnt up."

"So the narratives and emotional reality of human history are useless to us?"

"Yes, because we are *buying time* to exist. Are you used to it yet? The idea of dying in space?"

"Maybe Earth is too far at this point," said Lilet. "Did you think of that? The accidental jump could've taken us years past Katla."

"Of course. But what else are we going to stamp to if we're using consciousness travel instead of communication? When do we stop? When you're dead? And all the new women we vet? Dead women talking to dead women because they wanted to fill in a broken map."

"You relied on me too much."

"And you were worth it until a nice lake got involved."

"Just because I recovered every time you broke me open doesn't mean I didn't break."

A radiating quiet. There were no windows in the room.

"I'm sorry," said Nadya.

"I'm so tired of looking out the windows and seeing this sheet of nothing and nowhere," said Lilet, allowing the wall to revert to black.

"I've been tired since I was born."

"I remember," said Lilet. "When I'd see a planet far away and get excited. Look how corporeal it is. How *real*. But it was never Katla."

"We're baboons out here. We're snails. How is it possible no one on the whole ship can figure out where we are. *How*."

"Did anyone even try to get a location stamp on me?"

"The first time obviously. Nothing came up. Full Earth scan and nothing even lit up as likely. And we focused Nordic. The second time we were too busy saving all of our tech because it wasn't meant to be manned by one person."

"You say you're shutting it all down anyway, so who cares. Give me one more chance."

"You'll go into the same person and you'll stop breathing again."

"So let me stop breathing."

"Deathshitwish, Lilet."

"I've been thinking about it and I'm confident that if you keep me in there long enough, you'll get a location stamp."

"Your madrina doesn't make Earth any closer or location stamping any more sophisticated."

"You're not going to stamp me to Earth. You're going to stamp me to Katla."

Nadya blinked, and her voice became smaller.

"Descendant?"

PART VIII: DESCENDANT

10 November 3011

They were being lowered together into familiar water.

The hands that held them—utmost gentleness, careful fingers—were familiar too, at least to Avila. And the place was familiar. The light. The trees had somewhat shifted color, become bluer, though the water, when they tilted their mutual head to the right, was green as ever.

"May you always have beginning and end. May your feet always touch the ground. May you always find haven."

These were the words that Avila spoke to the circle of faces above her, some tearful, others ashen. Too many faces for Lilet to internalize. One person had green-hued skin and white hair, and dabbed at dark eyes.

Avila's vocal cords were dry and withered. Lilet could feel the immediate difference, the withering of their entire body. She had never entered the consciousness of someone so much older than her. She wondered if this was how it felt for some to become old, a vital mind trapped inside of a body that felt like a shell.

"Strange way to put it," muttered Avila. The ring of mourners had turned their backs to her ceremoniously and were walking away, disturbing the water.

"What did you come here for?" asked Lilet. Though she knew. Her weak heart seized.

"This is my deathday," said Avila. "We know ahead of time. Don't be concerned."

"I've never been inside of a dying body," said Lilet.

"I'm sorry. You won't be with me when I die. We know ahead of time. Also, you wouldn't be so rude as to stay here with me when I die. You saw how everyone else left. Death is a private matter. Who wants to see or hear anyone but their deepest self at the end?"

Avila had come back to the waterfall to feel like her deepest self. Here, her thin arms floated. Pain that radiated in her hips and shoulders soothed, at least a little. Her skydclan had known to bring her here.

"Something strange happens in your mind when I think the word *family*," said Lilet.

"That's because we don't understand family the same way, Lilet. You're still labeling blood relation. But the people I think of as relatives, my skydclan, are all chosen."

"None of those children were yours?"

"I didn't give birth to them. I found them, like I find wildberries by morning."

"So you mean . . ."

"Yes, Lilet. I am sorry. I'm the one dying, you will continue living, and yet I'm here to comfort you."

"I'm going to have children."

"And they're going to have children and children. This is the end of only one of your lines; who knows how far your other branches reach?"

"You aren't my madrina. You're my ahijada."

"You're weakening our voice. But you can think to me. You just have to learn to listen to my thoughts in return. They might be colors and feelings, but you speak that language. Yes. We learn the color code. Oatgrass. Twilight."

Lilet felt so tired in Avila's body. She couldn't fathom leaving, standing again, doing anything but resting. *What do I do now?*

Avila's thoughts came back like a starburst.

They found it already, while you were here talking to me.

I want to keep talking to you.

You thought that MADRINA would be about finding your lost god-mothers in the past, said Avila. *They were like fairies to you. But now you know: you too are godmother. Not only finding the world that was, but creating the world that will be.*

I want this to be my reality now.

I know. But now you have to let me sleep, butterfly.

◆

When she came back to her body, the first things she recognized were her pounding head and bloodless arms, which had gone numb and crossed over her chest in an X in the time she hadn't been breathing properly. The room around her vibrated with confused energy.

The plane in front of her eyes blinked with tech-light, in and out of darkness as her body was eased from the pool. A hushed path opened for her, and the world changed orientation as Nadya and Dabo carried her to the waiting cot.

The room was full of people she probably knew. Somewhere, a whisper rose to a wordless howl of joy, and then laughter and sound and applause erupted around her and made her head and eyes pound. She shook her head, mouthing *stop*. She closed her eyes, opened them, and saw Dabo as he inclined her bed to sitting. She noticed that Dabo had tears in his eyes.

Lilet thought she might faint. She felt like her body floated somewhere else and wasn't actually her body. She wanted water but couldn't summon the language to ask for it. Before she knew it, she had reverted to her first words, mouthing *agua*.

Nadya disappeared, a shadow gone from her side, and returned with a cup that she lifted to Lilet's lips. Lilet drank, though the first few sips hurt her throat.

The room had gone quiet and parted for her again, a red sea. When she looked up through the pathway that opened, she saw a beautiful, solid holo. It looked like a miniature planet, opaque and detailed enough to touch, floating in the air between them. A silver tinge to its atmosphere: its water appeared gray, but a stately slate gray, not grim or murky. A blue tinge to its earth.

"We aren't far, Lilet," said Dabo. "This whole time, we weren't far."

Once again, she couldn't find the language. She couldn't even say the word. She started to heave and cry, unsure if tears were coming from her eyes or not, and the whole room cried with her and laughed and clapped. Their bodies sang with sound.

Katla.

PART IX: WATERFALL

4 June 3015

The M.A.D.R.I.N.A. Project Casebooks: Mimicry Anthropology through Direct Reallocation and Intertemporal-Substitution by Neural Affinity

Verbal Agreement 00:00–00:10—4 June 3015
Entry by Dr. Lilet DeEsparza, PhD

My name is Dr. Lilet DeEsparza. I am a participant in the MADRINA Project. This is our first casebook entry to set up transition of MADRINA from the Bailey to Katla. First priority will be syncing assimilated data with our contact team EM-1 back on Earth, now that we have established communication again. EM-1 was keen to archive sociological data generated by MADRINA.

Our current timeline involves keeping MADRINA tech on board the landed Bailey for the remainder of scheduled trials, then moving to a secure location after we source one. Our new Katla-based team is enthusiastic to help us find such a space, though, understandably, very little has been constructed on Katla yet. We may also work remotely with Earth architects and Katla-based design teams to invest in designing a custom TimePool lab for MADRINA.

We are ready for our work to continue.

Verbal Agreement 00:00–00:13—4 June 3015

Entrev. Coady Ka-Vera, Katla MCOMM, c/ Dr. Lilet DeEsparza, PhD

I'm a child of Katla. Second-generation post-Noptera. The arrival of the Bailey was something we anticipated for years. The first settlement team here was only that: settlement. A sampling of Katlan specialists and citizens with Oran certification. All our tech essentially came from the dismantled ship. My parents built from scraps and learned to live off the land again. We were paving the way for you, the real heroes of the story.

What's it like for you, learning about Earth? A world you never knew?

Earth is a fantasy to me. A dark and glorious and decayed and beautiful dream.

A containment field of history. It felt that way to me too. Only, Katla also felt that way. It's like I was born in a gap. Like my whole life is a transition between people who will have true lives.

But aren't you happy to have landed?

Of course. I've seen the promised land. Who wouldn't be happy? But it doesn't feel *mine.*

You haven't been here very long.

I've been going back to the Bailey just to feel like myself.

Isn't there any part of Katla that you've started to feel an attachment to? Or even an attraction to? I know you toured our settlement.

There is one place. I just haven't been there yet.

◆

It took pulling up the initial location stamp.

A strange afternoon: Lilet, Dabo, and Nadya onboard the Bailey again a month after the interview. The TimePool room had taken on a sleepy, rusted feeling, even though it was still used every few days. Lilet herself hadn't used it. She hadn't used TimeWire since her last visit with Avila.

Dabo was rubbing his hands and scratching at his scalp. He'd dealt with a slew of allergic reactions since arriving on Katla. Lilet suspected it was from the fibers of Katlan clothes, which he still insisted on wearing. They'd all had their new things since coming to Katla, things that made them new people. Dabo, always the pleaser, had a need to be Katlan, and he marked this by the clothes he wore. So Nadya and Lilet stood in black and red Bailey suits while Dabo wore draped beige layers.

"You look like a monk," said Lilet.

Dabo's dimples started to show: his distinct grin that preceded a joke. "In the gardens of the Noptera settlement there's a crinkly little turnip," he said. "There's a grub that guards the turnip bulb, and it glows and blinks red. Bioluminescent! The entomologists can't wait to figure it all out."

Nadya had turned on the tech and the room hummed dreamily to life. A red light pulsed somewhere. "Is that what I look like?" asked Lilet.

"That's what you look like," said Dabo.

She beamed for him, trying hard to erase insincerity from her face. He looked away from her to swear and scratch his hands. For the first time, Lilet felt a pulsing sadness, a part of her life blinking away. It was the first time she didn't get the joke.

"Got it," barked Nadya, her voice stressed and utilitarian as ever. Since their arrival, Nadya had taken the helm on assimilation and on assigning scientists to different habitation zones in the Noptera settlement.

And Lilet? She hadn't settled anywhere yet. The endless desire for interviews and conversations (as the face of the Bailey's "Katlan Salvation") overwhelmed her, left her feeling like a drifting, stripped leaf. So she drifted back and forth between the settlement that felt like a fantasy zone and the empty, cavernous Bailey. She walked its halls and recognized herself in the echo of her own footsteps. She felt her way through the darkness and imagined being swallowed by a whale.

"Lilet. Did you hear me? I found your waterfall."

❖

They offered to go with her but she wanted to go alone.

The hike took two hours. Two Bailey hours, equivalent to four Earth hours. Lilet wasn't accustomed to Katlan hours yet.

Two Bailey hours of battling steep, muddy, unmarked ground that rose through a forest on an incline east of Noptera. Dabo had given her a location injection so that he and Nadya could keep track of her from the Bailey. At the beginning of the hike, trees with blue trunks and fanning turquoise leaves scattered the cold light of the Katlan sun. Red and blue worms gnawed at leaf mulch beneath her feet (and hands, when she had to crawl). The tree limbs warped and dipped in knots; she hadn't noticed them much in Avila's body, maybe because Avila didn't notice them.

Lilet turned her Ayelid off. Avila hadn't (wouldn't) use one, and Lilet wanted to experience all of this with unencumbered eyes.

The air felt dewy. After an hour of climbing, the incline leveled out and the ecosystem shifted. Trees emerged barkless, their trunks and branches shiny-smooth, charcoal-black. Lilet stood breathless at the sight of them, tunneling away from her. Their leaves were emerald snowflakes. Diamonds of light fell on the fern-lapped ground. Sun rays twinkled white.

Beyond the trees, she saw a wall of stone and shadow shrouded by white mist: the first hint of cliff and water.

◆

There was always a discrepancy between the sensory experience of being inside a madrina and being in her own body. Even if sensations felt vivid while in the madrina, they were always more vivid when experienced firsthand.

And so the waterfall assaulted her with its color, its fullness, its size.

The slate cliffs surrounded the pool in a towering promenade carpeted by Katlan ferns and mosses, interspersed with low canopy trees. The white spray of the falls broke through at different intervals along the cliffs and cascaded to meet the waters she knew so well. Someday Avila would be born near these waters. She would float on her back and look up at the sun in her billowing white shirt and speak to Lilet for the first time. Later, she would choose this place for her most private, internal moment, her deathday, and Lilet would be the last person she spoke to.

Lilet walked forward. Wet leaves draped and tickled her shins. This was Katlan springtime, and she wore thin black stretch pants from the Bailey through which she could feel the leaves. They grew dense as she approached the water's edge. When the water kissed her fingers, thick and silt-laden as she remembered, she felt an ache she hadn't felt before, something she didn't even feel when returning to the sanctuary of the Bailey. The ache of return. Homeland, homeplace, heartplace.

Lilet stood, turned, and looked back the way she came. She could picture it now: the clearing, the stone walls, the Bailey tech blinking at the door, the arms that encircled other arms and carried goods in preparation for a meal.

As she imagined the future, Lilet no longer felt she was drifting. She had found the home-that-would-be, and there was much to build.

Bad Sun

SCOTT RUSSELL DUNCAN

It was not the day for going outside, the boy was told again and again. Grandma did the curtains and heaved up the flat pieces of cardboard over the window with the crack as Mom taped over any gaps. Please? Not today. Grandma told him the sun was new, at its strongest. Light wasn't lucky today. They all had to sit in the dark. Grandma hummed some, told one story about foxes, and Mom just lay there. Sit still she yelled at every rustle. It was the dark of nap time all day and after an hour or two both Mom and Grandma were snoring, the boy sighing. Some cardboard fell off from the gap between the door and the doorjamb. The tape didn't stick so well to the dusty wall. The boy opened the door and ran out. It was a normal day. The entire world seemed orange and empty, no one yelling at him. The field was hot and he tore off his shirt. Sweat flung off his arm as he swung a sword stick against a sapling, who was the evil zombie general for the afternoon. The sun slumped and touched the top of scraggly trees in the meadow. The boy knew he had to go back. He opened the door slowly and lay down in the dark. Grandma and Mom were quiet. Were they still there? They came out of the back room with candles and told him to sit for now. Knocking came from the door. A man in a hat that had candles circling it talked to Mom. She grabbed the boy's arm and held it up to him. The man in the hat said the inauspicious sun had taken residence in the boy's skin, it had been infused with evil. Grandma took the boy's other arm. They pulled him outside; the boy asked why, why? Grandma said you were outside, in the sun, and now your skin is bad luck for us all. We must take it out.

Beacon

SCOTT RUSSELL DUNCAN

At first there wasn't any problem with the light. Then the bishop poked a group of kids in the chest and said, "Is that where your light is?" Most giggled and said, "Yes, Father." Others, the little ones, were confused and pointed up at the sun, delighting the bishop with their innocence and the double meaning he drew from the simple gesture. One kid, however, said, "There can't be light inside my chest." The bishop gripped the kid and repeated his question. "Inside the skin is dark!" The bishop shook the kid more but every time he got the same answer: light can't be inside someone.

Of course, the bishop had a talk with the kid's parents, teachers, and local preacher and outlined a rigorous discipline including hot and cold showers, humiliating clothes and haircuts, spiny paddle boards, and rote recitations, but these only wound up spreading the problem since people asked the parents, why's the kid being punished? Oh, he said light can't reach inside someone's chest. Wow! What a little . . .—Wait. That actually makes sense. And so before the bishop could reassure anyone (he was moving on to collect tithes from other towns), temp workers between calls, grocery clerks with degrees, and people who said they freelanced but were really unemployed were poking themselves hard in the chest, asking, hoping, wondering, where is the light?

The town originally had a name in the language of the local Indians, then in the language of the Franciscans, then in that of the Pioneers, all having to do with the pain of the Lord, but then the town council ditched them all in favor of something more cheery—Beacon—though the landlocked provincial town had no lighthouse and had never been a beacon in any sense of the word. Still, it sounded nicer than God's Torment in whatever language. And so the cause célèbre of "no light" seemed to threaten not only the latest town name, but the worth, the heart, of the town itself.

Retirees formed groups where one would be still and the others would poke hard with their canes and then squint, waiting to be blinded, but never seeing anything but the fronts of sweaters. Teenage boys, of course, took girls to the edge of town and told them that they wanted to find their light and the worried girls said, yes, please try. The boys examined the girls' chests with long, lingering, groping pokes, but of course, no light came forth and the boys said they would have to try once more.

Everyone called out the "No Light" kid, as if he had any more information than they. "Hey kid, what happened to the light?" But he kept quiet. He didn't want more lessons or to do anyone any favors by poking them in the chest.

No one thought things were that bad until they noticed no one was doing anything, everyone was going around holding their sore chests, hoping no one was going to look for any more light. And when the sun rose everyone ran out naked in the middle of town, hoping light would get in, but their skin only got darker. At sunset everyone ran back inside and covered up in case any light leaked out. The local preacher said the town was damned on a cloudy day, and boys and girls who looked for each other's light made suicide pacts. Their fathers and mothers lit candles to their spirits, then more candles so they could see to light even more candles, but it was never enough, darkness came every night, inside, outside, everywhere.

Of course, since no one was making or selling anything, there weren't any tithes and the bishop finally read the old emails from the local preacher that only said, "No light. No light." He then drove fast to the town.

It wasn't like before, no one crowded the bishop's car, tapping the glass and asking for forgiveness or blessings. Only a few noticed around noon that he had grabbed the kid who said there was no light in his chest. On the hilly part near the middle of town, the bishop was talking about the town living up to its name. The local preacher and some guy held the kid with no light in his chest flat on his back. The bishop cut hard and then put his hands together like he was opening double doors. The chest was open. The bishop pulled out the thing inside and held it to the sun, bathing it in light.

Her Number

SCOTT RUSSELL DUNCAN

Mary Ann had dogs and Tom had coyotes. Martha had deer. Andy had eagles. Everyone in the office had a different animal decorating their cubical. Raven mousepad. Coyote stickers on monitors. Fish calendars. Deer sweaters. Wendy thought it was weird, though she expected her first day to be a little strange because getting to know new coworkers always came with adjustments. She thought about making a joke that she liked cats when Judy the boss made her do the rounds and say hello, but the employees hardly looked up from the screens that showed nothing but the numbers they were scrolling through. The rest of the day, and the rest of week, they kept to themselves. Accountants were predictably normal and boring, but they also predictably overcompensated by doing things they thought were wacky. At least at Wendy's other accounting jobs. The lull of having work be work and play be play appealed to her and she didn't get annoyed that all the coffee cups had each coworker's animal on it. *It's what these people do to seem interesting*, she thought. *In a boring, sweater-suburbanite, hausfrau way.* So Wendy did her work, her numbers. Weeks went by. And her coworkers went by, never stopping to chat, even when they stayed late. They all seemed a little sweaty, anxious. *Sedentary jobs, fatty foods.* Wendy did her numbers. The patterns came slowly. Numbers formed pictures at times. At first like looking up in the clouds and seeing people. Or a paw. Or a tail. She would have pointed them out, but she had not made any friends. The numbers also formed coordinates . . . pixels. Once she found a program to map them, there were even full pictures of cougars. She didn't mention it to anyone. She did her job and canceled on friends, and just stayed at home looking up numbers, seeing pictures in numbers, and cougars. She went through numerology, astrology, Chinese year of the cat. She read, googled, searched till she came to the year of the jaguar. Mayan time keeping. And the reconstructed calendars of Stonehenge and the Sumerians. Time is cyclical. Ends and begins again every few thousand years, depending on which calendar you follow. Some say it will end in the year of the eagle. Deer. Dog. Jaguar. Months or years named after gods and gods represented by animals. She saved pictures of jaguars, trying to see them in a new light, get an edge on the numbers. 2012 came and went, just one apocalypse missed. Wendy wondered: *Does that mean the cycle will end in the year 2064 or in a thousand years or is it not the jaguar at all? Are all calendars off in their representation of reality? What does the end of the cycle mean? The end of time? People. Jaguars. Me.* Coworkers walked past her, one maybe nodded quickly before sitting down to work late as well. Wendy searched through new numbers, new clues, finding new pictures she printed off and put up in her office. Though every new pattern she found, as she drank out of her jaguar coffee cup and looked past the numerical coordinates to the picture underneath, was the wide maw and upturned eyes of the jaguar, her animal, her number.

Old Folks

SCOTT RUSSELL DUNCAN

This one was little Manny. Esther worried he was too young. Pearl thought he was darling.

"Come over and give me some sugar, sweet pea."

Pearl clutched him in her fat arms and didn't let go. "I want to eat him all up," she giggled. Frank patted Manny on the head with his prosthetic hook.

"So how old are you, amigo?"

"Twelve," Manny said and eyed the curved metal.

"Well, welcome to Sunset Springs retirement facility."

"The old folks' home," George grunted.

"No need to tell him that," Esther gasped out.

"He can tell with all the geezers, can't he?"

"Oh, George." Pearl fumbled with the card pinned to Manny's chest. "You got a purple card. That means you are especially special."

"I didn't want a card."

"Then you wouldn't have been able to come see us, amigo," Frank laughed.

"You can have one of mine, too." Pearl reached into her bag and pulled out a laminated white card.

Frank poked her in the arm. "Don't be so greedy, Pearl. Wait your turn. He's here for everyone."

Manny wiggled in Pearl's grip. "What happened to your hand, mister?"

"Don't ask about such things Manny, it's rude." Pearl held him tighter, giving Frank a mean eye.

"You mean this hook?" Frank asked. "Well, the doctors took it. They thought it was yummy so they lopped it off and ate it."

"Now, don't tell him that."

Esther wheezed. "He's not that young, Frank."

The old man scratched his pant leg with the tip of his hook.

"I got a bad heart, amigo. Esther can't breathe, and George got a liver that's no good. Pearl needs everything. We're old. We all need new parts."

"I don't want none of it. I'll keep what I got."

"You always say that, George."

"Each and every time," Esther said through her oxygen mask.

"He'll say that when he walks out of here." Pearl grimaced.

"Hey, want some candy, amigo?" Frank reached into his pocket with his good hand and pulled out hard green candy. "Take as many as you like."

Esther whispered loud to Frank, "The nurse is here."

Pearl unfolded her fat arms and the nurse took Manny by the hand. "Tell the doctor he'll be fine." Pearl patted Manny on the shoulder. "You go on now, baby."

"Whelp, see you, amigo." Frank's hook waved goodbye.

Manny, teeth green from the candy, dutifully waved. He then turned back to say, "My name isn't 'amigo,' mister." The nurse shushed him and took him inside the elevator. The door closed with Manny watching Frank's hook.

"He'll do," George said.

Ester hacked and turned blue.

"You see, I told you. Every time."

Soledad

EZZY G. LANGUZZI

Soledad chanted under her breath. *Hago tamales, soy cocinera como mi madre.* She labored in a trance, her hands wrist-deep, fingers squishing through ground corn, melted lard, and warm broth. She repeatedly plunged her hands into it, kneading it with great care. The ritual gave her a sense of purpose, helped her cope with the loss. It comforted her that Mamá lived on in the old kitchen. Its crumbling brick walls and Oaxacan floor tiles, cast-iron skillets, potted herbs, knives and cleavers meant everything to her. She didn't know what she'd ever do if she were to lose them.

Right on the US-Mexican border, the restaurant had provided a generous livelihood for three generations of Olivas women. It allowed them the space to create without outside influence. People had traveled from far and away to enjoy their succulent tamales, handmade tortillas, and savory birria.

Over time, truckers and vacationers replaced vaqueros and Zapatistas.

No más.

Soledad peered out the window, over a sink stacked with pots and pans. The family cemetery sat up on a hill. White rose bushes bordered the grassy area peppered with alabaster stone crosses. A statue of La Virgen de Guadalupe, as tall as her, nestled in a carved-out granite stone wall, and purple bougainvillea fringed every surface. There, Mamá rested alongside Abuela and Bisabuela. One day,

Soledad would be the fourth and last of the Olivas women laid to rest there.

Hago tamales, soy cocinera como mi—

"¡Cervezas!" her husband Felix called from the restaurant's dining room.

Bastard. She wiped her hands on her apron and hurried to the walk-in icebox. Sides of beef, pork, and goat were suspended from metal hooks on one side, and cases of Mexican beer and soft drinks were stacked to the ceiling on the other.

She took two *Bohemias,* his favorite, and set them outside the door on a large wooden barrel filled with sacks of beans. She ran her hands over its rough lid, felt the grain and dime-size holes Mamá had carved.

Soledad had barely fit inside the last time she'd hid there.

By five she'd grown accustomed to her parents' fights, the broken dishes, Papá needing stitches because he'd been whacked with a pan. What did he expect, returning drunk and smelling of another woman's perfume after being gone for days?

"Are you dead, mujer?! Where's our beer?!"

Soledad slammed the stainless-steel door shut and gazed at her reflection, her eyes. Abuela had told her a person's eyes always told the truth. She smoothed back a wisp of hair that had come loose from her ponytail and adjusted the lemon-print apron. "Ya voy, cochino," she muttered under her breath.

God forbid he should wait thirty seconds.

She hesitated in the doorway with her back to the kitchen, where cornhusks softened in a bucket of warm water, and a molcajete shaped like a pig's body cradled chile ancho, ajo, and cebolla, the ingredients to the spicy red sauce she'd make.

Felix and his new best friend lounged in a corner booth, under a ceiling fan that creaked like the springs of a well-worn mattress.

Oh, if only it would lop their heads off. She wished it—willed it—but no amount of concentration ever sent the fan's blades flying.

Her grip tightened around the beer bottles.

Soledad had left much of the restaurant intact after her mother's passing, sensing her approval amidst its shabby, red vinyl booths, warped wooden floor, and especially the hand-painted sign on the storefront window. As a little girl she'd withered under the hot sun, clutching a water-filled tin cup for Mamá to clean her paintbrushes.

She'd loved being her assistant.

"Mijita, un día este restaurante será tuyo, for you to pass to your daughter," Mamá had said. "Same as Abuelita did for me."

Soledad had accepted it as truth and anticipated one day owning the restaurant. She'd spent her formative years there, watching Mamá, absorbing every detail and lesson.

Never rush. Save the juice to make broth. Less is more. Never cut corners.

What now? Her situation filled her with angst and made her physically ill.

She approached the men and handed each his beer.

"Where do you think you're going?" Felix asked when she turned to leave. Heat rose in her cheeks at the tenor of his voice.

"To finish my work. I have another pot to make before we open."

Water in a stock pot burbled and boiled in the kitchen. A five-pound seasoned pork butt, with Abuelita's favorite meat cleaver stuck in its side, flashed before her eyes. She'd always enjoyed the feel of the cleaver's lacquered pearl handle in her hand, how the sharpened blade sliced through meat with ease. "You can't leave pork out for too long, you know?"

Timing was important, in love as in cooking.

She met Felix's gaze. The few gray hairs peeking through his temples, and crow's-feet crinkling the outer corner of his dark eyes, made him more handsome. Droplets of amber fluid dribbled down his chin as he chugged his beer. He wiped it with the sleeve of his white guayabera. He'd not worked in months. Is this who he'd been all along?

If she didn't take care, she'd end up in her grave before she turned thirty.

"Come sit for a minute," beckoned his amigo Louis, a savvy young Americano with sandy brown hair and hazel eyes. He'd recently purchased the liquor store across the road and held the note on a loan she'd agreed to let Felix take out against the restaurant.

Pendeja.

"Mi Mamá, she's sick," Felix had said. "We must send some money to Guadalajara to pay the doctors." She'd never even seen a photograph of the woman. What he'd actually done with the money, Díos sabe.

"You must be tired," Louis said, patting the seat cushion next to him.

"I really shouldn't. The tamales—" She glanced at Felix, who sat peeling the label from his beer bottle. The situation she found herself in was of her own making. She'd married him after a courtship of three months and succeeded at putting her future and livelihood in peril. How much could you learn about a person in that short time?

They shared nothing in common. Back when her mother owned both the restaurant and ranch, Soledad had learned the meaning of *work*. Early to rise. Milk the cows and goats. Fetch eggs before the cocks crowed. Then cook, serve, and clean.

"Tamales, tamales. The tamales aren't going anywhere, Cielo." Louis leaned over, pulled her by her apron strings, and sat her next to him. The smell of stale beer and cigarettes on his breath turned her stomach. He hooked an arm over her shoulders and leaned into her, pressing the crushed velour of his leopard-print blazer against her bare arm.

Felix seemed too comfortable, too familiar with him. How could her husband allow someone else to touch her, when he was so possessive?

"Be nice, Soledad," her husband said, frowning from across the table. "Where are your manners? We owe him my mother's life."

Did the woman even exist? "Do you need something else?"

The temperature in the room dropped. She shivered, as though she were back in the icebox. Everything became still. She no longer heard the fan or their voices—only muffled noise, as if her head were being held under water. Her mother's words came to her:

Good-wives-do-not-leave-their-husbands.

Good-wives-do-not-leave-their-husbands.

Good-wives-do-not . . .

Loyalty, she'd inherited from Mamá, too.

Ribbons of thick mist seeped through cracks in the wall near the bar. She looked at Felix and Louis to see if they noticed it, but they continued arguing about a recent boxing match.

The mist floated through the bottles of mezcal and tequila, over the booths, swirled before the antique jukebox, and disappeared into the kitchen.

She rubbed her eyes.

Damn, fatigue.

◆

Soledad prepped for bed at her vanity. Candle flames danced in the gentle breeze. She loved sitting by the open window, so she could hear the creatures of the night, flapping and scurrying about, and smell the cemetery's roses.

The steaming bath she'd taken had brought back some color to her cheeks. She touched the delicate skin under her eyes, noting the appearance of dark circles. Rubbed peppermint-scented cream into her hands and elbows. Loosened the knots at the ends of her long hair with a wide-tooth comb. Prayed an Ave Maria to La Virgen, asking for guidance and strength.

A framed photograph of Mamá glowed under the candles. She stood against a backdrop of flowering cacti and green mountains, shading her eyes as she watched a golden eagle circling above. She was nineteen, more full-figured than Soledad, her face rounder, with shiny black hair that spilled to her waist. The other half of the image had been torn away. A lock of Mamá's salt-and-pepper hair, tied with ribbon, an aluminum milagro cut and hammered in the shape of a heart, and pressed white rose petals filled the void in the frame.

Whiskey and a wandering eye had robbed them of Papá, Mamá'd always said.

Their fortunes changed soon after Felix entered their lives. Ovarian cancer decimated Mamá in the time it took Soledad to become consumed by passion. Things might've turned out differently had Mamá not sent her to the produce stand because they'd run out of garlic and onions that day. On her way back to the restaurant, she'd crashed into Felix on the sidewalk, as he left the barber shop where he apprenticed. Quite the caballero he'd been then, scrambling to help her gather the vegetables on the ground. Asking if he could walk her home.

Where others had failed to capture her attention, he'd succeeded by tantalizing her with stories about faraway places he'd visited in Latin America and the US. Places she'd only ever seen on television or in magazines. Places she'd hoped to visit one day.

Truth be told, she could never leave the restaurant—not even to see the world.

What would become of her now?

Something tugged gently at Soledad's heart and she felt a deep longing. She ran her fingers over the picture frame's jagged wooden edges, wishing she'd had more time . . .

Felix and his friends hooted and hollered in the restaurant downstairs, where they smoked and played cards under the creaking ceiling fan. His nights out—or *in*—with his friends had become more frequent. At the beginning she'd had trouble falling asleep with all the noise. Not anymore. She'd bury her head under her pillow, grateful they'd clean up after themselves.

She opened the vanity drawer containing the paperwork Louis had drafted for the loan. An oddly shaped bottle of mezcal Mamá had given her rolled over the fat envelope.

The bottle was still two-thirds full and glistened.

"Here, put this somewhere safe," Mamá had said to Soledad on her wedding day.

She remembered that day with perfect clarity, her bouquet's redolent roses, Mamá's tuberose and sandalwood perfume. She'd sat at the same vanity in her white dress, waiting nervously for the church bells to ring.

"Why would you give this to me?" Soledad had asked, startled by the odd gift. "You know I don't drink. Hard liquor makes me sick."

"It's more than that."

"More?"

"Trust me. Keep it. If you're worthy, it may grant you a wish one day."

Soledad had taken it, reluctantly. At the sound of church bells a heaviness filled her heart and doubt shadowed her thoughts.

"I don't understand, Mamá."

"When the time comes, you will drink from it once, and *only* once. You must never drink from it again. Do you hear me?"

"Yes, yes, I hear you," she'd responded as she secreted it in a vanity drawer, the last place Felix would look.

"I'm serious, Soledad. This is serious. What I'm about to tell you is most important. You will pass it along, preferably to a daughter, or another female in the family. The person must be deserving of it."

"Why?"

"It's believed to have the opposite effect on them if they're not."

"What if there's no one else?"

"Then you must bury it in the desert on a night that there's a full moon."

Soledad shivered in her robe thinking of that afternoon and the urgency in Mamá's voice. The men's ruckus faded in the restaurant downstairs and her vanity mirror rippled. She gasped. A scene from her childhood appeared on its water-like surface. Abuela reclined next to her in bed, while Soledad took a bottle of warm chocolate.

She couldn't have been more than five years old and looked like a muñeca in her flannel nightgown and long hair twisted into two thick braids.

"Buela, tell me a story."

"But it's time for bed mimi, Mija. Your mami will not be happy if she comes home from work to find you awake."

"I'm not tired!"

Abuela had never needed a lot of convincing to tell a story.

"Esta bien. Dejame pensar," she said, tapping her plump chin. "Hmmm. I've not told you the one about the magical agave, have I?"

"Nuh-uh," Soledad chewed on the bottle's rubber nipple. "What's an agave?"

"It's a prickly succulent that sprouts from the ground like an angry octopus." Abuela waved her fingers in front of Soledad's eyes.

"Ewww. They have giant heads."

"That they do. Now promise you'll go to sleep?"

"Promise."

Abuela sighed. "One day a beautiful young woman ran away from home to get away from her unkind husband. She ran and ran until she reached the mountains. Once there she climbed, dragging her clay water jug behind her."

Soledad frowned. "Why was he mean to her?"

"No se, mi amor. Perhaps his own Papi had been mean too and he did not know any better. Anyway, when the young woman reached the mountaintop, she discovered an agave plant so big," Abuela said, stretching her arms out wide for effect, "the young woman had to lean back and stretch her neck to see how tall it grew."

"What was the plant doing there?"

"It had been planted hundreds of years earlier by her village's ancestors to give birth to baby agave that would grow and be used for medicine. The young woman did not want to return home, so when it started raining, she sought refuge under one of the agave's gigantic leaves. The sky grumbled and thundered," Abuela said, pounding with her closed fists on the bed, "and lightning struck the giant agave, setting it aflame."

"Wasn't she afraid?"

"Not at all. The plant warmed, wrapped its plump, velvet-like leaves around her, and protected her from the cold. It cradled her and lulled her into a deep, deep sleep."

"Oh," Soledad said, her eyes hooded. She yawned.

Abuela took the bottle she'd finished and continued, "The young woman slept for three days and three nights. During that time, the giant agave sang to her, and shared its secrets. It told her that wisdom came to those who drank its amber tears, but only if they had a pure heart and good intentions. Strength springs forth from those who believe in themselves. When the young woman woke from her deep sleep, she found herself lying in a pool of sweet liquid that seeped from the giant agave's heart. She emptied her clay water jug and collected the elixir, as hundreds of moths flitted about her . . ."

Tears streamed down Soledad's cheeks when the image in the mirror vanished.

She pulled off the cork and lifted the bottle to the candles. If she had to choose between Felix and the restaurant, she knew which she'd choose. Her future—the Olivas family legacy—depended on repayment of the loan. She opened another vanity drawer and was startled by a flurry of moths that fluttered out. She waved them away and searched for something to pour the mezcal into. A small glass holding her earrings seemed the perfect size.

She poured herself a shot and sniffed its smoky essence.

"Here's to *freedom.*" Fire rushed down her throat as the silky liquid went down. Notes of honey, anise, and something earthy lingered on her tongue. She clutched the front of her robe and coughed uncontrollably, as pins and needles erupted throughout her body. Warmth flooded her torso and calm enveloped her in its warm embrace. She poured herself another, wishing to prolong the feeling, and set the glass before Mamá's photograph.

Two had to be better than one.

She stood and stepped back from the vanity, untied her robe, and contemplated her figure from various angles in the candle light. Aside from a softening around her belly, her slight frame had remained largely the same. She turned sideways, straightened her posture, and cupped her soft midsection. Maybe it was a blessing she'd not been able to get pregnant.

How long she stood in that state, she didn't know, because when Felix appeared in the bedroom, it was peaceful downstairs and the candles burned low. It had started to rain and the curtains waved in the breeze.

"You're still up?" he asked, approaching her. The smell of cigarettes and beer reached her before he did.

"I was about to go to bed," she replied, closing her robe.

He pulled her toward him and wrapped his arms around her waist. "I don't deserve you," he said, as he buried his stubbly chin into the crook of her neck.

Her insides melted. "You should shower." She tried to nudge him toward the bathroom, but his feet remained planted.

"What's this?" He picked up the filled shot glass on the vanity behind her and smelled it over her shoulder. "Holding out on me?"

"No—never." She grabbed hold of his wrist—then reconsidered. "It's delicious," she said, lifting his hand toward his lips. "Try it."

❖

Soledad overslept. Sunlight spilled into the bedroom and warmed the foot of their bed. The shot of Mamá's mezcal combined with everything else Felix drank with his buddies had affected him. There'd been other times, sure, similar promises and fervor, but nothing like what happened the previous night. He'd promised to start being a better husband, to return to his apprenticeship, pay back the loan. Help her around the restaurant, bussing tables. Maybe they'd adopt a baby? He'd matched his words with passionate kisses, soft caresses.

The waitstaff would arrive within the hour. She'd have to hurry.

Her belly tingled. It gave her reason to pause.

Felix, who'd never snored in their five years of marriage, started making noises she could only describe as wheezing. Like he had trouble breathing.

She turned over, and hugged him over the covers. He slept with his head buried under a pillow. No wonder.

He snorted. Loud.

"What's the matter with you?"

Snort wheeeee! snort wheeeeeee!

She removed the pillow.

A fat pig with floppy ears covering its eyes slept in Felix's place with its mouth open. Its big snout twitched.

Her scream got stuck in her throat. The mist from the day before reappeared. It drifted out from behind her mother's photograph, danced at the foot of the bed, and disappeared into the floorboards.

Oh my God.

"Mamá!"

❖

Daffodils. Soledad thought of daffodils when she'd put on the pretty yellow dress she'd worn on her first date with Felix. Its delicate eyelet material strained against her belly. With her black hair swept up into a bun and red lipstick staining her lips, she looked a lot like Mamá.

Felix nudged her bare leg.

"¿Qué quieres, mi amor?"

Snort snort snort.

His rotund belly nearly touched the ground. His ears shaded his eyes the way his black hair had. She scratched his chin and led him to the back door. "Go on now. You know what to do," she said, smacking him on the butt. "You'll eat and have your beer when you're done."

Felix squealed. He ambled out the back door up the hill to the cemetery and began to turn the soil of a new flower bed with his huge pink snout. His coiled tail wiggled with his every move.

"Hey, where's everybody?" Louis called from the restaurant. "The closed sign's up, but the door's unlocked."

The kitchen smelled of steaming masa. Soledad stood on a stool humming a Mexican lullaby as she arranged freshly wrapped tamales in her biggest stockpot. She'd concocted a new chile colorado recipe in celebration of new life and beginnings. She worked with her back to the corner of the kitchen, where she'd sat as a little girl, dressing her cardboard dolls, while Mamá cooked. One day her own daughter would sit there, too.

"Morning. Where's Felix?" Louis, who'd been away a couple of days, approached the stove.

"He left—early." She did not meet his gaze.

"You look very nice. I've never seen you dressed up."

"Thanks."

"Wow. What smells so good?"

"Are you hungry? Go, sit. I'll bring you a plate. I've prepared something *special.*"

Felix squealed, ran in circles outside, then crashed into the wrought-iron back door.

"When'd you get a pig?" Louis asked, startled. "Big guy."

"Yup. He was a gift," she answered.

"Felix was okay with that?"

"Mmmhm." Because of course, she'd need his approval. Things would be different moving forward.

Louis shrugged and left the kitchen. He sat in the corner booth, beneath the creaking ceiling fan. "You'd never know it was ninety degrees outside. It's chilly in here." He shivered and pulled the collar of his blazer up around his ears.

"It's the brick."

The mist descended from above his head and hovered over the table.

He was oblivious.

She set before him a plate laden with two tamales, leaking red sauce, flanked by rice and beans, and garnished with a sprig of cilantro.

"These look delicious," he said, licking his lips. "Aren't I a lucky guy?"

She smiled and set an empty shot glass before him.

Felix squealed as if he were being slaughtered and repeatedly crashed into the back door.

"What the hell's wrong with that pig?" Louis asked.

"Don't mind him." She raised her voice as she uncorked Mamá's bottle of mezcal. "He'll stop if he knows what's good for him."

Felix's portly silhouette became still on the other side of the wrought-iron door.

She didn't have to say another word.

Contraband

PATRICK LUGO

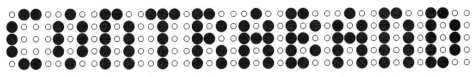

BY PATRICK LUGO

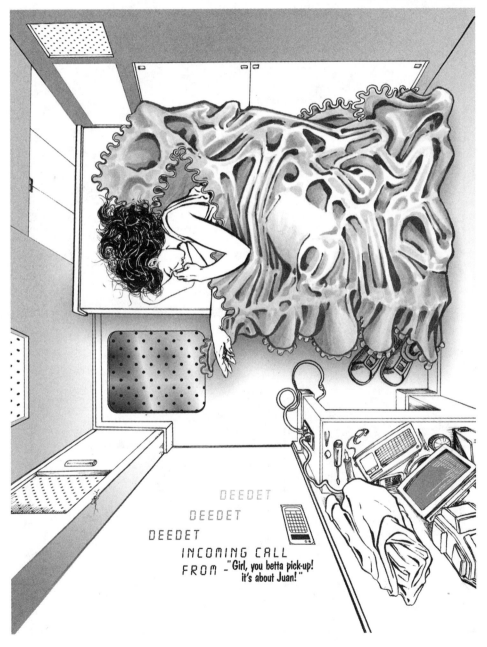

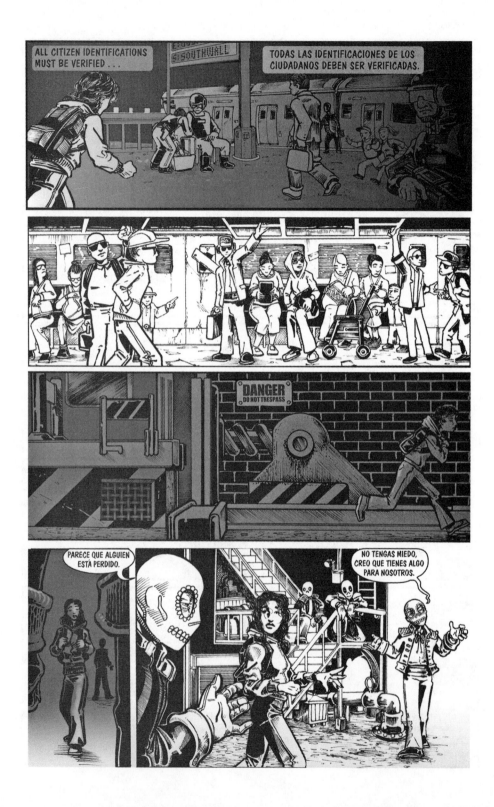

The ENCRoach Program

GRISEL Y. ACOSTA

tinier water bugs and crickets make fun of me,
my slavery, my burden,
metal on my back, nearly half my weight,
the death of me, looming,
cracked exoskeleton under encrypted data,

but they're next.
I heard the conversations, and that's my job.
they said they'd make smaller chips
for smaller bugs' backs,
little loads for *all* of us to carry.

I originally thought, why not give back?
work for the community that feeds me.
instead I see I betrayed the poor
suckers who inhabit the dirty neighborhoods
where I'm usually at, scrounging around
the tenements for an unnoticed crumb.

This poem quotes sections of the essay "Cockroaches Equipped as Wireless Networks" by Olga Kharif.

what's to listen to? lovers, despair, hours of TV—dull!
so we got together, revolted, the roaches, the vermin,
kept the mics on the abusers who attached the radios,
themselves, to us; the masters,
those who invented the chemicals that used to kill
us, those who would use us

now, to supposedly save the troubled,
the buried, the victims of natural disasters.
they do not see that we are buried under their desires.
our backs become thinner under cadmium, gold, silver, zinc,
and their words: "It has the potential for being
a redundant communication system at a low cost."

military men and university scholars
have many words to record; I've heard them all,
like "$850,000 from the US Army"
and "these are real bugs that can do bugging"
and "I always thought roaches were icky, but these are really cute."

my enslavement, the anvil on my back,
forcing me to steal words from the same population I steal food from,
never asking me if I wanted to move up to a federal offense.
it is a curse, a forced vigilantism.

we, the roaches of the world, once fed freely.
conducted our business unfettered
now we must listen to our victims
hear them say, "Can we make the rent this month?"
while well-rested men listen on their computers
and the record is on our backs

Homebound

TABITHA SIN

When Luca asked me if there was one thing that I wanted most in the world, I think he wanted me to say him. We were lying next to each other on his bed, his satin sheets making my hair staticky. I felt strands cling to the sheet with every movement. We were both fully clothed because even though I enjoyed kissing him, the Heraplon implant killed my sex drive. Sometimes, I felt the implant throb next to my tricep. Maybe before, I would have said I wanted him, but I think that still would have been a half-truth.

"I don't know," I said. It was hard to want anything deeply, when I couldn't even envision a future for myself.

"There isn't anything?"

Money? Stability? Family? What kind of answer could I give to someone who was not capable of giving me those things?

"I guess I would like a dog," I said and sat up from the bed. My fingers shocked the top of my head as I pushed my hair back. "I've got to go. I'll talk to you later."

He lingered a little by the door as I put on my sneakers. He was so pale, *Russian heritage*, he said. Technically, he came from a once-independent satellite country, but that's been a long time now. Russia invaded all those old lands like a phagocyte devouring a stray particle. He looked ghostly at that moment. My nose bumped into his sternum when he went for a hug and I went to pat his shoulder.

He leaned down and missed my forehead, or maybe my mouth, and planted his lips on my eye. I kept it closed and didn't look back as I headed to work. I didn't know if the heat that percolated upward from my stomach was from embarrassment or the implant working. I heard him sigh right before his door clicked shut.

It was hot—hotter than the weatherman's prediction—even though Luca lived in a central midtown location. Far enough from the deep end of the MalTides where the fumes of the Hudson mixed with other fetid organic odors, but not elite enough to be farther uptown with the specialized heat-resistant buildings. He was making his own money, at least, and didn't get a dime from his parents. And so, even though he worked for one of the top cybersecurity firms, he wasn't offering to pay for my ride back home.

There was no cool wind outside to temper the secondhand embarrassment. Sweat rolled down the back of my neck. My skin tingled, like a precursor to sunburn, despite how little time I spent outside. The politicians kept saying climate change didn't exist but it was 103 degrees Fahrenheit now in New York in late November. My office was a couple of blocks from Luca's apartment, but the walk felt like slogging through an oppressive fog. Reaching my office building was only a temporary relief. There was already a quiet crowd of patients in the waiting room. I hated that room and its offensive faded pastel pink walls.

My office had a glass door, an illusion of privacy. Jenny always knew everyone's business whether the door was closed or not. I leaned back in my chair, turning on and propping up the tablet on my desk. My eye began to throb—from memory or from the remains of Luca's saliva, I didn't know. I imagined the microscopic bodies that formed in his spit lingering on my eyelashes, and each time I blinked, it mixed into my sclera, invisibly invading my vision. I closed my eyes for a brief moment—*one, two*—until I heard Mirabel's nail tap against my desk. I hadn't fully closed the door in my rush past the waiting room.

"If you're tired already, you're going to have a bad day." She was also a rep, like me, but more senior. Only by a few months.

"All I ever have are bad days."

"Ay, please, I can't handle your self-pity this early. I'm telling them to let the appointments in."

I opened the first file and scanned through the information. Rivera, Paloma. Twelve days past her birthday. She almost didn't make the deadline. Curly black hair. First period at eleven years old, parents deported around that same time, genetic predisposition to osteoporosis, came from a family of five.

She was smaller than her headshot implied. Like most of them. Us. We were undernourished in our formative years.

"Hi, Paloma. Please have a seat. I'll explain the preliminary process, and if you have any questions at the end, I'll be more than happy to answer them."

The speech was always the same. Even at my own appointment years ago, Mirabel hadn't wavered from the script.

The Heraplon is a hormonal implant surgically shot right into the inside of your arm. Your arm will feel sore for a few days, which is normal, but if it continues to be inflamed, then you will need to set up a follow-up appointment. The hormones are released throughout your body in a timed, controlled manner. While this is an effective contraceptive, please continue to practice safe sex. This implant also has a built-in tracker for location and biological thermodynamics. You can think of it as your Social Security number—each day you show up to work, this ensures you some kind of retirement.

If your financial situation changes, such as getting a promotion or a significant pay-grade increase, you will have to report it to the Department of Health and Education and us as well. You are responsible for renewing the implant every six months. I suggest marking it on your calendar, but your rep will also remind you a month before to set up another appointment. It is strongly advised that you recommit, as failure to do so may result in penalties under federal law.

There are a few things that can happen during the first couple of weeks. You may feel tired or more energetic. You may spot a little—you'll be given sanitary napkins, free of charge, after the procedure—or it may last for a while longer. If any bleeding continues after two weeks, contact your rep first. If you have not had any children, it will be an easier transition. If you have had children, the hormones may seem strong; in that case, once again, make sure to contact your rep. We are available at any time you have any questions. If there is continual bleeding or an emergency issue, please go to the emergency room and tell the doctors that you have the Heraplon. We know it's an adjustment—it's not difficult, we'd like to reassure you of that. The majority of our users don't experience side effects, but we want you to be aware that there is a slim chance of discomfort. Any questions?

Paloma's eyes were wide like most patients'. I bet I looked the same. The information took a long time to process. It was a sudden addition inside our bodies that we couldn't control, one the government said was for our benefit, but it was really an all-seeing eye.

"Do you have one?"

"I do," I said and resisted rubbing mine. I felt it shift like a sleepy cat among my muscle fibers. "Getting it didn't hurt. It was like a vaccination shot."

"Do you feel different?"

"Different? I feel . . ." Like I sometimes forgot that my hands and fingers were connected to me and when I held them up to the light, I wondered who they belonged to. Sometimes when Luca would slide his fingers from my belly to the center of my thighs, a quick nausea rolled through me before settling into ambivalence. Even when it was my own hands traveling down my body, I would forget why I started in the first place. "No, I don't feel different. You could say I feel better now."

She nodded, staring at my tablet. There was an anger coiling in my throat, and I swallowed it down. I wanted to tell her to ask more questions. I wanted her to point out the absurdity of my answer. I wanted her to understand that this was government-sanctioned population control against our people. Instead, I asked her the rest of the questions needed for the procedure and told her to set up an appointment with the front desk. I gave her my card and said, "Welcome to the family."

I had to clock 39,000 hours to pay off my debt. As a ward of the state, that was the stipulation for my education and essentially, my life. Shilling Heraplon meant half the debt would be forgiven, and committing to the implant was an extra 15 percent off my hours. All temporary salves and mind games when work was a life sentence. Calculating how many hours I had left and my remaining debt was inconsequential in the long scheme of my life.

Paloma was easy and the rest of the day was turning out to be similar. During my lunch hour, I locked my office door, turned off the tablet, and ate the vegetarian kimbap Hemy had left in the fridge at home. I clicked open the aesthetically pleasing nude photo Luca sent. He liked to show off his abs in natural sunlight. I was able to discern he was in his own bathroom when I zoomed in and saw the shower curtain.

As I was trying to figure out an appropriate way to respond before my interest disappeared completely, my tablet buzzed and turned back on.

I looked up and saw everyone else was chatting into their head-sets or to a potential patient. No one bothered to look over at me. I felt almost invisible. It was nice.

How did the tablet turn on? I never used it outside of work nor took it anywhere outside the office. Although it buzzed, the screen was still black. I pressed the home button and still, nothing. If I sent this to a repair tech, it would be docked from my salary. I searched for instructional videos on my phone, promising myself I would respond to Luca later, and found a mini-toolkit in one of my draw-ers. How hard could it be to fix a tablet?

"Eliana?" A tinny voice cut through the room. It repeated my name, stronger this time. I jumped. "It's me, Gina. Me oíste?"

My fingers were already pushing against the implant by the time I remembered to breathe again. It was hard against the surface of my skin, like an embedded splinter. I felt like I could squeeze it out if I really tried. Were hallucinations a possible side effect? I couldn't remember. Out of all the speeches I had made, the speeches I had listened to, I couldn't remember if auditory hallucinations were on the list. How was I hearing my sister's voice?

Was Luca suddenly exhibiting childish behavior because I hadn't responded quickly enough to his photo? I never told him about my family, but because of his job he *did* have access to all my data. I knew Hemy would never do anything this cruel. Or what if it was a test from immigration officials to make sure I wasn't trying to escape before my time? The implant knew where I was. It would register this spike in adrenaline.

"Eliana, if you're there, tell me. We want you to come home."

Home? I circled slowly around the tablet and saw a grainy figure, lit in a high green like night vision, looking down. What home was this person referring to?

"I know it's been a long time since we were—" the words garbled into static. I detected that her English had developed an accent. "We tried to reach out to you before this. Tell me you're listening, and you're ready to come home."

Home? The last home I loved ended with dirty dishes abandoned in the sink, the half-folded clothes on the couch, my father's cologne still a cloud in the bathroom. A snapshot right before they were taken away by immigration officials. We didn't even know what happened to them for the first few weeks. Their presence still strong in that house for the first week, and then their absence overflowing from every room and decision. Home after that was the empty apartment I arrived at when she was supposed to pick me up from school. That time the dishes were washed. That time she wrote a note *I'll be back for you,* and I held onto it for years before ripping it up and dropping it in the Hudson. I watched it disintegrate. I still wasn't sure which was worse: our parents deported or my sister leaving of her own accord.

I clicked on the microphone button to the tablet.

"Eliana?" The figure looked up, and it could have been her.

"Fuck off," I said. My voice was not tinny. It was real. I shut the tablet off.

◆

The MalTides were what was left of the southernmost tip of Manhattan. The subway stations here flooded ages ago when the levies were not replaced in time from the last hurricane and the Hudson rose. The old tenement-style buildings survived best—the loft and redesigned buildings celebrities bought were abandoned quickly. It became a first-come, first-served living situation, and then transformed into a communal space as more stragglers showed up. Stragglers were forced out here, to the very edge of the city where the Hudson licked at our feet. It was all we had left to claim.

Hemy and I were lucky—her parents had already settled on a place long before the celebrity evacuations began. It was a trek from the last stop to the apartment complex where we lived. I was sweating puddles by the time I reached our apartment.

Hemy wasn't home when I arrived. While I worked regular hours at the clinic, she normally didn't get back until it was dusky outside. I peeled off my wet shirt and let it air out by our tub. I opened the windows to the apartment before cooking dinner and aimed the fan toward the crack in the window, hoping it would abate the smell and the heat.

I heard Hemy's slippers sliding against the floor before turning around. The whirl of the fan had drowned out any other noise. The kimchi was already cooked and mixed with rice and ham, and the egg yolks were two small suns wavering in the pan.

"Kimchi bokkeumbap?" She opened the fridge, the harsh light inside revealing bleached eyebrows. A new change from when I last saw her this morning. "Is it Luca again?"

"Luca is Luca," I said, ladling the fried rice into a larger bowl. She made a face, and I shrugged. Hemy's mother used to make this for me every day when she found out what happened to my parents and then my sister. "I had a weird day at work. Have you—"

"I had a weird day, too!" She placed the bowls and chopsticks down on the table. "There are some rumors going around at work. I heard one of the field teams has been seeing crazy shit like their patients reanimating. I mean, I wouldn't be surprised if there was another pilot program out there for more than just vestigial organs."

"Reanimating? What does that mean?"

"That's what I'm saying! It could be a joke. Maybe someone trying to stir up intrigue. As far as I know, we're only snipping off topical vestigial organs. And that's all local anesthesia. I had a really gross one today, too."

"No surgery talk at the table, Hemy. The last time you talked about the tail moving around, I had nightmares about octopus arms with large suckers squeezing my whole body like a wrapped sausage." I poked at my egg and the yolk collapsed. That nightmare was one of the worst. I was suffocating, and Hemy had to shake me awake.

"All I'm going to say then is that I'm really glad we're eating rice and not noodles."

I rolled my eyes. "Have you gotten your implant yet?"

"No, I don't have to." She shoved an extraordinarily large amount of rice into her mouth. It was her way of giving herself time before explaining anything. I had seen this technique countless times. I waited.

We were both living in the MalTides, and if Hemy was making more than what she was making at her last job as a research assistant, her lifestyle didn't show any difference. We still lived in this studio apartment, shared a bed together, and heard our neighbors fighting every night. She should have been required to undergo the same procedure as me.

"Technically, I'm still an international student," she said after gulping down her food several times. "Last time my parents went to Korea, they exchanged their citizenships and applied for me, too. They tried to do it for you, but the authorities denied it because . . . you're not blood Korean . . ."

"Of course," I nodded. I mixed the egg yolk and watched the reddish rice turn barely orange. There was a bitterness creeping into me, and a longing, as well. It was a feeling that began when Hemy's parents officially adopted me, years after I came home to an empty house. I believed Hemy that her parents had tried to create some sort of safety for me. Unfortunately, that would never be my fate here. Parentless, no family, my future tethered to this implant—

"What were you saying about work today? I'm sorry for interrupting."

"Well," I glanced up quickly. Should I tell her? She shoveled more rice into her mouth as she stared at me. Yes. She was like a sister to me, blood or not. I grew up with her family. She looked like a cartoon chipmunk with all the food in her cheeks. "I think Gina tried to contact me."

Hemy spit out the water she was drinking. I grabbed a napkin and dabbed my arm and placed it on the small puddle forming in front of her.

"*Gina*? Your *sister*? How? What did she say?"

"She asked me if I was ready to come home."

"Home?" Her brow furrowed. In the light with her bleached eyebrows, she looked similar to an egg. "But isn't this your home?"

I looked around our cramped apartment: our rickety table with a leg too short and currently standing on one of Hemy's old anatomy textbooks, the pots and pans stored in our tiny oven, our unmade bed with clothes piled on one side of it (so typical of her), the stack of books, papers, and unopened mail in a corner next to our broken-in couch. There was so much of it, we had unintentionally converted it into a table stand. My implant throbbed. What did I really possess that tethered me here?

"I'm home when I'm with you," I said to her. That was the truth. I had never lied to Hemy outright before, and I didn't want to start now. She was the only one who had stayed with me. What would it be like, though, to dream of a future?

◆

"Eliana? Are you there?"

The tablet buzzed again, but this time I was with a new patient. I quickly muted it as I continued with my speech. This patient, Rebecca Ng, didn't say anything. Her dark hair hung thickly over her face. Her mother sat next to her, and her knuckles were white around her purse handles. Rebecca came in with only one day left before her deadline, but I didn't mention that to her. Realizing that it was required to get this procedure was nerve-racking. It wasn't a choice made lightly, and in the end, it was never our choice.

When Rebecca and her mother left, I turned to the tablet. Eight days had passed since the first contact.

"You left me," I said to the hunched figure on the screen. I opened up my lettuce wrap.

Her head shot up and there was a familiar flicker of annoyance on her features. She managed to smooth the look out as she pressed her fingers between her eyebrows. The same reaction she used when I refused to go to school some mornings. While I barely had a temper, Gina always had trouble trying to reign hers in.

"I thought I had to. Eliana, I'm sorry. I didn't know it would take this long to get everything ready. Please."

"Please what?" The lettuce wrap had fake meat in it. Slimier than I expected. This wasn't the same fake meat Hemy usually bought.

The fingers shot up again. Rage flared within me at the same moment.

"Do you know what it was like to come home and see no one? Mami and papi okay, but you too? When I knew, even at that age, that you could have stayed? You abandoned me, Gina. You left me on my own so don't act like I'm suddenly the problem."

"I can't take that back. Ya lo sé. I thought I was doing what was right, for the both of us."

"For you."

"For *us*. You don't have to believe me now," she looked behind her. "Mira, I don't have much time. Neither do you. This is your last chance, the last time I can contact you. Life is better here, I promise. We miss you so much. Come home."

Home. What a strange word. I didn't know the home Gina was talking about. Yes, that was our ancestral origins, where our parents came from, and even Gina's earliest memories were there. I didn't have that. Only stories and blood claims.

I looked at my schedule and noticed my next patient wasn't for another fifteen minutes. Only a little less than 38,934 more hours to clock in. Did I want to continue spending the rest of my life counting down grains of sand?

"What do I have to do?"

Her face lit up and she leaned forward. I took notes until the screen went black again, and it was only my reflection staring back.

I had eighteen hours to disappear. I opened Luca's picture again and studied the shadows of his obliques, the prominent vein straining against his bicep. I finally responded.

❖

Luca's stomach felt like a cavern. When I pressed my ear against his belly, I felt his ribs enclose around my ears. I was soothed by the rumblings and waves inside him. They reminded me of the ultrasound before the implant. His fingers lightly combed my hair. I knew it was one of his favorite things to touch—even on our first date, he curled an end around his fingertips. When we kissed, he always reached up my nape to let my hair cascade down.

This was better than last time, and we both knew it. Better than the first time he left the country, better than any time since the implant. My body hummed against his lips, and I felt—I *felt* his body. I was aware for the first time in so long of the tautness of his skin, the smell from his neck, the sweat that slicked between our bodies. I only dissociated a few times but was able to push the nausea aside. My fingertips coasted his coarse happy trail, and he shivered. Goosebumps rose against my cheek. This awareness had come back in such an explosive way that I wanted to cling to it before I forgot it, but the Heraplon worked quickly. It was like mercury in my veins.

"Can I ask you something about your job?" I looked up at him and grinned, "Or is it confidential?"

His hand paused for a second before resuming. "Are you really interested in what I do?"

"Of course," I said.

"You weren't that interested two weeks ago." Luca opened one eye and peered back down at me. His face was made of sharp angles. "Why now?"

I pressed my lips against his oblique. "We've known each other for a few years." He sucked in a quick breath as I tried to gather more time. "I want to make sure I'm correct about what you do. I know that for certain cybersecurity programs, a shadow folder is created. It logs when you're at work, accessing which websites, and tracks the time spent, right?"

He shifted to his side and brought me up to his chest. Instead of the waves of his insides, I heard his steady heartbeat. "Most private companies do that. That's like first grade, entry-level basics, though.

We provide other facets, but I can't say which ones yet. Well," he kissed my forehead, "just one thing, mainly because it's not entirely unknown. Typing patterns are also tracked so there's a subfolder of the words you mostly use including your typing speed. If anyone signs on with your name past a certain time frame that you're usually not on, the AI system logs it. But once you start typing and it's asynchronous to your usual pattern, that's when we get alerted. That's just one of the things we provide to the government."

My head shot up and grazed his face. "The government?"

"I told you about the contract a long time ago." He rubbed his chin.

"That means you have access to anyone's folder. You could delete someone forever. Erase them from existence."

"It would be really difficult, but yeah, there should be a way."

"Could you do it? For me?"

His eyes widened and his eyebrows almost disappeared into his hair. He started laughing, a nervous chuckle shaking his body. "That's insane, Eliana. Do you know what you're asking of me? I would lose my job. I'd go to jail. My entire life would be ruined. The same for you, too." He cupped my face. "If you're in trouble, I can help you, legally."

It was disappointing to stare back into his eyes. I knew there was a very tiny chance he would do it willingly. I had hoped he would say yes to make my escape easier, but I could still figure out a way.

"Fuck. I can see it on your face."

Our paths collided from time to time, but I didn't think he ever knew me well enough to notice anything, especially if I was determined to do something.

"I don't know if I can do it. Deleting someone's existence entirely is a lot more time-consuming than you think. It's not like I hit the delete button and you're gone. The most I could do right now is clear out any kind of debts you have since money is the first thing they trace. If you don't have any debts, you're usually placed at the bottom of the pile of importance."

"I trust you. You can visit me in South America when you have another existential crisis. I know you haven't been there yet."

He smiled weakly but his arms tightened around me. It felt good to be held like that.

❖

I knew the best way to get Hemy to do something was by ambush. If the situation was presented as something spontaneous, not as a reaction to rules and restriction, she was always more willing to wreak minimal havoc. We weren't the best influence on each other growing up, but her parents never singled me out whenever we were caught. We were punished equally, kneeling on rice with our hands above our heads. Hemy was my partner, another sister. She would help me. She would put her life on the line for me, I knew that. I would do the same.

I set a bucket next to the chair. On the table was one of Hemy's scalpels she left in the bathroom, and a bottle of vodka for me to dull the pain. The last step in the plan was dependent on Hemy's participation. It was crucial. I had to get the Heraplon out. I barely passed anatomy and physiology in high school, but Hemy had trained to become a surgeon. Some nights I saw her poring through her old textbooks and examining her limbs. Her current internship with one of the skin-care companies was utilizing her surgeon skills.

And so I waited. I flexed my bicep, and the implant shivered. I sorted through our dishes and arranged them by color. I packed a small bag with a change of clothes, socks, and toiletries. I tucked my passport inside though I wasn't sure if I needed it. Gina said to be at the airport by 4:30 a.m., arrive at Terminal 3, and ask for Sebastian to check in. I kept touching the implant, pinching and prodding until I turned my skin a bright tomato red. It felt hot and sensitive, and I wasn't sure if that would make the incision worse.

Hours passed, and I was still alone in the apartment. Hemy should have come home by now. I texted her and waited another hour before sitting in the chair. A scalpel is surprisingly dainty for an immensely sharp object. I took two shots of vodka, one after the other, trying to relish the burn in my throat and stomach. I was fighting the fear bubbling up: could I cut it out myself, and what had happened to Hemy?

The implant was a white bulge against my irritated skin. I took another shot and then slashed into my arm. Blood immediately ran down. I had skimmed the surface and was barely close to getting it out. Another shot, and I dug deeper this time. It felt like I was slicing through stale layered cake. Blood pumped quickly out of the incision, pushing against the scalpel. I continued through until I tapped against metal. The blood was making my fingers wet and sticky. I fumbled trying to create a flap in order to push out the implant and dropped the scalpel into the bucket.

Wine-red blood poured out quicker as I tried to squeeze the small metal tube out. I was losing a lot more than I thought would happen. Vodka would do nothing for the pain at the moment, but I took another shot. It tasted like blood, and my stomach almost revolted. When I dug my finger into the gap and skimmed smooth, pulsing muscle, I passed out.

◆

A shadow in front of me. My arm at my side. Stiff.

I have to go.

Shut up, the shadow said.

I lifted my head. Light filtered through. It was Hemy. Her whole front was splashed red.

Mine?

Cool hands settled on my arm. The implant tugged lightly before it popped from my skin. The sensation reverberated in my head.

I'm leaving with you.

Everything went black.

◆

"You're awake now? Great. You are so stupid. Or stubborn. Actually, stupidly stubborn. Mostly stupid, though. You almost bled out. Not that we would ever see it now, but we won't get our security deposit back."

"Where are we?" My mouth was dry. I had woken up because of a bump where I felt like my stomach had risen into my throat. It tasted of iron.

"We're on our way to the airport. This is for you," she handed me a new passport. It had all the same details as my old passport except for my ID number.

"Where did you get this?" Hemy brought my bag with me, and I searched through it. My old passport wasn't inside.

"Luca. He was there with you when I came home. He definitely doesn't look like his photos nor is he as weird as you make him sound, by the way. He wanted me to tell you that he tried his best.

Oh, and that he might have an existential crisis soon within a year and you owe him dinner. I didn't know what that meant, but I told him thanks. He also helped get you into the cab."

Did I get blood on him? I checked my arm and flexed my fingers. They all functioned. I was wearing new clothing as well.

"You should have waited for me. You almost cut into muscle and damaged your nerves."

"I wasn't sure when you would get home."

"Again, stupid or stubborn. I dumped the Heraplon into the Hudson. It started to smoke by the time we left." She sighed before smiling excitedly. "Our first vacation together!"

I laughed and squeezed her hand. My arm ached at the motion, and a quick jolt of pain shot up. I turned to look through the rear-view window and watched us leave behind the MalTides. I didn't know if I was heading home or leaving it, but at least I had someone who felt like home by my side.

At that moment, it was the one thing I wanted most.

CONTRIBUTORS

GRISEL Y. ACOSTA is an associate professor at the City University of New York–Bronx Community College, a Geraldine Dodge Foundation Poet, and a Macondo Fellow. Her book *Things to Pack on the Way to Everywhere*, forthcoming from Get Fresh Books in 2021, is a finalist for the Andrés Montoya Poetry Prize. She is the editor of *Latina Outsiders Remaking Latina Identity* (Routledge, 2019), and her recent creative work can be found at *Best American Poetry, The Baffler, Split This Rock, Acentos Journal,* and *Kweli Journal.*

STEPHANIE ADAMS-SANTOS is a Guatemalan American writer whose work spans poetry, prose, screenwriting, and other swampy, hybrid forms. Her full-length poetry collection, *Swarm Queen's Crown* (Fathom Books), was a finalist for the Lambda Literary Awards. More about Stephanie and her work can be found at http://www.obscurobeach.com.

FREDERICK LUIS ALDAMA is an award-winning author, editor, and coeditor of forty-eight books, including his recent *The Adventures of Chupacabra Charlie*. He is University Distinguished Professor at The Ohio State University. He is founder and director of LASER (Latinx Space for Enrichment and Research), a Latinx high school college-readiness program.

WILLIAM ALEXANDER writes science fiction and fantasy for young audiences. His six novels include *Goblin Secrets* (a National Book Award winner) and *Ambassador* (an International Latino Book Award finalist). He serves as the faculty chair of the Vermont College of Fine Arts program in Writing for Children and Young Adults.

NICHOLAS BELARDES is a dual-ethnic Chicano writer. He recently launched Coalition Now, a Chicanx and allies coalition of writers, educators, artists, and GIS computer mappers committed to active social justice in Central California. An avid birder in San Luis Obispo, California, Belardes has been an ABC News managing editor, professor of history and writing, and 3-D animation writer. He can be found at http://www.nicholasbelardes.com, or on Twitter: @nickbelardes.

LOUANGIE BOU-MONTES is a Puerto Rican writer who lives in western Massachusetts with her two cats. When not writing or reading comics, she can typically be found advocating for reproductive justice, playing video games, and writing books.

A queer Tejana transplanted to Iowa, **LISA M. BRADLEY** writes speculative fiction and poetry for venues such as *Strange Horizons, Uncanny, Beneath Ceaseless Skies,* and *The Moment of Change: An Anthology of Feminist Speculative Poetry.* Visit http://www.lisambradley.com to learn about her first collection, *The Haunted Girl* (Aqueduct Press), and her debut novel, *Exile* (Rosarium Publishing), or follow her on Twitter: @cafenowhere.

ELIANA BUENROSTRO is a writer and scholar from Southern California and currently resides in Chicago. She forms part of the collective @pochapunks, which focuses community archiving for punks of color from every transbarrio.

DIANA BURBANO is a Colombian immigrant, an Equity actor, a playwright, and a teaching artist. Her plays focus on Latinx protagonists and reclaiming/taking/owning theatrical space. More information can be found at http://www.dianaburbano.com.

The author of more than a dozen books and hundreds of articles and essays, **PEDRO CABIYA** is one of the most beloved writers in the Hispanic Caribbean. His most notable books include *Trance, La cabeza,*

Historias tremendas, Historias atroces, Malas hierbas (*Wicked Weeds*), *Reinbou* (now a major motion picture), and *Tercer Mundo*.

STEVE CASTRO's debut poetry collection, *Blue Whale Phenomena,* was published by Otis Books (Otis College of Art and Design) in 2019. His birthplace is Costa Rica.

FERNANDO DE PEÑA writes for comics, animation, and film. He was born in Chile, studied film and screenwriting in Cuba, and lived in Mexico and Guatemala. He specializes in comedy, horror, sci-fi, and historical fiction with a Latin American perspective and a decolonial approach. He currently lives in Puerto Rico, the oldest colony of the world.

The fiction of **SCOTT RUSSELL DUNCAN,** a.k.a. Scott Duncan-Fernandez, involves the mythic, the surreal, the abstract—in other words, the weird. He is Indigenous/Xicano/Anglo from California, Texas, and New Mexico and is senior editor at *Somos en escrito* literary magazine. More information can be found at http://www. scottrussellduncan.com.

SAMY FIGAREDO (*he/him* and *they/them*) is a proud multihyphenate: Lebanese American, Puerto Rican, actor, activist, aerialist, consultant, pianist, public speaker, puppeteer, singer, and more. For more information, visit their website at http://www.samyfigaredo.com.

TAMMY MELODY GOMEZ is a writer, interdisciplinary performance artist, and collaborative arts producer. She earned her BA in Maryland (at Goucher College); studied permaculture on an organic farm (in Basalt, Colorado); trekked in the Himalayas alone (in Nepal); and has not owned a car since 2008.

MATTHEW DAVID GOODWIN is a visiting scholar at the Institute for Advanced Study in Princeton, New Jersey. His work focuses on the ways that science fiction, fantasy, and digital culture have been used to express the experience of migration. He is the editor of *Latinx Rising* and the author of *The Latinx Files: Race, Migration, and Space Aliens*.

J. M. GUZMAN is a Dominican American who writes about ghosts, coffins, and all the things in the dark. He has fiction that appears in *Apex Magazine, Fireside, Liminal Stories,* and other venues.

ALEX HERNANDEZ is a Cuban American science fiction writer. His work often explores themes of migration, colonization, and posthumanism, while blending the subgenres of space opera and biopunk. His first novel, *Tooth and Talon*, was published by EDGE. He lives in South Florida with his wife and two daughters.

ERNEST HOGAN is known as the Father of Chicano science fiction because of his novels *High Aztech, Smoking Mirror Blues,* and *Cortez on Jupiter,* and his many short stories. His mother's maiden name is Garcia and he was born in East LA during the Atomic Age, so he can't help it.

Originally from Los Angeles, **PEDRO INIGUEZ** now lives in Sioux Falls, South Dakota, where he spends most of his time reading, writing, and painting. His work can be found at http://www.pedroiniguezauthor.com as well as in various magazines and anthologies, such as *Space and Time Magazine, Crossed Genres,* and *Dig Two Graves.*

EZZY G. LANGUZZI is a speculative fiction author whose Mexican American heritage informs her storytelling. Her writing has appeared in *Strange California: An Anthology of Speculative Fiction, Broad Knowledge: 35 Women Up to No Good, Sovereigns of the Blue Rose,* and *Zorro(TM): The Roleplaying Game,* and will be in the forthcoming *Eldritch Century* by Draco Studios.

New York–born artist **PATRICK LUGO (PLUGO)** has now spent nearly half his life making a living in the San Francisco Bay Area providing illustration and design work for comics, kid's lit, magazines, textbooks, album covers, and countless T-shirts. The next children's book to feature his illustrations will be *Lucy Veloz: High-Flying Princess,* published by Cosmic Ray Press.

ROXANNE OCASIO is a graduate of the University of Southern Maine's Stonecoast MFA program and a two-time Voices of Our Nation Arts Foundation workshop fellow. She has written several articles about the local Latinx community for the magazine *Fresh-Water Cleveland.*

DANIEL PARADA is a Salvadoran American artist who lives in San Francisco. His work focuses on historical and Mesoamerican comics and illustrations that reconstruct the past in various ways to make it more accessible to modern audiences.

STEPHANIE NINA PITSIRILOS is a public health advocate and writer with work featured in anthologies such as *Insider Art, COVID Chronicles: A Comics Anthology,* and *Unlikely Heroes Studios,* among others. She is also a cocreator of the Webtoon series *DR163.* She's a Manhattan native with Puerto Rican and Greek roots and holds degrees from the University of Michigan and Columbia University. She is on Twitter @zoehealth and Instagram @TheNinaGalaxy.

SARAH RAFAEL GARCÍA is the author of *Las Niñas* and *SanTana's Fairy Tales.* She is also the founder of Barrio Writers and LibroMobile as well as coeditor of the anthology *Pariahs*

REYES RAMIREZ is a Houstonian of Mexican and Salvadoran descent who's won the 2019 YES Contemporary Art Writer's Grant, 2017 Blue Mesa Review Nonfiction Contest, and 2014 River Sedge Poetry Prize, among other distinctions. Read more of his work at http://www.reyesvramirez.com.

JULIA RIOS is a writer, editor, podcaster, and narrator. Currently the fiction editor for *Fireside Magazine,* she won the Hugo award in 2017 as poetry and reprint editor for *Uncanny Magazine* and was a Hugo finalist as a senior fiction editor for *Strange Horizons.* She has narrated stories for *Podcastle, Pseudopod,* and *Cast of Wonders.*

SARA DANIELE RIVERA is a Cuban/Peruvian artist, writer, translator, and educator from Albuquerque, New Mexico. Her speculative fiction, which focuses on desert ecologies and Latinx futures, has previously appeared in *Embark Literary Journal, Circuits & Slippers,* and the *Easy Street Mag* Portal Prize anthology. More information can be found at https://saradanielerivera.com/.

ROMAN SANCHEZ is a graduate student getting his MFA and PhD at the University of Massachusetts Amherst and teaches as an adjunct professor of material culture at Southwest School of Art in San Antonio, Texas. He is currently working on his master's thesis, his first novel exploring the collective Latinx dream for a socially just future. He lives in San Antonio with his wife and two daughters. Follow him on Instagram @madfarmersanchez.

TABITHA SIN is a Chinese/Colombian speculative fiction writer whose head is always in the clouds. You can find her work here: www.tabithasin.dev.

ALEX TEMBLADOR is the Mixed Latinx author of the award-winning young adult novel *Secrets of the Casa Rosada* and the upcoming adult magical realism novel *Half Outlaw*. The Dallas-based author is a public speaker, creative writing instructor, moderator of the Dallas author panel series, LitTalk, and a freelance travel, arts, and design writer for internationally known publications.

RODRIGO VARGAS is a comic book artist based in Santiago, Chile. You can read his and Coni Yovaniniz's webcomic at http://walkingtodo. com. His co-created (with Coni Yovaniniz) middle-grade graphic novel, *The Do-Over*, will be published with Houghton Mifflin Holt in 2022.

LAURA VILLAREAL is the author of the poetry chapbook *The Cartography of Sleep* (Nostrovia! Press, 2018). Her writing has appeared or is forthcoming in *Grist, AGNI, Black Warrior Review, Waxwing,* and elsewhere.

SABRINA VOURVOULIAS is an award-winning journalist based in the Philadelphia area. She is the author of *Nuestra América: 30 Inspiring Latinas/Latinos Who Have Shaped the United States* (Running Press, 2020), *Ink* (Rosarium Publishing, 2018), and short stories that have appeared in multiple anthologies and online magazines. More information can be found at http://www.sabrinavourvoulias.com.

KARLO YEAGER RODRÍGUEZ is originally from Puerto Rico but now lives near Baltimore, where he tests electronic documents for accessibility. His speculative fiction has appeared in such places as *Uncanny* and *Beneath Ceaseless Skies*. More information can be found at http://www.alineofink.com.